Fif

Going On

Fifteen

Going On Grown Up

Stephanie M. Turner

Matador
9 Priory Business Park,
Wistow Road, Kibworth Beauchamp,
Leicestershire. LE8 0RX
Tel: (+44) 116 279 2299
Fax: (+44) 116 279 2277
Email: books@troubador.co.uk
Web: www.troubador.co.uk/matador

ISBN 978 1780881 676

British Library Cataloguing in Publication Data.
A catalogue record for this book is available from the British Library.

Typeset in 12pt Bembo by Troubador Publishing Ltd, Leicester, UK

Matador is an imprint of Troubador Publishing Ltd

Printed and bound in the UK by TJ International, Padstow, Cornwall

To my husband Stephen and my children Jason, Damon, Holly and Harriet for their support, encouragement and inspiration.

CHAPTER 1

Fifteen

On the morning of her fifteenth birthday Hally Mackeller stood in front of the mirror in her bedroom. The reflection looking back was still a surprise to her, long blonde hair, bright big blue eyes and as the eyes travelled down the reflection full breasts a small waist and curving shapely hips ending in long slim legs.

The reason the reflection made her eyes open wide like she had just opened one of her birthday presents was simple. Only a few months before she had been a five foot four teenager with long shapely legs and round hips but her breasts had been small and out of proportion to the rest of her body. Because of this she had had to endure months of name calling by the popular crowd of both girls and boys at her school. Hurtful names such as pasteboard and pancakes and sometimes omelette. Hally's small group of close friends had told her to ignore it, but that was easy for them to say so she believed; because they were all shapely and had had boyfriends so knew about kissing and so on. However within a short time and to Hally it seemed overnight her figure blossomed almost like a rose bud opening up into full flower.

Hally slowly traced the shape of her body with her hands examining it inch by inch. At the back of her mind was a little fear that kept telling her what she was seeing must be a trick of the mirror. In reality she knew this wasn't true because now the names had changed to "tissue bra" and "gel tits". It seemed to Hally that the popular group just had it in for her and no matter what she looked like or what sort of person she was they were always going to find a reason to ridicule her and be hateful. Mum had told her countless times that they were just jealous, but jealous of what Hally couldn't fathom.

All right she got very good grades at school, she was well liked by her teachers and had predictions for high results in her exams next year, but every teenager knew that these were not things to be jealous of, popularity and looks were far more impressive and cause for the old green eyed monster to appear. Hally gave a huge sigh, a small frown and in a firm but quiet voice told the reflection

"It's your birthday so get dressed and go downstairs for your presents."

Mum had already laid out bowl, cereal and milk on the table, this was not usual except on birthdays as she was almost always in a hurry in the morning. Today was different, mum was not rushing around and dad was going to break off from work so he could be there when the birthday girl opened her presents.

Just as Hally started on her cornflakes dad came in and planted a big kiss on the top of her head.

"Morning Tink"

He said. He had called her Tink as in Tinkerbell ever since she had watched Peter Pan and announced she was going to be a fairy when she grew up.

"Hi dad how long can you stay?"

Dad mumbled something as he hugged mum.

"Didn't catch that dad"

Hally told him through a mouthful of cereal.

"He can stay whilst you open your presents."

Mum told her as she handed her husband a cup of tea.

For a short while the only sounds in the kitchen were Hally finishing her breakfast and mumbles from mum and dad as they chatted over cups of tea.

Mum got up and left the room. She returned shortly carrying a pile of presents which she placed in front of Hally. The top present was long and thin and tied with a silver bow. A small tag told Hally it was from Gran and Granddad. Inside the package was a gold charm bracelet which she recognised as her grandmother's. Mum raised her eyebrows to dad but said nothing. Hally stared at the bracelet and felt tears beginning to well up in her eyes. Nobody said anything but all knew that it would probably be the last present she received from her grandmother; as she was now in the advanced stages of secondary cancer and probably wouldn't live to see Hally's sixteenth birthday, and as Hally was her only granddaughter she had promised the bracelet to her a few years ago.

"Your Granddad brought it round last night because they had to go to the hospital early today and your Gran wanted you to open it first thing this morning."

Mum told her gently as Hally let each charm slide through her fingers.

The next package was wrapped untidily and held together with a lot of cellotape. As Hally tried to pull the wrapping off her little brother Nathan called out

"That's from me"

spraying chewed up cereal everywhere.

"Thanks Natty"

Hally said as she pulled a packet of jelly babies from the paper and planted a kiss on the top of his head.

"Urg getofffme."

Nathan grumbled knocking his bowl at the same time and sending milk and cornflakes spilling across the table.

"Nathan, be careful"

Mum told him.

"Wasn my fault"

He mumbled with his head down.

Other presents included perfume and chocolates from various relatives and the last package was from her parents. Hally opened the box and found a new mobile phone with touch screen and various internet applications.

"Wow, thank you mum and dad this is fabulous."

She kissed and hugged both her parents and dived off to her room to start putting all her numbers into the new phone. As she left the room mum called after her

"Don't spend too much time on that now, you've got school."

"O.K."

Hally threw back over her shoulder.

"Well let's hope nobody gets hold of this one."

Dad said to mum. He was referring to Hally's old phone that now had a cracked screen because a group of girls in Hally's year at school had taken it out of her bag and had been throwing it to each other, one of them had dropped it. These were the same group who had been teasing Hally about her figure.

Back in her room Hally quickly entered the numbers of her few close friends and put the phone in her bag with her other school things. She would play with it later but for now she knew she had to get to school. A quick look at her reflection, a flick of her hair and she grabbed her jacket and bag and headed back downstairs. She kissed both her parents and headed for school.

Just like any other day Hally met up with Corrinne and Clia where their two roads crossed. These were Hally's two closest friends who had stuck by her through everything. The three girls had first met at toddler group, then went to nursery school together and become inseparable over the years. Unusually, there had never been the split often seen when three girls grow up as friends. This was probably due to the fact that all three were very similar in character and neither one tried to control the trio. They just enjoyed each other's company and were as close as sisters. Each had different ideas about what a boyfriend should be like so they never got into an argument about one fancying the same guy and everything else they shared, makeup, clothes, bags and hair products. Sometimes, especially in the middle of the night Hally became afraid that when they all left school they would eventually drift apart, but so far all discussions between them pointed to a lifelong friendship.

As the school gates came into view Clia whispered

"Oh no look who's standing outside school."

The other two noticed Dana Edwards and Penny Cuthbert huddled together obviously getting ready for a tirade of insults. Although the abuse would be directed at Hally the other two felt it personally as Hally's best friends. However just as the outburst was about to begin Mr Clark, one of the Maths teachers came out of the gate and asked Dana and Penny to go into the school with him. The reason was at the time not obvious to Hally and the other two but it was a welcome interruption.

The three girls continued into the school grounds and found a bench to sit on until the bell went. Corrinne heaved her bag onto her lap and began pulling items out.

"I still can't believe the stuff you bring Corrie"

Hally told her laughing.

"Oh you know me, always ready for any event."

She said this as she pulled out a pair of socks. The other two burst into giggles.

"What you got those for?"

Clia asked her.

"Well what if my feet get wet?"

Hally and Clia looked at each other grinning. It was in fact a beautiful bright May morning with sunshine forecast for the rest of the week. They didn't say any more, they knew Corrinne well and this sort of thing was what made her the funny and somewhat eccentric girl they had loved like a sister for many years.

Eventually Corrinne found what she had been looking for. An oddly shaped package tied with multi-coloured ribbons. Not the foil kind but real satin ribbons. She gave the present to Hally.

"This is from both of us."

Hally smiled and unwrapped the gift. Hally felt a lump in her throat as she looked at the present. It was a silver chain with three silver letters, H, C and C. She hugged both her friends and whispered thank you and the bell went for registration which put a stop to the tears that threatened to spill from her eyes. Silently Hally told herself to get a grip, this was the second time today that she had been on the verge of tears; she was turning into a right wimp. She knew she was being too hard on herself and gaining her composure she linked arms with Clia and Corrinne and went into school.

The school day started normally with registration, a few interruptions from Ryan Cleaver (the most annoying boy in the whole school) and a few more happy birthdays from other members of the form. Mrs Jacobs, Hally's form tutor gave her a small card signed with her usual indecipherable signature and for a while everything was the same as any other day. There was a knock on the door and in stepped a year seven student, the day's message runner. Shyly he walked up to Mrs Jacobs and handed her a note. The teacher scanned the message, handed it back with a thank you and turned to the class as the year seven student left.

"Your attention please."

She said this in a soft gentle voice standing at the same time and though no louder than normal speaking volume the students responded immediately. Mrs Jacobs was well liked and commanded respect from her students with her personality and charisma.

"We have an extra assembly this morning, so if you would please stand quietly and make your way sensibly to the hall."

The students looked at one another, some with frowns others with shrugs. This was a very unusual event; assemblies were set at the beginning of the term and always planned well in advance.

As Hally's form entered the hall the mystery of the unexpected assembly deepened when it became obvious that the entire school was crammed in. The Head Teacher Mr Hopkins was standing on the stage and another man unknown to the students was standing next to him. Slowly the students squeezed into every available space. Mr Hopkins raised his right hand and the students' voices gradually died down to silence.

"Good morning everyone. We will not be keeping you long. We realise this is an unusual situation and thank you all for your patience and understanding. We also realise you are all rather cramped and will soon become hot so we will get straight to the point."

It was customary for Mr Hopkins to speak as a collective.

"We have with us today Inspector Miller who has some very serious news to pass on to you."

He stood back and the Inspector stepped forward.

"Good morning. Some of you may be aware of a series of burglaries at off licences recently. Well today we have apprehended a group of teenagers who we believe to be involved. Some of these people are students at this school. What we would like you to do is inform either us or your Head Teacher if you have bought or know of anyone who has bought alcohol or cigarettes from anyone. We would like to stress that any information you give us will remain strictly confidential and if you have purchased any of these goods and come forward you will not be prosecuted. Thank you, if you have any questions two of my officers will be at the school throughout the day to speak to."

The inspector stood back and Mr Hopkins again spoke.

"We are sure you are all aware of the seriousness of the situation and therefore any help from you will be greatly appreciated. Teachers, would you like to begin dismissing your classes from the back and front of the hall."

A murmur arose throughout the hall as the students began to file out and head towards their first lessons.

The first part of the morning was quite unsettled and by break time both students and teachers were glad of a rest. Hally and Clia hurried to meet up with Corrinne. The three girls were in the same sets for all of their lessons except Maths. Hally and Clia were in the second set and Corrinne was in the top set. Her Maths was outstanding and she was predicted an A star grade in her exams but she was not in the least big headed about it. Whenever anyone mentioned it she just brushed it off with

"Oh I just have a knack for it."

The three girls made their way to their favourite bench in the courtyard and sitting down rummaged through their bags for snacks. As they passed them to each other Corrinne exclaimed to the other two.

"On my way to Maths I heard Clarky talking to Double O Seven. He said Dana and Penny were with five oh."

Double O Seven was the nickname the students had given to Miss Wateley the head of year ten because she always seemed to know exactly what was going on even when the students tried to keep something from her.

"So that was why Clarky called them over this morning."

Exclaimed Hally.

"Wonder how involved they are?"

Answered Clia. Corrinne shrugged.

"I only heard that bit but I bet they're in deep. You know they're always hanging out with Cob's crowd and he's been inside at least three times already."

"Well it might keep them off my back for a while then."

Hally replied with a smile.

"They won't be able to spoil this birthday for me."

She was referring to last year when Dana, Penny and several

other girls had cornered her at breaktime on her birthday and thrown tampons at her because she had only just started her period the day before.

"Speaking of which, what are you doing tonight?"

Asked Clia. Hally missed the sly wink she gave to Corrinne.

"I think mum and dad are taking us out for a meal but that was only mentioned in passing at breakfast this morning."

Hally replied.

"Oh ok but when you get back give us a call and we can come round."

Clia told her.

The bell went that ended their conversation and after putting their rubbish in the bin they began to stroll towards their next lesson. None of them went enthusiastically; it was History and not a favourite subject with the threesome. However it was greatly cheered up by the absence of Dana and Penny which gave the whole class some interesting conversation in between the discussion on the Second World War.

The rest of the school day was uneventful and to Hally a little disappointing as nobody was able to shed any further light on the Dana and Penny situation. So when the final bell went signalling the end of the school day Hally, Clia and Corrinne happily left and made their way home.

No one was at home when Hally got there, this was not unusual. Nathan would almost certainly be dawdling home from primary school with his friends and kicking a football about on the way with mum strolling along with him. Mum went most afternoons to Hally's grandparents and picked Nathan up from school after. Depending on how much playtime mum let Nathan have on the way home, they would not be in until at least four o'clock. Hally loved this little bit of quiet time by herself. She dropped her bag on the table, kicked her shoes into the cupboard in the hall and dived for the fridge. Moments later she emerged with a can of cola and an apple and settled on the sofa with her favourite music channel on the television.

Just after four mum and Nathan came in together and the usual bustle of evening family life began. Nathan was typically covered in dirt with green stains on his elbows; and mum was as usual, trying to unpack shopping she had picked up on the way home whilst listening to Nathan gabble on about the next school football match with his head half covered with the sweatshirt he was removing to throw into the laundry. Hally knew if she waited just ten minutes Nathan would be in his room getting changed and mum would be free to listen to her day. It was only the last year that Hally had realised that a little patience with her brother would give her and her mother time to talk without interruption. Her mum had noticed the almost sudden maturity in her daughter and welcomed it, as the squabbles between her two children competing for her attention at the same time was always stressful. Now she was able to ask Hally what sort of a day she had had without one of them screaming at her that they had been trying to tell her something.

Hally poured water from the kettle she had boiled into two cups and squeezed out the tea bags. Handing one to her mum they both sat at the kitchen table and Hally relayed the events of the day. Her mum listened attentively and when Hally finished said to her daughter.

"I knew one or both of those two would end up in serious trouble. Neither of their parents seems to care what they do or where they go. It's funny, Mrs Teety was only talking about the break ins when I went with your granddad to the post office today. She said the police had caught some people."

"Well we have all been trying to find out where Dana and Penny fit in but no one at school seems to know. I 'spect it will come out soon, stuff usually does at school."

For a while the two sat drinking their tea in silence, then mum said.

"Changing the subject, we thought we would go to Gesslers tonight, how's that with you?"

"That sounds great, thanks mum."

Hally replied. Gesslers was a local restaurant and a favourite with most families because it had three sections. One was secluded and intimate with booths rather than just open tables. There was also a formal dining area with white linen and candles and the third and biggest section had large tables that could accommodate groups. The menu was wide and catered for all tastes and occasions.

Mother and daughter chatted for another half hour and then Hally made her way to her room to get changed and do some homework. She had got into the habit of doing her homework straight away right from the beginning of secondary school, so she would have the rest of the evening to herself and so the homework didn't pile up. Most of the other students she knew thought she was mad and left theirs to the last minute but Hally was a very organised girl. Clia had followed Hally's habit but Corrinne had a fixed homework timetable and stuck to it rigidly.

By six thirty Hally was in the shower preparing for her birthday meal at Gesslers. Lately she spent quite some time on getting ready for an evening out, styling her hair and applying makeup. Mum had given her many good tips about her makeup so now she wore enough to enhance her natural beauty but didn't overdo it like some of the other girls at school who ended up looking like painted dolls.

Gran and Granddad arrived at just after seven and Hally wrapped her arms around each of them, holding her Gran for some time.

"Thank you for the bracelet."

She whispered to her Gran.

"I knew you would like it angel, especially keep an eye on the compass charm. It's very old and will help you find your way."

Gran replied lovingly.

At eight o'clock the whole family arrived at the restaurant. They were taken to a long table that was already occupied and very quickly Hally realised that her parents had arranged a surprise for her. Corrinne and Clia were at the table along with six close friends from school. Hally sat down opposite Clia and smiling said.

"You crafty pair you kept this quiet."

Clia and Corrine just grinned and that completed the wonderful birthday Hally had that year.

CHAPTER 2

The Party

Saturday morning was cloudy and damp. Hally looked out of her bedroom window and groaned. They had all been hoping for a nice dry day as the party was planned mainly for the garden. Her actual birthday had been terrific and now her parents had agreed to let her have a party at home so other friends from school and outside of school could celebrate with her too. This was to be Hally's first grown up party. She hadn't had a birthday party since she was in year six and about to leave primary school so she was looking forward to this immensely.

Outside Hally could see her dad arranging chairs and tables and erecting a couple of large gazebos. At least there would be shelter if it did rain later. The barbeque was all set up too and without even going down Hally knew her mum would be in the kitchen organising food and drinks. Hally truly believed her parents were first class party organisers. Each year they put on a party for family and friends on their wedding anniversary and it was always a great success.

After showering and drying her hair Hally made her way towards the kitchen in search of food.

"Don't go getting in my way now."

Mum told her. Giving her mother a wide berth Hally opened the fridge and stood for a while looking in. She couldn't find anything she fancied so moved on to the cupboards. With a slightly irritable note in voice her mum said.

"What are you looking for?"

"I don't know, I'm hungry but can't find anything to eat."

This was obviously a contradiction as the cupboards and fridge were always full. Hally's mother knew her two children enjoyed their food but tried to make sure they didn't eat too much junk food, so she bought a huge variety of products that they could nibble on but were healthy at the same time. She wasn't a health fanatic and did provide her off spring with the usual tasty snacks all youngsters enjoyed but tried to balance these with others that did not have as much fat or sugar.

Finally Hally settled on a bowl of cereal followed by an apple and toast with marmite. Whilst munching her toast Nathan came flying into the kitchen from the garden yelling.

"MUM, MUM, DAD'S CUT HIS FINGER AND IT'S BLEEDING ALL OVER THE PLACE."

Mum put down the colander she was shaking and rushed into the garden to her husband. Hally, taking her toast with her followed. Outside Hally saw her parents underneath a gazebo and heard her father saying to her mother.

"It's alright May it's only a little scratch."

"Let me have a look Colin."

Her mother replied taking his hand in her own. As Hally got near she could see a smear of blood on her dad's hand. She heard her mother sigh and tell her father.

"When I get hold of him…"

Hally knew this meant Nathan and knew he was in trouble. She grinned and made her way back to the kitchen still eating her toast.

"Oh you're in for it Natty."

She told her brother whose rear end was sticking out of a cupboard as he delved for a packet of crisps.

In a muffled voice he replied.

"Why what have I done?"

As Hally began to explain Nathan emerged from the cupboard with two packets of crisps and a handful of breadsticks. At the same time her parents came through the back door and mum, already annoyed with Nathan marched over to him with a serious frown on her face.

"Those breadsticks are for the party and when are you going to stop exaggerating everything Nathan. Now I suggest you take yourself off to your room for a while and let me get on with things down here."

"Aw mum…"

Nathan began but the look his mother gave him stopped him complaining further and dropping his head and with hands clutching his snacks he stomped off towards the stairs. As soon as he was out of the room Hally's parents looked at each other and grinned.

"Well he's got to learn."

Mum said to no one in particular. Dad kept quiet as he washed his hands and applied a sticking plaster to the small cut on his thumb.

By seven that evening the garden had been transformed into a perfect party venue with chairs and tables scattered around and nets of lights inside the gazebos. Tea light lanterns rested on each table and there was a cooler filled with ice and loaded with bottles of soft drinks.

In her room Hally put the finishing touches to her makeup and perused her reflection in the mirror. She had a new mini skirt and top which showed off her curvy figure and long slender legs. Her mother came in and looked at her.

"You look really lovely darling."

She told her daughter. Hally screwed up her face and said.

"Do you really think so?"

Her mum nodded with a smile and Hally shrugged and grinned back.

"Oh well I suppose I'm not a Rachel Rover."

She told her mother. Mum burst out laughing. Her husband had invented that saying when they had been dating and used it to describe any girl he found unattractive. It was very amusing to hear her daughter use the saying.

"Come on, your guests will be arriving soon."

They walked downstairs chatting about who was coming to the party and as they reached the bottom they heard Corrinne and Clia's voices. Hally went to greet them and mum went out into the garden. She heard the girls squealing excitedly to each other about how they looked.

An hour later the garden was beginning to fill up with Hally's friends. Groups of girls stood admiring each other's clothes and groups of boys stood admiring the girls. Hally moved amongst her guests chatting and dancing and thanking individuals who handed her presents. She had decided to wait until later to unwrap her gifts and the pile was rapidly getting bigger.

By the middle of the evening the garden was humming with the sound of talking, laughing and music. Most of the girls were dancing and several of the boys were beginning to join in. Everyone was having a great time and Hally's parents were very popular with her friends as they joined in with the party spirit.

Everything was going really well until a commotion was heard in the corner of one of the gazebos. A small crowd gathered as Hally's parents quickly moved in to intervene. Hally pressed between two girls and came across a furious argument between Kerry and Anna. The girls who were friends of a friend of Hally's, were leaning so close together their faces were almost touching. Both were jabbing their finger at the other and were shouting so loudly it was difficult to determine what was being said.

"….you COW!"

"…bitch…you said…you KNEW!"

"NO I SAID……"

"What on earth is going on!"

Mum had forced her way to the girls and was trying to get between them. Both girls turned angrily and started shouting at the same time so no one could make out what they were saying. Hally squeezed in beside her mother and tried to help and dad joined in as well. Quite a large crowd had gathered around the group and mum, dad and Hally had a difficult time trying to calm the situation. Then quite suddenly everything went quiet and it became obvious that someone had turned the music off.

"That's better."

Dad said in an exasperated voice.

"Now will someone….." he raised his hand as the girls were about to start speaking both at once. "…tell me what is going on. You first."

He pointed at Kerry.

"She, SHE, I told her, but still she…" and she burst into a flood of tears.

Dad turned to mum and frowned.

"I think we had better get these two inside, the study should be quiet and kid free."

Without asking for an explanation mum nodded and began to lead Anna towards the house with her husband leading Kerry. Hally turned to her guests and was about to tell everyone to carry on with the party when Nathan jumped in.

"Shall I put the music back on now Hal?"

Hally grinned.

"Was that you who turned it off?"

"Yeah well I just thought those two yelling was a bit much with the stereo on as well."

With that he bounced back off to the house and a few seconds later music was again blasting out into the garden.

Clia and Corrinne had made their way towards Hally.

"What's that all about?"

Enquired Clia. Corrinne was nodding her head and looking intently at Hally.

"I don't know. But it must be something sort of serious for mum and dad to take them off."

As Hally finished her sentence she was bumped from behind and tumbled into Clia.

"Hey watch it you idiot."

Clia told the culprit. But it soon became obvious to the three girls that the bump had not been intentional but was because the girl who did it could not stand up straight.

"Oops sooo sorry."

Hally stared at the girl and recognised her as Kerry's cousin. She remembered Trish, a girl in her tutor group, asking her if she could bring Kerry and Anna and Kerry's cousin because she was staying with her. Hally had agreed adding them to the list. Now she regretted that decision very much as she realised the girl was quite drunk.

"I think you had better leave."

Hally told the girl.

"I can' I'm stayin at Kerry 'ouse."

The girl slurred.

"Right then I'm taking you to my parents."

She took hold of the girl's arm and with difficulty and help from Clia and Corrinne led her into the house to the study where her parents were.

Inside the study both girls were sitting on chairs in floods of tears. Dad was on the phone talking quietly to someone and as Hally and her two friends eased into the room with the drunk girl her mum put her finger to her lips indicating that Hally wait. Dad finished on the phone and turned to his daughter.

"So what have we got here?"

He asked. Hally pointed to the girl.

"Dad she's completely hammered and she's with these two."

"That explains a few things then. We can't get a word from these two. They just keep crying."

He told his daughter.

"Who were you phoning?"

Hally asked.

"Your mother managed to prise a home phone number out of one of them but her parents are not in. I was speaking to her older sister and asked her to tell her parents to phone us as soon as they get home."

The girl Hally had brought in made a loud belching noise.

"Oops. Don't know where that came from."

She muttered.

Hally's mum took the girl's bag and opened it.

"Hey you, you can't do tha' tha's my pers… my bag."

"Oh be quiet."

Mum told her firmly and at the same time pulled out a bottle of almost empty vodka.

"And where did you get this from?"

She demanded. Kerry suddenly stopped crying and this caused everyone to look straight at her. She was shaking her head rapidly at the girl. As soon as she realised everyone was looking at her she stopped and covered her face with her hands and began making a sobbing noise again.

"That is not going to work young lady."

Mum told her very sternly.

"Now where did this alcohol come from and have any of you got any more?"

Kerry and Anna both reluctantly handed over their bags and mum found inside a bottle of whisky and a bottle of rum. Both bottles had a lot more inside than the vodka.

"So I'll ask again where did it come from?"

Anna genuinely began to sob again. Kerry gave her a fierce look but she ignored her and quickly spilled out the truth.

"We got all of it from Dana. She sold it to us for a fiver a bottle. But she made us promise not to say where we got it from, she said…" At this point Kerry jumped up and grabbed Anna.

"Shut up you stupid cow, he'll kill us."

Dad stepped forward and pulled Kerry away.

"Now calm down, we'll have none of that sort of behaviour." And looking at Anna he said "Go on and tell us everything."

With her eyes wide and obviously terrified Anna began to explain.

"Hally you know that stuff about the nicked booze, well Dana and her lot got a load of it off Cobby and when she knew we were coming to your party she said we could buy some off her. Only she said there was a condition attached, like we could have each bottle for a fiver if we made sure the bottles were stashed somewhere in your house. And we was supposed to get a bit drunk and later she's gonna call five oh anonymously and tell them there was trouble at the party and they would come and find the booze and and …."

She burst into fresh sobs. Kerry stared at Anna furiously, but Hally felt the anger just bubble up and burst out of her.

"WHAT HAVE I EVER DONE TO YOU?"

She shouted. Mum put her arm around her and pulled her close.

"Hush hush baby. We will deal with this. You, Corrinne and Clia go back to the party and enjoy yourselves."

"But mum…"

"Go on love do as your mum says. I'm going to call the police myself."

As he said this both Kerry and Anna started to protest but he told them both to be quiet and sit still. The other girl in the meantime had slid down the wall and was snoring very loudly.

Hally was extremely angry as she marched back to her guests in the garden. Passing Nathan he linked his arm through his sister's and demanded.

"What's goin' on sis?"

"I'll tell you what's going on. Those idiots in there were not only going to ruin my party but get mum and dad into trouble at the same time."

Hally told him in a hard but very quiet voice, walking rapidly at the same time. Corrinne and Clia were almost running to keep up with her.

"Calm down Hally. Don't let them see that they have upset you."

Clia told her in a breathless voice.

"Don't worry. I'm perfectly calm. But you realise that Trish must have something to do with this 'cos she was the one who asked if they could come with her."

"Look Hal. I know you're really angry and so am I but you know Trish might not be involved. Just go and ask her but don't, you know, go steaming in with accusations."

Clia told Hally. Hally stopped and looked at her friends. Nathan was still clinging to her arm. She seemed to have forgotten he was there. For a few seconds she stood motionless, thinking, then she nodded slowly at the two girls. She knew Clia was right, how many times in the past had one of the popular group come and accused her of something she hadn't done? How many times had she been accused of saying something to someone when she hadn't even been there? No, she knew she had to deal with this carefully and diplomatically. Suddenly she realised her little brother was still attached to her elbow.

"Nat, get off."

She told him shaking her arm a little. With a groan he let her go but tagged along with the threesome as they made their way toward Trish.

Several people tried to get Hally's attention but she managed to deter them by whispering "Later,later." She spotted Trish amongst a group and moved towards her.

"What's up Hally?"

Trish asked as they came level. Corrinne and Clia stood either side of Hally and Nathan tried to peer around the girls.

"Trish why did you want Kerry and Anna here?"

Hally asked softly. Trish gave her a puzzled frown.

"Kerry asked me to ask you. She said something about not wanting to miss such a cool party. Why?"

"Did you know Dana had made an agreement with them?"

Hally enquired.

"What!"

Exclaimed Trish.

"Hally what do you mean, what's going on?"

Trish looked genuinely upset and concerned. In an instant Hally knew that Trish had not been privy to the setup and quickly informed her of the night's happenings.

"Oh my… crikey, that's just…Hally I'm so sorry. If I'd had any idea."

Trish stammered. Hally shrugged.

"Hey, look, it's not your fault so let's just leave it to my parents and enjoy this party."

Hally told her. She then turned to Nathan who was still hovering beside her.

"Go and turn the music off for a minute please Nat."

Without question her brother dashed off and a moment later all went quiet. Several people looked around questioningly, especially those who were dancing. Hally moved to the edge of the deck and raising her arms called for the attention of her guests.

"Everyone sorry to interrupt your fun but I need to tell you all something that has happened. Without going into too much detail at the moment a couple of girls have started some trouble and my parents have had to call the police."

There was a general murmur and a few exclamations of "What!" and "No!"

"So I think we should all try and get on with the party and let my parents and the police sort it out"

Hally finished speaking and sent Nathan back to the stereo. A few friends came over to ask what was going on but Hally refused to explain fully. She wanted the police to deal with it before it hit the grapevine.

A short while later mum came and found Hally in the garden. The party was in full swing and most of the guests were now dancing and having fun. The light was fading and as the moon came up big and full and glowing, the lanterns which Hally had lit a little earlier began to give off a warm romantic glow.

"Well everything is sorted sweetheart, the police have spoken to the girls and taken them home."

"Are they going to speak to Dana?"

Hally asked her mother.

"They're sending someone round…" and as Hally began to interrupt "…and they have informed control about the expected phone call. I gather from what I heard that they will wait until that has been made before they go to see her."

"Well I hope she gets the shock of her life."

Hally told her mum with a furious frown on her face. Then they both looked at each other and smiled.

"Come on, let's enjoy the rest of the party."

Mum told her and taking her arm pulled her into the middle of the deck and started to dance. Mum could dance well and kept up with the latest dances and before long several of Hally's guests had joined in as well.

The rest of the party went very well. The barbeque was a real hit and by the end of the evening everyone had had a most enjoyable time. As her guests began to leave in twos and threes the garden quietened down and by eleven thirty there was just Corrinne and Clia and Hally's family. Nathan had decided he was hungry again so dad put some burgers and sausages on the barbeque and the little group pulled up chairs close together.

"That was a great party."

Clia told Hally stifling a yawn behind her hand.

"Absolutely marvellous."

Corrinne chipped in putting on her posher than posh voice. Everyone laughed. Mum and dad handed out food and (protesting loudly) hauled Nathan off to bed leaving the three girls to gossip and gossip they did. Between them they worked out who was now going out with whom and who had broken up, or had a row or just had a kiss and a cuddle.

It was two in the morning when the three girls finally made their way to Hally's room. They had talked themselves out and were quite ready to just go to sleep. As Hally turned out the light Clia mumbled.

"Just think what your sixteenth will be like."

The other two giggled but soon all three were sleeping soundly and Hally was dreaming about her fifteenth birthday party.

CHAPTER 3

Study Leave and Mocks

As soon as everyone started arriving at school on Monday morning Hally was questioned about her party and what Dana had planned. Everyone seemed to know more about it than Hally herself and at one point the rumours had got so out of control that Hally overheard someone telling another that her house had been raided and six people had been arrested including her dad.

By lunchtime Hally, Corrinne and Clia had given up trying to explain the truth and let the rumours spread as they wished. The only piece of information that the girls could glean from everything was that Dana had been questioned by the police on the night of the party but had denied any knowledge of the incident. Apparently she had also done the same thing when the police questioned her at school about the robbery. So no one really knew what the situation was anymore about the proposed planting of the stolen alcohol. Hally made it clear that she was going to ensure her parents find out from the police what was going on and that she wasn't going to take anything she heard at school as the truth.

Actually Hally didn't have to ask her parents to do anything because early that evening they had a visit from the local constable anyway. Mum was just about to serve the dinner when there was a knock at the door. Nathan as usual dashed to open it before anyone else could get up and as usual came rushing back into the kitchen gabbling who was at the door.

"mumdadit'sthepolice."

He said it as one long word practically skidding to a halt in front of his parents. Since the word "police" was quite discernible all three stood up.

"Stay where you are Hally, I'll go."

With a loud groan Hally sat back down and mum began putting lids back on saucepans and food back into the oven. A moment later dad came into the kitchen with PC James Duston.

"I'm sorry to interrupt your evening meal."

He told them.

"I thought you would like to know what the present situation is."

Nathan nodded his head quickly and grinned widely.

"We have spoken to Dana Edwards at length but she is adamant that she knows nothing about the stolen alcohol. However the three girls who were in possession of the bottles at your party have all told us Dana sold them the drink and insisted they plant the empty bottles here. We did receive a phone call but it came from a call box so we don't know who made it. We do know she was out that evening but we don't know who with. As yet we haven't been able to trace anymore of the stolen goods and we think it's probable that it has all been sold on. I'm sorry that I can't give you any more positive news."

"So she's going to get away with it then."

Hally spoke vehemently.

"No, but it is going to take a bit of time. We believe Martin Cob is heavily involved and we have officers dealing with that. I will keep you up to date as much as possible."

Hally opened her mouth to protest again but mum put her arm around her and spoke before she had a chance.

"Thank you PC Duston, we would be grateful if you could do that."

"Well I'll leave you to your meal then, good evening."

Mum led him to the door and as she returned she put her hand up because she could see her daughter was about to explode.

"Now Hally, I know you're angry but we are all going to have to be patient. The police know what they are doing and in situations like this they can't rush in they have to get as much evidence as they can."

Hally slumped into her chair with her arms folded.

"Come on Tink." Dad said tickling her in the ribs. "This will all get sorted."

Hally couldn't stay angry with any of her family for long and as dad continued tickling her she began to giggle and sat up straighter at the table.

"That's better."

Dad told her then he got up to help mum with the dinner.

Later that evening Hally sat curled up watching a movie. She had finished her coursework and had helped Nathan with his homework. Her parents were in the study looking something up on the internet, they often did this and also had a wide group of friends that they talked to either by email or instant messaging. She felt quite relaxed and peaceful and was able to stay up later than usual because she didn't have to be in school in the morning. The next four days were devoted to studying for the mock GCSE exams the following week. Hally always became nervous when taking exams and didn't find revising easy, however she knew Clia would undoubtedly have created colour coded revision timetables for all three of them so she put it out of her mind for the rest of the evening.

Corrinne and Clia arrived at Hally's just after ten in the morning. As predicted Clia handed Hally an A3 laminated revision timetable.

"I've already got mine."

Corrinne told her.

"Well you want to do well and you know how hopeless you both are at revising."

Clia stated matter of factly. All three girls laughed and made their way into the kitchen. Mum had left a plentiful supply of snacks and drinks for them and they quickly set out their books in readiness. Hally quickly told her friends what PC Duston had said the previous evening and for a while they discussed what might happen next.

"Right, that's enough chit chat it's time to get on."

Clia announced. The other two looked at her and laughed.

"What?"

She asked.

"You look so serious and business like."

Corrinne told her.

"Well this is important, you know that."

"OK, chill a bit Clia, we are going to study our little socks off."

Hally told her. Clia smiled and leaned forward to point out on their timetables where they needed to start.

By one thirty the girls were ready to take a well earned rest. Between them they made ham and salad sandwiches and as they ate the talk turned again to Dana Edwards.

"I wish there was some way we could get her to own up."

Hally mumbled through a mouthful of sandwich.

"Well she's just one of those nasty little bitches that take pleasure in hurting other people. She'll get her comeuppance soon."

Corrinne stated.

"I wish I could be so sure."

Hally replied. Clia had remained quiet, silently munching her lunch. Then she put her sandwich down purposefully and said.

"Look, let's go out for a bit and get some fresh air. Besides I think I have an idea."

The other two both began to ask what she had thought of but Clia put up a hand and insisted that she would explain later.

The three girls made for the local park and saw several other students there in small groups. These they avoided and headed for a bench surrounded by large oak trees. It was a spot they had used many times when they wanted to discuss something serious and didn't want to be inside. A few birds were pecking the ground around the bench and took off as they approached. Clia who had brought her sandwich with her in a paper towel crumbled some of it and threw it in amongst the trees and watched the birds swoop down to feed.

"Well, come on tell us."

Hally said excitedly. Corrinne rubbed her hands together and nodded at Clia.

"I think we should go and see Dana..." the other two began to protest that that would be useless. "...just listen. I think we should go and tell her that we are going to start a very strong rumour that she has grassed on Cobby to get herself out of trouble with the police if she doesn't admit what she did to you. I think she'll fall for it."

Hally frowned with uncertainty.

"What if she just goes and tells everyone that it's us."

"We deny any knowledge. Anyway she's pretty thick. If she does tell the police what she did to you she's gonna have to tell the police where she got the stuff, so in a way she will be grassing on Cobs but I reckon she's more scared of him than the police and they will probably be able to pick him up without bringing her into it."

Corrinne didn't look convinced.

"I dunno it's a bit risky and we shouldn't really interfere with the police investigation, we could get into trouble ourselves."

"We are not interfering!"

Exclaimed Hally

"We are just trying to make her tell the truth. Well Clia I'm game. We might as well go and try it now."

Corrinne knew she was outvoted and so did not try and change their minds but supported their intention. Clia tossed the rest of the sandwich to the birds and the girls headed for the northern gate of the park which would take them to Dana's house.

"I just hope she's in."

Hally told the other two.

"She's probably still in bed. She's hardly likely to be revising and we all know she stays out to what time she likes."

Corrinne commented.

They arrived at Dana's house and Hally pressed hard against the door bell. There was no response, so she knocked hard on the door itself. After a short wait the girls heard an upstairs window opening.

"What do you lot want?"

They looked up and saw Dana leaning out of a window.

"We need to talk to you."

Hally called up.

"I got nuffin to say to you."

Dana replied and was about to close the window when Clia called out.

"If you don't it will be worse for you."

The window stopped moving and Dana's head reappeared.

"I'll be down in a minute."

After several minutes wait the front door opened just wide enough for Dana to peer around.

"Well?"

"We are not going to talk to you through a crack in the door."

Clia stated very firmly. With a sigh Dana opened the door fully and stood clutching her dressing gown around her.

"I 'spose you better come in."

She mumbled moodily. The three girls stepped into the hallway and Dana led them into the kitchen. Hally looked at her friends with a small frown. The kitchen was a complete mess. There were dirty dishes and pans piled in the sink, bread and butter left open to the flies and a pile of laundry spilling out of a laundry basket in the corner. Dana found what appeared to be a clean glass and filled it with water; then she leaned against the table and waited.

"I want you to tell the police what you did."

Hally told her. Dana gave a short harsh laugh.

"On your bike."

She replied snappily. Clia stepped forward slightly and looked directly in Dana's face.

"Well actually, this is not really a request."

"Oh really, so you're gonna make me, is that it?"

Dana sneered back, placing the glass on the table and crossing her arms.

"No we can't do that, but there is something else we can do."

Clia told her examining her finger nails as though Dana's comment hadn't bothered her at all. Dana looked disconcerted

"What…what are you on about?"

She mumbled hesitantly.

"Well…" Clia paused for effect. "…we just put it about that you have already grassed on Cobs and the police know everything."

Hally had to try very hard to keep a straight face because Dana's expression gave her a moment of pure pleasure.

"You do that an' 'e'll kill me!"

Exclaimed Dana. Her eyes were so wide open they looked like two saucers.

"Well, you go to the police and tell them everything you know and they will lock him up; so he won't be able to get at you will he?"

Clia told her firmly.

The girls could see Dana battling the problem over in her mind. For a full two minutes she remained silent and motionless except for the odd little frown that appeared on her forehead. Suddenly she just crumpled before them. Tears spilled down her face and she slowly sank to the floor wrapping her arms around her knees and hugging herself closely. Hally quickly dropped down beside her, the other two followed suit.

"Dana it's not that bad, just tell the truth!"

Hally exclaimed in a very worried voice.

"You just don't understand."

Dana sobbed. All the hardness and cockiness had gone from her voice.

"What don't we understand?"

Hally asked.

"Well just look at this place. I'm on my own here and I don't know what to do. I needed…" her voice broke as fresh tears flooded down her face. "…need needed the money. There are bills all over the place, I just managed to keep the electricity on but I think, I think the umm gas has been cut off and the umm telephone."

"But where are your parents?"

Hally asked, a look of astonishment on her face.

"My mum found another bloke, some American fella and she went with him to the States and my dad hasn't been around in years. I don't even know where he is."

"Your mum just left you here on your own?"

Hally couldn't believe what she was hearing and did wonder if Dana was making it all up to get out of the situation. She glanced at Clia and Corrinne and from their expressions thought they were thinking the same as her. Dana must have caught their suspicions because she quickly glanced from one girl to another.

"Honestly it's true, I can show you all the letters asking for money and all my mum's stuff has gone."

Hally stood up and looked around her. The kitchen certainly

did look as though it had been left unattended for some considerable time.

"When did she go?"

She asked without looking around. At first there was no response, and then as Hally turned and looked at Dana she saw her staring at a calendar on the wall and then she spoke in a flat sad voice.

"One month, three days and five hours."

All three girls let their eyes wander to the calendar and there marked in red marker pen was a large circle around a date. Corrinne walked over and read aloud the words written next to the circle. 'MUM GONE'

Hally glanced down at Dana and back at her friends. She felt useless and desperately sorry for the girl who had caused her so much hurt and suffering over the past years. She had no idea what to say or do. Dana was no longer crying she simply sat huddled with her chin resting on her knees. Hally looked at Clia.

"What should she do Clia?"

At first Clia shrugged her shoulders then she chewed lightly on the corner of her bottom lip, a sure sign that she was mulling over an idea.

"Well I think maybe she should call social services."

Dana's reaction was totally unexpected, she just froze. Hally kneeled down in front of her, fearful at the look of pure terror on Dana's face.

"What's the matter?"

"Please not, no not not social services. They'll just put me into another foster home and I can't bear that!"

Dana pleaded.

"What do you mean again?"

Corrinne asked.

"I had to go into foster care two years ago 'cos mum left me on my own and went on holiday. Some neighbour I think reported her and social services came and took me away. When mum got back she had to go to court and everything to get me back. The people I got put with had three kids of their own and it was just horrible being with people I didn't even know. Besides I'm gonna be sixteen in just four months, so if I can just hang on 'til then..."

Dana shrugged and her meaning was quite clear to Hally and her friends, she wanted them to stay out of it. Hally hated the idea of not doing anything but knew Dana would not thank her for interfering.

"Alright Dana, we won't say anything about this to anyone but will you please go to the police and tell them what really happened?"

Dana looked at the three girls sadly and then slowly nodded her head.

"Might as well 'cos my life can't get any worse than it is now."

"Thanks Dana and if you need any help please come and ask, my mum's great at giving advice and stuff like that."

Dana didn't reply she just stared at the floor. Hally signalled to her friends and they turned towards the door. As they reached the front door Hally paused, she then went back to the calendar and using the large marker pen hanging from a string wrote down her mobile number in large writing, Dana watching silently. She then turned and with her two friends left, quietly closing the door behind them.

"Well what do you make of that?"

Clia asked.

"I don't know but it doesn't seem right to just leave her to it."

Hally replied, a note of helplessness in her voice.

"I know what you mean Hally but she was quite insistent that we don't get involved."

Corrinne told her.

For a while the girls walked in silence, each deep in their own thoughts about Dana's predicament. Hally especially couldn't stop wondering if she should tell her mother about it and risk upsetting Dana if social services got involved. In the end she told herself that she would keep Dana's secret for now but if she thought things were getting worse later on she would tell her mother then. With that she linked arms with Clia and Corrinne.

"Come on let's get back to mine and do some more revision."

For the rest of the week the girls studied hard and had little time to think about what was happening to Dana. Hally and her family heard nothing from the police until Friday evening. Hally and Nathan were sitting in the lounge watching television and their parents were in the study. Both heard the door bell but neither moved to answer it. After a short time they heard voices from the hallway and curiosity won over the programme they were engrossed in. Quietly, they moved towards the door which stood slightly ajar and leaned into the gap to listen. Quickly they realised it was the police and boldly moved into the hallway to find out what was happening.

"Hally, Nathan, the sergeant has some news" and looking towards the police officer, "shall we go into the lounge?"

Holding her arm out to show the way, mum led them all back into the lounge. She indicated a seat for the police sergeant who sat down and looked towards the family.

"We have apprehended Martin Cob and have found a large quantity of stolen goods, including some of the alcohol and cigarettes from the recent burglaries in a lock up he has been using. There were several other youths involved who are also being questioned but Martin will be appearing in front of the magistrate tomorrow."

Hally let out a long breath.

"Did Dana Edwards have anything to do with this?"

She asked softly.

"I can't discuss the details I'm afraid. I can only let you know about Martin Cob because he is over eighteen and has been linked with the trouble you had at your party."

Hally nodded and her mother turned to the officer.

"Well thank you for letting us know what you can. At least one of these hooligans will be off the streets."

Hally stood up.

"I think I will go to my room, ok."

Her parents nodded and she quickly left, anxious to phone her friends and tell them the news.

The following week was too busy and full of exams for anyone to gossip about what had happened to Martin Cob. Hally heard a few whispers around the school and Dana seemed to be keeping a distance. Even the usual name calling and teasing that followed Hally around had ceased. It seemed everyone was concentrating hard on their work. Even during break and lunchtimes year ten students could be seen dotted about the school with their noses buried in books for last minute revision.

At the end of the week the year tens had a special assembly half an hour before school finished. Mr Hopkins stood at the front of the hall and the murmur died down as he prepared to speak.

"We realise this has been an extremely stressful time for you all, made even more so by the events of late. However we would all like to congratulate you all on a week of very hard work and concentration. We have not seen such effort put into mock exams for several years at this school and we are sure you will all put as much into the finals next summer. The next few weeks will be hard as you will be receiving your results and will know what level of papers you are likely to be entered into for the GCSEs, but please be assured the final decision will come later."

Students from all year groups flooded the gates of the school as they all left for the day but none were as pleased as the year Tens. Hally, Corrinne and Clia filed out amongst the crowd which began to thin outside the gates as students departed in different directions and towards the school buses. Most of the conversations were about the exams and how each thought they had either done well, not bad or that things had gone horribly wrong. Hally and her friends had already discussed their feelings about the exams and were now planning the weekend.

"We could go shopping, I need some tops."

Corrinne suggested to the other two.

"Yeah and we could go for pizza after, then back to mine."

Clia said enthusiastically. Corrinne laughed, pizza was Clia's absolutely favourite food especially from Pepe's Pizza in the town. Hally made no comment but asked.

"So, we staying at your house this weekend then?"

Clia nodded yes in reply.

"I thought we were staying at yours Corrinne?"

"Well remember, mum and dad are going to Nan's 'cos she's not well. I told you yesterday."

Hally frowned ever so slightly.

"I must not have been listening."

"Hally, is something up?"

Corrinne asked worriedly. Hally didn't reply and Clia had to nudge her with her elbow.

"Mm what was that?"

Hally asked. Her two friends looked at her with puzzled expressions on their faces.

"OK Hally spill."

Clia told her firmly. Hally looked at both her friends. Then with a big sigh she said.

"I just keep thinking about Dana. You know it's only a few weeks until we finish for the summer and then she will be stuck in that house on her own all the time."

"Well knowing Dana, she will be sleeping all day and out most of the night."

Clia replied nonchalantly.

"I know that's how it probably will be, but..."

Hally didn't get the chance to finish. Both her friends linked her arm and chimed.

"Don't worry about her!"

The three girls giggled and marched off with their arms still linked in the general direction of home. At the junction where their roads crossed Clia and Corrinne parted from Hally and she continued the short way down her street home.

Although not one of those teenagers that spent half the weekend in bed, Hally did usually enjoy an extra hour on a Saturday morning. However this Saturday she was up much earlier than usual much to the surprise of mum. The piece of toast was half way to her mouth when her daughter walked into the kitchen.

"Are you feeling alright Hally?"

Mum frowned putting the toast back on the plate and rising to place her hand on Hally's forehead.

"Mm you don't seem to have a temperature."

Hally giggled.

"Very funny mummy."

Mum smiled and switched the kettle back on adding a teabag to a mug at the same time.

"So why up so bright and early?"

She asked. Hally slid into a chair at the table, her mother poured boiling water into the mug and placed the freshly made tea in front of her. Just like her, Hally couldn't get motivated in the morning until she had drunk at least one cup of tea.

"I just don't want to miss the day. It's so nice outside and the last week has been chaotic. It feels like I've been stuck inside for ever doing the exams."

Hally explained to her mother. Mum was again taken aback by how mature her daughter was becoming. For a moment she bit back a feeling of tears as realisation came that her baby girl was closer to womanhood than childhood. So not to let Hally notice she quickly said.

"So what have you got planned for today?"

As she sipped her tea, Hally imparted the plans she had made with Corrinne and Clia. Mum smiled and then reached across the table for her bag.

"Well I think you have worked really hard this past couple of weeks, so take this and get yourself something nice."

She pulled a twenty pound note from her purse and handed it to her daughter.

"I don't need that mum. I still have some birthday money to spend."

She had been brought up to accept praise and pride for working hard at school and didn't believe in financial rewards for doing her best to learn.

"Hally, I know we don't give either of you money for being good, but just today I want to give you this. OK, it's not for doing well at school then, I'm just feeling generous; and before you say anything (Hally had opened her mouth to interrupt) we're taking your brother into town for new football boots."

Hally grinned and took the money from her mother. She stood up and taking her mug with her leaned over and planted a kiss on her mum's cheek.

"I'm off to get ready."

CHAPTER 4

Summer Begins

For the next few weeks everything at home and school was normal. Each day came and went with school, homework and friends. The usual name calling had restarted at school now the exams were over but without Dana's input the impact was less. At times, when the group of girls who delighted in teasing Hally were nearby; she noticed that as they started to shout abuse they looked towards Dana for encouragement, and when they didn't receive it closed their mouths as though they had been struck dumb. This amused Hally and her friends but they made no comment, simply enjoying the bemused and somewhat agitated expressions of the name callers.

The last week of term was given to sports day, the six form barbeque and various other events including the teacher's show. This was always an event to look forward to. Miss Drayman, the head of Drama, along with Mrs Walker, the head of English put together a show that consisted of various comedy sketches and acts (talented and untalented) played by the teachers. The untalented usually being the funniest along with scenes such as the whole IT department (which just happened to be all men) dressed as Can Can girls trying to do the splits.

At the end of the day and after the usual speech from Mr Hopkins about being sensible young adults in the community, Hally, Corrinne and Clia left the school premises for a long and hopefully enjoyable summer. They began by heading for the Hotspot café that all the teenagers loved, where they ordered coffees and muffins to celebrate the beginning of the holiday.

Hally noticed there were several boys that she didn't recognise and very soon the three girls were huddled together discussing which of the boys was the fittest. One boy in particular caught Hally's eye and he seemed to be glancing over at her frequently too, but Hally shyly avoided these gazes. Corrinne noticed this and tried to engage Hally in a conversation about the boy but Hally wouldn't be drawn in. Instead she tacitly avoided the subject by asking Clia if she was going to Corfu with her parents. Clia gave a small frown and said.

"You know I'm not Hally. Don's home from uni and mum and dad said I could stay at home this year with him."

"Oh yeah, I remember now, just forgot. You know I haven't seen your brother in ages."

Clia looked at Corrinne and gave her a very small frown. Corrinne gave an almost indistinct shrug back, both girls were confused at their friend's behaviour, they both knew that Hally had seen Clia's older brother just four weeks ago when he had been home visiting from university. He had taken all three girls to the cinema and thoroughly spoiled them for the day. Neither mentioned this to Hally and Hally didn't seem to notice anything amiss, so they ignored it and turned the conversation to what they planned to do that evening. Hally's parents were going out so the girls were staying at Hally's to look after Nathan.

"Shall I bring that new DVD mum bought me?"

Corrinne asked the other two.

"Ooh yes please."

Hally quickly replied. Corrinne giggled.

"Thought that would get your attention Hally."

"What do you mean?"

Hally asked, blushing as she said it.

"We both know you've got the hots for that well fit actor in the movie."

"Yeah" Clia added nodding her head. "You couldn't stop talking about him the last movie we watched him in."

"I wasn't that bad…"

She stopped as she saw her friends break out into giggles and quickly joined in.

"Well, so what, he's an actor, not like I'm gonna meet him or anything is it."

Hally managed to say in between giggles.

The girls finished their drinks and cakes and stood up to leave the café. Hally took a little longer than usual to straighten her top and pick up her bag, which Clia noticed but didn't comment on. They then made their way out. Just outside the coffee shop the girls stopped suddenly when they heard someone calling out.

"Girls, hey girls, wait!"

All three looked around to see who was calling them. Hally blushed to the roots of her hair when she realised it was not just one of the boys they had been discussing, but the very one she had been looking at.

"You left your jumper."

The boy said looking directly at Hally.

"Oh, erm." Hally mumbled, trying to hide her blush with her hair. "Uh thanks."

The boy held the jumper out for her to take. She didn't move. Corrinne gave a little cough and Hally jumped slightly. This seemed to shake her out of her embarrassing freeze, and quickly she held her hand out for her jumper. As she took it her fingers touched his very lightly and Hally felt her insides go to mush. She just didn't know what was happening to her. Holding the jumper tightly to her she mumbled a hurried thank you and turned to walk away. She felt as though she wanted to run, but managed to keep to a fast walk as Corrinne and Clia caught up with her.

"What?..."

Clia began.

"Don't, please, I know I just made a right plank of myself."

Hally replied. She hugged the jumper to her and looked at the ground as she walked.

"But why were you so embarrassed?"

Corrinne asked.

"I don't know. I just..." she sighed deeply "he was, um, looking at me in the café and...oh look can we just forget it. What a great start to the hols."

Her friends just nodded and accepted what she said knowing she would explain later.

It was much later when Hally finally had a chance to tell her friends how she was feeling. Mum and dad had been gone for half an hour and Nathan was in his room playing on his play station. He had strict instructions from his mother that he had to pack it away at eight thirty and could stay up until nine, so long as he didn't annoy Hally. Downstairs the girls were settled on loungers on the deck. It was a hot summer evening and though they were keen to watch the movie the heat was too good to miss by sitting indoors. Each girl had a tall glass of lemonade with slices of orange and lemon floating amongst the ice cubes, a large jug with more of the beverage on a table in between them.

"I just love your mum's lemonade Hally."

Clia commented between sips.

"Well actually, I made it. With mum's supervision."

Hally told her friends.

"Well she taught you well. Is it some sort of family recipe passed to the girls?"

Hally giggled.

"Nah, nothing like that, she just sort of chucked it together once and remembered what she had put in. She showed me so we can take turns making it."

"Well, I think you and your mum should keep quiet about how you make it 'cos someone will find out and then mass produce it and make a mint."

Corrinne said this so seriously that the other two burst out laughing.

"Well it's true"

She exclaimed indignantly. This only caused the other two to laugh even harder.

"Oh go on take the mickey out of me."

She told them sulkily. Hally and Clia knew their friend too well to know this was just a charade. This was confirmed when Corrinne looked up and burst into giggles too.

For a while the girls sat quietly sipping their drinks just enjoying the warm evening. Hally looked at each of her friends, hesitated a moment, took a deep breath and said.

"He's gorgeous."

Corrinne and Clia looked straight at her. They knew Hally

would say more if they stayed quiet. They didn't have to question her for information. After a short interlude Hally continued.

"That boy in the café, he is gorgeous. I have definitely fallen head over heels in love."

Clia looked across the deck to Corrinne and raised her eyebrows. Both the girls knew this was unusual for their friend. Hally was always very cautious when declaring her feelings for any boy, let alone one she had only seen once and for a less than an hour.

"Hals, we don't get it. Who are you talking about?"

Clia asked.

"You know, the guy that gave me my jumper."

She stopped, again looked at each of her friends and then continued.

"I don't know who he is. I just know that when he looked at me I…I…well, I just, I've never felt like this before. I know I haven't had many boyfriends, well let's be honest, actually boyfriends is an overstatement. I went out with Josh for a day and a half, and that was a joke on his part with his mates. Then I went out with Dan for a week. I saw him precisely three times, we had one date to the cinema and when he couldn't get into my pants he dumped me. So, considering my limited experience with lads, well, I just feel completely different about this one."

Corrinne sighed.

"Sounds like you really have it bad Hal."

"Look, let's just think about this a moment."

Clia said.

"First we need to find a way of finding out who he is. I mean he could be visiting someone."

"Don't say anymore, please, Clia. He's just got to have a girlfriend, a guy like that. No way is he gonna be interested in me."

Hally choked back a sob and brushed a hand across her face. Her two friends looked at her with concern on their faces. They had never seen Hally this worked up about any boy before. Usually she just took a fancy to a boy but if he showed no interest she just giggled it off with Clia and Corrinne and moved on. This time was so different and Hally's two best friends were unsure of how to deal with it. Clia, however soon took charge of the situation.

"Come on Hally, don't cry darling. We can sort this out."

Corrinne pulled a handful of tissues out of her bag and handed them to Hally as Clia continued.

"Right. This lad is obviously very important to you. So, I am going to find out who he is right now."

Hally dabbed her eyes and in a shaky voice said.

"How are you going to do that?"

"Contacts my dear, contacts."

She said this in such a grown up voice, even Hally, who was still teary laughed.

"What?..."

Hally began, but Clia held up a hand as she pulled her mobile from her bag. None of the girls spoke as she quickly scrolled to her phonebook and put the phone to her ear. After a short wait she spoke.

"Hi, how you? Yeah I'm good thanks. Listen can you do me a favour? There's this new lad in town, prob' about eighteen or nineteen, yeah that's him. Do you know who he is? Hey, that is brill'. Look, Don's home in a couple of days. Yeah, he did, but he went surfing with some uni mates for a bit. You know you should come round. I know, but he still chats about you. (she giggled) O.K ta for the info, see you soon."

She hung up her phone with a satisfied look on her face.

"What was that all about?"

Corrinne asked.

"Tell all in a bit. The important thing is I know who he is."

Hally gripped her hands together in front of her, her fingertips close to her lips.

"Go on."

She said tentatively.

"His name is Wesley Robinson, he just moved here from Oxford, he's eighteen and he's going to sixth form in September. Oh, and he does not have a girlfriend."

"How on earth did you find out all that?"

Corrinne asked, with raised eyebrows.

"Well, you remember that girl Don had a bit of a thing with a while back. The sister of one of his mates, well we sort of keep in touch, you know on the net and text. Well I figured she would probably know who this guy is 'cos they would be about the same age."

"You are such a genius Clia."

Corrinne said. Hally had remained silent throughout. She sat with her hands in front of her as though she were frozen.

"So now we have to work out a plan to get you together."

Clia stated matter of factly. However, Hally was not listening.

"Hey, Hally."

Clia called gently.

"Oh, What? Did you say something?"

Her two friends burst into giggles.

"OK, back track. We know who he is, now we are going to plan a way for you to meet him."

Corrinne told her.

"You're gonna do what?"

Exclaimed Hally.

"No, I don't, I can't ..."

Hally could not find the words she wanted to say. With a big sigh she let her fingers drop into her lap and looked at her two friends.

"OK, I give in. what are you going to do?"

Corrinne looked at Clia and raised her eyebrows. Clia frowned slightly, and pinched her lip between her thumb and forefinger. For a few seconds the only sound that could be heard was the humming of the bees in the lavender that grew around the edge of the deck.

"Got it!"

Exclaimed Clia.

Hally and Corrinne jumped so much that Hally knocked her glass over nudging Clia who let out a loud "Ouch!" as she bit her lip where she still held it pinched between her fingers.

The three girls folded up with laughter. Corrinne, who was still holding her glass drenched herself in lemonade; this only made the situation more funny to the girls and a fresh tide of giggles followed. After a few moments the giggles gradually subsided and Hally went into the kitchen to get paper towels for Corrinne. When she returned the other two had calmed down. Hally handed Corrinne the paper towels and topped up her drink before sitting back down.

"Well?"

She looked to her two friends questioningly. Clia smiled.

"Tomorrow we go back to the café at lunch time. It's always busy then and everyone goes there, so if he's new in town he will probably be there."

Hally frowned. Corrinne saw this and quickly jumped in.

"You know statistically Clia is right."

Hally giggled at her friend's mathematical reference. Clia pounced on Hally's happier look and continued.

"So we go to the café for lunch."

"And then we…?"

Hally asked moving her hand in a circular motion to prompt her friend.

"Well we, we, well we will know when we get there."

She said with a rush. Corrinne and Hally sat silently for a few seconds, then they all burst into giggles again.

"Great plan."

Hally told Clia.

CHAPTER 5

Wes

After a very restless night Hally woke early and was showered and dressed long before anyone else in the family. Even Nathan was still in bed asleep, which showed the unusualness of Hally's situation as he was normally awake and in front of his play station before going down to breakfast. Hally made herself some tea and toast and settled at the table to eat. She hadn't touched either when she was startled by her mum coming into the kitchen.

"Didn't expect to see you down here."

Mum said as she touched the side of the kettle to see how hot it was.

"Oh, had a bit of a rough night that's all."

Hally replied. Mum frowned a little as she lifted a mug from the cupboard and waited for the kettle to re-boil.

"Hally, is something wrong baby?"

She asked her daughter gently.

"No, not wrong…" she paused taking a sip of tea. "just…different."

Hally told her mother, looking up at her. With her mug of tea made, mum sat opposite Hally.

"What do you mean sweetheart?"

She asked very gently. Hally smiled at her mum but her lower lip trembled a little as she tried to explain.

"Well there's this boy. I don't know him but Clia found out his name and how old he is. He's called Wesley and he's eighteen and we are going to the Hotspot café today to see if he's there."

She said the last bit quickly, took a great swallow of tea which resulted in her choking and spluttering.

"Careful babe, so what's bothering you about this? Don't you want to see him?"

Mum asked.

"Yes I do, that's the trouble. What if he doesn't even notice me?"

Hally said with real tears in her eyes.

"Maybe if you start at the beginning I will get a better idea of what you mean."

Mum said with a little smile. Hally looked at her mother and tried a little smile herself. Then with a very big sigh she explained everything. When she finished mum stood up and made fresh tea. Placing a mug in front of her daughter she smiled and said.

"Hally you are a very beautiful young woman with very little experience of boys. (Hally opened her mouth to comment) But that's good because it adds to your charm; and you also have a maturity that this boy can probably see. You are, fifteen going on grown up. If you like this boy, then make sure he notices you."

"But how?"

Hally asked sounding panicky.

"Well you know, when I first saw your dad he didn't know I was there. So, I simply walked into him. I sort of made out that I hadn't seen him but, well it did the trick."

Hally laughed. She had heard the story before, but it always made her laugh, and since her parents had been married for seventeen years and were still just as happy she figured it was a good plan.

"I just don't know if I'm brave enough to try something like that though."

She told her mother.

"Well you don't have to do exactly that. I mean you probably won't even have to. You are so pretty he's bound to notice you anyway."

Mum told her giving her a little hug. Hally lifted her shoulders and sighed a very deep sigh.

"Well… I had better go and get ready then."

She said this in such a way that her mum burst out laughing.

"You sound as if you are going to an interview or something."

She said. Hally stood up, took her tea and left the kitchen.

"Hally!" mum called "It's only half past seven."

Hally came back into the room with a deep frown.

"Oh cripes, that only leaves me like two and a half hours to get sorted."

With that she spun around spilling tea down her front and took off upstairs.

In her room Hally sat on the edge of her bed for several minutes not doing anything. Her mug of tea sat untouched and cold on the bedside table. She simply stared at the picture on her wall. She had had the picture since she was tiny. It was a christening present from her grandparents. It showed a tiny baby in a soft pink crib being watched over by two beautiful angels resting on pure white fluffy clouds. Hally had always believed the angels were her grandparents. Thinking of her grandmother brought tears to her eyes; she knew she was over emotional at the moment and with a big sigh sat up straight looked in her mirror and said.

"Right girl, get a grip and sort out what you are gong to wear."

She then laughed at herself for talking to herself, stood up and went to her wardrobe. Glancing through her clothes she debated on two outfits. Should she wear a denim mini, strappy top and flip-flops as it was hot, or jeans and T-shirt? She decided on jeans and strappy with flat sandals. The last thing she wanted was to wear heels and then go tripping over and making a real idiot of herself.

An hour later Hally stood in front of her mirror applying her makeup. She was always careful with this, her mum having shown her some time ago how to put it on to look natural and not like a painted doll. Today it seemed to be a real effort to get it just right, or so it seemed. Her eyeliner kept smudging and before long Hally realised her shaking hands were causing the problem. She abandoned the eye make-up to open her window and stand for a while just wondering why she was so nervous. He was after all just another boy, worse still one she didn't even vaguely know.

Breathing deeply, Hally closed her eyes and let the warm morning sun shine on her face. She stayed like that for several minutes. After a while she opened her eyes and looked out across the garden. A few birds were pecking at the feeders and bird table. It was peaceful watching them, almost mesmerising and for some time her thoughts were just on the little sparrows and starlings. Each little bird furiously fighting for seed or breadcrumbs, constantly aware of the danger of predators. A squawking fight between two starlings brought Hally out of her reverie; she turned back to her room which for a few seconds appeared very dark after the glaring sun; walked back to her dresser and began again to apply her eye make-up.

Hally walked into the kitchen a half hour later, saw it was empty and carried on out to the garden. Her mum was hanging washing on the line and Hally without talking began handing her items out of the basket.

"You all sorted then sweetie?"

Mum asked. Hally looked into her mother's eyes and nodded.

"Well you look very pretty."

"Oh, does it look like I've gone over the top?"

She asked quickly.

"No, not at all, you just look very pretty."

Mum assured her quickly.

"What time are Corrinne and Clia coming for you?"

"Well they'll be 'round at about ten and then we are going into town first then the café at lunchtime."

"So what are you going to do whilst you are waiting?"

Mum asked holding a towel to the line and pegging it at the same time.

"No idea. Is there anything you need help with?"

She asked, hoping her mum would have something to occupy her for the next hour.

"Mmm…well you could go and drag your little brother away from his play station; (she laughed at the look on Hally's face) only joking. No, actually, you could finish this off for me. Hally nodded and took over hanging the washing. But no matter what she did, her mind was in turmoil over the possibility of meeting Wesley.

"Wesley."

She said his name out loud, realised she had and looked about to see if mum had heard. She breathed a sigh of relief when she saw her mum inside the kitchen. She had shocked herself saying his name out loud and realised that it was in fact the first time she had actually thought about his name. Up until then he was just this boy whom she had taken a real liking to. By speaking his name it all suddenly became very real and she began to tremble.

Mum gently took the shirt out of Hally's hands and shook it out before hanging it on the line. She then took her daughter by the hand and led her into the kitchen. Hally didn't speak, she just let her mum gently push her into a chair.

"My darling, what a state you have got yourself into."

She told her.

"You were scrunching your dad's shirt into a ball. It would have been impossible to iron."

She finished with a small laugh. She then filled a glass with water and gave it to Hally who slowly sipped it.

"You seem more terrified than nervous about meeting this boy Hally."

Mum told her. For a few seconds Hally just sipped. She then put the glass on the table and told her mum what had happened outside.

"You know what I think?"

Mum asked. Hally shook her head.

"I think you have built this meeting up into such a big thing that you don't really feel you can cope. I mean he might not even be there, have you thought of that?"

Hally looked at her mum and a wide smile spread across her face.

"Yeah, course, he probably won't be there. We can just have an ordinary day in town and go to the café as usual. Oh what an idiot I am. I should know better than to get all dippy about meeting a guy who might not even be there. Thanks mum."

And she stood up and gave her mum a big kiss and a hug.

Hally was watching television when Corrinne and Clia arrived. Both girls were dressed in jeans, this made Hally feel much better about her choice of clothes.

After saying their hellos and goodbyes to mum the three set off for the town.

"What shall we do first? Do either of you need anything specific?"

Clia asked.

"Yep, I need new mascara, lip-gloss and eyeliner."

Corrinne stated.

"That's cool 'cos I need Chandlers too."

Clia told her. Chandlers was a small chemist where the girls could buy all their cosmetics and perfumes.

"What are you buying Clia?"

Hally asked. She asked this because Clia wore very little makeup and usually only went to Chandlers when Corrinne or herself needed to.

"Oh, I just want to have a look at some stuff."

She told her friends. This puzzled them because Clia was normally very open about her actions.

"OK, give."

Hally said to her. Clia looked at her and grinned.

"You know me too well Mackeller."

The use of Hally's surname was not rude, it was something the girls often did to each other, a bit like using nicknames.

"I want to check out some eye make-up advertised on television." Hally and Corrinne raised their eyebrows. "I know that's a surprise, but I just thought it was about time I started to look more like a woman."

Hally and Corrinne giggled. They found this remark more than just funny. To them it was hilarious since Clia looked older than both of them and had developed her figure quite some time before either of them. She was also very pretty with dark thick hair and big brown eyes.

"Clia, you are stunning and you already look like a woman."

Hally told her friend.

"Well sometimes, one has to simply enhance what one has already got."

Clia told them with a very straight face. This made the other two giggle again and then Clia herself joined in. Still laughing the three girls made their way towards Chandlers.

After spending some time shopping and window shopping the girls made their way towards the Hotspot café. As they neared the café they could see it was very busy. Hally slowed her pace, dropping behind her friends a little the nearer they got. Corrinne not only noticed but knew exactly what was bothering Hally.

"Hey Hally, don't look so petrified. Everything is going to be ok."

Corrinne and Clia also slowed down so they were level with Hally and on either side of her. They linked her arms to give her encouragement. Together the three girls approached the café door.

Just as they were about to push open the door, it was pulled from the inside and standing in front of them was the very boy they had come to see. Hally felt herself blushing and tried to pull away from her friends. All she wanted to do was turn and run. Inside she felt embarrassed and shaky, she simply did not know what to do and since the girls were still linked they were blocking the entrance. However the boy didn't seem to want to get past, in fact he moved to one side and held the door for the girls to pass through. As they separated to get through the open door, Hally dared a glimpse at his face and to her horror he smiled and spoke.

"Hey, you were here yesterday, how are you?"

Hally could only stare back. She seemed to have lost the ability to talk, inside she was churning and thinking he must think she was dumb. Clia came to her rescue.

"Oh hi, yeah we did drop in yesterday. Hally how's your throat?" Turning back to the boy. "She has a bit of laryngitis so her voice keeps coming and going."

The boy looked at Hally and stretched his arm out indicating a table near the window.

"Oh, I'm sorry to hear that. Why don't you sit by the window and I'll get you some cold drinks."

Hally still couldn't respond. She wanted to run and hide but at the same time she wanted to speak to him. Here was her chance, the boy she had taken a serious liking to was actually speaking to her, (or was he? she thought, maybe it was Clia that he wanted to talk to) but no, he was looking right at her. Taking a deep breath and forcing herself to smile, she finally managed to find her voice.

"Oh, thanks…so…so do you work here then?"

Behind her Clia and Corrinne were beaming.

"Yeah, I wanted a part time job and luckily I found this one, it fits in well with my plans. I'm starting sixth form in September."

The boy told Hally this as they moved towards the table.

"So what drinks can I get you girls?"

He asked them smiling brightly as they settled at the table. Hally sat so she was facing into the café and could see him walking back to the counter. Clia and Corrinne sat opposite her. Breathing a big sigh of relief, she turned to her two friends.

"Thanks Clia. I froze. It was awful, I couldn't speak. He must think I'm really stupid."

"Nah, I reckon he guessed you were nervous."

Clia told her matter of factly.

"So, what should I do now. Maybe 'cos he works here he was just being polite and doing his job, you know showing us to the table."

"Well if that's the case he's very conscientious. No one else is serving people at their tables."

Hally looked around, and sure enough, other customers were queuing at the counter.

"Look, when he comes back say thanks and sort of pause then ask his name."

"But I already know his name."

Said Hally.

"Yeah, but he doesn't know that does he?"

Clia replied patiently. Hally put her face in her hands, then slowly composed herself. As she looked up she saw the boy on his way back with a tray of drinks. As he neared she noticed there were four glasses not three.

"Here we go." He said, placing the tray on the table. "Would you mind if I sat with you? It's my break."

Hally nodded as he slid onto the seat next to her. She tried very hard to stay calm, but since she felt like she was trembling inside she was sure this would be visible to him. So she took a little sip of her drink and put on what she hoped was a natural smile.

"So, hello. I'm Wesley Robinson, but just call me Wes, everyone does."

"Oh, um, hi, I'm Hally and…these are my friends Clia and Corrinne."

After an unsteady start Hally finally found her voice and was relieved to discover that she sounded quite normal. Wes held his hand out to Clia and Corrinne and smiled at all three of the girls. There was a little silence whilst they sipped their drinks and then Wes spoke again.

"Have you got any plans for the holidays then?"

Hally wasn't sure if he was speaking to all three of them or just her.

"Well, we haven't really sorted anything out yet, have we?"

She answered, looking to Clia and Corrinne for support.

"Uh, no, not yet."

Corrinne replied a little taken aback for they had made some plans for days out and the cinema.

"What about you?"

Hally asked, now feeling quite confident.

"Well mostly working here. Days that is. But then we have only just moved here, so I don't really know many people. We moved here from Oxford. I failed my first year at sixth form, passed the re-sits, but it put me a year behind. So I'm doing that here. It means I will be a year older than most of the others, but, well that's cool."

Although he was looking around at all three girls, he seemed to be directing his words at Hally. Trying very hard not to blush, Hally took a long sip of her drink and found it going down the wrong way. Desperately trying not to cough and spray everyone with cola she tried to swallow, unsuccessfully. In a very undignified way she started to splutter and cough, her cheeks puffing out as she tried to keep her mouth closed. Clia saw at once what was happening and quickly grabbed a handful of serviettes from the dispenser on the table and pushed them into Hally's hand. Luckily this at least stopped Hally from spraying cola over everyone, however the splutter soon became a definite painful cough and tears poured from Hally's eyes. Wes turned to her and gently patted her on the back, but she could feel her mascara and eye liner running. Gradually the cough eased and with a real sore throat mumbled.

"I…I'm just going to the ladies."

Without waiting for any reply she quickly stood up and headed for the loo.

Standing holding the edge of the basin, Hally looked at herself in the mirror and saw two panda eyes looking back. She giggled which turned into a sob and two tears rolled down each cheek. She took a deep breath and told her reflection.

"Well great impression you made."

The door to the ladies opened and in walked Dana and her friend Penny.

"Nice show Hally."

Penny said with a sneer.

"You really showed yourself up there. Gave us a real laugh. Are you here to touch up your clown makeup for the next half."

Before Hally had a chance to respond Dana spoke in a flat but hard voice.

"Knock it off Penny. I'm not in the mood."

Penny was about to make some remark back but Dana grabbed her by the jacket and pushed her up against the door.

"WHEN ARE YOU GONNA GROW UP!"

She bellowed at Penny.

"Hey cool it Dana, it was just a …"

She didn't get the chance to finish.

"Joke? Yeah everything is just a joke to you. What do you know anyway?"

Her voice had returned to its former flat hardness. She glanced at Hally who was standing still, shocked by Dana's reaction, let go of Penny and walked back out of the toilets. Penny straightened her jacket and without a word stormed out after Dana.

Hally again stood looking in the mirror. This time though her mind was on what had just happened and not on her embarrassment. Thinking about Dana's outburst she quickly repaired her makeup and tidied her hair. Just as she turned to leave Clia came in.

"Are you ok honey?"

Clia asked gently.

"I'm fine." Clia frowned. "No seriously, I'm ok, but I bet Wes just couldn't wait to get away from the table and back to work."

"Actually, he's still there. In fact he suggested one of us come and see if you were alright."

Clia said this in such a way that Hally couldn't help but laugh.

"Well, I best see if I can get his attention in a better way then. Come on let's go."

The two girls returned to the table and as Clia had said Wes was still there. He and Corrinne were chatting but as soon as he saw Hally he looked up and smiled.

"You ok?"

He asked very gently.

"Just feel like the world's biggest idiot, but other than that no harm."

She replied as she slipped comfortably into the seat beside him. Clia sat next to Corrinne and smiled.

"Wes has been talking about Oxford."

Corrinne said.

Hally looked to Wes and he spoke as if she hadn't left the table at all.

"Sometimes I miss the place, but mostly am glad to be away. It's great to live in a new place though, you know new friends and well, just somewhere new."

Hally thought that he seemed to be stumbling over his words a bit, especially about being glad to be away from his home city, but she didn't feel she should question him, it was too soon.

Hally felt herself relaxing and soon the four of them were happily chatting about school, the holidays and the town. Wes seemed genuinely interested in everything and though he spoke to all three of them he seemed to glance and smile more frequently at Hally.

"I saw Dana and Penny go into the ladies when you were in there Hally."

Corrinne commented. She didn't ask any questions but said it casually to give Hally the option of telling them all if anything had been said or to leave it until later for just her and Clia.

"Oh yes, we were just coming out as they came in"

Hally told her. Corrinne knew then there was more because she had noticed the other two girls coming out before Hally and Clia.

"Are you talking about those two by the juke box?"

Wes asked. Corrinne looked over her shoulder.

"Yes, do you know them?"

She asked warily. Hally frowned, immediately worried about where the conversation was leading.

"No, I don't know them, just have sort of found out about them. They come in here a lot. Bob, my boss just told me to keep an eye on them when they come in 'cos they like to cause trouble. They're usually with a bunch of lads, older I think. I'm surprised to see them on their own."

Hally felt the tension drop from her shoulders and she very nearly let out a deep sigh, quickly disguising it with a wave in front of her face.

"Bit hot isn't it?"

She said to no one in particular. Both her friends nodded their agreement even though she could tell that neither of them thought this was the case, especially since they were sitting next to an open window. To change the subject Clia asked if anyone wanted any more drinks.

"I'll get them."

Wes said, casually standing up.

"Same again?"

The girls all nodded and replied with thanks and Wes moved towards the counter which was now clear of customers.

"Well what do you think?"

Hally quickly and quietly asked her friends.

"Oh, he's interested."

Said Clia.

"Definitely interested."

Corrinne confirmed. They didn't get the chance to say any more, or for Hally to tell them about Dana because Wes was already on his way back with another tray of drinks, and again there were four glasses.

"My boss has told me to take the rest of the day off since it's gone really quiet."

He told them as he again sat next to Hally.

"So, were you planning on spending the whole day in here?"

He had a wide grin on his face as he spoke and Hally had the feeling he knew she had come in to see him.

"Uh, no, we uh…"

"We did some shopping and thought we would decide what to do after we had had a drink in here."

Clia jumped in rescuing Hally.

"Well, do you mind if I tag along?"

Wes asked. Hally nearly knocked her empty glass off the table and only just caught it as it rocked alarmingly.

"Whoops, I am so clumsy today."

She said with a giggle, hoping to disguise her nervousness, which seemed to be coming and going today.

"Of course you can."

Corrinne told him, and she stood up to take the lead in leaving the café. Clia quickly followed Corrinne leaving Hally to walk with Wes.

For the rest of the afternoon the four of them wandered about town, checked out the cinema listings and helped Wes buy new jeans and trainers; since he announced that he needed them but hated shopping alone. This made all three girls laugh. All of the boys they knew were so vain they wouldn't let a girl come anywhere near them when they shopped.

By five when the shoppers began to go home and the town began to get quiet, Wes told the girls he had to head off home. Hally felt a jolt in her heart and a churning in her stomach. She was enjoying herself so much she didn't even consider the day could be over. She tried a smile and found it worked.

"Oh, ok, well I guess we'll see you then."

Wes' smile faded and Hally realised she had made a mistake. For a moment they looked at each other and then Hally took a deep breath to speak and Wes did the same.

"I…"

"Would…"

They both burst out laughing and then Hally said.

"You go first."

"Well, I have to get home, my mum will be expecting me, but I would like to see you again. So can I have your number and I will call you."

Hally was sure if she gave him her number she would not hear from him again but she knew she would give it to him anyway. Wes seemed to understand this and said.

"I will call, I just need to check when I'm working 'cos I don't have regular hours yet and will need to check with Bob."

Hally looked at him and this time the churning in her stomach was excitement.

"I'll give you my home and mobile if you want."

Wes nodded and took out his own mobile ready to key in Hally's numbers.

Corrinne and Clia stood either side of Hally as Wes walked away, turned and walked backwards as he waved and then turned and began to jog towards the other side of town to where the girls lived.

"Well."

Corrinne said.

"Well what?"

Asked Hally dreamily. Her friends linked her arms and turned her around in their direction. She went reluctantly, she wanted to stand and watch the exact spot when Wes turned a corner and went out of her site. She felt the girls tug her and slowly let them lead her towards home.

CHAPTER 6

Parents Approval

They all strolled into Hally's kitchen still chatting about the day. At least Corrinne and Clia were chatting, Hally had said very little on the way home. She had mostly listened to her friends' conversation, occasionally adding a bit to it herself, but much of the walk home she had spent thinking about Wes. Once or twice one of the others had tried to ask her a question or get a response from a comment but had given up trying when she just replied with am "Um" or "Mmm". Now they stood in Hally's kitchen and watched their friend gently sit down at the table and rest her chin in her hands.

"Hally, Hal. Wake up girlie."

Clia said to her friend. Hally looked up and blinked.

"Yes, it's us, your best friends. Are you back on earth sweetie?"

She said with a smile and no malice. Hally giggled, which made the other two giggle too.

"Oh, I'm so sorry you two you must think I'm terrible."

"Yeah you're really awful Hals."

Said Corrinne with a smirk.

"So give. When he calls what are you going to say to him?"

As if on cue Hally's mobile rang. It took a moment for Hally to realise this, then she fumbled around trying to get it out of her bag. At last she grabbed the phone, didn't recognise the number and answered it.

"Hello."

"Hi, it's me Wes."

Hally felt her face getting warm. At once her friends realised it must be him and began bouncing up and down silently clapping their hands. She grinned at them and tried to keep her voice normal when she spoke.

"Oh, hi Wes. Did you get home ok?"

She saw the look on Corrinne and Clia's faces and squirmed at her own question. She felt like an idiot, he was a guy, well almost a man and she was asking him if he got home ok. She thought he would probably bail out of the conversation and find a girl who didn't ask stupid questions. Wes, however didn't seem to mind.

"Yes thanks. So how would you like to meet up with me tomorrow evening?"

Hally's ability to speak left her and she sat holding the phone and willing herself to respond. What seemed like hours later but was actually just a few seconds, she finally managed to voice a reply.

"Um, uh… that would be…I mean, yes ok."

"So, shall I pick you up at seven?"

Wes asked. Hally began nodding and realised he couldn't see her. Her friends were creased up with silent giggles and Hally placed a hand over her face in embarrassment.

"Ok."

She said, her voice little more than a whisper.

"Sorry, I didn't get that."

Wes replied.

"Um, I said ok. Yes tomorrow evening at seven."

"We can decide what to do when we meet up."

Wes told her. Hally was still finding it difficult to speak in a normal voice and found herself nodding silently again. This time Clia nudged her and this seemed to bring her back to her senses.

"Ok, that sounds good. I'll see you tomorrow then."

"Tomorrow at seven then…"

Hally didn't let him finish, she was so nervous that she hurriedly mumbled a goodbye and hung up. Clia and Corrinne eagerly started talking at the same time wanting to know what Wes had said. Hally took a deep breath to begin relaying her conversation, at least Wes' side of it since she had barely spoken when her mobile rang again. As she was still holding it, it startled her and she dropped it on the table. She grabbed it up and answered.

"Hi it's me again. You didn't give me your address."

He spoke so calmly and gently that Hally knew he wasn't

teasing her or upset with her and at last she found the same confidence she had in the café.

"Oh, I am so sorry. Look you probably think I'm a right idiot I…I was just surprised that you called and was a bit nervous too."

"It's alright, I was nervous calling you too."

This shocked Hally as he had not sounded in the least bit nervous. It also made her smile. She couldn't imagine how she Hally Mackeller could make any boy nervous. This news boosted her confidence.

"Well at least you managed to speak to me normally."

Wes laughed a deep resonant sound and Hally felt her insides wobble.

"So, let's start again. Hally would you like to come out with me tomorrow evening?"

"Yes I would like that very much."

She felt very proud of herself that she could now speak normally.

"Good. I will pick you up at seven so long as you tell me where you live."

She could hear the humour in his voice and this made her smile too, it also gave her enough confidence to tease him a little.

"Well, you know my father might object to me giving out my address to a stranger."

Both Clia and Corrinne frowned, not understanding what Hally was doing and wondering why she should be saying such a thing. They both knew Hally's dad would not be like that. However their dismay turned to humour when they realised Hally was grinning widely.

"So should I call him and ask his permission then?"

Wes asked Hally, completely taking her by surprise. She then burst out laughing.

"No, I'm only teasing, my dad is well cool, my mum too. So, I live at twenty two Oak Road. Do you know where that is?"

Hally went on to give Wes directions on how to find her house. The conversation ended and her two friends both started speaking at the same time wanting to know what had been said.

Hally felt like she was walking on air as she bounced across the kitchen to put the kettle on. Corrinne and Clia were still rapidly asking questions.

"Come on Hal, tell all, stop keeping us in suspense."

Clia finally managed to get across to her. Hally turned and looked at them whilst taking mugs out of the cupboard.

"Coffee?"

She asked, holding up the jar. Both girls sighed deeply.

"Oh come on MacKeller. Stop being so annoying."

Corrinne exclaimed. Hally finally gave in and with a smile told her friends the whole conversation.

Handing each of them a mug and sitting at the table with her friends, Hally sipped her drink and smiled contentedly. The day could not have been more perfect. At least the outcome of the day couldn't be more perfect. Her face flushed as she remembered all the embarrassing moments.

"Hey, what's up sweetie?"

Clia asked. Hally put her mug down on the table and smiling told her friends why she was suddenly blushing, shortly after all three were giggling and retelling each other Hally's moments in the café.

A few minutes later the giggles eased off and they sat quietly with their empty mugs in front of them. Hally stood up and switched the kettle on again. As she was spooning more coffee into their mugs Corrinne suddenly spoke.

"Oh yeah, what was going on with Dana and Penny in the Hotspot?"

Carrying fresh mugs of coffee to the table Hally relayed the events in the café toilet.

"Well what do you make of that?"

Corrinne asked.

"Sounds very weird to me."

Clia said with a frown.

"I wonder what's going on with her now? You know I still feel really bad about just leaving her that day and not telling anyone."

Hally told the other two. The excitement of the day and the warmth she felt from her interaction with Wes was pushed to the back of her mind. Clia noticed her change of mood and quickly tried to ease her distress.

“Hey Hally, sweetie, Dana is not, absolutely not your problem. She and her little pet bitches have given you grief for a very long time. Whatever is going on in her life she has to deal with.”

Clia told her very firmly. Hally nodded and sipped her coffee but didn’t really feel any better. She tried to push Dana to the back of her mind as they chatted and since the other two were determined to chat about Wes, found it not too difficult.

“Well, home for dinner, I think.”

Corrinne announced a short while later.

“Yep, I’ll walk with you.”

Clia said. So Hally walked her friends to the door and arranged a time for them to come around the next day.

Later that evening mum had the usual battle with Nathan over his bath.

“But muuuum!”

“No buts Nathan. It won’t take long if you do it now and then you can have free time until bed.”

She told him in a firm but soft voice. Nathan turned to his father but before he opened is mouth Colin spoke.

“Don’t even try it son. Do as your mum tells you.”

Hally could see he wanted to smile and turned away so she wouldn’t giggle. It was the same every night, even worse in the holidays. Nathan simply hated having a bath or shower. He loved the swimming pool, the rain, puddles, in fact any other water except where he had to get clean. Putting on an exaggerated sulk and stomp Nathan headed for the stairs, mumbling and grumbling under his breath. As soon as he was out of hearing range mum turned to Hally.

“Well?”

She asked. Dad stopped reading his paper and looked at his daughter and wife.

“Going to let me in on this?”

He asked with a smile.

“Hally’s met a lad.”

Dad raised his eyebrows but waited for Hally to speak.

“Well, his name is Wes and he’s eighteen…” She paused but her parents didn’t comment. “and he’s taking me out tomorrow.”

"Well, just be careful and keep your mobile switched on. Oh, and let us meet him before you go out."

Dad said. Mum nodded in agreement and Hally knew her parents were giving her the go ahead to go out with Wes, but were still keen to see him and check out who he was. Hally didn't mind this at all. She knew her parents loved her very much, and felt she was a lot better off with her parents taking an interest in her social life than not. This brought back thoughts of Dana and she opened her mouth to mention it when dad spoke again.

"So, how did you meet this lad then?"

Hally went on to explain and was soon deep in conversation about Wes with her parents, all thoughts of Dana gone from her head.

After spending the evening pretending to watch the television, when really she was day dreaming about Wes; Hally stood in her bedroom looking out of the window. It was still light but she could see the sun was beginning to go down. The sky was a beautiful red orange with streaks of tissue like cloud. She had always loved sunset even in the winter, she opened her window wide and breathed in the summer air.

There was a small tap on her door and mum came in. She had two glasses of iced fruit juice, she handed one to Hally and sat on the edge of the bed and sipped her own. Hally stayed by the open window but turned to her mother.

"So, I expect you are excited about tomorrow are you?"

Mum asked gently.

"And nervous. I've never been on a proper date."

Hally replied. Mum nodded but didn't speak straight away. Then she asked.

"Is there anything in particular you are nervous about?"

"Well, I suppose 'cos he's so much older."

Hally confided.

"And what if he? well you know, being older."

She asked hurriedly. Mum smiled, put her glass down and put her arms out to her daughter. Hally crossed to her mum, sat down and let herself be comforted. Stroking her daughter's hair mum spoke gently.

"Baby, if he is a nice boy he won't even give you that worry. You will know quite quickly what he is hoping to get out of the date. Just remember, always, it is your choice and decision. Never allow yourself to be pressurised into anything. Only go with what you feel comfortable with, and remember, if things go wrong we can come and get you."

They stayed like that for a short while, Hally letting her mother continue stroking her hair.

"I think he is a nice boy."

Hally said matter of factly.

"He just seems open and honest."

She sat up and sipped her juice. Mum smiled and sipped her own drink.

"Sometimes you can just tell can't you?"

She asked her mum who nodded and kissed her daughter on the cheek.

"Yes, sometimes, but still be careful."

Late into the night Hally awoke from a dream. She couldn't quite remember all of it and the bits she could were fading quickly. She lay still concentrating on what she could remember. There was a vague recollection of Dana chanting something at her and of Wes laughing and pointing at her. When she turned to the mirror that seemed to be hanging in front of her, she saw the reflection of a heavily made up girl that didn't look anything like her.

Hally threw off the cover and walked over to the window. It was a very hot night and everything outside was silent. As her eyes adjusted to the dark she saw the time was a quarter past three. She opened her window wide and breathed the summer air deeply. Standing still and quiet she let the remains of the dream flow from her, and as she stood quietly she heard a slight rustling in the shrubs below her window.

Carefully and as quietly as she could, she leaned out of the window and looked into the plants. At first she couldn't see anything, the shrubs dark against the moonlight. Then she heard another rustle and a little snuffle and emerging from the shrubbery she saw a hedgehog. She watched with a smile on her face as the little animal quickly scurried across the lawn and disappeared into the darkness of the rear of the garden. Hally kept watching for several more minutes but she didn't see the hedgehog again. However, the pleasure of seeing it completely wiped out the fear of the dream and Hally returned to bed and soon fell into a deep and dreamless sleep.

CHAPTER 7

Holiday Romance

At six thirty in the evening Hally sat at the kitchen table desperately trying to control her nerves. All day she had managed to contain her excitement and keep busy wishing the time away. Corrinne and Clia had spent most of the day with her and together they had decided on her outfit for the date. Now she sat waiting and wondering if Wes was going to enjoy her company or decide she was just too young to have as a girlfriend.

"Girlfriend"

She said out loud to the empty kitchen. Mum and dad were in the study, and Nathan was due home from his friend's house at the same time Wes was due to arrive. That thought set her nerves jangling. Nathan was bound to cause chaos; he always did when he came home. She smiled to herself knowing she was thinking too harshly about her little brother. Nobody could dislike him; he was just a very active, normal little boy. She was just so unsure of herself and the confidence she had found yesterday had now deserted her.

Just before seven Nathan came running through the back door, diving for the fridge at the same time the front door bell rang. Hally tried to get up and get to the door first, but Nathan managed to whiz out of the kitchen clutching a carton of juice and opened the front door.

"Hello, who are you?"

Nathan asked nonchalantly. Wes looked down at him and was about to speak as Hally arrived behind her brother.

"He's my little, (rubbing the top of his head) very annoying brother."

Hally managed before Nathan could utter a word.

"Hey…"

Nathan sputtered, as Hally gently turned him away from the door and pushed him back down the hallway. Nathan turned and walking backwards called out.

"I'm telling mum."

Hally giggled, the nerves melting away.

"Hello, please come in."

She stood back as Wes stepped into the house.

"Come through to the lounge, or we can go into the kitchen. Would you like a drink?"

Hally gabbled as she led the way. Suddenly she stopped and Wes bumped into her. He put his arms out to steady her just as she jumped out of the way and ended up sprawling down the hallway. Completely red faced and embarrassed her one thought was that her decision to wear jeans was absolutely right. Her face became an even darker shade of red when she imagined the scene if she had chosen the denim mini instead. Oh what a sight then; with her knickers displayed thirty seconds after he had arrived. However, sighing deeply and trying to regain some composure; Hally got to her knees. As she was about to stand up, strong arms were lifting her to her feet.

"Are you alright?"

Wes asked her gently. He had a very small smile on his lips but his face was all concern. Hally felt herself melt and started blushing all over again.

"Uh, yes, I'm fine, thank you. Oh crikey, you must think I'm a right klutz. First the café now…"

She didn't finish the sentence. Wes was fully smiling now and still holding her.

"No Hally, I don't think that. Believe it or not I'm just as nervous. But still, it's a great ego boost when a girl throws herself at your feet."

She could see he was trying not to laugh and this made her giggle; then they were both laughing. Hally's nerves again disappeared and she very lightly tapped him on the arm with her fist.

"Excuse me Wesley…"

she began, which made him laugh even louder.

"Oh telling me off now are you?"

They were interrupted from continuing by Nathan charging back into the hall, heading for the stairs.

"Hah, you two are gonna kiss aren't you."

He announced bluntly. Mum was following behind him.

"Nathan."

She said in a warning tone. Nathan looked at his mother with downcast eyes.

"Whaaaat…"

He began, but mum's look quieted him as she pointed up the stairs. Without another word he trudged up the stairs as slowly as he could.

"Why don't you two go into the kitchen; your dad is just making some drinks."

Twenty minutes later Hally and Wes were on their way into town. Hally found herself chatting happily as they strolled along, and when Wes took her hand in his it seemed the natural thing to do. Her dad had been friendly towards Wes, and when mum came back downstairs with a slightly subdued Nathan, they sipped coffee and chatted. Now they were walking hand in hand and Hally felt completely at ease and very happy.

"So, what would you like to do?"

Wes asked, swinging her arm gently.

"Well, it's a really warm evening, so…"

Hally didn't know what else to suggest and felt herself getting embarrassed at her lack of decision making. However Wes didn't seem to notice; instead he chipped in.

"OK, how about a drink at the Hotspot and then maybe go to the park. I could get some left over bread and we could feed the ducks."

He suggested. This seemed like a really good idea to Hally, although the thought of being at the Hotspot with a boy in the evening was a little daunting. There was bound to be people there who would not be happy that Wes had chosen her.

The café was as Hally expected quite full. Surprisingly though there were very few people she recognised. She spotted a few girls from the year above her and they gave her curious, but not unkind looks. There were a few boys from her year and a couple from her form. She said a small hello to them and then Wes was asking what she would like to drink. Quite a few people spoke to him as he went behind the counter and got their drinks himself. Some laughingly joked about bringing his date to work, but he made it clear he wasn't working and would not be serving them.

They sat by the window sipping their drinks and chatting comfortably. Hally had no attack of nerves, nor did she spill or choke on her drink. She had a small moment when the door
opened and Penny Cuthbert walked in with a boy Hally didn't recognise. Hally was surprised Dana wasn't with her, they always hung out together. Penny gave her an evil look; then without a word she walked to the counter and started chatting to some other older boys. The boy she was with seemed to know these boys and before long they were all laughing loudly.

Wes looked at the group with a frown. Hally was about to ask why when he spoke.

"That group are heading for trouble."

"What do you mean?"

Hally asked.

"From what I've heard they were all part of that thing with Martin Cob. Somehow though they managed to get away with it. Gave each other alibis or something; just goes to show there's no loyalty among thieves since they didn't help out their mate Martin."

"You must hear a load of gossip in this place."

Hally replied. She hoped he hadn't heard any about her. He smiled at her warmly and said.

"Yes I do, for instance, I know about the trouble you had at your party. I had only just started working here and a few guys came in and I overheard them talking about this really cool party that a couple of girls tried to ruin. I sort of asked a bit about it and they told me who you were. I got the impression that they sort of fancied you."

Hally felt the blush spreading up her face. She felt a mixture of shock and embarrassment. None of the boys she knew fancied her, or at least she didn't think they did. She was a bit lost for words.

Before she could work out what to say, he spoke again.

"So, when I gave you back your jumper I asked some of the customers in the café if they knew who you were. A girl said your name was Hally and it clicked you were the girl whose party the boys had spoken about before. I knew then I wanted to get to know you; and luckily for me you came in here yesterday."

Hally sat for a few seconds unable to speak. To cover this up she sipped her drink slowly. Finally she felt able to speak normally.

"So, you knew my name already when I saw you yesterday. Why didn't you tell me?"

She wasn't annoyed, just curious.

"Well I didn't want to freak you out. You know you might have found it a bit weird; a complete stranger calling you by name. Then, you seemed so nervous, I didn't want to scare you off, so I let you introduce yourself. Actually, I liked that because you got your confidence back really quickly and I ..."

Wes stopped as Hally began giggling.

"Now you're the one who's gabbling."

She told him confidently. Then they were both laughing. When their laughter subsided to a comfortable silence, Hally spoke shyly.

"Actually I fancied you the moment I saw you. I just didn't have a clue what to do about it. Then Clia called a friend of her brother's and she told her who you were. So we sort of planned to come in here yesterday so I could see if you were here and somehow get you to notice me."

Hally couldn't bring herself to look up, instead she studied the drink in her glass. Then she felt Wes' warm hand cover hers. She finally looked up and was thrilled to see he was smiling warmly.

"What are we like?"

He asked. Then they were laughing again. Hally felt like she had known him for months rather than a few days, and it felt so right being with him.

Later, armed with a large bag of bread they strolled through the park; chatting and feeding the ducks. Wes explained that his dad had moved jobs and since he had to re-sit his A levels anyway was quite happy to move to a new town. Hally didn't think she should ask why he failed his exams this soon into their relationship, but made a mental note to ask about it sometime. She did however tell him all the details of her party and the full story behind it. She even felt comfortable telling him about her past problems with Dana and her gang; blushing furiously when she told him about the name calling. Wes stopped walking, turned and looked down at her and took her hand squeezing it gently.

"Well you certainly don't have to worry about any of that now."

He gently told her as he looked into her eyes. For a panicky few seconds she thought he was going to kiss her then and there; but he just smiled as if he could read her mind, and still holding her hand carried on strolling around the lake. She didn't know whether to feel relieved or disappointed, but it felt nice to have him holding her hand.

At just after ten thirty they arrived back at Hally's house. Now the nerves came back strong. Should she ask him in, would he expect that? She had no idea. However once again Wes seemed to know the inner turmoil she was feeling and saved her any embarrassment.

"Well Hally, I have to get home now. It's been a really wonderful evening. Can I see you again?"

She was both shocked and excited. She actually hadn't thought beyond this evening, and now he was asking to see her again. It just hadn't crossed her mind that there would be more dates. She didn't know why, it just hadn't entered her head. Now she smiled and nodded. He leaned down towards her and gently took her face in both his hands. He then slowly kissed her on the lips. It was soft and brief and when he lifted his head and looked at her he was smiling.

"Goodnight Hally. I'll call you tomorrow."

He waited until she opened her door, then turned and walked down the path. He looked back and waved as she went inside and closed the front door. For a moment she leaned on the door, then sighed deeply and went to find her mum to tell her about her evening.

CHAPTER 8

Dana's Note

The summer holidays slowly moved on with a combination of days and evenings spent with Clia and Corrinne, Wes and sometimes all four of them together. Hally always treasured her time with her friends and never put them off to go out with Wes. He told her one evening that he would never expect her to choose between seeing him or her girlfriends and his maturity was something she found very attractive. Most boys her own age would be peeved that they didn't get their own way.

Clia and Corrinne loved spending time with Hally and always pressed her about how things were between herself and Wes. She always told them everything about their dates and found it very comforting to confide in her friends.

One evening the three girls were sitting on the deck in Hally's garden sipping lemonade. It was another really hot night following a very hot and humid day; storm clouds were slowly building up and the air was heavy with the impending storm. The girls were gossiping about some of their school friends, who was dating whom; who had recently broken up and more importantly which girls had gone all the way with their boyfriends. The conversation lapsed into a comfortable silence for a few minutes. Then Hally spoke.

"You know, there's just one thing bothering me about Wes."

Corrinne and Clia immediately sat up straight in their loungers all ears and interest.

"Hals, what do you mean?"

Clia asked gently and with a frown. Up until now, all they had heard about Wesley was how gorgeous he was; how mature he was and how he never tried it on with her.

"Well, I find it strange that he's never taken me to his house. In fact he hardly ever mentions his family at all"

"Mmm…maybe he's a bit nervous of you meeting his parents."

Clia offered as a way of explanation.

"Have you asked him about it?"

Corrinne said matter-of-factly.

"Nooo…to tell you the truth I'm a bit nervous."

"Mackeller, you dipstick."

Corrinne announced with a grin. Then all three girls were laughing. At that moment Hally's mobile rang. She reached for it and saw it was Wes calling; all thoughts of his parents gone from her mind.

"Hi." She said breathlessly. "How are you?"

"I'm good thanks. You sound out of breath."

"Oh, we were just laughing about something."

Hally felt herself blush, glad he couldn't see her since the topic of their laughter had been him; although not in a nasty way she told herself.

"Ok…anyway I called 'cos I wondered what you were doing tomorrow. I know we arranged to see each other on Thursday; but my boss just called and told me I don't have to work tomorrow now."

Hally's heart gave a flutter. It did that every time he rang her. She was still surprised that a guy like Wesley would be interested in her, and still felt the relationship was fragile. Her mum and friends had told her it was her confidence, or rather lack of it that made her feel this way; but she couldn't help it. However, whenever they were together she felt both secure and confident.

"Hally, you there?"

Wes asked. She realised she hadn't answered him.

"Sorry Wes. Uh…we, that is Corrinne, Clia and me, we planned the pool and then a picnic in the park."

"Oh, Ok no problem…"

Hally noticed Clia making hand signals to her.

"Just a sec Wes, Clia is doing some sort of sign language."

She looked to her friend who was now silently wording "Invite him." She nodded her understanding and turned back to her phone.

"You could come with us, the girls don't mind."

She told him.

"That's great, and listen, leave the picnic up to me. I'm a whizz when it comes to organising *al fresco.*"

They arranged the time and Wes said he would meet them at her house.

"Well I'll see you tomorrow. Enjoy your evening with the girls. L…night night."

He hung up before she had the chance to reply. Her excitement was palpable and her friends caught it quickly.

"Hally?"

Said Corrinne.

"Oh, um, crikey."

Was all she could get out.

"Hally what is it?"

Corrine demanded.

"I'm not really sure, b..but he..he was about to say something and quickly changed his mind. Then he said "night night" and hung up."

Hally stammered.

"Well what do you reckon he was going to say?"

Clia asked gently.

"He started to say something beginning with el."

She replied in little more than a whisper.

"What you mean something like elegant."

Clia asked without really thinking. Hally shook her head.

"No, I mean the letter L, like at the beginning of love."

As soon as the words were out, Hally blushed to the roots of her blonde hair. Both her friends were speechless. Clia recovered first.

"Wow Hally, that boy is smitten."

This comment brought all three out of their shock and they burst into laughter. Only, very quickly Hally's turned to tears as well.

"No, look; I probably got it all wrong. I mean he's like a grown man, he wouldn't just fall for me like that so soon. It's only been a few weeks."

"Stranger things have happened."

Stated Corrinne.

'Stranger things had happened.' This thought kept intruding on Hally's mind as she got herself ready for bed. Her friends had left after a lot more deliberation on Wes' words, or rather lack of them; so Hally kept telling herself. Surely, no way was he going to say what she had thought. But, stranger things had happened. "Like what?" Hally asked her reflection, as she examined her face in the mirror. So far she had been lucky not to break out in a multitude of teenage acne like some of the girls her age. But still, she kept checking expecting an imminent eruption. However, for now her skin remained smooth and tanned.

"Dana and her crew leaving me alone. That's really strange."

She again spoke to her reflection. With everything going on with Wes, she hadn't thought about Dana for a while. Now, a small pang of guilt invaded her thoughts. She had worried so much about Dana's situation at first; but that seemed such a long time ago. She had seen her briefly during the holidays, but Dana kept her distance and didn't even seem to be that interested in her own friends. Even in the Hotspot, she sat slumped alongside Penny and the usual lads, but had little to say. Hally even remembered one afternoon, Dana simply got up and walked out without a word to anyone. Hally's mobile beeped indicating a message, and bringing her out of her reverie. Picking up the phone she saw it was from Wes. Quickly she opened the message and holding her breath read it.

hi just wanted to say goodnight and very much looking forward to tomorrow. x x x x x.

Hally read the message several times then quickly tapped in a reply.

me too night night x x x x.

All thoughts of Dana went out of her mind as she pressed the send button. She then settled into bed and let her mind drift into fantasies of Wes telling her he loved her in a variety of settings, all extremely romantic.

The storm that threatened arrived through the night fierce and furious, but had completely passed over by morning. Hally woke to bright sunshine casting tiger stripes across her bedroom walls as the sun filtered through the partially open blinds. After showering and dressing (she spent a long time choosing an outfit) Hally made her way downstairs. The house was strangely quiet. Normally mum would be busy in the kitchen; usually trying to keep Nathan in his seat at the table to eat his breakfast. However, this morning Hally found a very empty kitchen and a note on the fridge.

Hally sweetheart. Have taken Nathan to the summer play scheme and then going straight to your grandparents. Don't panic, all's ok.

Love you and see you later mum xxxxxxx.

Hally slowly released the breath she hadn't realised she was holding. Mum went to see her grandparents every day; but she didn't rush off first thing in the morning. So for today to be different Hally had immediately thought something must be wrong. Her grandmother's cancer was rapidly getting worse and the family were sure it would not be long before she had to be cared for professionally. However at the moment, mum and her granddad were doing it between them, but it was getting much harder.

As she made herself tea and cereal, Hally pondered over why her mother had gone out so early. As she ate her breakfast she kept telling herself the note had said all was ok, but she was becoming more and more unconvinced as she ate. Eventually she put down her spoon, took out her mobile and rang mum's number.

At first, there was no answer; just ringing then the messaging service. Hally shakily rang again and this time mum answered.

"Hello darling."

"Mum is everything alright. I know your note said so, but I'm worried."

Hally gabbled quickly to her mother.

"Everything is alright angel. Your gran had a rough night so I came early so granddad could get a bit of rest."

"What sort of rough night?"

Hally asked suspiciously. Mum sounded a little too bright.

"Oh, she got out of bed a few times but couldn't get back in again. So, granddad had very little sleep."

"Shall I come over and help?"

Hally asked, not even considering how it would affect her

plans; but mum told her it wasn't necessary and that she should enjoy her day.

"You don't have much of your summer holiday left, so have as much fun as you can. We'll be alright, I'll see you later. Ok darling?"

Her mum told her. Reluctantly Hally agreed and said goodbye.

She still worried as she got her things ready for the day and when Clia and Corrinne arrived they sensed something was awry.

"Is it Wes?"

Asked Clia after seeing her friend's distress.

"Oh no, it's just gran. She's getting worse really quickly. Mum's over there already."

She went on to explain to them what her mother had told her. When she finished Clia spread her arms, palms up and said.

"Well your mum is always really open with you Hals, so when she says everything is fine, then that is exactly what she means. I mean, if it was serious, she would have definitely told you. She's never kept your Gran's illness from you in any way."

Hally realised her friend was quite right and smiling said.

"Well I think I have everything, bikini, towel, shower gel and moisturiser. Have I forgotten anything Corrinne?"

"Um, extra undies, spare top…"

Hally and Clia burst into giggles.

"What?"

Corrinne asked innocently.

"You just have to be prepared for any event."

She told them matter-of-factly.

Wes arrived around eleven and the four set off for the swimming pool. They planned to spend a couple of hours in the water then the rest of the day in the park.

"I will have to call in at the Hotspot because I stored the picnic there."

Wes told them as they strolled to the leisure centre.

"What delights have you prepared for us?"

Clia asked.

"Now that's a surprise."

He told them grinning.

After a very enjoyable and amusing (Clia's bikini top came

undone in the pool) session swimming, the four set off for the hotspot to collect the picnic. As they were not eating at the café and since it was lunchtime and busy; the girls waited outside. Wes soon appeared carrying a real wicker hamper. All three girls were surprised, they had simply expected a plastic bag with wrapped sandwiches.

Before any of them spoke however Wes held out an envelope for Hally.

"What's this?"

She asked. The envelope simply had her name on it.

"No idea. Apparently someone left it behind the counter yesterday."

Wes told her.

Hally was very curious and wanted to open it immediately, but decided to wait until they were at the park. Besides, there was something about the writing that seemed strange. It was very child like in style and Hally had a feeling she had seen it before, but couldn't remember where. So she put it in her bag and turned to Wes instead.

"Where did you get that from?"

She asked, indicating the hamper.

"It's mum and dad's. They've had it for years. Mum said I could borrow it."

This was one of the few times Wes had actually mentioned his family. Hally felt that strange sensation again that she was missing something but could not figure out what. She pushed it to the back of her mind and smiling said.

"So to the park."

The others burst out laughing and joined her as she pretended to power walk towards the town park.

Unsurprisingly, there were a lot of people the girls knew at the park. Some were in large groups laying and sitting on various rugs and jackets. Some had phones and iPods playing, with the result that as they strolled towards the lake it was impossible to work out exactly what music was what. They found a spot of sunny grass and Wes pulled out two rugs from the side of the hamper. He spread them on the ground and Clia and Corrinne quickly dropped their bags next to one and sat down. Hally settled herself onto the second rug, and Wes kneeled next to her. The hamper had old fashioned leather straps and for some reason this brought a small lump to the back of Hally's throat. For a few seconds she visualised her Gran's face but swallowed hard and pushed it to the back of her mind. Now was not the time to dwell on why mum had really gone there so early.

The hamper opened to reveal one side with crockery, cutlery and glasses strapped neatly in and the other side with food.

"It used to have real linen napkins, but they disappeared years ago; so we will have to make do with paper."

Wes told them as he began to unwrap various packages. This reminded Hally about the envelope. She took it out of her bag and turned it over; but there was nothing else on it. She gently slit it open and pulled out a single sheet of lined paper, which looked torn from a pad like they used in school. It was untidily folded several times as though it had been stuffed in the envelope in a hurry.

Corrinne and Clia were happily chatting to Wes as he began to lay food out and at first didn't notice Hally holding the note.

"Look at this yummy picnic Hals."

Said Corrinne. When Hally didn't answer her friend became concerned.

"What is it Hally?"

She asked. Clia and Wes then both looked up and saw the frown on Hally's face.

"Hally, what's the matter?"

Wes asked her, gently putting his hand on her shoulder.

"It's from Dana."

Hally replied. Corrinne and Clia both audibly took a breathe and though it was obvious by his expression that Wes had no idea what this meant, he did not ask any questions.

"Hally, what does it say?"

Clia asked, deep concern in her voice. Hally handed the note over for her friend to read out. It was poorly written in a very childish hand writing.

'HalY i aM reely sorrY for wot I done to You i no wot i got to do noW
Dana '

"What is that supposed to mean?"

Corrinne asked, as she took the note from Clia and read it herself. Hally shrugged, she had no idea.

"Well it's about time she realised what she's put you through all these years; now her own life is in a mess."

Clia stated without much sympathy in her voice.

"I suppose so."

Hally replied, taking the note back and putting it away.

"Come on girls, lets eat before it dries up in this lovely sunshine."

Wes chipped in lightening the mood. The girls laughed, but Hally felt somewhat unnerved by the note. However, when Wes handed her a plate it looked so delicious and his smile was so warm and comforting that she put everything except him out of her mind.

The rest of the day was truly wonderful. They fed the scraps of the picnic to the ducks and Wes surprised them again by pulling some old board games out of his backpack; which they had enormous fun playing. Several times throughout the day people passed and spoke to Wes casually. Much to Hally's joy when he politely introduced them he referred to the girls as "My girlfriend Hally, and her two friends Clia and Corrinne."

As the day turned to evening they mutually agreed to go back to Hally's.

"Have you sampled Hally's homemade lemonade yet?"

Corrinnne asked Wes. Hally gave her a wicked look, but her friend chose to ignore it.

"You make lemonade Hally?"

He asked her. For some reason this made her blush. It was such a small thing, but it sounded so domestic and to Hally really uncool.

"Uh, well, my mum does and …"

Before she had the chance to decide what to say both her friends chimed in with "You do too Hals, and it's gorgeous." Wes laughed and put his arm around Hally's shoulder.

"Sounds like you have a fan club." Then in a mock posh voice. "Come then, to Hally's for lemonade."

Even Hally couldn't help but laugh at this, so forgiving her friends they made their way back to her house.

The house was quiet when they got back. At first Hally's heart skipped a beat thinking something was wrong; then she remembered her parents had promised to take Nathan to the cinema. Relaxing, she sent the girls and Wes out into the garden whilst she put together the lemonade.

"Well I can't have any of you recording my secret recipe."

She told them playfully. Wes patted her gently on her behind and said.

"One day I will know."

Then with a laugh he joined Clia and Corrinne.

Hally tried not to mull over what that meant as she took the already cooked and cooled lemons out of the fridge. Luckily for her, her mum kept a stock.

As they sipped their drinks, Wes asked Hally what Clia had meant about Dana; so the three girls recounted many tales of the bullying Hally had had to endure over the years.

"Most of the time it was just bitchiness."

Hally told him, but there had been times when it had got bad enough for Hally's parents to visit Mr Hopkins the head teacher. On these occasions, Dana and her friends had been subjected to detentions, calls to their parents and even temporary exclusions. However, the situation was never truly resolved. "Until now, Dana seems to have stopped by herself, for whatever reason." Hally finished.

"My poor baby."

Wes said, wrapping his arms around Hally, and though it shocked her to hear him call her this she felt like she was in heaven.

"Mmm, look at the time Corrinne. Think we should get going."

Said Clia, standing and pulling her friend from the other sun lounger.

"It's not that late…"

Hally began, but Clia put up a hand to stop her and obviously faked a yawn.

"All that swimming, delicious food and fresh air has totally worn me out"

She claimed.

"Me too"

Announced Corrinne, faking her own yawn. Hally laughed as she stood up too.

"Ok, I'll see you out."

The three girls walked down the garden to the back gate.

"I know what you two are up to."

Hally told them.

"What?"

They both exclaimed innocently. Hally shook her head lightly and the three girls gave each other a hug as they said goodnight.

Hally then nervously made her way back up the garden. She had spent evenings alone with Wes quite often over the holidays, but she still got wobbles in her tummy each time. She always wondered when Wes, being so much older would expect their relationship to move on, but as yet he had not tried to push her at all. Most of the time she was very relieved by this, she was, she kept telling herself only fifteen. However, there were times, and naturally, she told herself; when he was holding her and kissing her; that she felt a fiery sensation deep inside her. It was then that she wished he would just move his hands to somewhere else on her body, like her breasts, she would say in her mind, or even somewhere else.

These thoughts always brought heat to her face, and she dreaded Wes seeing this. But he seemed to understand and sense her feelings because he would back off a bit as though he knew she wanted more; but also knew she wasn't really ready. She would then feel disappointed and worse, her body felt bereft, but relieved at the same time. These feelings created a great deal of confusion within her and she knew at some point she would be having a long chat with her mum.

Now though, she was going to enjoy the rest of the evening and try not to get herself into a state about what may or may not happen.

Wes was leaning back on a sun lounger with his hands behind his head and his eyes closed. Hally crept over to him and tickled him in the ribs. He grabbed her so quickly and pulled her onto his lap that she believed he had only been pretending to have his eyes shut. They both laughed. As Wes tickled her back, his fingers just brushed over the lower part of her breast. Hally felt a sensation so strong in her lower body that she could hardly breathe; her heart began to beat very fast and she leaned into him waiting to be kissed. Wes obliged and took her face between his hands, kissing her deeply. Too soon, the kiss ended and as Wes pulled away from her she saw a slight frown on his face.

"Hally, I'm sorry, I didn't mean for that to happen. I really was just tickling you."

He looked so miserable that her first reaction which had been to tell him not to be stupid, was rapidly replaced with concern.

"Wes, it's alright."

She put a hand on his arm, but he still seemed unhappy.

"No, it's not. I should know better."

"But..."

Hally began, but Wes moved so she had no choice but to stand up, as he stood also and moved away from her a little. He stuffed his hands in his pocket and looked at the ground.

"I have to go."

He told her and moved towards the door. With tears beginning in her eyes, Hally followed him into the house. At the front door he turned to her.

"Goodnight Hally."

Then seeing the glistening on her cheeks he pulled her into a hug.

"It's alright baby, don't cry. I will call you tomorrow, but I must go now."

Hally buried her face in his shoulder and in a muffled voice that shook when she spoke said.

"You, you're nnot bbbreaking up with me?"

She felt him shake his head and relief spread through her when he said.

"No, definitely not. I just need to go home now. Ok."

He leaned back and planted a small kiss on her lips; then he let go and turned to walk down the path.

CHAPTER 9

Back to School

Despite his reassurances Hally went to bed feeling miserable. She wanted to call her friends and talk but couldn't bring herself to do it. She wanted to wait until her mum came home and talk to her, but she knew Nathan would be excited and rebellious about bedtime; so she took herself off to her room and when she heard her family come home stayed in her room quiet.

After a very restless night, Hally wandered down to the kitchen in her dressing gown and relief spread through her when she found her mother alone. Turning to look at her daughter, mum knew something wasn't right.

"Hally, angel, what's up?"

Her words were enough to set the tears flowing and before she knew it mum had her wrapped in her arms.

"Muuuummm I'm…"

"Not now Nathan"

Her mother told her brother as he was about to come bounding into the kitchen looking for food. Hally didn't look up from her mum's shoulder and to her surprise Nathan withdrew from the kitchen for once without asking why.

Minutes went by where Hally simply sobbed into her mother's shoulder. She didn't ask any questions, just held her and let her cry herself out. Slowly the flow stemmed and then Hally murmured in between sobs.

"I think Wes is going to to bbreak uup with…"

She couldn't finish the sentence as a fresh wave of tears flowed. Without releasing her hold mum gently said.

"Why do you think that sweetheart?"

With her face still buried in her mother's shoulder Hally replied.

"Because; something sort of happened last night."

Mum eased back slightly, brushing Hally's now damp hair from her face. She took her daughter's face in her hands and said.

"Sit down my angel. I'm going to make some tea and then we can sort this out."

Hally nodded and folded herself into a chair. She felt wretched, never having felt like this about a boy before. Mum put a mug of tea in front of her and pulled another chair around the table so she was sitting next to Hally. Hally took a sip of tea then turned to her mum.

"We were playing, just tickling each other."

She stopped and sipped more tea. Her mum nodded to keep going and then it all spilled out. In a rush Hally told her mum everything; all the feelings she had been having and the ones she'd had the night before.

"Then he left."

She finished the story and swallowed the remainder of her tea. Mum had kept quiet throughout but now put her own mug down and took Hally's hand.

"My little girl, you are growing up. Everything you are feeling is normal and perfectly ok. What you have to do is make choices. These are really difficult times for you. Your body and your mind are in chaos and conflicting. One is telling you one thing and the other is saying something different. Now, Wes told you he wasn't breaking up with you; well if he meant that then he will call you today as he promised. He is a lot older and that is something you have to think about; but from the sound of it, he is sensible and believe it or not, he did the right thing. Baby, he realised what was happening and made sure it stopped. I think he knows you are too young yet and not ready for that sort of relationship."

Hally looked at her mother and tried a little smile.

"I'm scared mum."

"I know baby, unfortunately that is part of growing up. But, being scared will be what helps you keep things in perspective. It's your mind telling you you're not ready for anything else. If Wes is as decent as he seems, he will understand."

Hally sighed deeply.

"Thanks mum. I'm so glad I can talk to you about this stuff. There are so many girls in my year that can't tell their parents anything and I think some of them have already done it, but you know from what we have heard, they don't seem to have a clue about it. They just seem to be seeing it as some sort of competition; like it makes them more popular the more boys they go with."

Mum smiled at Hally.

"That my darling is the same as it was when I was your age. But you know, the fact that you and Clia and Corrinne can see that; just shows how much more mature you are compared to those other girls. You will know when the time is right for you whether Wes is a part of it or not."

At that point Nathan put his head around the door to the kitchen.

"Please can I have breakfast now, before I starve to death?"

He said it in such a sweet little voice that both Hally and mum burst out laughing. Hally stood up and headed for the door.

"Come on squirt, we can't have that can we." Then turning to her mum. "Thanks mum, I'm going to get ready."

Mum nodded and smiled, a little lump in her throat aware that her daughter was truly growing up.

Hally was in her room drying her hair when her mobile phone chirped indicating a message. Quickly she grabbed it and saw straight away it was from Wes.

hi hope you are ok this morning im really sorry about last night i really want to see you today but chris has gone sick so I have to work i will call you later xxxxxxxx

Hally's first thought was that he was giving her the brush off. Then, furious with herself she told herself to stop being stupid. He had texted her and that was more than she'd expected. So she quickly tapped in a reply.

hi im really glad i heard from you. xxxxx

She was about to press send when she decided to add what she was really feeling, "or some of it anyway," she murmured.

i really thought you might think i am too young for you and wanted to break up xxxx

This time she pressed send before she could change her mind.

After the message went she stood holding the phone tightly with her eyes closed terrified she had said too much. However, within a few seconds it chirped in her hand nearly making her drop it.

no hally I don't want to break up i knew how old you were from the start its not a problem i will try and see you later if can xxxx

Feeling like she was on cloud nine Hally pulled on her clothes and bounced out of her room. She suddenly realised that she was hungry and decided toast was needed. Mum was still in the kitchen clearing away Nathan's breakfast dishes. She smiled when she saw her daughter was looking much happier.

"You've heard from him then?"

She asked with a smile. Hally nodded as she placed bread in the toaster.

"Yep, he texted me and everything's ok."

"Well that is good to hear. I hate seeing you so upset." Then in a more serious note. "But… sometimes relationships have ups and downs, unfortunately it's part of life and growing up."

Hally hugged her mum and sighed.

"Yeah, I know. But, for now I am going to enjoy what I have."

The toast popped before her mum could reply; Hally buttered it, and seeing her so cheerful mum decided not to say any more.

With just two days and the weekend left of the school holidays Hally was not going to waste a moment. As she finished her toast she dialled Corrinne's home number knowing Clia had stayed the night before. Without telling her friends what had happened between Wes and herself she quickly arranged to go round to Corrinne's house.

"I'm taking Nathan to play scheme then going to your grandparents."

Mum told her as she gathered her bag and put on her flip flops. Hally stopped and looked at her mother.

"Is everything alright with gran?"

She asked tentatively.

"Hally…"

Hally felt a jolt of panic right in the middle of her stomach, and a coldness spread through her. Mum watched her daughter pale and immediately put her arm around her.

"Baby, it's ok. I didn't mean to frighten you and I'm not keeping anything from you. Your gran is getting worse, we knew this was going to happen. Granddad is struggling, but neither of them want her to go to the hospice yet. So a nurse who is qualified in this type of care is going to be there. I haven't met her yet she's coming today."

Despite knowing how ill her gran was, Hally still felt a sense of shock.

"Can I come round a bit later?"

Hally asked. Mum smiled.

"Hally, darling of course you can. You don't have to ask. Bring the girls too, you know your gran loves them, and even though she's very ill, she wants things to be as normal as possible."

Hally hugged her mum.

"Ok, I'm going to Corrinne's now. We will be round a bit later."

She kissed her mum on the cheek and left for her friend's house.

At Corrinne's, Hally quickly brought her friends up to date with both her news about her gran and about Wes. As expected the girls were very interested in everything Hally had to tell them.

"Well, you will know when the time is right for you and Wes Hals."

Clia told her as Corrinne nodded too.

"Just don't rush into anything 'cos you think it's what he wants or to stop him, you know, getting pushy."

Hally smiled at her friends.

"Don't worry. I have no intention of doing anything I'm not ready for, and you know, even though I want to when I'm with him, I know deep down it's not what I want. Do you get me?"

Both her friends nodded they understood.

"Now, what are we going to take your gran today?"

Clia asked. The other two giggled, because over the past few months they had taken to presenting Hally's grandmother with a variety of unusual gifts; which gran had enjoyed immensely.

"Mmmm, I have the perfect idea."

Corrinne told them.

After walking into town to get Gran's gift, the girls arrived at Hally's Gran's early afternoon. They walked into the kitchen through the back door and came face to face with a woman who looked exactly like Mrs Doubtfire. When she spoke though she had a soft sweet voice and a soothing smile.

"You must be Alice's Granddaughter."

It was directed at Hally and a statement not a question.

"You have her eyes."

The woman said before Hally could ask.

"I'm Mrs…"

"Doubtfire." Whispered Corrinne behind Hally. The woman obviously heard her and burst out laughing; a lovely sing song laugh.

"No, my dear, I'm Mrs Mildred Clattercote. I'm a nurse, here to help."

Corrinne blushed scarlet to the roots of her hair.

"I'm so sorry, I really didn't mean to be rude."

Mrs Mildred Clattercote waved her hand briefly.

"Oh, don't worry." And at the look of concern on Corrinne's face. "Honestly love, in this job you have to have a very good sense of humour. Come on, let's go and see the person you have come to visit."

They followed the nurse into the lounge and Hally immediately felt the day chill. Her Gran was propped up on the sofa with a footstool and cushions. She looked comfortable in position, but she had lost weight since Hally had last visited, which had only been a week ago. Her skin was a strange colour, a sort of greyish yellow and her eyes. *Oh her eyes* Hally said wordlessly. They looked so dull, whereas before they always sparkled with youthful mischief. Hally felt tears threaten but forced them back as Gran held out a hand to her.

"Hally, angel, come here and let me look at you. Your mum has been telling me all about this lad of yours. And girls, what have you brought for me today?"

Hally smiled, despite how she looked, the mischief was still there.

The three girls settled themselves around Gran giving her fragile body hugs and kisses. Then Corrinne pulled her bag onto her lap and began removing the usual bits and pieces to find the latest gift. She pulled out an irregular shaped package, wrapped in purple tissue and tied with purple ribbon. Hally's mother, Granddad and nurse Mildred all gathered around them to see what the present was. Gran carefully unwrapped the gift and burst out laughing, the others joining in when they saw it.

"Oh how wonderful, a bubble kit. I don't remember the last time I played with one of these; probably when Nathan was little."

Granddad gently helped her undo the packaging, his eyes sparkling a little from unshed tears; and handed her all the different pieces to make different size bubbles.

"I'd like to do this in the garden please."

Gran said. Nurse Mildred was right there.

"Of course Alice. It's warm outside but I think you should wear your cardigan."

Deftly she helped Gran up and into her cardigan. Then taking her arm gently led her through the patio doors into the garden. To everyone looking, it did not seem as though the nurse was taking most of Gran's weight, even though they knew she was. It simply looked like she was offering her arm for a bit of support. At that moment Hally knew this was a wonderful lady who was going to make her Gran's last remaining time as comfortable as possible.

A little while later Hally and the girls were back in the lounge with Gran. The adults had left them alone; but Hally knew Nurse Mildred especially was alert to her Gran's needs despite not being in the same room. Hally sat on one side of her grandmother, Corrinne on the other side and Clia on the floor leaning against Hally. Gran looked at Hally and the old sparkle was there.

"So am I going to meet your beau?"

The girls giggled at her choice of words.

"Of course."

Hally replied. Gran gave her a huge smile and for a few seconds she didn't appear ill at all. Again Hally had to force back a lump in her throat.

"So, tell me all."

Hally took a deep breath and told her all about Wes. When she finished Gran gave her a deep and knowing look.

"Well I definitely want to meet him now."

She stated. Mum came back into the room with Granddad and behind them Nurse Mildred carrying a tea tray. Everything seemed just like a normal afternoon tea except for the little plastic cup holding a variety of pills.

After tea the girls decided Gran needed some quiet so they left and set off back to Hally's. On the way they chatted about the visit and when Hally would broach the subject to Wes about her Gran's wish to meet him. She was a little worried because although she had spoken about her Gran and how ill she was, they had never discussed him getting to know her grandparents. Now, talking to Corrinne and Clia, Hally realised that in the back of her mind she had thought introducing Wes to her grandparents would look like she was getting too serious.

"I think you should just tell him your Gran wants to meet him, and see what he says."

Clia announced as they walked into Hally's kitchen. Hally began pulling cold drinks from the fridge.

"Mmmm, yeah, I suppose. After all it's what Gran wants that is important. She hasn't got much time…"

Hally couldn't continue. The tears that had been threatening all day came in a flood. As she sank into a chair at the kitchen table; Corrinne and Clia wrapped their arms around her and she sobbed and sobbed. None of the girls spoke for some time, then Corrinne quietly pulled a wad of tissues from her bag and handed them to her friend.

"Shh, shh Hals. We are here for you all the way."

Hally was shuddering as the sobs subsided, her face puffy and red. With a tiny smile she said to her friends.

"I probably look a right wreck."

"You look like someone who has a very sick grandmother whom you love very much."

Clia told her. The way she spoke brought a bigger smile to Hally and Corrinne. At that moment there was a knock on the backdoor.

"Oh yikes, I can't answer looking like this."

Hally gasped. Clia stepped forward.

"I'll go."

She opened the door and immediately stepped back to let the person enter. Hally was horrified when she saw Wes coming into the kitchen. It was the first time he had used the back door, usually knocking on the front. However, when he saw her he rushed to her side and stooping so he was level with her, took her hands in his.

"Hally?"

"It's ok Wes, I'm ok. We, well we have just come back from Gran's and she's so fragile, well, it just got a bit too much for me."

Wes pulled her to him and held her.

"Is there anything I can do to help?"

He asked sweetly. Hally felt relief flood through her. She leaned back and looked into his eyes. They held genuine concern. So she simply said.

"Gran wants to meet you."

"Ok. Whenever you want."

Corrinne and Clia glanced at each other, then quietly took their drinks into the garden. Hally noticed her friends disappear and was very grateful to them.

"So how come you are not at work?"

She asked him.

"Well it was really quiet, and since school starts in a couple of days and I will have to reduce my hours anyway; my boss said I could leave early since I was doing him a favour today. So I thought I would surprise you instead of ringing."

"Well I think you got the surprise, seeing me looking like an overripe raspberry."

She told him. Wes laughed and pulled her to her feet.

"You look gorgeous." Which made Hally blush on top of the tear induced redness. "Let's go into the garden with Corrinne and Clia."

Not long after, mum came home with Nathan in tow. As they came through the garden mum said hello to everyone as Nathan kept up a stream of chatter about what he had done at play scheme.

In between, mum was able to invite the girls and Wes to stay for dinner and still respond to Nathan. The sun was still warm and Hally began to feel better about everything. Wes was his normal self and she was able to put her fears and doubts to one side.

Over dinner the conversation turned towards Gran. Mum had already brought dad up to date and told him all about Nurse Mildred, so the discussion was fairly light, which was just right with Hally. She didn't think she could stand bursting into tears again. Casually the subject of Wes meeting her was raised. Hally still had a little twang of nervousness about this; but Wes seemed relaxed and keen. He had completely won over her parents during the weeks she had known him and he chatted animatedly with both of them. But still he never seemed to mention his own family.

"Do you have any grandparents?"

Mum asked as she served dessert. Nathan was already rapidly spooning his into his mouth, keen to get to his play station.

"No, unfortunately, both sides died a few years ago. It's just mum, dad, me and well, my parents' little surprise."

Hally looked up suddenly, as did both Corrinne and Clia. This was something new and she was a little taken aback that he had not told her before. Mum smiled.

"How old?"

She asked. Before Wes had a chance to answer, Nathan chimed in.

"Please can I get down from the table."

He was so sweet and polite, Hally felt like hugging him. Usually he would gobble his food as fast as possible and gabble out the request to leave the table. It seemed Wes was having an influence on him too. Mum gave him permission and even more unusually, he pushed his chair in and walked from the kitchen. However, it seemed he couldn't contain himself after that, because they heard him thundering up the stairs to his room. They all laughed then turned to Wes for his answer.

"She's just turned two."

"That must have been a bit of a shock to your parents to have such an age gap."

Mum commented. Hally sat feeling stunned by this

information, and made a mental note to question Wes as to why he hadn't told her about his very little sister.

Hally got the opportunity a little later. Corrinne and Clia had both gone home, mum and dad were in the study chatting to friends on the internet and Nathan was still in his room. Hally was curled up on the sofa with Wes' arm around her watching television. It was very comfortable but Hally couldn't help the nagging feeling in her mind that Wes was keeping secrets. As casually as she could she said.

"So what's your sister's name?"

He paused before answering.

"Ellie, well she's really Eleanor, but I, we, call her Ellie. It's much sweeter, and she really is very cute."

He was just as casual with his reply, but Hally still felt something wasn't quite right.

"Wesley…"

She didn't get any further.

"Uh oh. The full name. Am I in trouble?"

He asked with a big grin on his face. Hally gave a little laugh.

"No of course not. It's just, well, you have never taken me home and I hardly know anything about you. I mean it was a huge surprise to find you have a teeny tiny sister. Why haven't you told me before?"

Hally gabbled all of this out in one breath. She felt a little embarrassed but looked right into his eyes waiting for his reply. She felt him take a deep breath then he replied.

"My parents are a little over protective, but you're right I should have introduced you to them. I have told them about you, I'm just nervous about you meeting them."

Hally didn't give him time to say any more before she jumped in worriedly with.

"What, won't they like me?"

"Hey, it's ok. Of course they will like you. I… it's…well, my last girlfriend took off and…like I said they are over protective."

Wes stopped speaking and looked away. Hally was extremely confused. Of course parents were over protective, but this seemed very odd. Wes had gone very quiet and didn't seem to want to look at her.

"I'm sorry. Have I said something wrong?"

She asked tentatively. Wes looked down at her and she felt a jolt through her heart as she saw moisture in his eyes. She could feel he had tensed against her too. She reached up and placed a hand on his cheek.

"What's wrong?"

She asked in a small soft voice. Wes covered her hand with one of his and tried a small smile.

"I'm the one who should apologise. This is not your fault."

A thread of fear went through Hally; but before she could speak, Wes continued.

"I went out with this girl for like two years and mum and dad thought the world of her. Everything was fine, then she told me she didn't want to be with me anymore. Just like that. No reason, she just turned cold and nasty. My parents were as cut up about it as me. Then we heard she and her family moved away. She was my first real girlfriend and well; I haven't had a serious relationship since, until I met you. I mean I went out a couple of times with a couple of girls, but that's all. So as much as I want you to meet my family, I suppose I'm scared."

Hally felt overwhelmed by this information and at first couldn't think of what to say. Then taking a deep breath she asked.

"So, are you over her?"

Hally felt Wes relax next to her, but he tightened his hold around her.

"Oh my Hally. I am so over her. Even before I met you. I came to realise that she wasn't a very nice person. Moving here made me realise lots of things. We discussed moving away from Oxford to give us all a fresh start and it has worked out really well."

He then leaned down and kissed her, and that was all the reassurance she needed.

The weekend went by in a haze of spending time with the girls, Wes and getting ready for school on Monday. The first day back always made Hally nervous. She had a fear of everything being different and more difficult, but this year there was a big difference. As usual she met Corrinne and Clia where their roads joined but Wes was there too.

As they all entered the school gates, the usual teachers were present but Dana wasn't. At first Hally didn't even notice, Wes was holding her hand and quite a few girls were looking on with interest. However, Corrinne gave her a nudge when she saw Penny Cuthbert coming toward them.

"Hey, have you seen Dana?"

Penny asked in what she obviously thought was a tough voice, but to the others just seemed childish. Before Hally answered, Clia cut in.

"Now why oh why would we have any idea where your mistress is?"

They all laughed except Penny who looked from one to the other with a very confused expression.

"I… what, what is that supposed to mean?"

Without replying they all laughed and walked away from her making their way to their favourite bench.

The day was uneventful. The usual welcome back assembly, sorting timetables and teachers lecturing them on how important this year was going to be. Hally briefly saw Wes during morning break, but as he was in sixth form his timetable was a lot more flexible and he would have more study time than lessons, so she wouldn't be seeing much of him actually at school.

What was strange was not seeing Dana at all. She often skived some lessons, but was nearly always at school at some point during the day, even if it was only to meet up with her friends at lunchtime. Hally felt a small pang of guilt for not trying to contact her after her note, but as Corrinne told her, their summer had been busy and enjoyable. Why should they spoil any of it on the likes of Dana who had only ever given Hally grief. With this is mind Hally put Dana out of her thoughts and instead thought how good this school year was going to be. She had Wes and it looked like at last she would have no more trouble with Dana and her gang.

CHAPTER 10

Mr Austin

The new term was indeed busy and though not particularly stressful the workload was quite intense. Hally's favourite subject, English proved to be challenging but interesting. The students were given a list of books that they would be reading throughout the year and a list of recommended reading that would support the set books. Several of these, Hally had already read as had Corrinne and Clia, so re-reading them was recreational rather than studious. Mr Austin, their English teacher was very pleased with this and sent letters home to all their parents congratulating them on their dedication to the subject.

However, in class Mr Austin treated the girls the same as all the other students. He had been very aware of the problems Hally had incurred from Dana and her friends, and although none of these girls were in the same group as Hally, he knew what they were capable of outside the classroom. Still, he knew Hally was one of his brightest students and that English was her strongest subject, so he was determined to give praise where it was due.

This became very evident at the beginning of the third week back in school. The students had been given a writing assignment. They had to compose a poem about dread, and Hally had chosen her Gran's illness as the topic of her poem. She wrote straight from her heart and was given an A star grade. On top of this Mr Austin asked if he could read it out in the year group assembly. Hally agreed, but felt very embarrassed.

It seemed very strange to hear someone else reading her thoughts to her peers. At the start there were a few snickers from Penny and her group but a scathing look from Mrs Wateley quietened them very quickly. As he read on, Hally glanced around and saw her peers were giving her work their full attention. It might have had something to do with the way Mr Austin read it out, but they all seemed really moved by her poem. Even the boys, who usually stared at the floor seemed interested. When he finished reading there was a moment of silence then applause. Hally felt herself blush, then an overwhelming sense of pride.

"Well done Hally. That is an excellent piece of work."

Again there was applause. After, as they were leaving to go to lunch several people passed Hally and complimented her. She had always been able to write well but this was the first time it had been made public and shyly she enjoyed the moment.

Wes was waiting for them when they came out, and Clia launched into a detailed account of the assembly. Wes hugged Hally and told her he was very proud of her. Then he whispered in her ear.

"Can you come and meet my family this evening?"

Hally felt herself glow with pleasure and quickly nodded. She only hoped the meeting would go as well as the assembly.

Hally dressed carefully for the visit to Wes'. She had told mum all about it and how nervous she was. Mum had held her and tried to reassure her but knew Hally would only feel better once she was there. As arranged Wes called for her at seven and hand in hand they walked across town to where Wes lived. Hally was actually surprised to find he lived quite some distance from her home, and chatted comfortably about in on the way. Wes explained that they had chosen the house because it was old and had a huge garden. His dad was a builder and his mum although a trained accountant did interior design as a hobby, so between them they had begun renovating.

As they got nearer, Hally began to feel tense. Wes sensed this and put his arm around her. But as they turned the last corner and Hally saw the house her nerves disappeared. It was gorgeous, not because it was huge, but because it was set behind wrought iron gates; surrounded by lawns and shrubs and bordered with big old trees. These were just beginning to change colour and the reds, oranges and gold of autumn glowed in the evening sun.

Wes took Hally around the back of the house explaining that

they rarely used the front door and Hally gasped when she saw the rear garden. It was big and open and overlooked the fields on the edge of the town. Hally had lived in the town all her life but didn't even realise there were houses like this. She and her friends mostly stayed in the newer part of Colingford, but silently she resolved to find out more about her home and to encourage Corrinne and Clia to do the same.

Wes led Hally to the backdoor and her nerves flooded back. She was sure his parents would either dislike her or think she was too young. As she stepped through the door she saw a wide open, but modern kitchen and a small, round, dark haired woman tending pots on the cooker.

"Mum, we're here."

Wes announced. His mother turned and smiled so warmly Hally felt her tension disappear. Both stepped towards each other, Wes' mum spoke first.

"Hally, it's lovely to meet you at last."

She gave her son a serious look, but he smiled brightly and put his arm around her shoulder. He towered over his mum, but he had her eyes and hair.

"It's lovely to meet you too…"

Hally paused and felt her face heat up. She had no idea what to call her.

"Kate, I'm Kate and Wes' dad is Michael." She frowned at Wes. "You didn't tell her our names."

Wes gave a pretend pout.

"Oh dear, I'm in trouble. Sorry mum, I thought I had."

"It's not me you need to apologise to, it's Hally, poor girl. Now don't be embarrassed Hally. Sometimes I can't believe I brought him up with manners."

Hally smiled at the chastisement of her boyfriend, especially as she could see both mother and son were grinning at each other.

"I am so very sorry Hally."

Wes said with mock exaggeration. Hally found this very amusing and soon they were all laughing.

"Someone going to let me in on the joke."

A tall, stocky man with a deep voice came into the kitchen.

Hally was quite shocked at how much Wes sounded like his dad.

This time Wes introduced Hally impeccably and soon they were ushered from the kitchen by Wes' mum; who was adamant they would ruin dinner if they didn't get out of her way. Wes led Hally into the lounge which was very comfortable and showed definite signs of a small child. Though very neat and clean there were toys in a wooden box and some still on the floor, and a small child size bookshelf with lots of big colourful books. At first, Michael chatted with Hally asking about her family. Then he suggested Wes take her on a tour of the house. He was obviously very proud of what they had done so far.

Each room Wes took her into showed signs of renovation, but it was clear there was still much to be done. There were four bedrooms, his parents' which Hally glanced in through the door; Wes' room which she would have like to linger in, but thought it was better not to; a very pretty spare room and a closed door which he explained was Ellie's room.

"I won't open the door 'cos sometimes she wakes up when the light shines in."

He told her. Then to finish he took her up a narrow staircase to a large attic with windows looking out over the fields.

By the time they returned to the lounge, Kate came in to tell them dinner was ready. To Hally's relief they ate in the kitchen at a big farmhouse table.

"Thought this would be more cosy and less formal."

Kate told her as she served the food.

"It's lovely Kate. Thank you."

Over the meal Hally felt very relaxed. Michael and Kate made her feel very much at home and the only slight pause in the conversation came when Hally mentioned Ellie.

"It was a shame I didn't get to meet Wes' little sister."

She said casually. Kate quickly glanced at Wes then turned back to Hally.

"Yes, our little gemstone."

Hally noticed the look and thought she had said something wrong but couldn't work out what.

"Have I said something wrong?"

She asked concernedly. Kate smiled warmly.

"No of course not my dear. It's just, well there's such a huge gap between Wes and Ellie, well it was a bit of a shock to us when she came along, and of course you will meet her very soon. We just thought meeting you without a toddler demanding my attention would be better. At least at first. Besides, she's very attached to Wes and she would probably be a bit put out that someone else was getting his attention."

Wes laughed and added.

"Yes, she does tend to dominate my time when she can."

Hally could see that having the attention of a grown up brother as well as parents would be very nice for a toddler.

The rest of the evening passed pleasantly and without incident. On the way home they chatted whilst walking hand in hand. The evening was a little chilly but clear and the stars shone brightly. When they reached Hally's house they saw a police car parked outside. Hally became very anxious and rushed around the back to see what was happening, Wes close behind her.

"Mum, dad!"

She called out as she dropped her bag and coat on the table.

"The lounge baby."

Mum called back. Followed by Wes, Hally went through the door. Both parents were sitting on the sofa and PC Duston was sitting in a chair. Mum held a hand out to Hally and dad moved along to allow her to sit between them. Wes settled himself on the floor to the side of the sofa.

"What's happened?"

Hally asked in a small voice. Mum took her hand and held it gently.

"PC Duston has been waiting for you to come home. He needs to ask you something."

Hally was scared and puzzled at the same time. She hadn't done anything wrong so wondered what this could be about. She looked worriedly at PC Duston. Gently he spoke.

"Hally, do you know a girl called Dana Edwards?"

Hally nodded, still confused, she thought it was about the trouble at her party.

"I haven't seen her in ages."

She told him. Then she remembered the note she had received.

"Oh, but she sent me a note; a few weeks ago."

"A note; do you still have it?"

PC Duston asked. Hally felt something ominous, she began to tremble and dad took hold of her other hand.

"Um, yes, it's…"

She looked at Wes as though he would know where she put it. She remembered the day she received it, remembered reading it, but where had she put it? Wes stood up and came over to her. He knelt in front of her and put his hands on her knees, gently squeezing them he looked directly into her eyes.

"We had been swimming, then the picnic. It was warm so you didn't have a jacket, just your big bag."

Wes' voice was soothing and almost hypnotising, so much so she suddenly remembered.

"Yes, my big bag, the side pocket."

Hally leapt from the sofa and dashed from the room and upstairs to her bedroom. She was visibly shaking as she delved into the pocket of her bag and found the envelope with Dana's note. When she returned to the lounge, she held the envelope out to the police constable and in a voice she hoped was steady asked.

"So what is this about?"

PC Duston opened the envelope and took out the note as mum indicated to Hally to come and sit back down. As she moved back to the sofa PC Duston scanned the contents of the note. Then very gently he spoke.

"Hally, Dana was found earlier today at her home. She committed suicide."

All of the breath went out of Hally. There didn't seem to be any air in the room either. Between her parents and Wes on the floor she felt herself go cold; her cheeks tingled and a darkness began creeping in from both sides of her head. She could hear all their voices saying her name, but they sounded as though they were very far away and muffled. She felt herself sway and slip and then there was nothing.

A soft hand was on her cheek and a cool damp cloth was on her forehead. She was lying down, but unsure of where. As she opened her eyes everything came flooding back. Mum was sitting by her side on the sofa, dad was standing at one end of the sofa and Wes was kneeling at the other end. He was the person holding the cloth to her brow. She tried to sit up quickly but mum shushed her and held her back.

"Baby, take it slowly. Here have a sip of water but take it a little at a time."

Hally did as she was told and gradually eased herself into a sitting position. With more water she began to feel more in control of herself again and looked over to PC Duston.

"Oh God. Did I really hear you right?"

She asked in a very small voice.

"Yes Hally, I'm afraid so. Are you ok?"

He asked.

"Um; I think so. I mean, probably not but I'm not going to pass out again. What happened?"

Hally's voice became stronger as she spoke but inside she felt torn up with guilt. She knew this was irrational but it was still there. PC Duston looked towards her parents to see if he should go on with such devastating information. Dad stood straight and nodded that he should. Wes had moved to the sofa and was now sitting on one side of Hally with mum on the other. He had his arm securely around her and mum held her hand. PC Duston took a deep breathe.

"Well, one of her friends, a girl called Penny went to her house as no one had seen her in days. She thought Dana may have run away from home because apparently she doesn't have a very nice home life. However, when she got there no one answered, but the door was unlocked. Penny went in calling out to Dana, but she didn't get an answer. Penny was worried by now because Dana and her mother always locked up when they were out. She went upstairs to Dana's room and found her lying on her bed. Unfortunately, it was quite obvious to Penny that Dana was already dead. She ran screaming from the house and all but hammered down the next door neighbour's door. The neighbour rang us."

He paused and sipped the mug of coffee Hally had not noticed before. Strangely what came to her mind then, was that the drink must be very cold by now. Since he quickly put the mug back down she assumed she was right; and a giggle tried to bubble up out of her. She held it back, knowing it would be totally inappropriate. Mum seemed to sense this and patting her daughter's hand said.

"Why don't I go and get some fresh hot drinks for everyone."

Dad nodded and took her place on the sofa taking Hally's hand in his big warm one. This had a wonderful calming effect on her. For a short while they were all silent, waiting for mum to return with the drinks.

"What I don't understand is what this has got to do with me. I mean why are you here telling me?"

Hally asked, and was relieved to find her voice was now normal. Mum came back into the room with a tray and placed it on a small table. She handed Hally hers first, then began passing out drinks to the others. PC Duston sipped his now steaming coffee then replied to her question.

"We found a mobile number written in marker pen on a calendar. We thought it was Dana's mother, but when we checked it was registered to you." He paused to sip more coffee then added as though an after thought. "We don't know how to contact her mother."

Without even thinking about it, Hally jumped in with.

"You won't be able to. She's somewhere in America. She left Dana by herself and went off with a man."

Everyone looked at Hally, surprise on their faces. Mum spoke before anyone else.

"Hally, how do you know this? Dana is not one of your friends."

Hally took a deep breath and a large gulp of her drink which burned her tongue, but she ignored this and said.

"Oh I wish I had said something earlier. I so wanted to, I wanted to tell social services, or you (she looked at her mother) so you could; but I promised her I wouldn't. She was so scared they would put her in foster care again, and…and (tears began to flow down her cheeks) she was going to be sixteen soon."

She broke down into sobs, her body shaking with shock and

guilt and a sadness she couldn't comprehend. Dad squeezed her hand gently.

"Hally, honey; I think you had better tell us everything."

He said.

For the next hour Hally told them everything that had happened from when the three decided to confront Dana, to when they went to her house and how Dana had finally stopped bullying her. She told them about the time in the Hotspot when Dana had flown at Penny and how she had put her out of her mind over the holidays. She was too shy to explain that her knew relationship with Wes was the cause of this, but a quick glance in his direction confirmed to all that this was the case. She explained about the picnic and how the note had been left for her at the Hotspot and a nod from Wes confirmed this too. She finally finished by saying.

"But, I had absolutely no idea what she meant by it. Ask Corrinne and Clia, they'll tell you. That's the truth."

Tears began to well up again as she turned to her father.

"Daddy is this my fault? Could I have stopped her?"

Wes relinquished his hold on her as dad pulled her into his arms and held her whilst she cried.

"No my angel Tinkerbell; nothing about this is your fault. The girl had problems, huge ones by the sound of things. No wonder she felt there was no where else to go. If anything you tried to help her, but she chose not to accept that help. That's right, isn't it PC Duston?"

The constable nodded and realising Hally was too distressed to notice this cleared his throat and spoke.

"Your dad is quite right Hally. I'm so sorry you had to be put through this, but we had to find out. I think I have all I need here so I'm going to leave you with your parents and boyfriend. I have to take this note, (Hally looked up with fear in her eyes) it's ok, not because of you, but the coroner will need it. Well I won't go into any more detail."

He stopped talking. Hally thought she had missed something but couldn't work out what; but at that point she didn't think she could cope with anything else so she didn't ask any more questions.

Instead she stayed snuggled in her father's comforting arms whilst mum saw PC Duston to the door.

After the constable left, Hally went to her room and changed into cosy pyjamas and a fluffy dressing gown. Mum made hot chocolate and the four of them sat quietly drinking the soothing beverage. Wes stayed close to her and when their drinks were finished he told them he should go home and let Hally get some rest. He wouldn't let her get up and see him to the door but gave her a light kiss on the lips before he left. He showed no signs of embarrassment at doing this in front of her parents and she felt just as comfortable. Mum followed her to her room and sat with her as she settled into bed.

"Could you stay with me for a little while?"

She asked mum. A small lump came into her mother's throat at the pain in her daughter's eyes.

"Of course I will my baby. You close your eyes and try and sleep."

Hally didn't think she would sleep at all that night; but she woke from a dreamless sleep to autumn sunshine. It seemed very late and when she looked at her clock she saw it was ten thirty. She jumped out of bed wondering why mum had not woken her for school. As she rushed from her room the events of the previous night flooded back into her mind and she stopped on the landing, realisation coming that this was why mum hadn't woken her.

"Hally, are you alright?"

Mum called from the bottom of the stairs. Hally trotted down to meet her mother.

"Um, yes, I think so. How come you let me sleep in. I should be at school."

She said as she got to the bottom.

"Don't worry, I rang Mr Hopkins and explained everything. He agreed it was best for you to have a day at home and rest. And before you ask, I rang the girls too. They both wanted to come straight round but I insisted they speak to their parents first."

There was knock on the backdoor, so Hally followed mum through to the kitchen and saw Corrinne and Clia through the glass. Hally felt her day brighten with the sight of her friends as mum opened the door for them. They dived at Hally with hugs and a huge box of chocolates.

"I'm not ill."

She told them laughing. Together they said.

"We know."

"But you need pampering" From Clia

"And chocy comfort." From Corrinne

They all laughed then and Hally raising her hands in submission said.

"Ok, but first I'm going to have a quick shower and get dressed."

The girls explained how their parents had agreed to let them have time off school to support Hally, and as they were all three very able students, Mr Hopkins had given permission too. Feeling secure that Hally would be alright with her friends, mum left them to visit her parents.

Settling on the sofa with a DVD, hot chocolate and the box of chocolates, the three girls began to discuss the dreadful news of Dana's death.

"I just wish I had said something before."

Hally said solemnly.

"I know Hals, we feel the same way. But, really, there was nothing any of us could do. Obviously Dana was in a very bad way, but even her own mates didn't know anything or do anything."

Clia stated.

"What a horrible life to have."

Corrinne said in a soft voice. This brought tears to Hally's eyes. Tears because of the loss of such a young person; tears because of the desperation and loneliness of the girl who had treated her with such hatred and tears because she felt privileged to have a family and friends who loved her. Corrinne and Clia hugged her from either side and for some time the three sat huddled and quiet.

"Hello!"

A voice called from the kitchen. Hally leapt up recognising the voice as belonging to Wes. As she reached the kitchen she saw him holding the back door slightly open with his head poking through the gap.

"I knocked a couple of times, but I don't think you heard."

He told her as he came fully into the room.

"Your mum rang me and said Corrinne and Clia were with you, but I wanted to see for myself how you were doing."

"My mum rang you. how?"

Wes hugged her and laughed.

"Uh, they call it a phone."

He said jokingly. Hally play thumped him on the arm and giggled.

"I meant, how did she get your number?"

"I gave it to her last night when you went to get changed and asked her to call me anytime, even through the night if she wanted me to come round."

Hally hugged him tightly, all the joking put aside.

"That is so very lovely."

She whispered into his shoulder. Wes hugged her back, then with his arm around her led her back to the girls in the lounge, where Hally took her place between her friends and Wes settled on the floor resting against the sofa. They watched the film and ate chocolates and though Dana's suicide was very much in Hally's mind; she kept pushing it back and tried to enjoy the company of three of the most important people in her life.

The next morning Hally walked into school with Corrinne, Clia and Wes feeling very apprehensive. She knew how quickly news got around the school and she was sure everyone would know about Dana. What she wasn't sure about was whether anyone knew about her involvement. There was no sign of Penny or any of the other girls in Dana's gang and the boys who usually hung out with them seemed to have drifted away to other groups.

Registration went ahead normally but Hally could see some of the students giving her sly looks. However none dared question her with Mrs Jacobs commanding silence throughout. But, as soon as she dismissed them for their first lesson she was bombarded with questions.

"Did you find her Hally?"

A girl called Rachel asked.

"Yeah, what happened?"

Asked a boy she only knew was nicknamed Pickle. Clia and

Corrinne saved her, they linked arms on either side of her and marched her through the throng calling out as they moved.

"No she wasn't there, and she doesn't know anything about it, even if you have heard different."

It was a relief to arrive at English and settle down in the classroom. Mr Austin was there so no one had any chance to question Hally further. The lesson progressed normally, but it seemed to fly by to Hally and she was quite disappointed when the bell went indicating the end of the lesson. As she gathered up her things Mr Austin came over and said quietly.

"Could I just have a quick word?"

"We'll wait outside Hals."

Corrinne told her. She gave her friends a thankful smile and waited whilst the remaining students left.

"Mr Hopkins has explained what happened Hally. All I want to tell you is that I am a trained counsellor in trauma. The school believes it's important for the students to have someone to talk to about things like this, so if anytime you feel it's getting too much or you just need to talk about how you feel about this; well just let me know."

Hally was a little taken aback about this. She hadn't thought at all about herself needing support, if anything she imagined Penny would need it. She didn't voice this though but instead shyly thanked him and went to meet the girls outside.

As English had been a double lesson, they went straight to break and much to Hally's relief Wes was waiting on their bench. This completely discouraged any other students from coming over to question her. However she knew it was only a short reprieve; that she would undoubtedly have students coming up to her throughout the rest of the day wanting to know any little titbits she could impart.

Somehow, Hally got through the rest of the day without too much trouble. She had one really uncomfortable moment when at the end of the day outside the school gates she saw a van with the local news logo on the side. Milling around was a television crew interviewing a few students, and when they saw her, a few pointed at her. The reporter immediately headed towards her. Wes who had been waiting outside her last lesson of the day tried to steer her away, and when he failed to accomplish this put his arm around her protectively instead. Corrinne and Clia closed in on either side too, so the reporter was unable to get too close. Trying to get as close as possible the reporter leaned in. He was short with thick dark curly hair, an orangey looking tan and brows that looked like caterpillars wiggling across his forehead as he raised them when he spoke.

"Hello, my name is Daly Fesandelo. Could I ask you about Dana Edwards?"

He thrust a large microphone towards her.

"No, I don't know anything."

Hally replied nervously. Daly tried to inch nearer and she backed away. His eyebrows really did look peculiar and she felt laughter bubbling up. Help came with the deep authoritative voice of Mr Hopkins.

"Really. This is unacceptable. I cannot have you trying to interview my students outside the school gates."

As Daly Fesandelo turned to the head teacher Hally and the others made a quick escape. They knew all the cut throughs away from the school and were able to put some distance between themselves and the television crew.

They headed for Hally's and were all relieved to find mum already at home when they got there. Hally flopped onto a kitchen chair and miserably told her mother about the day. Mum gave them all drinks and snacks and gently massaging her daughter's shoulders said.

"It was bound to happen baby. But it sounds as though you all handled it well." She turned to Wes and the girls. "And thank you for taking care of her."

Nobody said anything, they knew they didn't need to.

"Think about what Mr Austin said though darling. I know you have all of us to support you, but he has had professional training and you never know, it might help."

Mum told Hally. Hally swivelled in her chair to look up at her mum.

"But I feel ok. I mean it's really sad and it was a huge shock at first, but it really doesn't have anything to do with me."

"I know baby, I know. But he's there just in case."

Mum told her as she squeezed her shoulders gently. Hally nodded and left the subject there. There was a loud crash from upstairs which made them all jump and mum quickly moved towards the hallway.

"Nathan, what have you done!"

She called on the way. Hally and the others laughed. Hally was grateful to her little brother, the diversion was a relief, even though she knew he had probably created an enormous mess for her mum to clear up.

After dinner Hally sat with her family watching the television. The local news was on and though she was looking at the screen, she wasn't really concentrating on what was being said. Her mind was all over the place. Thoughts of Dana just kept invading her little daydreams about Wes and this annoyed her. Mum and dad were partly watching and partly chatting, and Nathan was playing on the floor with his cars. Suddenly her attention was brought back to the television when she heard one of the newsreaders say Dana's name. Everyone except Nathan, went completely quiet and watched with full concentration. It was a short piece, and showed the reporter Daly Fesandelo outside the school. There was a brief moment when Hally saw herself, then the report cut to Daly solemnly telling the viewers about the tragic suicide of Dana. They watched in silence, and after mum quietly came over to the chair Hally was curled up in and wrapped her arms around her.

That night Hally had the worst nightmare of her life. She awoke sweating and frightened and lay for some time as real life replaced the horrors of the subconscious. She didn't want to wake her parents, but wished she wasn't alone. She looked at her clock and saw it was just after three. Debating what to do she finally reached for her mobile phone. Before she could change her mind she rang Wes. He answered quickly.

"Hally what's wrong?"

The panic in his voice made her feel very guilty.

"It's ok. Oh I feel stupid now…sorry to wake you…"

She stammered, her face heating up even though he couldn't see her.

"Hally, babe, what is it?"

He asked quietly. There was such gentleness in his voice that tears began to flow.

"I just had the most horrible nightmare."

She whispered. He sensed she was crying and replied.

"I'm coming over. Can you wait in the kitchen? I don't want to wake your family."

Hally tried to protest but he wouldn't hear it, so she nodded then realised he couldn't see her.

"Ok, and thank you."

Then he was gone.

As quietly as she could Hally slipped out of bed and put on her fluffy dressing gown and matching slippers. She tip toed out of her room and down stairs. She didn't turn on any lights until she reached the kitchen, and because of this the nightmare invaded her thoughts and she began to shiver with the fear of it. She partly wished she had woken her parents instead of ringing Wes, but the thought of seeing him helped alleviate her terror.

Much to Hally's surprise Wes arrived in record time. He was a little breathless and felt somewhat sweaty when he pulled her into his arms.

"I jogged most of the way."

He told her by way of explanation in a hushed voice. She felt exhilarated that he had gone to so much effort just because she was afraid and upset and held onto him tightly, tears beginning again.

"I woke up and it seemed so real."

She mumbled into his sweatshirt. He rubbed her back gently murmuring soft words of comfort. Then he led her to a chair and turned to put the kettle on. When they were both sitting with hot chocolate, Wes asked her to tell him about the dream.

"I was back in Dana's house, but on my own this time. I could see my number on the calendar and it seemed to be much bigger and it was flashing red. Everything was really quiet and there didn't seem to be anyone there, just me. Then I heard a sound from upstairs. I realised someone was calling my name. It was weird, like a radio station slightly out of tune, it seemed to come and then fade. I had to go up the stairs, yet I knew there was something up there that I didn't want to confront. I went up and only one door was open. Dana was standing in the doorway, she was grey and was pointing at me. Then she said in that weird voice. "Hally why didn't you help me?" then she sort of floated towards me with her hands reaching for me, and that's when I woke up."

She shivered at the memory of the nightmare and Wes came around the table and put his arms around her. He whispered gently.

"Maybe you should go and see Mr Austin."

Hally nodded into his forearm.

"I think maybe I should. I'll speak to him tomorrow. Oh cripes, it already is tomorrow, it's gone four. Oh Wes I'm sorry, you must be shattered."

Laughing softly Wes kissed the top of her head.

"I'm alright." And at the disbelieving glance she gave him. "Really, I am, and I will stay with you as long as you want me too."

They were still sitting in the kitchen quietly talking when dad came down at half past six to get ready for work. He gave a startled "Oh!" as he saw them. Hally stood up and refilled the kettle for her father.

"I had a really bad nightmare and didn't want to wake you and mum, so I rang Wes and he came over."

Dad nodded, accepting the explanation, but answered with a little frown.

"Darling, we wouldn't have minded you waking us."

"Waking who? Oh, hi Wes"

Mum said as she came into the kitchen too.

"Have I missed something?"

Hally made tea for them all and explained to her parents why Wes was there so early, and though it gave her more tremors, retold the nightmare to them.

"I'll call the school and tell them you won't be in today."

Mum stated matter-of-factly. Hally quickly shook her head.

"No it's alright mum. I want to go in, and I will go and see Mr Austin. I'm sure the dream was just a reaction to yesterday, you know the questions and that reporter. I don't want to sit around all day it will probably make me think about it more than I should."

Mum didn't argue, instead busying herself with breakfast preparations.

Hally saw Mr Austin before lunch. She was surprised by how comfortable she felt sitting and bearing her soul. For an hour, she talked about the bullying she had suffered and the trouble Dana had caused at the party. She talked about how her relationship with Wes had helped her become more confident; and she poured out all her fears about the guilt she felt over Dana.

Mr Austin sat and listened, rarely commenting or questioning. By the end of the session he had made a few notes which he went through with Hally.

"I just have to keep a brief record of this meeting, but it is all confidential and kept locked in the main office."

He told her as he placed the notes into a new folder with her name on the front. Hally wasn't at all worried about this; she felt like a huge weight had been lifted from her.

"I think you are very strong Hally. You have a supporting family and friends and having nightmares is a way of our minds dealing with our fears. By talking about it, you are helping yourself analyse it. I won't make formal appointments for you to see me because I think you will find a way to deal with this yourself. But, I would like to stress, that you should keep talking to your family and friends, and any time you need to see me, I will be available."

The fact that this statement didn't bring tears to Hally's eyes showed her how far she had already come. She thanked him and made her way to meet Corrinne and Clia from their respective maths lessons.

CHAPTER 11

Wes and Gran

Over the next two weeks, interest in Dana began to wane and Hally found herself being bombarded with questions less and less. Although this was a great relief, it also filled her with a deep sadness. It was like people were forgetting who Dana was. There was no one to care, she had no other family and her friends, though sometimes seen huddled together holding tissues; were more often seen causing trouble for the teachers or other students.

Despite what Dana had put Hally through over the years, she had asked PC Duston to let her know when the funeral was. Hally's parents expressed concern over her intention to go, but respected their daughter's wishes and mum said she would go with her. Corrinne, Clia and Wes all said the same and so it was on a very cold, dull Friday morning late in October; that the small group made their way to the local church. The hearse was already there, the coffin still inside. Hally could see two wreaths laying on top, one she recognised, a simple arrangement of white lilies, which they had ordered; and wondered who the other was from.

Quietly they made their way inside and pitifully saw just two people there who were not from the funeral directors. One was Reverend Hayward, and the other was Mr Hopkins. Now Hally understood the other wreath must have come from the school. There was no sign of Penny or any of the other girls Dana had been friends with, and Hally realised that friends was obviously not a word Dana knew much about. The complete loneliness and aloneness of the girl brought tears to Hally's eyes and she leaned into Wes and quietly let them flow as they took seats in the front pew.

The service was short and poignant, so too was the burial.

Hally was all cried out by then; and simply stood in the cold next to her mum, friends and boyfriend on one side of the grave with Mr Hopkins on the other. When it was over, Mr Hopkins spoke briefly with the Reverend, then thanked Hally and the others for coming. He told them he did not expect them to come into school for the rest of the day, then he turned and left them so that he could return to school.

The Reverend also thanked them and left them and for a while they just stood looking into the grave. Mum put her hand on Hally's shoulder and gently said.

"Come on love. Let's go."

Hally looked up at her mum.

"Can I just have a minute here by myself?"

Mum glanced worriedly at Wes and he answered.

"Ok babe, we'll just wait by the gate. Don't get cold."

He kissed her gently on the cheek, then they all turned and slowly walked towards the arched entrance to the church.

Hally stared into the grave at the five red roses they had dropped onto the coffin. She felt numb and not just because the day was so cold. She just could not comprehend how a mother could leave her child so alone to fend for herself. Nor could she understand how so called friends could not even come and say a last goodbye. She sighed deeply, so grateful for what she had.

"Sorry to disturb you love, but we have to get on here."

Two men in work clothes with shovels stood nearby indicating the open grave. Hally gave a little start and then a shudder. She did not want to be there when they filled in the gaping hole with the heavy soil, which she only just realised was close and covered with what looked like a green grassy looking cover.

"Oh! Um, sorry, I'm going now."

She mumbled, and quickly turned and walked hurriedly away from the grave. She reached the others without looking back. Wes took her hand and together they all made their way back to Hally's home.

Over the next two weeks Hally plunged herself into her schoolwork. Although not really behind, she felt the time she had taken away from school had impacted on her studies. Corrinne and Clia had the same attitude and the three friends spent evenings studying together, sometimes Wes joined in, but most evenings with him she spent alone. Occasionally, Hally got scared that the time she gave to Wes was time away from the girls, and during the night when she was alone in bed; she would imagine Corrinne and Clia getting closer but further away from her. In the mornings, when she was fresh and rested and they all met up for school and they were just their normal selves; she pushed these fears deep down and away.

On a very cold and damp Saturday afternoon early in November, Hally met up with Corrinne and Clia to go into town. Wes was working in the Hotspot and the girls had decided to start looking for Christmas presents. They had decided that they wouldn't buy anything yet because they all agreed it was still a bit early, and Hally had spent quite a bit of her money on Wes' birthday present at the beginning of the month, but thought they would browse the shops and get ideas. After traipsing from one shop to another, they stopped in a coffee shop for a rest. Over hot steaming coffee and general chat about their presents ideas, the conversation became more serious.

"So, how is your Gran?"

Corrinne asked Hally.

Hally sipped her drink and smiled.

"She's really good at the moment. Nurse Mildred says she's stabilised and they're managing her pain quite well. You know how Gran is, won't let on to us how she feels 'cos she doesn't want to worry us. Like we're not out of minds most of the time anyway."

The girls nodded their understanding.

"Sorry we haven't visited her in a while."

Clia said bashfully. Hally's night time fears crashed into her mind. She actually hadn't realised the girls hadn't been to Gran's in a little while. She put her cup down shakily. It rattled in the saucer and the girls noticed straight away something was wrong.

"Hally?"

Clia said.

"Corrinne, Clia, are you drifting away from me?"

The girls looked shocked, Hally felt shocked too. She had not intended to ask that very question, it just came out, like her subconscious had taken over. Corrinne leaned forward and grabbed one of Hally's hands, Clia grabbed the other and said.

"Hals, sweetie, never, I mean never, ever, ever. We have been best friends for like, as long as I can remember. Nothing will change that. Even if one of us emigrated to Mars, we would still be best friends, you know chat on the phone, email."

This brought laughter to all of them.

"What made you think that anyway Hally?"

Corrinne asked seriously.

"It's just something that crept up on me in the middle of the night. You know, I spend quite a lot of time with Wes and I got scared that you two would... well..."

She couldn't bring herself to say what was in her mind. The girls seemed to be able to read her thoughts anyway and Corrinne answered.

"Hally, we love it that you have such a great boyfriend, and honestly, it's really only the odd night that we get together when you are with him. Mostly, we stay at home and do other stuff, we really treasure our time when the three of us are together, but Clia and I..." She looked at Clia. "Well, it's just not the same when it's not all three of us."

Clia nodded in agreement.

"And, well we are still hopeful that your hunk will turn up one day with a couple of dishy lads for us."

Clia added with a giggle. This made them all laugh again and Hally felt relief wash over her.

"Perhaps I will have a chat about that to him then."

She told her friends. This brought big smiles to their faces and so they continued drinking their coffees and chatting. The topic of conversation had now changed to what Clia referred to as a 'boy recipe'. For the next half hour, with fresh coffees, they put together Corrinne and Clia's 'ingredients' for their perfect boyfriend. Some of it was completely wild, like owning a yacht and a Ferrari, and some of it quite realistic, like being faithful and caring.

"Anyway, Hally, back to your Gran. We haven't been round in a while only because we didn't want to get in the way. You know, too many people at one time. But, we miss seeing her, so if it's ok could we come with you next time?"

Clia asked. Hally relaxed in the leather chair and smiled.

"Of course you can. Actually, Wes is coming round with me tomorrow and I know he's very nervous, so maybe if we all went together he would feel a bit better."

The girls agreed to this.

"But only if he finds us our own hunks."

Corrinne said jokingly.

"So now Gran gift. What shall we get her?"

Clia stated matter of factly as they finished their drinks and got up to leave.

The rest of the afternoon was spent choosing the perfect gift for Gran. After much deliberation they all settled on a bumper colouring book and crayons.

"She's going to love this."

Hally stated.

"Yeah, and you know she will have Wes right next to her joining in."

Clia said.

That evening Hally sat with Corrinne and Clia all snuggled in pyjamas and fluffy dressing gowns watching a very girlie DVD. Mum and dad were out for a meal with friends and Wes was working the evening shift at the Hotspot. He had agreed with his boss to do the overtime telling Hally he wanted the extra money for Christmas. Hally didn't mind although she did miss him, but thought he probably wouldn't really enjoy the film they were engrossed in. Nathan was tucked up in bed and they hadn't heard a peep out of him. They had feasted on popcorn, tortilla chips and dip and were starting on a box of chocolates when Nathan appeared in the doorway. He stood rubbing his eyes. Hally jumped up and took her little brother by the hand.

"Natty, what's up?"

She asked gently. Nathan blinked and looked up at his sister.

"Hally, where's mummy?"

He whispered.

"Mum and dad are out, but we are here to look after you."

She said. Nathan looked around the room, Corrinne and Clia smiled. Suddenly he burst into tears. Hally knelt down and pulled him into her arms where he leaned close and sobbed.

"Natty, darling, what's wrong."

She asked as she rubbed his hair.

"I had a horrible dream, and I want…want…mummy."

He wailed. Hally lifted him up and carried him to the sofa. It wasn't easy, he wasn't quite so little anymore. Corrinne shifted over to give her some space and she sat down with her brother on her lap, cuddling and shushing him. He sobbed for some time and gradually the tears abated until there was just the odd hiccough. Hally waited before asking him any more questions. When the tears had subsided enough for him to hear her, she asked very gently.

"What did you dream little one?"

Nathan looked up at the girls and in a shaky voice said.

"The Gripper came out of my toy box. He grew and grew and tried squashing me in bed."

To most people this would have made no sense, but to Hally she fully understood. The Gripper was a character toy from Nathan's favourite children's television show and DVDs, 'The adventures of Crewman and his Team'. Gripper was the baddy in the film and Nathan had spent hours and hours on his own and with his little friends; with other character toys formulating their own stories. Always in their play, Gripper had been foiled but now it seemed Nathan's imagination had just got the better of him. Hally hugged him close and Clia said she would go and make him some hot chocolate. Neither of her friends had younger siblings, so they treated Nathan as their little brother too.

Mum and dad came home shortly after and found Nathan snuggled between the girls on the sofa. The chocolate had eased him and he was drifting in and out of sleep. Hally explained why he was up and smiling, dad lifted him gently and carried him back to bed with mum following.

"He's all settled."

Mum said as she returned.

"What about Gripper?"

Hally asked.

"Oh, a good telling off from dad and being sent back to the toy box satisfied Nathan. No one defies dad, not even the toys, so Nathan believes."

Mum said with a smile.

"Did I hear my name mentioned?"

Dad said, as he came back into the room. Hally nodded as he leaned over and plucked out a chocolate from the box.

"Hey, you can't have that."

Hally told him in mock indignation as he took a bite. He held out the other half.

"Want it back?"

He said laughing.

"Ug, dad, you are so gross."

They all started laughing then and Hally handed the box around for all of them to share.

It was late by the time the girls went to Hally's room for bed. Wes had texted her saying goodnight and that he had missed her. She texted the same back. They had already arranged what time he would come round the next day to go and visit Gran so she was quite surprised when he sent another text. This one simply said.

cant wait to see you tomorrow and to meet your gran sleep soundly my little darling xxxxxxxxx.

After showing Corrinne and Clia the text and discussing it, Hally thought she would be awake all night; but she quickly dropped into a deep and peaceful sleep.

In the morning the girls left Hally's to see their families before returning for the visit to Gran's. They arrived a few minutes after Wes, tapping on the kitchen door and grinning like Cheshire cats because Hally and Wes could be seen through the glass locked in an embrace.

Mum had gone earlier and dad was going to take Nathan to the park with his football. The family tried to make sure Nathan got to spend as much time as possible with his grandmother, but he didn't really understand how ill she was. Also it was difficult to keep him occupied when he visited. Although he was a very well behaved child he was still just a little boy, his toys could only keep him settled for a time. Because of this, mum and dad tried between them to make sure he had as much parent time away from the situation as possible.

Hally led Wes and the girls into her grandparents' house via the backdoor. Granddad was in the kitchen and gave her a huge smile and an even bigger hug. Hally introduced Wes who held out his hand and received a strong handshake, a smile and a very scrutinizing, but friendly look. He then turned to the girls and holding out both arms gave them a hug at the same time. Granddad then turned and led the small party into the lounge where mum was sitting with her mother, and Nurse Mildred was standing at a small cabinet preparing some medication.

"Gran."

Hally called gently. Gran looked up and it tore at Hally's heart to see how fragile she looked. Gran smiled and held out a thin frail arm to her granddaughter.

"Come here my angel." She said softly. "And is this him?" she asked with some of her old cheekiness.

Hally led Wes towards Gran. He was holding her hand quite tightly and she realised he was very nervous. Mum stood up to allow some room, but much to all their surprise Wes didn't sit on the sofa, he knelt in front of Gran so he was the same level as she was. To Hally he visibly relaxed and letting go of her hand reached forward and very gently took both of Gran's hands in his.

"It is such a pleasure to meet you."

He told her in a soft and humble voice. Gran smiled and gave a small girlish laugh, her blue eyes lighting up.

"It's lovely to meet you too. You are a very handsome young man."

Wes blushed at the compliment, Hally giggled and the others joined in. Corrinne and Clia came forward with the gift, and delighted, Gran insisted, as predicted that Wes should choose which picture to colour and to help her with it.

"My fingers are not so nimble these days."

She told him, then in total contradiction to this held a crayon firmly and began colouring in the picture neatly and perfectly to the edges.

"So, tell me about yourself."

Gran said to Wes as she coloured. Wes looked at Hally.

"What, Hally hasn't told you all already?"

He asked with a little smile.

"Oh yes, everything. But I want to hear it from you."

Gran answered mischievously.

"Everything?"

Wes asked with his eyebrows raised, and even though the question was aimed at Gran, the look was given to Hally. It was Hally's turn to blush.

"Um, think I'll go and help mum with some drinks."

She said hurriedly and jumped up and trotted out to the kitchen where mum was chatting with Nurse Mildred. Not long after, Corrinne and Clia came into the kitchen too.

"She thinks it takes all of us to make some tea."

Corrinne announced as they walked in. Hally grinned.

"Poor Wes."

They all laughed and explained to mum what was going on. Mum turned to Nurse Mildred.

"She did exactly the same thing to me the first time I brought Colin home. She'll know his entire family history three generations back by the time we take the tea in."

This made them all laugh. With the tea made and on a tray they made their way back into the lounge. Wes was now sitting next to Gran and both looked relaxed and happy. Hally was relieved to see her boyfriend sitting so comfortably next to Gran and though he offered to give up his seat, both Hally and Gran insisted he stay where he was.

"Wes has told me all about Oxford and why they moved. I would say that it was very lucky for you Hally angel that they did."

Gran announced with a twinkle in her eye, as Hally carefully held out a cup to her.

"You know Gran, I think you are absolutely right."

"So what about you two?" Gran looked towards Corrinne and Clia. "I bet this gorgeous man here, (she lifted Wes' hand indicating him) has two really gorgeous friends who would very much like to get to know you both."

Not only did Corrinne and Clia blush, but Hally did too. It was like Gran had been a party to their conversation the day before.

"Did you…?"

"What did…?"

"I didn't…"

They all spoke at the same time then burst out laughing. No one except Gran seemed to have any idea what was going, but to Hally's relief, it was Wes who spoke.

"Well you know, there are a couple of guys I know who are single; and when they came into the café last night we were chatting; they asked me about you two. Maybe we could all get together soon."

Corrinne and Clia beamed, Gran looked at them all as if to say she had arranged the whole thing.

They all spent most of the day at Gran's. Dad arrived later with Nathan who jumped into his Granddad's arms and announced.

"I had a very bad dream last night."

He then went on to tell Granddad in full detail about the dream and how dad had made sure Gripper didn't scare him again.

"I looked in the toy box 'smorning and he was right where dad put him, so he knows now not to scare me 'gen"

Granddad hugged him and told him that next time he was around he would have a word too, just to be sure. He then took Nathan out to his workshop. Nathan loved going in there to look at Granddad's carpentry tools and to be shown how to work the wood.

Mum and dad were in the kitchen putting together a buffet. Since Gran's appetite was now so small and since she needed small meals and often; it was decided that a buffet would suit everyone, and wouldn't be as demanding as preparing a cooked meal for them all. Nurse Mildred had settled Gran into a special reclining chair to have a sleep; so Hally took Wes, Corrinne and Clia into the garden even though it was now very cold; to show Wes the tree house Granddad had built her when she was little. He had maintained it perfectly over the years and it was mostly Nathan who used it now, but occasionally Hally and the girls still went up, usually in the summer time. Crouching slightly to get through the door, they all squeezed in. Granddad had built child size furniture and so they perched on the little chairs.

"This is wonderful Hally."

Wes told her.

"Yes, Granddad is very talented. There used to be little cushions and a table cloth that Gran made, but I think they are indoors in the loft. They got quite worn and stained but I wouldn't let Gran make new ones or throw the old ones out, so as I got older I think she just washed them and stored them away. Nathan just plays up here sometimes with his toys. I don't know what Granddad is going to do by himself."

No tears came, but she felt pain deep down. This was the first time she had voiced aloud the inevitability of her Gran's death. Wes hugged her in the small space and the girls got as close as was possible.

"We will all be here for you and your family sweetie."

Clia told her with sincerity. Corrinne and Wes nodded in agreement and for a while they sat quiet and still in the little tree house that Granddad built.

It was the middle of the evening when they left Gran's house. Nurse Mildred saw them to the door whilst mum watched over Gran in the bath.

"Alice was sparkling today."

She told them.

"She has such spirit in her, she won't let the pain get the better of her and though she tires quickly she's still very much the matriarch. Today was very good for her and for your Granddad, it's very hard for him."

"Having you here is a big help."

Hally told her. She smiled at Hally, but there was a sort of sadness in her smile.

"Thank you, I appreciate that. It's more than just a job for me because I know that when I'm called in it's because time is limited. I like to think that I can give my patients and their families as much comfort and pleasure as is possible given the situation."

Hally leaned forward and gave the nurse a hug. She realised how strong Nurse Mildred must be to do her job. She wasn't just there to look after Gran medically but to look after the welfare of all involved. Hally decided then and there that if there really were angels, then this woman truly was one. They said goodnight and told Nurse Mildred that they would be back to visit very soon.

"Yes, you come back often."

She told them and as they walked away Hally wondered if there was deeper meaning in this tiny statement. She thought there was and tried to push it to the back of her mind, but like the moment in the tree house she finally voiced it to Wes and the girls as they walked home.

"I don't think my Gran has much longer to live."

She said quietly. Again, there were no tears just that deep, deep pain. Wes squeezed her hand but they all knew there was not anything they could say.

CHAPTER 12

Gran

Monday morning arrived very cold and foggy. Hally walked out of the backdoor and couldn't even see the gate out of the garden until she was very close to it. She carefully made her way along her road fascinated by the way the fog changed everything. Barely visible cars crept alongside her, their headlamps like huge yellow eyes, their engine noise distorted. Small high visibility bands bounced along the pavements, looking like luminous worms floating in the air; as young children togged up in reflective jackets, trotted next to their mothers who held them tightly by the hand.

Corrinne and Clia were waiting where the roads met, but Hally could barely make them out until she was almost next to them. They said their good mornings, linked arms and carefully made their way through the fog to school. Strange shapes greeted them along the way as they bumped, sometimes literally, into groups of people they knew; not being able to make out who was who until they were near or recognised a voice. Eventually, and without harm they reached the school gates, thankful that it was almost time for the bell as the fog was not just dense but very cold.

Hally had a very normal day at school. Lessons which she thought were going to be a lot more challenging; were in fact no more difficult than the previous year, and she was very relieved about this. She did find the workload heavier, but much more interesting. She felt she was completing tasks with more intensity and content, and so far all her assignments had been returned with high marks and very positive comments.

The fog did not clear at all throughout the day and the return journey home was a repeat of the morning. Corrinne and Clia had arranged to go with Hally to her house, deciding that they would all three complete their homework together. Mum was not home when they got there, and Hally accepted that she had probably picked Nathan up from school and gone to Gran's. With the kettle on, the girls unpacked their books from their bags and prepared to settle at the kitchen table. Soon, with hot coffee by the side of them, they were deep in concentration over their homework. Occasionally they spoke, asking each other a question, or seeking advice or approval on something they had written; but for the most part of an hour and a half, they worked quietly. They had just stacked their books and sat back with fresh coffees as mum came in the door with Nathan, followed by dad.

"Hi baby, Corrinne, Clia."

Mum said as she planted a kiss on top of her daughter's head.

"Hi Tink, girls."

Dad said, as he did the same. Nathan squeezed past them all dropping his bag and coat on the floor as he dashed past them.

"Hold it!"

Dad said in a firm voice. The girls giggled as Nathan skidded to a halt and meekly turned around, his chin on his chest. Dad pointed to the little pile without having to say anything, and Nathan, sliding his feet along the floor slowly and with a big exaggerated sigh picked up his things.

"And put them away properly."

Mum called after him as he plodded out of the room. Hally looked at her friends and together they giggled at her little brother's antics.

"He's so cute."

Clia announced. Mum nodded in agreement but added with a more serious note.

"But we still need to be firm with him. He sort of understands what's going on with his Gran, but we can't let that be an excuse for letting him get his own way. Mostly, he just needs reminding that we won't run around after him, that there are certain things he has to do for himself. It's just normal growing up really."

"Was I that much of a pain mum?"

Hally asked.

"Nathan's not a pain angel, he's just a normal little boy that needs a normal amount of discipline. But you, well…"

She stopped and looked at her daughter with a smirk on her face.

"Oh mum."

Hally said tutting. Dad gave her a squeeze on her shoulder and as he made his way out of the kitchen called back.

"Yep, you were a pain in the neck, back and arse."

He then laughed and jogged out before Hally could get up. This made them all laugh, and with a smile Hally said to all of them.

"I'll get him back."

Wes came over later that evening and as mum and dad were in the study chatting to friends on the internet, they had the lounge to themselves. Snuggled up against him watching television, Hally felt very content. Although Wes had kept his word and kept his affections to just kissing and cuddling, Hally's body was still very much in turmoil when he did this. She knew he knew this and she wanted to talk to him about it; but she still felt shy and didn't have the confidence to broach the subject. Unknowingly, she let out a really big sigh and was taken aback when he spoke.

"Hals, what's up?"

"Huh, oh…nothing."

She stammered. Sitting up a bit and turning towards her he said.

"Hally, I know you have something on your mind. What is it?"

Trying to bury her face into his jumper she shook her head and mumbled.

"Nothing."

He took her chin in his hand and lifted it away from his chest. Looking directly into her eyes he pushed for an answer.

"Tell me please. Have I done something?"

Quickly she shook her head.

"Oh no Wes. It's just, um, well. Oh cripes."

She felt her face burn, partly with embarrassment and partly pure shyness. Taking her face in both his hands he said very gently.

"You can tell me anything Hally."

"You will just think I'm some stupid little kid."

She told him, and much to her dismay felt tears welling in her eyes. Wes saw the tears and gently brushed them away with his thumb.

"Nothing you say or do would make me ever think that."

He told her sweetly.

"Well…"

She tried, but her voice came out as a whisper. He leaned forward and gave her a little kiss on the lips. At once she felt the burning low down in her body and she leaned in for a fuller and deeper kiss. Wes accepted her kiss and then pulled back, again looking deep into her eyes.

"I think I know."

He told her. Again she felt her face burn but this time met his eyes and clearing her throat said.

"I just feel like, well, you know, that time in the garden ages ago, well you have never done anything like it again. The thing is, I want you to, like most times when we kiss and we are on our own. Well I don't mind, I mean it's ok, it really is."

Still holding her face in his hands Wes took a big sigh.

"Hally, babe. I really want to as well. But for now I can't do that to you." Hally's face began to crumple. "Baby, please, it's not because of you. I just want us to wait, at least until you are sixteen."

"But that's ages away."

As she said this Hally realised how childish to her it sounded, like Nathan waiting for his dinner.

"Oh God, that sounded really bad, like a little kid. Wes, I'm sorry, oh I don't know what I'm saying." Then she realised what he had said. "So you think we will be together for my birthday then?"

Wes gave a small laugh.

"Well I have no plans to go anywhere, what about you?"

With a very big smile she shook her head and wrapped her arms around his neck.

"No I don't."

She said in a whisper, and although her body still ached and burned she set her mind to believe what he said and wait.

As Christmas approached the days settled into a pattern for Hally. She would come home from school, sometimes with

Corrinne and Clia, sometimes alone; complete her homework and wait for her parents. Some days she would detour from school and go to her Grandparent's house and frequently Corrinne and Clia joined her. Because of this busy schedule Hally had only re-visited Wes' home twice since her initial visit. She wasn't worried about this though, but as yet had still not met Ellie, as each time she had been to Wes' Ellie had been in bed. Wes told her he would make sure they would meet over Christmas.

Nurse Mildred had now become almost a part of the family. She was definitely the force that held them all together, always bright and smiling but always very gentle; completely aware of their feelings and fluctuating emotions. She could sense minute changes as though she were psychic and step in before something became too tense. This was especially the case with Nathan. He was after all just a little boy who wanted and needed to play, but was also in a position where he understood that he had to try and limit his activities. So, on rare occasions when mum was about to run out of patience, Nurse Mildred would take Nathan by the hand and take him into the kitchen and play a game with him. She would even take him out into the garden and kick a football around with him.

Many times when they were all together at Gran's, Hally would sit back quietly and just watch her family. She saw her Granddad pottering around the house or in his shed acting like everything was the same as it always had been. But when he thought no one was looking, Hally would see the pain and despair in his eyes. She would watch him push his food around on the plate and nibble at it as though it had no taste. She would hear him laugh out loud at Nathan's antics and play with him as usual but with an air of false enjoyment.

Watching her own mother tore at Hally's heart. She could not imagine life without her mum, so how could her mother get by without hers. But, mum always kept a brave face on. She was almost as strong as Nurse Mildred, no stronger, Hally told herself. Because, as caring and gentle as she was, it was Nurse Mildred's job, whereas mum was going to lose a part of herself. Hally silently observed her mum carefully and gently help Gran hold her tea cup, guide her knife and fork, or as though caring for a new born baby wipe her face with a soft cloth when something spilled. Never did she complain, or tire of looking after her so very sick mother.

Colin spread his time with work and supporting his wife and children. He had lost both of his parents many years earlier, his father who had a major heart attack and his mother soon after from a stroke. Hally had been small and Nathan not even born, so both children had grown up with just one set of grandparents. Because of this, Colin could see the impact of his mother in law's illness on all of them. At times he felt completely helpless, knowing there was very little he could do to relieve the pain they were all suffering so deeply. So, he made sure the day to day running of the home went smoothly. He was lucky to have a well paid job, and lucky that the job itself didn't demand more of his time than his usual working hours. This meant he too could spend time with his in laws, his wife and children and lend his support to all.

Hally saw her family as an arch, each holding the other up, she only hoped that the whole thing would not crumble and fall when one or all was weakened with sorrow. She resolved that she would make sure each of them would have the others to depend on when the time came; when they all had to cope with the ultimate loss, the death of her Grandmother.

On the Saturday two weeks before Christmas Hally awoke at seven feeling very much in the spirit of the season. She was going Christmas shopping with Clia and Corrinne and had a mental list of the presents she was going to buy. Wes was working a split shift at the Hotspot, so the girls fully intended to start out early, have lunch at the café (Wes had hinted to Hally that the two boys he'd mentioned would be there, but she hadn't told the girls just in case they were not.) then complete all of their shopping in one day.

Corrinne and Clia arrived at eight thirty shaking raindrops from their coats before coming in. The weather had been changeable for days; switching between freezing fog, to sleet, back to fog and ice and now to heavy rain. However Hally and her friends were determined not to let the weather deter them from their plans. Before they set off for town, Hally made hot drinks and the three sat at the kitchen table sipping from their cups and telling each other what they were buying for their families.

"Well I'm going to buy Nathan another character toy from his favourite programme. He's been going on about one called Tankman; he's one of the good guys and part of Crewman's team; so I told mum and dad I would get it. I have it reserved at the Toy Store because I think it's quite popular."

Hally told her friends. Both girls looked at her completely familiar with the characters Hally was talking about.

"Oh, I love that shop and we can get something for him too."

Said Corrinne.

"But you two don't have to buy him presents."

Hally tried to protest but Clia shook her head.

"We know we don't have to, but he's like our little brother too. So, well we want to."

Corrinne smiled and nodded, so Hally gave up trying to argue her case.

Mum and dad were already out, mum at Gran's and dad with Nathan at football training. Mum had insisted Hally take the whole day and spend it with her friends, just being teenagers. Hally had tried to argue, saying she would split the day, but mum wouldn't hear it, so Hally, feeling a little guilty agreed to her mother's wishes. Now, sitting with Corrinne and Clia, she was glad her mum had insisted. She realised that she did need a whole day away from the stress of her Gran's illness and she had her mobile with her if she was needed.

As expected, the town was very busy. Parents, with harassed and strained looks on their faces practically dragged their young children from shop to shop. People with umbrellas jostled and bumped into each other as they all fought for space along the pavements. Even in the pedestrianised shopping area, couples holding hands, families with children and buggies, groups or single shoppers rushed about or queued at checkouts. All the coffee shops and cafés were packed with shoppers taking a break, their windows fogged with steam.

At first the girls just wandered about various shops looking at the huge variety of products all designed especially for Christmas. They pushed buttons on musical gifts creating a complete racket as various snowmen, santas, reindeer and more sang or played different Christmas tunes or hymns. Some harassed looking shop assistants frowned, others smiled at the girls' mischievous antics. Giggling the girls dashed from shop to shop, sometimes being beaten by others, including adults doing the same thing. At one large department store, the girls stopped to play with some of the novelty toys on display and found themselves competing with grown men who were supposedly buying gifts for their wives or girlfriends.

After spending time playing in the shops, they settled down to serious shopping. They had worked out a strategy before setting out whereby they compared gift lists, so they wouldn't be traipsing back to the same shops if more than one of them was buying from a particular place. This worked very well and by the time they agreed to break for lunch, Hally had bought for Nathan and her dad, Clia for Nathan and her dad and brother, and Corrinne for Nathan and both her parents.

Feeling proud that their shopping trip was going as planned the three made their way to the Hotspot Café at the time Hally had arranged with Wes. Like other places it was jammed with shoppers, and unusually, more adults and families than teenagers. They entered the café and was very surprised when Wes came straight over and told them he had reserved a table for them near the window. They were very pleased and relieved by this as the café was very full.

"Sorry I can't come and sit with you, but as you can see the place is heaving."

Wes told them gesturing around the café.

"Wes, it's ok, we can see how busy you are, and thank you so much for reserving this table."

Hally told him smiling. He gave her a very big and cheeky smile back.

"That's alright my sweet girlfriend, just remember when you come to buy my Christmas present."

He then turned swiftly before Hally could retaliate and left them laughing and perusing the menu.

"Mmm, I think I will have a jacket potato with the chilli."

Hally said.

"Well I think I'm going for the fish pie."

Corrinne replied.

"And I'm going to have the steak and kidney pie."

Clia told them both.

"No surprise there then."

Hally said smiling. Clia nearly always opted for the Hotspot homemade steak and kidney pie, she simply loved it.

"Well it is just the best pie ever."

Clia exclaimed. Wes came over and took their order squeezing Hally's hand gently. Before returning behind the counter he said.

"I'll bring you hot drinks."

When he came back with a tray of drinks he was not alone. As he placed the tray on the table he said.

"Girls, I'd like you to meet two friends of mine."

Indicating to each of the girls.

"Hally my girlfriend, and her two friends, Corrinne and Clia, this is Gregg."

A tall, well built blonde boy with green eyes stepped forward holding out his hand to the girls. They shook hands and said hi but Hally noticed Corrinne blushing slightly as she said hello.

"And this is Rhys."

He was not quite as tall as Wes and Gregg and was more slightly built, but with dark curly hair and brown eyes he had an almost model look about him. He leaned forward to greet them too and this time Hally noticed he blushed when he spoke to them. She suspected he had a gentle shyness about him and could see this really appealing to Clia. Hally noticed Wes had placed five mugs on the table.

"Well got to get on."

He told them. For once Hally took charge of the situation as Gregg and Rhys were still standing by the table.

"Oh please sit down, Wes has brought you drinks too."

She then scooted off the bench seat and stood up.

"Just nipping to the ladies."

She told them all and quickly disappeared before her friends could protest. As she had been sitting next to Corrine with Clia opposite it meant the two boys could sit down next to each of the girls.

Hally fussed with her hair and makeup in the ladies long enough to give her friends some time with the boys. She didn't stay too long so as not to make it too obvious and when she returned to the table the four seemed to be getting along quite well. At least there didn't seem to be any awkward silences. She slipped onto the bench next to Rhys and smiling said.

"Queue."

Corrinne and Clia gave her such a disbelieving look that she felt herself blush; which she quickly covered up by sipping her coffee, and to her relief saw Wes coming over with their order. He beamed at her as he laid out their food, Gregg and Rhys' too. Hally was very proud of the way he had arranged this little get together for Corrinne and Clia and felt her heart swell with love. This sudden flood of emotion took her by surprise and did not go unnoticed by Wes.

"Hally, are you ok?"

He asked full of concern.

"You look all flushed."

"Um… oh…yes I'm fine, just suddenly got a bit too hot. Too many layers, it's cold outside."

Quickly she slipped out of her jumper even though the top underneath wasn't particularly thick. Wes gave a slight concerned frown but didn't say anything further. Corrinne however gave her a look that told her straight away she didn't believe what she had told Wes and that she would be questioned later.

After they had all eaten, Wes brought them fresh drinks and slid onto the bench next to Hally. He told them he was taking a quick break which pleased Hally. It did however mean that Clia and Rhys were a bit squashed together but from what Hally could see, neither minded. In fact her two friends were chatting to Wes' friends like they had known them for ages. In fact they were all chatting like the whole group had been friends for a long time. Hally was almost disappointed that they had to leave and carry on with their shopping.

"Why don't we all get together this evening?"

Wes asked as he stood up to go back to work and the girls prepared to go back to the bustle of Christmas shopping. Rhys and Gregg nodded immediately and Corrinne and Clia agreed too. Hally thought for a moment, not wanting to spoil what could be a great evening; but worried about visiting her Gran.

"Go and see Gran for a little while and then we will come and meet you there."

Wes told her, reading her mind.

Hally beamed relieved, and again felt her emotions building in her chest like a dam ready to burst.

"Thank you Wes. That's a lovely suggestion. Oh but aren't you doing a split?"

He gave her a quick peck and grinned.

"I came in really early and promised to work through until five, so I wangled the evening off."

The girls left the boys still sitting in the café and began the afternoon session of shopping. The rain had now turned to sleet and the temperature had dropped considerably. They tried to stay inside the stores as much as possible and chatted about Gregg and Rhys as they shopped.

"Wes is an angel."

Clia told Hally.

"He's an absolute angel."

Corrinne told her sincerely. Hally smiled at her friends and felt happier than she had in a long time. For just a few moments all her family's problems were buried beneath the tide of emotion she felt for her friends and their happiness and her boyfriend. Corrinne noticed the change in Hally.

"So… what happened in the Hotspot then?"

It took Hally a moment to realise what her friend was talking about, then felt her cheeks growing warm at the memory of her intense feelings.

"You'll think I'm crazy."

She mumbled.

"Sweetie, we know you are a crazy bird, so nothing will surprise us."

Clia told her in her ever so grown up voice. Both Hally and

Corrinne laughed and as Hally mulled over the two gifts she was looking at for her mum, finally came clean.

"I think, I really do think that I love Wes."

Both her friends gave a deep sigh. Then Clia, rolling her eyes said.

"We know that already. We thought something serious had happened to you."

Hally looked at them in pure astonishment. Her mouth formed a perfect O and she almost couldn't speak.

"What…what…do…you mean, you know?"

She stammered. Corrinne laughed heartily.

"Hals, we can see it in your face, your voice, everything about you, especially when he's around you."

"Oh, do you think Wes knows too."

Hally asked sounding worried.

"Probably."

Clia and Corrinne replied together, and at the devastated look on Hally's face.

"But hey sweetie, I think he feels the same way about you. Just because it's not said doesn't mean it's not felt."

Clia said. Hally remembered Wes nearly about to say something and then changing it and the smile returned to her face.

"Well, now it's your turn."

She indicated to both her friends. They all laughed and Corrinne and Clia nodded in agreement.

"So. Which one for mum? Oh I'm going to buy both."

Hally announced taking both gifts and putting them in her basket.

As promised Wes and the others picked Hally up from her Gran's that evening.

"How's Gran today?"

Wes asked gently.

"Mum says she's had a really good day and the time I spent with her she was quite lively."

Hally responded. Wes smiled took her hand and kissed her on the cheek.

"I'm very happy to hear that. So, if it's ok with you we thought we would go to Corrinne's. Her parents are out at a Christmas party so she asked if we could all go there."

Hally gave Corrinne a deep understanding look. Originally she was going to the party with her parents. As an only child she often went out with them rather than be alone, now Hally could see the excitement in her friend's eyes at the thought of having not just her closest friends round; but a whole group. Corrinne had had a couple of boyfriends before, but like Hally they had only been brief relationships and none to take home. With a deep sigh Hally realised they were all growing up and the fears she had experienced about drifting apart resurfaced. Determinedly, she pushed them aside and resolved to thoroughly enjoy the evening.

The evening went very well indeed. The six spent the time chatting and finding out about Gregg and Rhys. They had met Wes because they worked with his dad who was a builder, and both boys were training in the building business. They listened to a variety of music and played some board games, girls against boys, which the girls won most of the time. The boys insisted jokingly that they had cheated, but Clia indignantly told them it was because girls concentrated better than boys and since the games had required thought and tactics, it was obvious they would beat them. Hally and Corrinne agreed with Clia which started a playful argument and left everyone laughing.

The girls took themselves off to the kitchen still giggling to fetch refreshments. Hally knew it would be an ideal opportunity to question her friends about Gregg and Rhys. However she didn't have to start the conversation, as soon as they were out of earshot of the boys Clia put her hands together and raised them to her face.

"Oh my goodness!"

She exclaimed in a slightly hushed voice.

"Your Wes really came through. I mean Rhys is just so fit, but well, it's not like he knows it, you know what I mean. He's not vain with his looks, he's just so sweet and that accent…"

Clia stopped. She simply couldn't say anything more at that moment. Hally smiled at her friend's delight and raised her brows to Corrinne.

"What about you?"

Corrinne smiled a soft, sweet gentle smile.

"What can I say, I'm happy."

It was enough and all three girls giggled and hugged.

"Hey, have you three got lost or are you cooking up some new strategy for the next game?"

Wes called out.

"Just coming."

Hally replied. Hurriedly they put together a tray of drinks and snacks and returned to the lounge to continue the evening.

On the way home arm in arm with Wes, they chatted about the success of his two friends getting along so well with her two friends.

"How did you know they would hit it off so well?"

She asked.

"I didn't really. It's just, I've got to know Gregg and Rhys quite well over the past couple of months. I just thought well, they are quite a lot like me in some ways and since you and the girls are similar too, well I just hoped they would like each other. I think I sort of knew who would go for who too."

He told her. Hally smiled to herself.

"Well let's hope they work out as well as we did."

Wes stopped in the street and turned her into the circle of his arms. It was very cold now, the sleet had stopped and his breath came out in little clouds as he looked down into her eyes. There was just enough light from a nearby streetlamp for him to see her face.

"Your cheeks are all rosy and you have a little pink tip to your nose."

His voice was quite husky and Hally felt warmth spreading through her body despite the cold air. She pressed against him and as he lowered his head and kissed her, through the thick layers of winter clothes she felt something she hadn't experienced before. Wes' body was reacting in the way any normal young man's would. At first she felt a little afraid, but the warmth in her own body quickly turned to fire and she pressed closer, kissing him back. His kiss deepened and he wrapped his arms tightly around her pressing closer too. Quite suddenly she felt something build inside her and flood through her entire body, she shuddered involuntarily, gripped his shoulders tightly and felt her breathing quicken, and then the feeling began to subside. Wes stepped back releasing the contact between them but still holding her. Hally held onto him as the cold air began to seep back into her body. She didn't know what to think, she thought she knew what had just happened, but it was all so new to her that she felt confused and a little embarrassed. She didn't know if he knew, she didn't know if she could tell him and worse she didn't know if anything had happened to him too. Suddenly she felt so very young and inexperienced. All the times she had talked openly with her mum and friends had not prepared her for this moment and she did not know what to do or say.

"Hally it's alright."

Wes whispered. His voice seemed to come from far away for a moment and then she felt his gloved hand lift her chin to look at him. Then so very gently he said.

"I know what just happened to you, I'm not sure I should have let it but it is ok. Was it the first time?"

Hally felt tears sting her eyes and didn't know why. She let out a little sob which soon turned to a flood of tears. Wes wrapped his arms around her and stroked her hair soothingly. For a while they stayed that way and soon the tears began to lessen. In a shaky voice Hally finally replied.

"Yes… it's…I've never. What… did anything…you?"

She couldn't get out the right words, in fact she really had no idea what to say to him.

"Hally, babe, no I didn't (and at the worried look she gave him) but it's ok. I enjoyed it just the same. Look, it's getting very cold here, let's get you home and we can talk about this in the warm."

Hally didn't know if she would be able to talk about it in a nice cosy warm room face to face. But she knew he was right about one thing, it was getting colder and as they continued the walk home the first few flakes of snow began to fall.

Thankfully when they reached Hally's house, there were only a few lights on which told Hally her parents were already in bed. As usual they knew where their daughter would be and who with so felt comfortable going to bed while she was still out, and even though it was only just gone eleven had been going to bed quite early for a while now. Hally knew this was because of the stress and strain of Gran and also because everyone knew that a late night call could come at any time.

As they approached the back door Hally realised that she didn't want to have a discussion about what had happened. She needed to deal with this herself first and work out her own feelings about it. She unlocked the door and then turned to Wes.

"I think I need to be by myself."

She told him. Looking devastated Wes replied in a shaky voice.

"Hally…are you upset with me…I… did I…was it?…"

He couldn't finish his sentence and Hally realised that he sounded very close to tears. She wasn't quite sure how to handle this either, usually Wes was the one comforting her when she cried.

"Wes, I'm not upset or mad at you, I just feel a bit strange and need to be by myself."

Not since the first few weeks of going out with Wes had Hally felt so uncomfortable and nervous. Wes pulled her into a hug and whispered into her hair.

"Hally please call me tomorrow. I'm sorry."

Without moving Hally hugged him back and felt her heart wrench. He really did think he had done something terrible, but she really needed to be alone. She whispered back.

"Wes, it's alright, please don't say sorry…and of course I will call you tomorrow."

She kissed him lightly on the lips, wanting to give a fuller kiss but afraid she wouldn't be able to control her body. She then turned and stepped into the kitchen. Dejectedly, Wes turned and with his head down against the snow walked away.

Hally quietly went through the house and up to her room. She desperately didn't want her mum to wake up, even though she knew she could talk about it to her she didn't want to talk to anyone. As she began to undress she thought about the feelings she had experienced. Her body still tingled in places and standing in her underwear she looked at herself in her mirror, she almost expected to see something different, but her body looked just the same as it always did. It was how it felt that was so different.

Climbing into bed in just her panties Hally left her lamp on and lay in the semi-light thinking. Of course she knew about orgasms, she was after all fifteen and a half, she had read about them in magazines, talked to Corrinne and Clia millions of times, well lots anyway she told herself. She had even had conversations about the subject with her mum. She had also had some different but similar feelings the times when she had explored her body, though these were very few. But what she had felt with Wes was new, big and a whole different experience.

It wasn't just the physical response, how every muscle in her body tightened, how her breathing had got faster or the explosion inside that made her shudder all over; no, but how she had felt emotionally at the same time. She was completely overwhelmed with love for Wes; she wanted to cling to him forever, kiss him forever, never let him go. She wanted to laugh and cry and squeal with joy all at the same time. She could not comprehend how so many emotions could take place all in such a short time. Because, she realised, it had been a short time. Even though at the time it had seemed to last forever, to go on and on it had just been moments.

This thought brought on a whole new stream of thoughts. If her moment as she thought of it happened so quickly and made her feel like she was feeling what then would it be like if Wes touched her properly, or even if they went all the way. Laying in the dimly lit room Hally felt her face begin to burn. Even though she was alone she felt embarrassed thinking about that and then realised that she was also beginning to feel a heat low down in her body too. Turning onto her side she gave a little groan and whispered into her pillow.

"Don't think about that Hally. He doesn't want it to happen and you don't really either. It's not right yet, there's plenty of time. Think of something else or you won't get any sleep tonight at all."

Trying very hard to put all thoughts of Wes and how gorgeous and sexy he was out of her mind Hally finally drifted into a very restless sleep. She awoke several times during the night from dreams she barely remembered but which left her body throbbing and almost aching deep inside. When morning eventually came, she arose feeling as though she had hardly slept. She wrapped herself in her dressing gown and peeped through her blinds to see a deep white world outside. She glanced at her clock and saw it was only just after eight then glimpsed movement in the garden. Nathan was already outside taking over large steps to trudge through the snow. It was already up to his knees and snow was still falling. Hally smiled and decided to put last night behind her and go outside and build a snowman with her little brother. But first she would text Wes. She picked up her phone and quickly typed a message.

hi are you ok im fine everything is alright what are you doing today im going to play in the snow with natty for a bit will I see you later xxxxx

Hally pressed send and then went off to shower. When she came back to her room her phone indicated a message had come in. Still wrapped in her towel she read the message from Wes.

hi babe im so glad to hear from you i was very worried that you had gone off me mum and dad asked me to look after ellie so they could get some shopping done do you want to come round i would really love it if you did i have chocolate and hot chocolate xxxxxxxxxx

Hally giggled to herself and quickly sent a message back saying she would come round late-morning. She then dressed in jeans, jumper and thick socks and headed downstairs ready for some snow fun with Nathan. Her body felt normal and she felt very happy, she was going to see Wes later and more importantly she was going to meet Ellie at long last.

Hally arrived at Wes' house warm and a little out of breath. The snow had settled everywhere, in places quite deep and especially near Wes' home at the edge of town. Wes opened the door to her and pulled her into a tight hug as soon as she was inside.

"I am so glad you are here."

He told her as he squeezed her. Hally held him back and was glad that her body was behaving normally. He helped her out of her coat and sat her down and pulled her wellingtons off. They had no time for further discussion because a tiny dark haired toddler came waddling into the kitchen waving an empty cup.

"Pappy Es, dink ta."

She said offering the cup to Wes. He scooped her up laughing and took the cup from her tiny hand. He turned her towards Hally.

"Ok, Ellie this is Hally. Say hello."

The little girl studied her for a moment, then without warning leaned towards her reaching out both arms. Luckily Wes was holding her securely. Hally reached out her own arms and took the child onto her lap. Bouncing her slightly she smiled and said.

"Hello Ellie."

Ellie looked up at her and curled the fingers of one hand into Hally's hair. For a moment she studied Hally's face, twirling the ends of her hair but without pulling it. She placed the palm of her other hand on Hally's face and softly rubbed her cheek.

"Eyo. Me ike oo."

Hally giggled and looked to Wes for interpretation.

"She just said hello and she likes you."

"I like you too Ellie."

Hally told the little girl. As quickly as she had wanted Hally, she turned back and reached for Wes who was ready to take her back.

"Anyway tike, how did you get past your gate, you know you're not supposed to be in the kitchen."

Wes asked Ellie as he refilled her cup with one hand whilst holding her with the other. Hally watched interestingly, he obviously felt completely at ease dealing with his little sister's demands. As Ellie slurped on her cup Wes turned to Hally.

"During the day we have a child safety gate to keep her out of the kitchen but I think she's worked out how to open it."

He turned still holding Ellie and headed towards the doorway to the lounge. Sure enough the safety gate was open.

"The catch can be turned around, so that will foil her for a bit."

Wes told her as they made their way into the other room. Toys were strewn over the floor and as Wes lowered Ellie to the floor she waddled over to a little pink vacuum cleaner and started pushing it around the carpet whilst making vacuuming noises.

For the next two and a half hours Hally and Wes entertained and were entertained by the little dark haired girl. She was like a whirlwind picking up and discarding toys, flipping through picture books, pointing at pictures sometimes able to tell them what the pictures were, other times waiting to be told and trying to repeat what she'd heard. Most of the time it was "Pappy Es." this or "Pappy Es." that, occasionally throwing in "Ayee" which Hally now could interpret as her name.

"Why does she call you Pappy Wes?"

Hally asked.

"Well she calls dad Pappy Ikle 'cos she can't say Michael and mum Mam Mam Tate, for Kate. We can't get her out of it and mum thinks it's just a stage, that when she gets a bit older she will just start using the proper words. We're not even sure where she heard it to pick it up in the first place."

Hally left Wes to go to Gran's about mid-afternoon with the promise that she would call him later. They had not raised the subject of the previous night and Hally was relieved to keep it tucked safely away inside her own mind. She knew eventually it would resurface either because of physical contact between them or because one of them would broach it verbally, she suspected that would be Wes, but for now it wasn't mentioned.

Gran was in great spirits that afternoon. Even though she looked thinner and more frail and her skin had a grey pallor to it she was ironically the life and soul of the family, despite having to remain in her recliner. Nurse Mildred had placed a special piece of equipment just inside Gran's clothing, a pump system that Gran could control by pressing a button to deliver pain relief when she needed it. It was not too obvious and though Nathan had spotted it and asked about it, once they explained as simply as possible what it was for, they could for the most part ignore that it was there.

Granddad had already been in the garden with Nathan and built an entire snowman family, one for each of them, and Colin had taken several photos and uploaded them onto his laptop to show Gran who was too weak to venture even to the window. Whilst Gran was looking at the photos Hally wandered into the kitchen to find her mother. May was standing with her hands in a bowl of foamy water but was staring out into the back garden.

"Mum?"

Hally moved to her mother's side and saw tears pouring down her face. Hally took a towel from the rail and took her mum's hands from the water and wrapped the towel around them. As though she were the grown up she pulled her mum into a hug and let her sob on her shoulder for a change. Mum cried silently, but Hally could feel her pain shuddering through her. For a while neither said a word, Nathan poked his head around the door, but a quick small shake of Hally's head sent him back into the other room. Gradually mum's sobs lessened and slowly she stood up straight rubbing her hands across her wet face.

"I'm so..so..sorry my angel. I didn't mean for you to have to deal with that."

Mum told her in a very shaky voice.

"Mum, it's ok to let go now and then. You can't always be the strong one."

Hally swallowed back her own tears determined to support her mum.

"We are all in this together, a family, we have to prop each other up. We all know it's only going to get harder, even little Natty knows that. Look, sit down, I'm going to make you some tea."

As she was filling two cups Colin came into the kitchen.

"Nathan whispered you were crying."

He said to his wife as he placed his arms around her, and at her frown.

"Oh it's alright, he didn't let your mum hear. He was quite grown up about it actually."

Mum gave him a little smile, tears threatening again.

"Yes, he's being very sensitive about all this lately. I think he really does understand, and Mildred has been wonderful helping me talk it through with him."

Hally gave her parents both cups of tea and then made another one for herself. The three sat at the big old kitchen table saying very little. Mum was drawing circles with her finger on the table.

"You know, mum taught me how to make pastry at this table. I was too little to reach the work surface so she let me kneel on a chair here."

Hally looked at her father but stayed silent, she suspected there was more to come and she was right.

"Your dad asked your Granddad if he could marry me at this table too, only mum was listening at the door. She told me she nearly ran in to give her permission but managed to stop herself and let the men have their time."

Colin smiled.

"Yeah, I remember that, crikey I don't think I've ever been so nervous, at least not until I actually asked you."

Again, they sat in silence sipping their tea.

"And this is where I told mum I was going to have you."

This time a little sob came as well and Colin again leaned towards her and wrapped her in his arms. Hally wanted to cry too, but knew she had again to hold it back. Nathan again poked his head around the door and without a word indicated with his finger for Hally to come to him. Quietly she stood and went over to him and bent towards him so he could whisper in her ear.

"Gran wants you."

Hally looked back over her shoulder at her parents.

"Gran wants me, ok?"

Colin nodded to her and moved closer to his wife holding her hand and quietly uttering comforting words. Nathan strolled over to his parents and leaned against his dad's arm, not saying anything. Hally made her way to her Gran's side still holding her tea. Gran saw the cup and turned to Mildred.

"I can see Hally has some tea so would you be a real dear and fetch me a cup too?"

Mildred smiled and turned towards the kitchen. Hally suspected Gran wanted them to be alone.

"Sit close my angel. There are things I want to say."

She had to stop for a moment, a little out of breath. Hally perched on a soft stool near the recliner and leaned towards her Grandmother. Gran took her hand and Hally felt tears prick her eyes. Gran's hand felt bony and dry, but surprisingly still quite strong.

"You are my only granddaughter and you are nearly a grown woman. I think you have something special going on with your young man."

Hally had an uncanny feeling that somehow Gran knew what had happened to her the night before. Gran had to stop for breath and a squeeze on the pump button. She closed her eyes as the pain relief was released into her blood and then took another breath and continued.

"You are very mature for your age — but you are also still a child — this time in between a girl and a woman — when you want certain things."

Again she stopped to rest, closing her eyes for a short time. Hally sat waiting patiently. Gran opened her eyes and looked directly into Hally's. Her next words took Hally completely by surprise.

"I was just sixteen when I started courting your Granddad — he was so handsome and I was wild — I knew I loved him straight away — and I wanted him — but he wouldn't —he made me wait until we were wed."

She took a very deep breath and another squeeze of her pump, eyes closed in pain. Hally felt tears beginning but bit them back and waited. It was a while this time before Gran spoke again and Hally first thought she had drifted off to sleep.

"Of course these days things are — different — but don't rush my sweet child — when it's right — and make sure you really know him first."

Hally was a little taken aback by what Gran had to say. She had never had even a glimmer of a conversation like this before so wasn't quite sure how to respond.

"Ok Gran, thank you."

Was all she could manage, but Gran gripped her hand with surprising strength and now in almost a whisper said.

"Hally, I think there are things you don't know about him."

Hally was instantly alert and concerned.

"Has he told you something?"

She asked with a frown. Gran's fingers relaxed immediately, the burst of strength gone as quickly as it had come.

"No darling, it's just a feeling."

As though staged, Mildred came back into the room with Gran's tea.

"Here we are Alice, just as you like it."

She told her brightly, and very gently she sat beside Gran and helped her sip from the china cup. For as long as Hally could remember Gran had drunk her tea from a china cup with a saucer, now she needed help to hold it. Hally heard a noise behind her and saw Granddad standing near the door. He looked forlorn, so Hally stood and went over to him wrapping her arms around him. He hugged her back and whispered to her.

"It won't be long now, I know it."

Hally held him tighter, there was nothing she could say to give him comfort.

The final week of school started off with everyone struggling to get through the snow; but with many snowball fights on the way. By the time Hally and her friends reached the school gates they were all warm, damp and flushed. Harassed looking teachers struggled to get piles of books and papers from their cars without slipping over and the school caretaker was rushing about trying to make sure pathways and steps were clear of snow. Hally suspected he had been at the school very early to do this, and since the snow was still falling suspected he would be doing it all day.

Unlike some of the schools outside of the town, most of the staff lived in Colingford so were able to get into work; so the school remained open but with some disruption to the timetable. Both staff and students accepted this was probably going to be the way all week, and since Friday would bring an end to the term Mr Hopkins announced in morning assembly that some lessons would be cancelled; but that he would still expect discipline to be maintained. So by the end of the week everyone was totally ready for the Christmas holidays. The last day of term was as usual rather rowdy but with good humour all around and as usual finished at lunchtime.

Hally, Wes, Corrinne and Clia joined other students in a snowball fight on the way home and Corrinne and Clia were pleasantly surprised when they saw Gregg and Rhys coming around the corner toward them.

"We got off early, there's not much more we can do today with this weather."

Gregg told them as they met on the pavement. Hally could see her two friends were very happy with this news and invited the two boys back to her house as that was where they had been heading. They arrived back at Hally's all flushed, a bit breathless and with copious amounts of snow stuck to their coats, hands freezing cold, but all very happy.

The last few days before Christmas day were very busy for Hally. She divided her time between family, boyfriend and friends. All her presents were wrapped but still hidden away in her room because Nathan was still in the 'When is Father Christmas coming' stage so no presents would be put under the tree until late Christmas eve. She helped her mum with food preparations especially as they would be taking Christmas day round to Gran and Granddads, since Gran was now unable to leave the house at all. As Hally stood in the kitchen rolling out pastry for mince pies she thought of what her mum had told her about baking with her mother. She sighed as she began cutting rounds of pastry.

"That was a deep sigh."

Mum said.

"I was just thinking how normal things just keep going."

She replied.

"What do mean baby?"

Mum asked.

"Well, here we are baking, I'm making pastry the way you taught me, the same way your mum taught you and I hope one day I will teach a child of my own too. But Gran won't be here for that yet it's well just the normal thing to do."

Mum wiped her hands on a cloth and put her arms around her. She gave her a kiss on the cheek and said softly.

"I know, it doesn't seem right that everyday life goes on just the same when something so tragic is going to happen soon."

She gave her own big sigh and the two stayed like that for a while.

Hally was woken by two things on Christmas morning, first her phone chirping brought her partially out of sleep, then Nathan shrieking down the hallway for her to get up because Father Christmas had been. The phone was a message from Wes wishing her a happy Christmas and sending lots of love and kisses and that he would come round to Gran's after he had had Christmas dinner with his family. She quickly sent a message back then clambered out of bed, excitement welling at the thought of watching her family open their presents, and of the presents waiting for her to open. Nathan was waiting, very impatiently, but all the same waiting, but as soon as Hally appeared he looked at his mother who smiled and nodded. He then dived for presents under the tree excitedly pulling the wrappings from those with his name on. Lots of squeals of delight came from him as mum and dad more sedately handed Hally her gifts. The child in her soon came out as she unwrapped and found an assortment of items, all things she wanted but couldn't actually remember voicing.

"Granddad said they will give you two their presents when we go round."

Mum told her. Hally smiled and handed her parents the gifts she had bought them.

After breakfast the whole family climbed into the car and dad carefully drove them through snowy streets to Gran and Granddad's home. Normally they would walk but today they had far too much to carry. Nurse Mildred greeted them at the door and Hally wondered for the first time if she had any family since she had barely left Gran from the day she had arrived. Granddad gave everyone hugs and then they all clustered around Gran to give her hugs and kisses too. Mildred appeared with a tray of hot drinks and the festive day began.

Christmas dinner was a little cramped as the dining table had been moved close to Gran's recliner, but this is no way deterred the enjoyment of the whole family, more so because they all knew it would be the last all together. Hally again watched each member of her family, especially Granddad who had insisted that today he would assist Gran with her meals. Hally saw the love between them as though it were something tangible and wondered not for the first time how Granddad would cope when his wife was gone.

The rest of the day was spent playing games, watching

television, chatting together and enjoying being a family. Later when there was a knock on the door, Hally jumped up expecting Wes but had a surprise when she found him accompanied by Corrinne and Clia.

"We had to come and see Gran."

Clia announced.

"Yes definitely."

Corrinne chimed. Wes stepped forward and gave Hally a kiss as the three stepped into the warmth. The girls darted past them both and headed for the lounge to see Gran which gave Wes the opportunity to give Hally a warm hug too. Then together they followed the girls.

Gran was already unwrapping a package, her fingers struggling somewhat with the tape and ribbon. Granddad ever so gently and without fuss helped her and together they released the contents. Much to Gran's delight she found jelly babies, handmade chocolate truffles and a little teddy bear filled with lavender. But what made her laugh out loud was a red thong with fur trimming and 'Gran' written on it.

"You little devils."

She told them, a little breathless from laughing. The girls giggled as did the rest of the family except Nathan who was too involved in a battle between his toys, and oblivious to what was going on around him.

"How has your day been?"

Wes whispered to Hally.

"It's been wonderful and difficult at the same time."

She replied. Wes nodded in understanding.

"What about yours?"

She enquired.

"Oh absolutely crazy. Ellie was full of it. She doesn't yet really understand about Christmas, but she had great fun opening presents, sometimes not just her own, and playing with the wrappings and boxes."

He smiled and the look on his face made Hally realise that he obviously loved the little girl deeply. She supposed it was different to the way she reacted to Nathan because of the wide age gap.

Much later when everyone was tucked up in bed, Hally sat wrapped in her dressing gown sitting by the window looking out at the winter wonderland in the garden below. The night was clear, stars sparkling gems resting on a velvet pad. Everything was so quiet and still, the only sound her soft breathing. Hally gently touched the gold bracelet Wes had given her for Christmas. He had told her he didn't want to buy a necklace because he knew she always wore the one the girls had bought her for her birthday; and didn't want her to have to choose which one to wear or alternate them. Again she felt herself fill with love for him and the depth of her emotions frightened her. She felt consumed by her feelings almost to the point of suffocation and for a moment she leaned forward and held herself trying to give herself comfort. She was so afraid that if Wes did not feel the same way she would never be able to cope, or worse still if he broke up with her that her life would be over. Hally had never been one to indulge in dramatics, so the intensity of her emotions were as tangible as if someone had actually punched her. How could a person feel so much at one time, and how could a person be so happy yet feel miserable at the same time. All these thoughts wandered through her mind as she held herself and looked at the blanket of snow outside.

Even later, buried under her duvet, Hally closed her eyes and tried to sleep. It had been a long day and an even longer build up to the day. She felt a little deflated that Christmas was over, it had all been so busy, and Boxing Day was probably going to be hectic too. However thoughts of Wes continued to invade all of her other thoughts and again her body began to react to the day's memories. All innocent but still powerful, his touches, his light kisses, his smile and even just hearing his voice; all sent waves of emotion through the lower parts of her body, so intense she allowed her own hands to travel to those parts of her body and give herself release and pleasure. After, she was finally able to drift into a sleep full of dreams about Wes, her Gran and a whole host of strange events that can only take place deep in the subconscious.

CHAPTER 13

New Year

New Year's Eve dawned with the temperature well below freezing and snow still sitting deeply on the ground. All of the main roads had been salted so were relatively free of snow and ice, but everywhere else was like a skating rink. Most people were now using sledges to pull young children and shopping rather than risk their cars, and looked like circus clowns in overlarge shoes as they walked precariously along the pavements.

Hally and her family were going to Clia's parent's party, something they put on every year so that their friends could get together and celebrate without having to worry about arranging baby sitters. Hally was very excited by the upcoming event this year because for the first time she would have a boyfriend to go with, and even better, so would her two best friends. It was going to be a fabulous evening and she had a fabulous outfit to wear to it.

Mum and dad left early for Gran and Granddad's with Nathan and Hally planned to walk over later in the morning. Mum had again insisted she spend some time doing the things normal teenagers did over the holidays, but Hally was determined not to spend the day lounging around; so she made sure her room was neat and tidy, vacuumed the downstairs rooms so her mum wouldn't have to and laid her outfit out for the party. She phoned Wes and chatted for a while then togged herself up in warm clothes and made her way to her Grandparents.

Mum opened the door just as she reached it and this gave Hally a start. She instinctively knew something had changed by the look on her mother's face.

"What's happened?"

She asked, her voice quivering with a fear that gripped her

entire being. Mum took her hand and pulled her into a hug.

"She's in a bad way angel. Barely awake now, mostly because of the pain medication."

Hally yanked her boots off and headed for the lounge peeling her outdoor clothes off on the way. Gran was in her recliner with Granddad on one side holding her hand and Mildred on the other. The pump had been removed, no use to her Grandmother now as she was too weak and ill to administer the pain relief herself. A small disposable dish sat on a little table nearby, a syringe laid in it. Mildred looked at Hally and said very gently.

"I have to give her pain relief by injection now my dear. That's all we can do now, just make her as comfortable as possible. But she's a fighter and she's holding on."

Hally burst into tears as she knelt before her Gran, placing her head on the blanket which covered her Gran's withering body. As she sobbed she felt Granddad softly stroke her hair and they just stayed that way until Hally's tears finally subsided.

Throughout the day Gran drifted in and out of consciousness sometimes obviously aware of their presence, other times barely flickering her eye lids. Dad was doing his best keeping everyone together. He kept Nathan entertained as well as keeping him fairly quiet and informed as much as an eight year old could be informed. Nathan had a fair understanding of the situation and did his best to not get in the way. Mum wanted him to be as close to his Gran as was possible so gave him some leeway to play near to her without being a disturbance. Mildred was wonderful in helping with this and explained that Nathan didn't need to be completely quiet; that a degree of normality in his play was the best way for him to be able to handle his own feelings. Over a cup of tea in the kitchen she explained to mum that Nathan may feel he had made his Gran worse if they tried to keep him silent and as a normal child was not able to achieve this. From then on, there was a much more relaxed atmosphere in the home. Hally phoned Wes several times throughout the day which gave her a lot of comfort. Neither of them expected she would be going to the party that evening and Wes told her he wouldn't go either but would come around to Gran's if she wanted him to, which was exactly what she wanted.

However, just as she finished on the phone mum came into the kitchen and spoke to her.

"I know this sounds really terrible, but Mildred and your Granddad has told your dad and me to take you and Nathan to the party."

Hally started to protest but mum put her hand up and gave her a sad smile.

"I know baby, I was about to protest too. But, Mildred has lots of experience in these situations and she's told me that though mum doesn't have much time left, it's not going to happen straight away. Granddad is very insistent that we take you two out this evening and see the new year in. He even told me that since it's going to be the last one he has with his wife, he wants it to be as much like their first New Year, just the two of them. Of course Mildred will be there but..."

Her voice shook and she was unable to continue. Hally hugged her mum but had no words of comfort to give.

Hally spent quite some time getting ready for the party, doing her hair, applying makeup and pulling on the new dress she had for the event. As she looked at her reflection in the mirror, she smoothed out her dress, it was a black sequinned tube dress and hugged her figure beautifully. But in between her excitement she felt threads of guilt, that she should be looking forward to an evening of fun when her Gran was so close to death. Mum tapped on the door and came in, smiling at how beautiful her daughter looked. Then as if reading her mind she said.

"Hally darling, it's ok. I know your Gran wants us to enjoy this party. We all feel, well except probably Nathan, that we shouldn't be going, but dad and I have made sure Mildred has both our mobile numbers and Clia's house number. We will only be twenty minutes away, even in this weather."

Hally felt a little reassured by her mum's words and said.

"Ok, I know really that this is alright, so how do I look?"

They giggled together and for a moment it was just mother and daughter preparing for a family night out.

Wes came round at eight as he was going with the family to the party. Gregg and Rhys were going straight there from their respective homes and the six were looking forward to meeting up and enjoying celebrating the incoming year together.

"Wow, you look gorgeous."

Wes told Hally as he came into the lounge. Before she had time to respond Nathan jumped forward.

"What about me?"

Asked Nathan giving a little twirl. He was wearing a child-size dinner suit complete with bow tie to match his father.

"Wow, you look very handsome and grown up."

Wes told him, bending to his level. Nathan giggled and with another twirl sprinted off to the kitchen where mum was organising the packing of some dishes of food to take with them. Wes stood up and gave Hally a kiss just as dad came into the room.

"Hi Wes, can I get you a drink?"

He asked without raising an eyebrow. With no sign of embarrassment Wes nodded. Dad disappeared into the kitchen and returned with two open bottles of lager.

"Don't I get one?"

Hally asked batting her eyelashes at her dad. He came over to her and planted a kiss on the end of her nose.

"A shandy, alright, I'll go and get it."

Hally gave a pout as dad turned again towards the kitchen patting her behind on the way.

"You can have a glass of champagne at midnight."

He told her on the way. Hally beamed brightly, her eyes lit up in anticipation which in turn made Wes smile.

"Mum and dad let me have some wine, or a bottle of beer sometimes for special occasions."

Hally told Wes.

"Yeah, my parents used to do that and now I'm old enough to drink I don't find it so mysterious or exciting, or like some people I know, rebellious, you know, doing it just because you're not supposed to."

Hally nodded in understanding.

"Mmm some of the girls in my year are out all weekend just getting hammered. They think it makes them look all grown up and sexy. But all they end up doing is throwing up everywhere and looking stupid. Honestly, the amount of fights over this boy or that boy 'cos they've had too much to drink, and half the time next day they can't remember what they did. Some of the lads are just as bad, only they end up punching each other, just because they think it's clever to down as much booze as they can in one go. Yuk, I don't ever want to get so out of control."

"Hally my sweet girlfriend, I cannot imagine you ever being out of control as you put it. You are far too sensible."

Wes said in a slightly teasing tone. Hally looked up at him using her eyes to give him the sexiest look she could and said in a low voice.

"Oh I don't know, I can think of something that might make me lose a little bit of control."

Before Wes could comment, dad returned with Hally's drink. He looked from one to the other and thought he might have interrupted something but wasn't sure what, so he simply handed Hally her drink and turned to Wes asking about his family.

There were already quite a few people at Clia's house when they all arrived. Mum went straight to the kitchen to unpack the food she had prepared, dad behind her carrying it. Nathan headed for some children he knew and Hally and Wes made their way over to Clia. Corrinne, Gregg and Rhys had not yet arrived. Clia's brother Don was standing next to his sister and was introduced to Wes. They were soon chatting about Don's uni experiences and Hally wondered for the first time if Wes might be considering further study. They had never discussed his plans after he finished school, for some unknown reason the subject had never come up, but now Hally wondered and worried. In her mind she saw him going off to some university at the other end of the country, meeting girls his own age and forgetting about her.

"Earth to Hally."

She came out of her wonderings as Wes nudged her smiling.

"I don't think you were with us there babe."

He said putting his arm around her. Hally gave a little shudder and he frowned giving her a concerned look.

"Hally are you ok?"

She gave herself a mental shake and put a smile on her face.

"Of course, I'm fine."

She told him. Clia looked at her with her all too usual knowing look that something was out of sorts with her friend.

"Let's go and get some drinks Hally."

She said, taking Hally's hand and leading her towards the kitchen. Once out of earshot of the boys Clia said in a whisper.

"Ok, what's up?"

"Nothing really. Well, it's just, Don was chatting about uni and you know, Wes has never said anything about what he wants to do after he's taken his exams."

Hally told her worriedly. Clia gave her a look which told her straight away she was worrying over nothing.

"Sweetie, just ask him."

She told her matter of factly.

Carrying drinks, the two girls returned to the lounge. Wes and Don were still chatting.

"…three street cones and a cricket bat."

They heard Don say to Wes as they handed over drinks to the boys who were now laughing heartily.

"So what are you going to do after your exams Wes?"

Clia chimed in. Hally looked at her and felt herself blushing with embarrassment. She was sure Wes would know exactly what they had been talking about in the kitchen, and what had worried her earlier. But without hesitation Wes replied.

"Well I've looked at a few part time courses at the further education college. I think I might go for some sort of accountancy training. My mum's a qualified accountant and so she would be able to sort of act as a home tutor. I don't want to do full time because I still want to work as well, and I don't think it's fair to expect my parents to fully finance me when mum can't work full time now 'cos of Ellie."

Hally was surprised and relieved at the same time. She also felt a little let down that this was the first time she had heard of his plans and resolved to ask him later about why he had never mentioned it. She also remembered that a long time ago, or so it seemed, she had planned to ask him why he had failed his exams in the first place, and was determined now to discover the reason.

Wes looked at her and gave a slight frown as though he knew something was amiss but that for now it wasn't going to be broached. The entire subject was then put to one side with the arrival of Corrinne, Gregg and Rhys and as the six greeted each other, Don drifted off to chat with some other friends.

Before too long the house was full of people all enjoying each other's company. Clia's dad ensured that a variety of music was played to suit all ages and that the children were kept entertained and out of trouble. Her mum with the help of Hally's mum kept the food on the table topped up and the evening developed into a very noisy but happy night. Hally and her friends had a great time, especially watching some of the adults, who as they drank more loosened up more and began to dance more and more vigorously, often completely out of rhythm to the music.

By the time midnight approached everyone was hot but happy. With the help of Hally's and Corrinne's parents, Clia's parents handed out glasses of champagne to all but the younger children, who were given lemonade as the countdown to the new year began. The music was turned off and the television turned on and everyone stood close to their respective families as they listened to Big Ben chime in the new year. On the stroke of midnight, glasses were raised and kisses passed around. Wes gave Hally a lingering kiss which set her pulse racing and her heart swell with love. Then there were chants of 'Happy New Year' and everyone joining hands to sing Auld Lang Syne.

It was nearly two in the morning when Hally and her family finally said their goodnights, or goodmornings as dad merrily put it and made their way home. Wes had hugged and kissed her before he left with Gregg and Rhys and promised to call her later in the day. At home Hally gave her parents each a kiss and planted one on top of Nathan's sleepy head, and made her way to her room. She pulled off her clothes and climbed into bed feeling tired but happy. It had been a wonderful evening, dancing and snuggling with Wes, laughing and dancing with Corrinne and Clia, and watching her two friends so very happily cuddling and dancing with their boyfriends. It was a good start to the new year.

Hally was being rocked, then she was being tapped and then

she was falling. Falling away from a dream full of bursting champagne bottles, a huge room with high ceilings and crammed with people she didn't know. Quite suddenly she realised she was awake, mum leaning over her gently shaking her shoulder.

"Mum… what?"

She knew she didn't have to say any more. She had gone to sleep with her lamp on and in the soft light it cast she saw the look of fear and misery on her mum's face.

"We have to get over to your Gran's."

It was said without panic or rush and Hally knew from what Mildred had explained to them that they had some but not a lot of time.

"Ok, I'll get dressed, is Nathan up yet?"

"Your dad has gone to get him. Baby you do understand what this means don't you?"

Mum asked in a voice full of emotion. Pulling off the duvet and climbing out of bed, Hally nodded. She grabbed her bra, jeans, jumper and socks and began dressing hurriedly as she replied.

"I know what this means. Mildred told me that she would know when Gran was close to… to…you know…"

She just couldn't bring herself to say the word 'dying'

"She said she would let us know so we could all be… with… her."

Hally knew if she continued she would burst into tears and she didn't want to do that, not yet, for now she wanted to be strong for her mum, because although mum was holding it together at the moment, Hally knew she was very fragile and it would not take much for her shell to crack.

The family gathered in the kitchen wrapped in warm outdoor clothing to face the cold outside. Hally was surprised to find she had only been in bed for an hour and a half. Nathan looked sleepy and was somewhat grumpy, but dad had done his best to explain to him why he had to get out of his nice cosy bed, and although it didn't do much for his mood he understood enough to behave. They set out in the snow and ice treading precariously along frozen pavements. Most of the neighbourhoods they passed through were quiet and dark, but here and there they saw signs that the New

Year celebrations were still in full swing. At times they passed other people, some staggering and slipping, and were greeted with 'Happy new year'. With false smiles they responded in the same way and soon they arrived at Gran and Granddads.

The house was warm and quiet with soft lighting in the room where Gran lay on her recliner. Mildred was leaning over her as they entered gently sponging her face and one hand with warm water. Granddad sat at her side holding her other hand gently stroking her delicate fingers.

"She's holding on."

He told them in a flat voice.

"But now you're all here, I think it won't be long before she lets go."

Again his voice was lacking emotion and Hally knew he was struggling to maintain his composure and her heart went out to him. She knelt by his side and placed her hand over his, both holding Gran's hand gently. Mildred finished bathing Gran and stepped away so that mum, dad and Nathan could sit at her other side. Nathan leaned into his father, his eyes drooping with tiredness.

"Daddy can I go sleep?"

He asked with a wide yawn. Mum looked at her little boy and smiled as dad replied.

"Go and lay on the sofa little one."

He told him in a soft voice.

"What if Granny dies when I'm asleep?"

He said innocently but with obvious concern. Mum choked back a little sob and took her child's hand and led him to the sofa. Mildred as ever aware of the situation was ready with a fleece blanket.

"Natty sweetheart, have a little rest, it will be alright."

Mum told him as she laid him down and tucked the blanket around him. As his eyes began to close he said in a small voice.

"Is Granny gonna go to heaven?"

Stroking his hair away from his brow mum smiled and felt her heart shudder in her breast.

"My angel, I really do think your Gran will go to heaven and from there she will watch over you all of the time."

Mum had never practised any religion but at that moment she desperately wanted to believe that her mother was going to a safe and pain-free place, and if that was heaven then so be it. Hally still sat with Granddad but could hear her mum's loving voice speaking to Nathan. Her words brought to Hally's mind the picture on her wall. Her Gran would be one of those angels watching over all of them.

As dawn approached the family took turns sitting on either side of Gran, holding and stroking her hands. Mildred kept a supply of hot drinks coming for them all in between tending Gran. Although Gran was essentially motionless, Mildred made sure the covers on the recliner were neat and smooth. She ensured the little bowl of water and glycerine was always fresh that was used to moisten Gran's lips. She prepared some food for them all and sent them into the kitchen, except Granddad and Nathan who was still asleep, because she wanted Gran to have some privacy and dignity whilst she administered pain relief that she had to give by suppository. All of these tasks were completed without fuss and with the utmost gentleness and consideration for all involved.

At nine twenty, Hally was sitting on one side of her Gran and her mum was on the other side. Nathan was awake and dad was supervising his breakfast. Granddad and Mildred were sitting on the sofa sipping coffee. Hally felt a tiny movement in her hand and quickly relayed this to the others. Mildred was on her feet like a cat and mum called dad and Nathan in from the kitchen. Hally stood to allow Granddad to take her place, Granddad taking Gran's hand in his own. Dad stood near the bottom of the recliner one arm round Nathan, the other holding his hand. Standing close to mum, Mildred pressed her fingers to Gran's wrist and checked her fob watch as she monitored her pulse.

Hally stood watching her Grandmother's face, feeling that everything had been suspended in time, that no one was breathing. Then she saw Gran's eyelids open, her eyes two beautiful orbs, deep blue and clear as crystal. She felt Gran look at all of them, complete clarity and understanding in her eyes, a silent farewell to her family that she loved and cherished so much, and who in turn loved and cherished her too. Then a soft white cloud gently moved across the blueness and as in slow motion her eyelids began to close and then her chest rose once more and then stilled.

At first there was silence, Hally's vision blurred as tears began to fall down her cheeks, then she heard the soft crying of her mum and Granddad. Mum came to Granddad then the whole family wrapped themselves around each other trying desperately to comfort one another in their grief. For some time they all stayed just like that holding onto each other and holding each other up. Quietly and gently behind them Nurse Mildred continued with her job. Hally heard her soft voice speaking to someone and then there was again just the sound of the family's sobs.

Over the next few hours things were a blur for Hally. She had called Wes and before she could even begin to tell him what had happened she was sobbing uncontrollably into the phone.

"Hally babe I'll be straight over."

He told her. At first she didn't even realise he had disconnected. Shortly after her phone chirped and she saw the call was coming from Corrinne.

"Hals, do you want me to come over?"

She asked. Before Hally could respond her text alert went off and mumbling "Just a sec" to Corrinne quickly checked the message.

tried to call got busy signal wes called do you want me to come over

"It's Clia, she just asked me the same."

Hally told Corrinne. She felt completely detached from everything and couldn't even grasp the simplicity of her friends' question.

"So, shall we?"

Corrinne asked carefully.

"Shall you what?"

Hally replied.

"Come over Hals."

"Oh, yes, oh please, I really don't know what to do."

Sobbing uncontrollably again she didn't hear Corrinne tell her she would call Clia and they would both come over, and again was still holding her phone to her ear even though her friend had disconnected.

Later in the day Hally sat in her own home with Wes and her two best friends. Wes had taken charge and called Corrinne and Clia and asked them to meet them at Hally's instead of coming to Gran's. He explained to them that Hally's mum thought it might be too difficult for Hally to cope with the arrangements that had to be made.

So now, she had talked herself out about Gran, going over and over her last hours with her. Wes sat with his arm around her and Corrinne and Clia snuggled close on her other side. Mum and dad were still at her grandparents house as there was a lot to help Granddad with. When Wes arrived he first gave his full attention to Hally, then hugged the other members of the family. Nurse Mildred then took him through to the lounge to see Gran who looked just as though she were sleeping. Mum then told Hally to go home as she thought it might be too stressful for her to be there when the doctor came out to confirm the death and for Gran to then be moved to the funeral home. Without argument Hally agreed and offered to take Nathan, but mum told her Nathan was now upstairs sleeping. Hally was surprised at herself that she hadn't even noticed Nathan was no longer in the kitchen.

"It's ok baby, even though we expected this it's still a shock to you."

Mum told her, her voice choked with emotion. So, almost numb with pain and anguish, Hally hugged and kissed her mum, dad, Granddad and even Nurse Mildred and allowed Wes to wrap her in her coat and his arms and take her home. Now she sat huddled afraid she would never feel happy again.

The next few days were stressful for the entire family. Hally helped as much as she could especially with Nathan and she had Corrinne and Clia with her most of the time to help too. Wes divided his time between her and work and all this at least gave Hally a little respite from her feelings. However there were times, even when she had company that she simply couldn't concentrate on anything. She often found herself drifting away into her own world in the middle of a conversation, or when she was eating, or watching television, or anytime really.

There were brief moments when her mind would almost forget

and she would talk to her friends about normal things. She would laugh and share jokes, then suddenly her grief would come flooding back in and she would feel guilty for those tiny moments of happiness. Watching her mum cope was hard, watching her go about her normal daily routines with Nathan, the home, with her, all which she dealt with in her usual efficient way, yet with a sadness so deep, it was almost solid. Dad was a rock to them all and Hally watched him give his wife so much love and care without smothering her, she watched him play with Nathan and she soaked up the attention, love and comfort he gave to her. Together, they all supported Granddad. He had chosen to stay at his own home even though mum desperately wanted him to stay with them.

"No love. I need to be here where she was. This was our home for all our married life. I have to carry on though God only knows how I'm going to do that. But, somehow, I will. She wanted me to continue living, not to grieve for ever, although I will, but you know how strong she was…well… she…made me promise…to… look after you."

Granddad told mum, his voice cracking, after she had tried for the tenth time to get him to come and stay with them. Mum wrapped her arms around her father and together they sobbed and tried to give comfort to each other. Hally felt her heart breaking at this sight and took herself out into the still snow covered garden to shed more tears of her own. She felt alone and empty but didn't want to invade their grief with her own. She knew this was irrational, that they would give her love and comfort too, but she just felt they needed to have that moment to themselves.

As the days passed and the new term grew closer, Hally felt the loss of her Gran in so many different ways. At times she would simply sit in her room looking at the angels on the wall and remember growing up with her Gran nearby. Other times she would cry silently into her pillow, or sob loudly into Wes' shoulder, or the girls' arms. She would wander around the house as though sleep walking, not always remembering why she went into that room, or what she wanted out of the fridge. One time she found herself holding a full cup of tea that was stone cold and completely untouched. She wasn't even sure exactly when she had made it.

Sometimes she would crave company only to find herself wanting to be alone the minute someone came close, then desperately seeking solace in a hug from a family member, Wes or her friends. She was so mixed up she felt as though she had been thrown into a giant blender.

On the first day back to school, Corrinne, Clia and Wes came to Hally's house. Usually they all met up on the way but this morning the three had decided Hally needed support from the off. The weather remained freezing with hard snow packed solid on the ground making the journey treacherous. However, with great care the four made their way steadily to school. Hally tried her best to be cheerful towards her friends and boyfriend and at times accomplished this without having to fake it. But as the school gates approached she wondered how she was ever going to get through the day.

English was Hally's first lesson of the day and as she entered the classroom Mr Austin came straight over to her and quietly said.

"Hally, if you need to see me, here is a list of times when I'm not teaching. Just let which ever teacher you are having at the time know that you are coming to see me."

He handed her a folded sheet of paper and smiled gently. Hally just nodded, she didn't think she could speak, her emotions were bubbling to the surface and threatened to burst. She simply took the list and sat down in her usual seat. For parts of the lesson Hally was able to concentrate and absorb what was going on, but some of it went over her head and her mind wandered to memories of her Gran. These included Granddad and other members of her family and many of the things they had shared as a family. So, by the end of the lesson Hally felt disjointed and a little lost, not quite knowing what had been discussed and read. This happened throughout the day and by the time school ended Hally was exhausted and unsure of exactly what each lesson had been about. All her teachers had been sympathetic and understanding. They knew she was an excellent student and that she would catch up on anything she missed, but Hally felt she had let them and herself down.

"Sweetie, don't beat yourself up about it."

Clia told her on the way home. Wes' day had been shorter than theirs and then he had to go to the café, so it was just the girls who walked home with her, linking arms on either side.

"Everyone understands Hals."

Corrinne told her. Hally looked side to side at her friends and was about to reply when all three hit a particularly icy patch and slid to a heap on the ground. For a moment all was silent, then they all burst into giggles as they tried to untangle themselves from each other and stand up. This turned out to be more difficult than expected as each time one went to hold the other to stand, their feet slipped out from under them. A couple of boys from their school saw them and offered gloved hands to help them stand. Eventually and with lots of slipping and sliding, and the near fall of one of the boys; they finally got to their feet and away from the very icy patch. Flushed, hot and giggling, the girls thanked the boys and treading very carefully continued homeward.

Settled in Hally's kitchen with hot drinks, they relayed the event to mum who also found it amusing. For Hally to see her mum smile too gave her an emotional boost and she felt her spirits lift for the first time in days. Silently she told herself that she knew she could get through this. That it would be hard, but with support from her family, friends and school, it would happen. She decided then that the next day she would go and see Mr Austin.

On the Friday after school started back, Wes, Corrinne and Clia arrived at Hally's house early. It was the day of Gran's funeral and they wanted to be there to support the family in any way they could. Mum and dad had already left for Granddad's house and Hally had arranged with her mother to get Nathan ready and take him there a little later. The undertakers were going to be at Granddad's at eleven and they would all go from there to the church.

At ten thirty Hally stood with mum in Granddad's kitchen putting the final touches to the buffet they had prepared for the wake. Mum had remained completely composed all morning fussing over her father and making sure Nathan didn't mess up his suit. Dad constantly fussed over his wife, giving her little hugs and kisses, soft touches and gentle pats every time he passed her. She smiled at him and accepted his attention with so much love in her eyes. Wes was as attentive towards Hally, and in turn she gave her attention to Nathan and her two friends, as she knew that they were grieving too. They had known Gran for all their lives and loved and missed her too.

At exactly eleven o'clock the undertakers pulled up outside the house. Softly they knocked and told Granddad they were ready when he was. Hally saw the hearse carrying her Grandmother through the window, floral displays laid alongside the coffin. From where she stood she could only see one side, a beautiful display saying 'Alice' and another saying 'Mum'. But she knew on the other side she would see another saying 'Gran'. Her parents had asked her and Nathan what they wanted it to read and at first Hally had thought 'Grandmother' but then Nathan had announced quite strongly.

"But we always call her Gran."

His little eyes had filled with tears and Hally hugged him tight and replied.

"You are so right little brother. We do call her Gran, so it should say Gran."

In complete contrast to Dana's funeral, the church was filled to overflowing. People were quite literally having to stand in the aisles and at the back. There were wreaths and sprays and bouquets everywhere. Gran and Granddad had so many friends, both in the town and in various other parts of the country and it seemed they had all come to pay their respects. Hally, mum, Nathan and her friends walked behind the coffin as it was led by the vicar and carried by Granddad, dad and Wes and three pall bearers from the undertakers to the altar. They then all settled in the front pew as the service began.

Hally listened intently to the words from the vicar celebrating her Gran's life. Sometimes there was gentle laughter from the congregation other times there were obvious sobs. Granddad stood at the lectern and tearfully yet with a smile talked lovingly about his wife. He spoke of her strength, of their family and how she would always be with them to support their every need. Mum leaned into dad and cried, holding a wad of tissues to her face. Then Hally stood and approached the lectern. She didn't feel at all nervous even though she was about to speak to more people than she had ever done.

"There is so much I could say about my Gran, but it would take until spring. (light laughter came from the mourners) So, what I really want you all to know is that she was the most wonderful woman anyone could ever meet. (there were murmurs of agreement) She was funny, always gave advice that could be followed without hesitation…would talk about anything and everything…and put her family above all else. And…she approved of my boyfriend just as she approved of my dad."

Hally felt no embarrassment at this final statement, and as she returned to her seat saw Wes look at her with warmth in his eyes as he took her hand and gently squeezed it.

Tears flowed furiously from Hally, her parents, Nathan, her friends and many others as they stood by the graveside and the funeral was completed. Each of them took a small handful of the dirt offered by the vicar and gently dropped it onto the coffin. They followed this with red roses, their deep colour standing out against the white of the snow and ice laying deeply across the churchyard. When the service and burial was finished, people came over and whispered words of comfort to them. Many took their hands and held them, others gave hugs or gently pats, but all said the same, how sad that Alice was gone.

Back at Granddad's, the house filled with friends for the wake. Dad passed drinks out and Hally with Wes, Corrinne and Clia, kept a supply of tea and coffee going. By early evening there was just a handful of people left still reminiscing to Granddad and mum about Alice. Hally could see the exhaustion on both their faces and felt worn out herself, but no one wanted to suggest they all now get some rest. Finally dad turned to Hally and said.

"Baby, could you take Nathan home, and you need some rest yourself."

"I'm ok dad, but I will take him home. It's been a long day for him and he's been so well behaved I think maybe he will need to let off a little steam soon."

Hally replied. Dad smiled and pulled her into a tight cuddle.

"You are your Gran's granddaughter."

He said, his voice filled with emotion. He kissed her on the top of her head and as he turned she saw him wipe tears from his eyes. Hally kissed him back and turned to Wes and the girls to explain what they were going to do.

By the time they reached Hally's Nathan was in fact drooping, so instead of needing to calm down he compliantly went and changed into his pyjamas and dressing gown. Then he settled on the lounge floor and played with his new action character Hally had bought for Christmas. Hally and the others sat comfortably on the sofa and chatted about the day and how well it had all gone. It seemed to Hally that this kind of small talk was all any of them could cope with just then. Then for a while they sat in silence. Wes, his arm around Hally squeezed her gently and nodded towards Nathan.

"I think he's asleep."

He told her quietly. Hally lowered herself to the floor and softly crawled towards her little brother. Sure enough, Nathan had curled up still holding his toy and was fast asleep. Hally brushed his hair away from his face and gave him a little kiss on the cheek, he looked so sweet and didn't stir at all.

"Do you want me to carry him up to bed?"

Wes asked gently coming over too. Hally felt more tears welling in her eyes and she didn't really know why, so she just nodded and stood up as Wes lifted the child into his arms. Clia and Corrinne both stood and gave Nathan a kiss as well, then Hally and Wes took him up to his room. As Wes lowered him onto his bed and Hally covered him with his duvet he stirred ever so slightly, then rolled over still holding his toy. Hally didn't try to take it away even though she was worried it might dig into him, she thought as hard as the toy was it was at least offering him some comfort, so she left it where it was and left the room.

With the funeral over, Hally tried to bring some normality back to her life. Slowly and with the counselling from Mr Austin Hally caught up with her school work and found she could again concentrate on her lessons. She and her family were still deeply grieving but were beginning in tiny steps to move forward with their lives. Wes was a real bolster to her and because Corrinne and

Clia were also grieving arranged with Gregg and Rhys to spend as much time as possible all together.

"He's just so considerate mum."

Hally said one day after school when she was having tea with her mum.

"Yes, he is. I've seen how he is around you and how he gives Nathan lots of attention too. Perhaps having a toddler for a sister has helped him grow lots of patience."

Mum told her with a smile and a squeeze of her hand. At mum's words something stirred in the back of Hally's mind, something she was going to ask Wes about. She couldn't quite get the memory, it hovered just out of reach, something about New Year's eve, but it wasn't about the evening.

"Your tea's getting cold baby."

Mum said and the oh so near memory faded spirit like and disappeared. Hally smiled at her mum and finished her drink, but resolved to concentrate her thoughts later when she was alone and remember what she knew was important.

Wes was supposed to come round for dinner with Hally that evening but called to say he was going to be late because Ellie had picked up a tummy bug and was being sick. When he finally did arrive, he told her his mother had asked him to help take care of Ellie while she stripped off the toddler's bed and remade it. So he had bathed and changed her and tried to encourage her to take some liquids until his mum had been able to take over the care again. Hally hugged him feeling her emotions rising.

"You are so good with her. I try with Nathan, but well…(she struggled for words) maybe it's the age difference."

Wes held her tightly, smiled wistfully and said.

"She's just so tiny, and when she was being sick her little face was all screwed up and flushed. She didn't know what was happening really and she cried. It was heartbreaking to see her, her little hands holding her tummy and trying to tell us where it hurt."

Hally held him back, a little confused about the obvious emotion emanating from him. She got upset when Nathan was ill, but this seemed to go much deeper with Wes. Perhaps it was the huge age gap, maybe it made people react differently to their siblings, so hugging him, she decided not to question it, he was just a wonderful person she told herself.

Later when Hally was tucked up in bed she again pushed her mind to remember what she had been going to ask Wes about on New Year's Eve. However, too many other thoughts just kept crashing in, how Wes was with Ellie. How he was with her, since the kiss in the snow they had not really had any chance to get that close again. Hally was disappointed and relieved at the same time, but with everything that had happened she knew it was circumstances and not deliberate. Then there was the whole thing about his plans after school. Suddenly it came to her, exactly what she had wanted to ask. Why had he failed his exams? That was it. She would not forget that question again. Tomorrow, she told herself, she would finally ask that nagging question. For some reason she could not fathom, this question was so very important, she felt their relationship almost depended on the answer. This thought gave her more than a jolt of fear, it bombarded her entire being. What was it Gran had said to her such a short time ago 'I think there are things you don't know about him.' What could she have meant? But now she thought about it, Hally knew there had always been something there, she was just too afraid to ask.

CHAPTER 14

Roses and Chocolates

The almighty intrusion of thoughts kept Hally awake for most of the night, and when she did drift in and out of sleep strange dreams invaded these short periods of rest. So by the time she rose in the morning she felt drained and ragged. Her head ached, her throat was sore and she was oh so tired. She pulled on her dressing gown and made her way downstairs and into the kitchen. Mum was supervising Nathan's breakfast and looked up as she walked in. Her smile turned immediately to a frown of concern.

"Hally, baby, what's wrong?"

Hally opened her mouth to speak and found nothing came out, she had lost her voice. Mum came to her side and placed her hand on Hally's forehead. It felt so cool and soothing.

"Back to bed with you little girl. I'll call the doctor for an appointment and let the school know."

Hally turned back towards the door, then turned back to her mum.

"Yes, and the girls, and Wes, now bed." She leaned towards Nathan. "Eat your breakfast darling whilst I go with Hally and take her a drink."

With a mouthful of cereal Nathan nodded.

Tucked back up in bed with water and juice nearby, Hally felt miserable. She was rarely ill and when she was she hated it. Mum had made an appointment with the doctor for later that morning and was going to call in on Granddad on the way back from taking Nathan to school, so for the time being she was alone and felt very lonely.

Mum had also called her friends and Wes. Both Clia and Corrinne had texted her sending their love, but so far there had been no word from Wes. This made her feel worse and tears spilled down her cheeks. Her book lay next to her on the bed and as she reached for it she heard the back door close downstairs and was relieved that mum was home. Then she heard voices and thought Granddad must have come back with mum. Footsteps sounded on the stairs, too rapid to be Granddad, and too heavy to be mum. Then he was there, Wes, moving into her room and straight across to her bed. He held out his arms and she leaned into him.

"Babe. How are you feeling? stupid question, you've lost your voice."

As ill as she felt, this made her smile and she hugged him close, so much happier that he was there with her. Mum came up with hot drinks for them all and told Hally that Granddad was going to take them to the surgery in his car as dad had their car for work.

The doctor diagnosed laryngitis and told Hally she had to rest for a few days, drink plenty of fluids, take pain relief and not strain her vocal cords by using her voice too much.

"Ah, peace and quiet."

Dad joked with her that evening as she sat huddled on the sofa with a fleece blanket wrapped around her.

"Ha Ha"

Hally silently mouthed back. She was actually feeling quite a lot better with pain relief and soothing drinks supplied by mum and Wes throughout the day. She had worried that Wes was taking time off school or work, but he insisted he wasn't and that he would spend all day just taking care of her. This was very helpful to mum as she had shopping and Nathan to take care of when he came in from school. Now, Wes had gone home and dad was sitting with her as mum was busy getting Nathan ready for bed.

"Wes spent all day with you?"

Dad asked. Hally nodded and smiled again.

"That lad is really taken with you sweetheart. I didn't think boys were that considerate these days."

He told her seriously. Hally leaned towards her dad and let him cuddle her. At that moment, despite being ill, she felt like the luckiest person alive.

Corrinne and Clia called by early the next morning on the way to school to see how she was and told her they would come back straight after school. They were true to their word and sitting either side of her on the sofa, chatted to her about Gregg and Rhys and about school. Hally's voice was a little above a whisper now and so she was able to join in with the conversation a little. She told them how Wes had looked after her the day before and was surprised when Clia said.

"We saw him on the way to school. He was so worried about you, he couldn't get here fast enough."

Hally raised her eyebrows and whispered.

"Wow, he never said."

"Well I just hope Rhys is as caring if I get ill."

Clia replied.

"Me too, with Gregg."

Corrinne chipped in. The girls stayed for a little while longer and by the time they left Hally felt quite worn out. Mum had told Nathan to stay out of the lounge so as not to disturb Hally, and she was just dosing when Wes arrived. He came in and kissed her gently then sat next to her wrapping her in his arms.

"Go back to sleep babe."

He told her in a soft voice. Hally leaned into him her eyes closed and relaxed. Now was not the time to ask questions, that could wait until she was feeling better and could talk properly.

It took a whole week for Hally to fully recover and get back to school. Once again she had to catch up with her work but her teachers were insistent that she take it easy and not push herself too hard. Still, she was determined to catch up as quickly as possible. She didn't like the feeling of not being sure what was going on in lessons.

The end of January brought a thaw and February began with bright sunshine and a rise in temperature. The shops were suddenly full of everything red as they advertised Valentine's Day, from tiny teddy bears, to bottles of pink champagne.

"I just don't know what to get Wes."

Hally said to Corrinne and Clia as they sat on their favourite bench during morning break.

"Well, I'm going for something sexy for Rhys."

Clia told them.

"What about you Corrinne?"

Hally asked. Corrinne pressed her lips together and mulled over the question.

"Um…me…I think."

She told them boldly. Both Hally and Clia looked at her wide eyed.

"What?"

Hally exclaimed.

"Yeah, what?"

Replied Clia too. Corrinne burst into giggles.

"Oh priceless. You should see your faces."

Hally gave her a playful punch on the arm.

"You.."

She didn't know what else to say. Corrinne laughed more loudly and Clia and Hally joined in.

"Oh don't you look all carefree and guiltless!"

A girl's voice came from behind them. They turned on the bench and saw Penny Cuthbert staring viciously at them. She stomped towards them, came round to the front of the bench, pointed at Hally and all but screamed at her.

"You sit there all giggly with your little friends like nothing ever happened."

Hally stood up, but before she could speak, Penny, her voice rising to a screech screamed.

"You're a jinx. Everyone around you dies, first Dana, my best friend, then your own gran, probably be one of these two next, (she jabbed her finger towards Corrine and Clia) or that fancy boyfriend of yours. Or maybe even your little brother…or…"

She didn't get any further. Hally unusually and totally out of character saw blind fury. All of the years of bullying and ridicule from this girl bubbled to the surface as she brought her hand back and swung it as hard as she could at Penny's face. The slap sounded like the crack of a gun, then there was a moments silence, then.

"What on earth is going on?"

Mrs Jacobs was there. Her voice calm but authoritative. Penny stood holding a hand to her face then spun round and said.

"She just hit me. I only asked how things were."

Corrinne and Clia both started talking at the same time. Hally couldn't believe what she had just done and was unable to speak, not even to defend herself. Mrs Jacobs put her hands up.

"Ok. Enough. All of you to my office please."

"But miss… I didn't…"

Penny tried to argue but Mrs Jacobs silenced her with a look and pointed in the direction of the school buildings. Corrinne and Clia took one of Hally's arms each and gently led her along the path. Penny stormed past them and Mrs Jacobs silently walked behind them.

Once outside her office, Mrs Jacobs asked Penny to sit down and wait. She indicated to Hally to enter and Corrinne and Clia were about to follow when she said.

"I'd like you two to go back to your class and tell which ever teacher you have right now that you will be late, Hally too."

They were about to protest that they didn't want to leave Hally but Mrs Jacobs look was enough to deter anyone from disobeying. So, giving Penny a scathing look instead they made their way along the corridor.

Hally was still standing when Mrs Jacobs entered, still shocked by her own actions.

"Sit down Hally."

Mrs Jacobs said gently. Without a word Hally obeyed.

"Now please tell me why you hit Penny."

Hally looked at her form tutor and saw concern on her face. This brought tears to Hally's eyes, she thought she could cope better with anger. Wiping her face with the back of her hand she relayed the events that led to the slap. She left nothing out and ended by saying.

"I lost my temper. I shouldn't have. But you know, she didn't even go to Dana's funeral, some best friend huh? And all the years they kept at me…"

She couldn't say anymore. She noticed for the first time Mrs Jacobs writing and frowned a little.

"I have to put this in an official report Hally."

Mrs Jacobs told her.

"Will I get excluded?"

Hally asked, her voice a trembling whisper.

"No, I will speak to Penny and Corrinne and Clia, but you were seriously provoked and the pressure you have been under recently, I'm surprised you haven't cracked before. But I still have to report it officially, do you understand?"

Hally nodded.

"I'm going to call your parents and I think it's best if you go home today."

"But you said I won't be excluded."

Hally replied tearfully.

"You're not Hally. I just think you need the break, just for the rest of today."

Hally nodded wordlessly. Mrs Jacobs reached for the phone and quietly spoke to Hally's mum. Hally couldn't hear what her mother said and looked at her teacher questioningly after the call ended.

"She's coming to pick you up. You can wait in reception. I'm going to speak to Penny now and I will be making it clear that you are not being excluded, that I am sending you home for a rest not because of what you did. I have to report what she tells me, but I will also report what Corrinne and Clia have to say too."

Her meaning was very clear. She didn't think Penny would tell the truth but knew Hally's friends would.

As Hally moved away from Mrs Jacobs' office towards reception, Corrinne and Clia were coming towards her. As they met they heard Penny's voice rise to a shout from inside the office and they all knew she hadn't been believed.

Mum came towards her as she sat in reception, her arms extended. Hally stood and fell sobbing into them and let mum hug and then lead her from the building. Hally felt she had let everyone down, especially herself. All the years of torment from Dana and Penny and their gang and not once had she let her temper get the better of her.

"Mum I'm so sorry."

She said as she climbed into the car. Mum squeezed her hand.

"Baby, it's not your fault. Let's get you home then we can talk about it. Your dad's at home, I called him and he came straight home."

This news brought more tears to her eyes. Her daddy was her hero, what would he think of his daughter, so near to being grown up brawling in the school playground. At least that's how Hally thought of it anyway.

When Hally walked into the kitchen dad stood up from the table and came straight to her. He held his arms open wide and Hally fell into them crying so hard she could barely catch her breath.

"Tink…it's alright…shush…sh…sh."

Dad held her and gently patted her back. Mum came over too and put her arms around Hally as well.

"She's in a right state."

Mum said to her husband.

"And she thinks she's let us down. Even though I have tried to tell her she hasn't."

Dad nodded and continued comforting Hally and very slowly her sobs began to diminish.

Eventually calmed, dad led Hally into the lounge and settled her on the sofa. Mum followed with a glass of juice and together they fussed and comforted their daughter.

"So tell us exactly what happened Tink."

Dad said. Hally went on to explain in detail, even the conversation between her and the girls about Valentine presents. When she got to what Penny had said she saw her father's face darken with his own anger.

"That evil little bitch."

He said vehemently. Hally was quite surprised since her dad rarely showed anger. At the same time she felt an overwhelming sense of security. Her dad wasn't at all angry with her, he would protect and love and comfort her.

Corrinne and Clia arrived straight after school and at once informed her that of course the whole school knew what had happened.

"Penny has a fat lip and a huge black eye." Clia told her giggling.

"Oh and a sprained wrist, bruised shins and scratches down one side of her face."

Corrinne added giggling too. This all brought a beaming smile to Hally' face.

"So the usual gossip, rumour and exaggeration then."

Hally replied. The girls nodded and they all laughed.

"But seriously, what did happen after I left?"

Hally enquired. The girls looked at each other deciding who would tell and Clia took the lead.

"Well, we were still waiting outside Mrs Jacobs' office when Penny came out like a bat out of hell screaming. She just kept shouting 'I didn't do anything. It was her.' then she took off and no one saw her for the rest of the day. But some of the kids in our year reckon she was outside the gates at lunch with the bunch of lads she hangs out with. Some reckon they overheard her telling them that you beat her up."

Hally looked at her friend with fear in her eyes. Corrinne put her hand on Hally's arm and said.

"Hey, don't worry. Barry from the year above was there and he told us that Penny tried to blame you but none of them wanted to listen. They told her to shut up and leave them alone. That they didn't want to hear about a kid fight. Barry said Penny got really wound up and stormed off with the lads laughing and jeering at her."

Hally let out a very big sigh of relief. What she didn't need was another group of teenagers bullying her.

"Anyway, back to our conversation, what are we going to get the boys for Valentines?"

Corrinne asked. Clia and Hally burst out laughing.

The girls were still chatting about Valentine's Day when Wes walked into the lounge.

"Babe, are you ok?"

He asked as soon as he saw Hally. She nodded and gave him a smile as he leaned over and kissed her on the lips.

"I have been at work all day 'cos I didn't have any lessons. Some kids came into the café and I overheard one say you had gone home from school because something had happened. I asked what but they didn't know. Then I stupidly realised I'd left my phone at home, so I came straight over instead."

"I wondered why you didn't reply to my text."

Hally told him worriedly. Wes kneeled in front of her and took her hands.

"Babe, I'm so sorry. If I'd known earlier I would have come, honestly."

He kissed the back of her hands and smiled. She smiled back, forgiveness in her eyes, and went on to explain to him everything that had happened.

"So, can you stay with me for the rest of the evening?"

Hally asked, squeezing his hands for comfort. Wes leaned forward and said very sincerely.

"Of course I can."

As Hally walked into school the next morning she felt all eyes were on her. She tried not to look guilty but couldn't pull it off. Corrinne and Clia as usual walked by her side and fended off the occasional question from other students with.

"Don't ask, there's nothing to tell."

There was also no sign of Penny and this was a relief to Hally. Registration went as normal and when the bell went signalling the start of lessons Mrs Jacobs asked her for a minute of her time.

"Just to let you know, Penny won't be in school for the rest of this week. She didn't take too kindly to my questions, became far too aggressive and has been excluded for a few days."

Hally left for her first lesson feeling that the day had suddenly become much brighter. It brightened up even more during morning break when Wes came up behind her and wrapped his arms around her.

"Thought I would come in early. First lesson is a single before lunch."

He mumbled into her hair.

"Sometimes I wish Gregg was here at school."

Corrinne told no one in particular. They all squeezed on the bench, chatting and sharing their snacks with Wes.

"So have you girls got plans for Valentine's day then?"

Wes asked nonchalantly. Hally looked at Corrinne and Clia,

obvious disappointment on her face. So Clia chirped in.

"Well, we always spend the day together actually."

Wes' disappointment was tangible and this gave Hally a very real lift. She looked at him and with complete confidence said.

"Why do you have something else in mind then?"

Wes realised he was being teased and a smile spread across his face.

"Maybe…"

He got no further as the bell went indicating the end of break.

"Just have to wait."

He told Hally planting a kiss on her lips and heading off towards the library.

On Saturday Hally and the girls headed into town in search of Valentine cards and gifts. Wes was working at the café and they had arranged to meet up with Rhys and Gregg there later.

"Oh look at this?"

Hally turned to her friends holding up a red velvet teddy bear with 'My Lover' printed on the front. Clia raised her eyebrows at her friend.

"My lover?"

She asked.

"You know what I mean."

Hally replied blushing a little.

"Anyway, you can't buy it either, nor you Corrinne."

Hally told them.

"Well not yet, but who knows."

Corrinne replied mysteriously. Hally and Clia looked at their friend waiting for more.

"What?"

She asked them. Then blushing herself answered her own question.

"I don't mean… well not yet…just you know… touching and stuff."

"Corrinne Bryant what have you been up to you naughty girl?"

Hally exclaimed. Corrinne led them into a coffee shop and wouldn't say another word until they were settled in leather chairs sipping hot coffee.

"So spill."

Clia told her impatiently.

"It only happened last night."

She said quietly. Hally and Clia were surprised as Corrinne was the shyest of the three. They looked at their friend and waited.

"We were just snuggling and kissing, and well he…touched… um…rubbed…my boobs."

Hally felt herself beginning to smile but forced it back.

"On top of clothes or bare?"

Clia chimed in before Hally could speak.

"On top. But it was ever so nice."

She was now blushing furiously.

"Well, you are the lucky one. Rhys kisses great but so far he hasn't attempted anything else. Or maybe he's just not tempted."

Clia said dejectedly. Hally stayed silent realising that she hadn't told her friends what had happened between her and Wes so long ago before Christmas. She thought she had intended to but somehow had never got around to it.

"What about you Hally?"

Clia asked. Hally didn't know what to say. She hadn't deliberately kept it a secret from her friends.

"Come on sweetie, there's something you're not telling."

Clia coaxed. Hally took a deep breath and decided to tell just part of it.

"Well, I know he gets… well…excited when we kiss, and that… well it's kind of nice to feel it…"

She burst into giggles and so did her friends. It took quite some time for them all to be able to look at each other without giggling again, but eventually they were able to finish their drinks and leave the coffee shop for more shopping.

As usual the Hotspot was crowded and this day the girls had to wait a while before a table was free. Eventually they sat down and Wes was able to bring them drinks. They were only there a short time when Gregg and Rhys came in too. The boys glanced at their packages with raised eyebrows but the girls were not giving anything away.

"Phew, chaos."

Wes said, sitting with them for a short break.

"Everyone and his brother are out shopping today. So what have you bought me Hally?"

Hally had been expecting his cheekiness so delved into a bag and said.

"Well, I could only think of this."

She pulled a small paper bag out of her large one and handed it to Wes. He peeped inside and burst out laughing.

"You cheeky little…"

Rhys and Gregg leaned forward as he pulled a badge from the bag. It read 'Don't forget your phone' Wes pretended to tilt a cap.

"Never again milady."

He told Hally.

"So what about us?"

Rhys asked.

"What about you?"

Clia said back with a look that told him he would get no answers.

After the Hotspot, Gregg and Rhys left with the girls, with Wes promising to be around to Hally's by eight that evening as the group were babysitting Nathan. They spent the rest of the afternoon wandering around the shops and then headed in their respective directions to get ready for the evening.

Hally now spent quite a lot of time getting ready whenever she was meeting up with Wes, even if they were just staying home watching a movie. Mum and dad had bought her several outfits for Christmas and Hally had bought more since with money she had been given at Christmas. Now she felt her wardrobe was more than adequate to mix and match various items. Corrinne as an only child had a complete walk-in closet over spilling with the latest fashion and she shared all of it with Hally and Clia.

"I can't wear it all at the same time."

Corrinne had once told them, so all three girls always had something to wear.

This evening Hally had chosen one of her new outfits, skinny jeans and a purple top that showed how well her figure had developed. She carefully applied her makeup and fluffed her hair, then giving herself a final check in the mirror went downstairs to wait for her friends.

"You look lovely darling."

Mum told her as she walked into the lounge.

"And so do you."

Hally told her mother sincerely, as since the funeral mum had wandered around with a lost look, tiredness and grief etched into her face. But tonight, she looked brighter, there was more colour in her cheeks and the dark circles that had been present under her eyes were fading. Mum smiled a real smile.

"Thank you angel."

Dad came through from the kitchen and put his hands around his wife's waist nuzzling her neck affectionately.

"Tink's right honey, you look fabulous."

Mum hugged his hands to her, looking back and kissing him lightly on the lips.

"Thank you too Colin. It's your love and support that has got me here."

Hally watched her parents happily. Seeing them displaying their deep love for each other gave her a warm, safe and comforting feeling inside. She could never understand how some of the kids in school scoffed when they saw adults cuddling and kissing.

Mum and dad left for their evening out at the same time Corrinne, Clia, Gregg and Rhys turned up. They said their hellos and goodbyes as they passed through the kitchen. The five then went into the lounge where Nathan was playing with his action figures. Straight away the boys plonked down next to him and joined in his game.

"Do they ever grow up?"

Clia asked Hally and Corrinne. They all laughed agreeing that the answer was probably not.

"Well my dad is always playing with Natty with his toys. They make up such stories between them."

Hally said.

"It must be so nice to have a little brother or sister."

Corrinne commented a little wistfully. Clia adding.

"Yeah, I'm the youngest and now I'm all grown up (giggles

came from Hally and Corrinne) well I am, there's no play in our house."

Hally could understand how her friends were feeling, she couldn't imagine what things were going to be like when Nathan did grow up. Although sometimes exceedingly annoying and noisy, it was still a lot of fun having a younger child in the house.

Wes arrived exactly at eight o'clock and after admiring her outfit and kissing her on the lips joined the boys on the floor.

"Another half hour Natty, then it's bed."

Hally told her little brother.

"Oh but!…"

Hally gave him her most stern big sisterly look and said.

"No buts"

Nathan pouted at her but didn't argue further. Wes looked up from the floor and smiled but there was something in his eyes that Hally couldn't work out. She put it aside in her mind and concentrated on setting out the movie they had all chosen to watch. She kept the snacks in the kitchen for the time being knowing full well that it would be impossible to get Nathan to bed if he saw them on display.

With Nathan tucked up and quiet, the six settled down to watch the movie. Hally and Wes were snuggled on the sofa, Clia and Rhys in one armchair and Corrinne and Gregg in the other. The coffee table in the middle was loaded with popcorn, chocolates, tortilla chips and grapes. The movie was a real chiller and every so often Hally would notice Corrinne give a little squeal and bury her face in Gregg's shoulder. Hally smiled to herself because she knew her friend was faking her fear. Corrinne never got scared over a movie, in fact she was the one who laughed openly and teased the other two about scary or jumpy bits. Hally looked over to Clia to see if she had noticed and saw her and Rhys glued together at the lips, taking no notice what so ever of the film. At that moment Hally felt herself fill will complete happiness. She and her friends were content.

Over the next week Hally and her friends tried to prise out of each of their boyfriends what plans had been made for Valentine's day, but with absolutely no luck. They even tried being sneaky with no effect.

"You know we do actually spend the day together 'cos we don't usually have anyone else, and even though we have you guys this year we don't think we should change tradition."

Clia tried to goad the boys. It didn't work.

"Not a problem."

Rhys came back with giving nothing away.

"Ooh, you can be so…so…"

Clia couldn't find the right words.

"Gorgeous, handsome, loving, romantic…"

Rhys got no further as Clia playfully tugged the back of his hair.

"Ouch!"

He said dramatically, making them all laugh. Wes then took the lead.

"All we will say is, the day starts early and you will need wellies and waterproof coats."

Hally looked at him in astonishment.

"What do you mean? Valentine's supposed to be romantic where are you taking us?"

Wes burst out laughing. It was his turn to get his hair tugged.

"Sorry babe, couldn't resist that. No, but truthfully we have planned a full day, and before you ask you will need at least two outfits, one for the day and one for the evening."

The girls looked at each other with curious expressions.

As Valentine's Day got nearer Hally became more and more excited but with a mixture of nerves too. She had never spent Valentine's Day with a boy before. It was true what Clia had said, they usually did spend the day together eating chocolates and watching movies. Well this year they would still be together but with their own boyfriends too.

"Hally, your dad and I have been given permission to tell you that we have given our permission to let you stay out on Valentine's night."

Mum told Hally Friday over dinner. Dad looked at her grinning.

"What do you mean?"

Hally asked shocked.

"Wes asked us and told us his plans…we can't divulge… and we said it would be ok."

Dad added. Hally looked from one parent to the other, both were smiling secretively.

"What about Corrinne and Clia?"

Hally asked randomly. Dad looked at mum and raised his eyebrows.

"The girl gets permission to stay out for the night with her boyfriend, and all she can say is what about her friends."

He playfully shook his head whilst still smiling.

"It's alright Tink, we have spoken to the girls' parents and everything is organised."

Just at that moment Hally's phone chirped an incoming text message. Quickly she opened it and read.

mum and dad said i can stay out tomorrow night you and clia too

As she read her phoned sounded again. This time the message was from Clia.

mum said we are out for the whole night tomorrow do you know whats going on.

Hally rapidly typed messages back telling her friends she was as much in the dark as they were, and she only knew that they had all been given permission for a night out. Soon after sending the message she got a reply.

me and Corrinne on way round now.

Hally finished eating and waited for her friends to arrive. They had planned to spend the evening together anyway as the boys had told them they needed to put the finishing touches to the Valentine's Day arrangements, it was just a little earlier than arranged.

The girls spent the entire evening discussing the next day. They were settled in Hally's bedroom wrapping the boys' gifts and writing out the cards they had chosen. Each of the girls had bought a serious gift and a cheeky one for their boyfriend. They also chatted about outfits, Hally had asked Wes a few questions and got enough answers to help her choose. So Hally showed her chosen ones and the other two described theirs. Hally held up her outfits, jeggins, jumper and pixie boots for the day and a deep red chiffon dress with red strappy platforms for the evening. Corrinne and Clia's outfits were similarly casual for the day and sexy for the evening.

“What about night wear?”

Clia asked.

“Well I’m packing silk shorty pjs but with my big dressing gown.”

Corrinne told the other two.

“Mmm… I think I will just take my usual stuff, ‘cos Wes has seen me loads of times ready for bed.”

Hally replied.

“Well, I’m going for full on silk chemise and gown. Maybe Rhys will notice that.”

Clia told them a little sadly.

“Clia, is something wrong?”

Hally asked softly.

“Well…no…not really. It’s just he kisses and kisses really great, but that’s it, nothing. I wonder if he fancies me at all.”

To Hally’s dismay Clia’s eyes shone with unshed tears. She pulled her friend into a hug and Corrinne joined in.

“Clia, I’m sure he does, maybe he’s shy or just doesn’t want to be pushy. Have you asked him?”

Clia looked up shocked at the prospect.

“I don’t think I could.”

“Well you’re always telling me I should ask Wes about stuff that’s bothering me.”

Hally replied.

“I know I am, and you’re right, I’m probably over reacting. Let’s see what happens tomorrow.”

“Do you think it matters that we are not yet sixteen?”

Corrinne asked her friends. Hally answered.

“Actually yes I do.”

Corrinne and Clia looked startled at the seriousness in her voice, so she carried on with her explanation.

“Well, I know it all sounds sexy and romantic and grown up, but, well I don’t think I’m ready yet. I mean the thought of it is exciting, I get all sort of…(she blushed deeply and her friends nodded knowingly) warm inside. But then I think about Wes, how much it could cause him a problem, you know being over sixteen himself and that. Well it’s against the law isn’t it? and I know loads of kids that just don't care about that but I couldn't put him at risk like that."

Clia and Corrinne stared at her for a moment, then Corrinne said.

"So what about, you know touching and stuff? Can we do that?"

Hally frowned.

"I don't know. Oh it's hard isn't it…(Corrinne and Clia burst into giggles) oh you know what I mean, dirty girls."

"Well I think a bit of touching should be ok. On top of the clothes."

Clia announced. Hally looked at her friend knowing she was hoping Rhys would give her more attention, and knowing that despite her external show of maturity Clia was just like her.

"Well there won't be much clothing in between you if you go for the silk chemise."

Corrinne said with a laugh.

"Well maybe I will rethink that then and just go for pjs and dressing gown like Hally."

"Yeah, maybe that is best. We don't want to make the lads think they have to do something."

Corrinne replied. So, that decided the girls continued chatting about other things and more about the next day. Corrinne and Clia left for home at ten and after seeing them out went to say goodnight to her parents. Mum and dad were snuggled on the sofa watching a drama on television.

"I'm off to bed now."

She told them leaning down and giving each a kiss.

"Ok baby, sleep tight."

Mum said.

"Yes, sleep tight Tink, big day tomorrow."

Dad said with a grin. Hally gave him the kind of look only girls can give to men.

"Ooh the evil look."

He said laughing, which in turn made Hally laugh too.

"Oh you."

She said as she made her way back to her room.

With just her lamp on, Hally undressed and looked at the angels on her wall. She remembered what her Gran had told her and thought Wes was so much like Granddad, he wanted her to wait too, to be sure and ready. She moved over to the window and looked out across the garden. It was a beautiful clear night with stars twinkling brightly. There was a banana moon shining down and just the tiniest of wispy clouds floating in slow motion across the night sky. Everything outside seemed quiet and peaceful unlike her inner feelings. Hally sighed deeply, the conversation with her friends circling her mind. She knew she loved Wes, and she hoped he loved her back. But at fifteen and a half, she knew she was so very young to feel so much and it frightened her, how to cope with such intense emotion. She reached into her jewellery box and lifted the charm bracelet turning back to the window. She took hold of the little compass charm and whispered to the night.

"Show me the way Gran."

Hoping she could summon the answer from the night.

Turning away from the peace of the night outside, Hally climbed into bed and pulled the duvet right up to her chin. She wasn't cold, she just needed the comfort, how could happiness and sadness happen at the same time? She lay with her eyes open questioning herself silently. What was she sad about? The answer came easily. She was sad because she was afraid this wonderful time she was having with Wes would come to an end. What was she happy about? Well simply that he was with her. It was all so confusing and she knew no matter who she talked to about it, her mum, her friends or anyone, they would not be able to take the confusion away. She turned over and whispered to the angels on the wall.

"Goodnight Gran, Clia's right, let's see what happens tomorrow."

She then closed her eyes and drifted into a sleep full of dreams she wouldn't remember much about.

Hally arose early on Valentine's Day full of excitement and happiness. She looked out of the window and the sun was shining brightly, not a cloud in the sky. Down in the garden she could see a bed of pure white snowdrops and a few purple crocuses just peaking through the centre of the lawn. Her night fears had disappeared and to her it seemed this early show of spring was nature's way of telling her everything was perfect. Dad was in the kitchen when she came down filling two mugs with hot water.

"Just taking your mum a cup of tea."

He told her. Hally noticed a tray on the side laden with a red doily, a small vase with a single red rose, a small box and a plateful of croissants. Hally nodded towards the tray.

"Not just tea."

She stated and dad grinned. Hally had a sudden realisation.

"Dad, you usually take mum out on Valentine's night and I babysit. What are you going to do this year?"

Dad smiled at her.

"Sweetheart, first you have only been old enough to babysit for two Valentine's and second, your mum and I can have just as a romantic evening at home, perhaps even more so…especially with you out of the way."

He said the last part quickly and with a grin ducked out of her way as she flicked a hand at him in a mock slap.

"What's in the box?"

Hally asked him more seriously. Dad lifted the little box from the tray and held it to her. It was velvet with a hinged lid. Gently she raised the lid and nestled on a silky cushion was a gold and diamond eternity ring.

"Dad she'll love it."

Hally whispered. Dad smiled and closed the lid placing the box back on the tray.

"Do you want me to keep Natty out of the way for a bit this morning?"

She asked. Dad shook his head.

"No it's ok baby I've got it all in hand. Besides you need to get ready I'm told your day starts early."

At nine o'clock there was a knock on the back door. Hally was waiting with an overnight bag ready having been up and said her goodbyes to her parents. Mum had tears glistening in her eyes as she showed Hally the ring and both parents told her to go and have a great day. There were no words of warning or be careful, or be sensible, just smiles. Wes stood outside looking at the garden with his hands behind his back as she opened the door.

"Morning my sweet Valentine."

He greeted her. Then he brought one hand from behind him and said.

"Open."

She did as she was told and he popped a chocolate covered strawberry into her mouth which he followed with a kiss on the lips.

"The first chocolate of the day. Now are you ready?"

Hally nodded and stepped back for her bag which Wes took straight from her.

"Wow, are you packed for a week?"

He mocked, pretending the bag was over heavy. Hally giggled. He turned towards the gate and Hally followed.

The pathway at the back of her house led to the road and when they reached it Hally saw a large people carrier with Corrinne, Clia and Gregg sitting in passenger seats and Rhys in the driver's seat. Wes took her bag and stowed it in the luggage area and helped her climb into the car, settling in beside her.

"Ok Rhys, off we go."

Wes said. Without a hint of their destination, Rhys pulled away from the kerb and drove away from Hally's house.

"So where are we going?"

Clia asked from the front of the car.

"I've told you for the hundredth time it's a surprise."

"Whose car is this?"

Hally asked.

"My Parents."

Rhys replied. Hally glanced over the seat to Corrinne and Gregg. She was already tucked up close to him with his arm around her and didn't seem in the least bit interested in finding out where they were going. Wes put his arm around her and said.

"Just enjoy the ride. It won't be long."

That was all he would say about the journey.

An hour later they were driving through open countryside with fields of sheep on both sides. There didn't seem to be anything around them except the odd farm scattered about. Hally had never before taken much notice of what lay outside of Colingford, she had been on trips and picnics with her parents and Nathan but hadn't really taken it in. Now she was surprised at how rural her hometown actually was. Most of the conversation in the car had been restricted to general chitchat until Rhys turned the car off the road and headed down a rough track.

"Here we are."

Wes told them all. Within a couple of minutes they pulled up outside a stone cottage. There was quite a lot of building materials and equipment outside the house. Seeing the expressions on the faces of the girls Wes quickly stated.

"Oh don't worry about that stuff, inside is what's important."

"But what is this place?"

Hally enquired.

"My mum and dad bought it and dad's been doing it up. Gregg and Rhys have been giving him a hand. It's not complete yet (Hally gave him a concerned look) but don't worry, there's only small things left to do. It is perfectly habitable."

Hally was again shocked and she thought disappointed that she was again finding out something at the same time as her two friends. She gave Wes a little look that told him she was hurt that he hadn't told her about the cottage before and he frowned slightly in realisation, but said nothing at that point. Unwilling to spoil the day Hally let it go but again resolved to question him when they were alone. This brought back the fact that she still hadn't asked about his exams and was beginning to wonder what other things she would find out.

Inside the cottage was more than habitable, it was simply delightful. There was a small cosy sitting room with country style furnishings and an open fire. The ceilings were low with heavy wooden beams and the windows were small with deep cushioned window seats. Wes led them into the kitchen which was much larger than the sitting room with windows that opened onto an overgrown garden and fields.

"Dad opened this out, it was two smaller rooms originally."

He told them.

"This place is like a tardis, it seems to get bigger as you move further inside. You'll see when we go upstairs."

Gregg told the girls and indeed he was right. Somehow the cottage had three bedrooms and a small bathroom upstairs. Each room softly painted and furnished in wood. The girls glanced at each other unsure of what to say or do. Wes came to their rescue.

"Don't look so worried you three. Dad let us have this place on the strict understanding that we behave ourselves, by that I mean us three. We just want you all to enjoy this day, so choose your rooms and then come downstairs for surprises."

Hally, Corrinne and Clia looked at each other and it was Hally who made the first move.

"Ok, I'll take this room."

The other two smiled and they all moved to the hallway to decide on the other two rooms.

Back in the sitting room, Wes told the girls to sit down by the fire which the boys had lit whilst the girls were still upstairs. Then he, Gregg and Rhys went into the kitchen. It was quite some time before they returned each carrying something. Wes was holding a tray which he placed on the small coffee table in front of the sofa. On it was mugs of hot chocolate, a plate with chocolate muffins more chocolate covered strawberries and a dish of chocolate truffles. Rhys came forward and handed each of the girls a bouquet of red roses and Gregg came round to the front of the table and placed on it a red heart shaped box filled with fresh strawberries, red grapes and dipping chocolate. The boys settled themselves on the floor and told the girls to dig in.

After the chocolate feast the boys cleared away and indicated that the girls should follow them. At the back door they handed each girl a thick travel rug and a pair of wellington boots, Wes grinning widely at Hally's look of astonishment.

"Told you you'd need them."

He said to her as he donned his own boots and hauled a backpack over his shoulder. Then he took her hand and led her and the others out into the overgrown garden. They plodded through foot high grass and shaggy shrubs for what seemed like ages. Just when Hally was about to call a halt and demand to know where they were going the overgrown garden opened out on a small wooded area with the river running through. Attached to the trees were red heart shaped balloons and ribbons. The girls gasped at the sight and were then even more surprised when the boys led them towards the river and into a small arched summer house built from stone. There were more balloons over the entrance and inside stone benches lined the curved wall. The ceiling arched away above them and Hally was very glad of the rugs as it was rather cold.

"Sit down."

Wes told them. They did as he asked and then he pulled open the backpack and with the help of Rhys and Gregg unpacked a flask of soup, crusty bread, cheese, fruit, plates, cutlery and cups. Between them the boys gave the girls a lunchtime feast which they found very filling and warming on top of the earlier chocolate treats.

"What is this place?"

Clia asked.

"Well, it belongs to the cottage and dad was told it was built by the farmer who lived here like over a hundred years ago. Apparently he built it for his wife because she wasn't from farming stock but had fallen in love with him and been disowned by her family because she married him. This summer house was the only connection to her life as a lady that he could give her."

Wes told them all.

"Wow, how romantic!"

Exclaimed Corrinne.

"Were they happy?"

Hally asked solemnly. Wes took her hand and kissed the back of it.

"Very, so dad's been told. They had eight children and lived 'til they were very old."

Hally smiled, glad she was sitting in a place that had seen so much love and happiness.

After the lunch they made their way back to the cottage and the boys settled the girls in front of the fire and loaded a DVD player with a chick flick which they knew all three girls loved to watch.

"But you lads don't like these sort of movies."

Hally told them.

"Today we watch whatever pleases you girls."

Gregg told them pulling Corrinne close. The girls giggled and settled down, whilst the boys went into the kitchen and returned with fizzy drinks and snacks.

"We are going to go home ten pounds heavier."

Clia said with a laugh.

"Oh well, we will still love you."

Rhys replied then blushed furiously when he realised what he had said.

"Ooh film's starting."

Hally said to relieve Rhys' embarrassment, and all went quiet as they watched.

The rest of the day was spent in front of the fire watching a whole variety of girlie films, much to the delight of the Hally, Corrinne and Clia. The boys showed no signs of getting bored. Then around five in the evening the boys stood up and headed for the kitchen.

"You three stay just where you are."

Wes instructed.

"Oh we are not going anywhere, it's too cosy here."

Hally told him with Corrinne and Clia nodding the affirmative. But a short time later when they heard some clanging and banging and loud male laughter, they began to wonder what was going on.

"They must be trying out their culinary skills."

Clia said to the other two.

"Mmmm, strange, but Wes has never cooked for me before. In fact neither of us has, we always just eat with the family or go out."

Hally commented.

"Gregg is actually a very good cook. He's cooked for me quite a few times."

Corrinne told her friends.

"You've never said before."

Hally said giving her a quizzical look, but with that odd trembling inside she experienced before when she thought her friends were drifting away. Corrinne gave her usual smile which alleviated the fear.

"I really didn't mean to keep it from you, we just sometimes cook together when mum and dad are out."

Hally saw in her friend's eyes that everything was still right between them all.

"Rhys made me an omelette once at his house, but it sort of fell to bits."

Clia announced and all three burst into giggles.

About an hour later Wes reappeared in the doorway. His hair was damp and swept back untidily and his face was flushed and hot looking.

"Girls it's time for you to go and dress for dinner."

He told them with a smile. Hally stood up and walked over to him.

"Is everything ok through there? You look really hot."

She asked with concern in her voice. Wes leaned down and planted a sweaty kiss on her lips.

"Everything is absolutely going to plan. Now go and dress."

Hally giggled and turned as Corrinne and Clia peeled themselves off the sofa and all three headed upstairs to get ready.

The room Hally had chosen was warm and cosy as she began to pull off her day clothes and unzipped the dress from its cover. She changed her underwear into a beautiful red set that matched the dress and sat at the dressing table to put on her makeup. There was a knock on the door and Corrinne called out.

"Hals, you got a minute?"

"Of course, come in."

Corrinne came into the room closing the door behind her, a frown and a worried look on her face. Hally was immediately concerned.

"What's wrong?"

She asked turning from the mirror. Corrinne's eyes shone with unshed tears and Hally quickly went and put her arm around her friend. Corrinne rubbed her eyes and then said.

"Damn it, I've just come on. It's early, have you got some tampons?"

Hally immediately went to her bag and pulled a small container out loaded with tampons and handed them to Corrinne.

"Corrie, how come you haven't got a bagful?"

Hally asked gently.

"I know, usually I have everything bar the kitchen sink don't I? It's just I didn't want to look stupid to Gregg carrying so much unnecessary stuff. (She sniffed back tears) Should have just been my normal self."

Hally hugged her friend close.

"You know Corrinne, Gregg sees you all the time with your big bag, that's who you are."

Corrinne gave a smile.

"I know, I won't make the same mistake again. See you never know what's going to happen. Trouble is what if Gregg, you know, gets well a bit frisky tonight?"

Corrinne asked worriedly.

"Just tell him the truth, besides, I actually don't think any of them are going to be like that. I really do think they just want us to have a good time."

Hally replied. Corrinne gave her a look that was close to disappointment.

"Hmmm, ok."

"Corrinne you little…"

Hally didn't finish as both girls started laughing and Corrinne left the room looking a lot happier than when she entered.

Corrinne and Clia came to Hally's room before going downstairs. Corrinne was wearing a soft blue ruffle dress and black caged platform shoes and Clia was wearing a thigh length tiered black lace dress with black patent platforms. They admired each other's outfits and checking their makeup in the mirror carefully made their way back downstairs. Somehow the boys had managed to all get changed too and were waiting for the girls in the living room. They had removed all the packets and glasses from the coffee table and replaced them with a tray of champagne flutes.

"You look gorgeous."

"Wow."

"Mind blowing."

Each girl was complimented by her boyfriend. Then as the girls looked at the glasses.

"Alcohol free fizzy wine."

Wes told them as they handed each girl a drink. Then holding out an arm the boys led the girls into the kitchen.

They had transformed the country kitchen into a beautiful dining room that looked like an expensive restaurant. A deep red cloth covered the large table with soft candles burning at the centre. There were place mats and cutlery and glasses all laid out; and the wall lamps had been draped with squares of red lace giving a romantic glow to the large room. The boys pulled chairs out for the girls and settled them at the table. Hally noticed a huge range style cooker and realised why Wes had looked so hot and flushed.

With tea towels folded over their arms like waiters, the boys moved from the fridge to the table setting in front of the girls their starter and then sitting down opposite to join them. Hally looked at the dish, avocado pear filled with prawns in a sea food sauce, and wondered who had actually prepared it. Wes seemed to read her mind.

"Mum gave us some cookery lessons. She helped us put together this menu, she kept it simple so we wouldn't muck it up."

Hally smiled and felt her heart swell and race at the same time and for the first time that day contemplated what might happen later.

Wes, Gregg and Rhys continued waiting on the girls for three more courses, raspberry sorbet followed by chicken breasts in a white wine sauce with baby potatoes and vegetables and a dessert of chocolate mousse with strawberries and fresh cream. They finished with a pot of coffee and after dinner mint chocolates.

"Phew, I don't think I will eat chocolate for a month."

Hally announced at the end of the meal. Corrinne and Clia gave her a scathing look.

"Well maybe a week."

She told them.

"More like just about a day."

Clia told them all laughing. This brought laughter from them all.

"Well, now it's time for the clearing up. So, we'll just leave you girls to it and go and watch the television."

Rhys said standing and stretching.

"Ooof…"

Was all he could then say as Clia mock punched him. He started laughing as did the others.

"Suppose I deserved that."

He told them.

"Come on girls, off to the sitting room and let us poor guys clean up this kitchen. Such slavery."

Gregg announced kissing Corrinne on the top of her head. So the girls returned to the sofa.

A little while later Wes poked his head around the door and saw the girls settled together on the sofa.

"Um…could you three sort of sit on separate seats please?"

He asked unusually bashful. Hally looked over the top of the sofa and saw a shyness in him that wasn't usually there.

"Ok, we will."

She told him and he gave her a beaming smile. Hally stood up and moved to an armchair close to the fire and Clia turned to Corrinne.

"Where do you want to sit Corrie?"

"I'll go to the chair, give you and Rhys some room for those extra ten pounds."

Corrinne replied with a chuckle. Hally smiled at her friends loving them like they were sisters. They re-settled themselves and chatted for a while.

"When are you giving Wes his gifts?"

Corrinne asked.

"Oh, I don't know, what about you two?"

"Well what if we go and get them and bring them down because it sounds like they have something planned if they want us on separate chairs."

Clia said to them. They agreed and Hally popped her head around the kitchen door to let the boys know where they were going.

Hally and Corrine placed their wrapped gifts by the side of the chairs where Wes and Gregg wouldn't see them. Corrinne had to hide hers under a cushion as all sides of the sofa were easily visible.

"Shoulda opted for a chair."

She grumbled light heartedly. The girls chatted some more, the television playing to itself, and then the door opened and boys returned each carrying a gift bag. Wes turned out two of the wall lights leaving just a dim glow from the other two and the firelight. The boys then went to their respective girlfriends. Wes took Hally's hand and gently pulled her out of the chair, then sat down easing her onto his lap. Rhys sat next to Clia and Gregg squeezed into the chair with Corrinne, she lifting her legs and draping them over Gregg's knees.

Wes opened his gift bag and reached in taking a soft package wrapped in red paper and ribbons. He handed it to Hally who carefully but excitedly opened it. Inside she found a tiny pink teddy bear with a red heart on the chest. The words 'Be My Valentine' embroidered on. Smiling she kissed Wes and hugged the bear to her. Next he pulled a square package with the same wrappings and inside this one she found what was more like a book than a card, for it had several pages of Valentine messages and a hand written note that said.

Hally, the only girl for me. Your Wes. xxx

The last gift Wes pulled out was small and again in the same wrapping paper and trimmings. Slowly she unfolded the paper and found a small box. She lifted the lid and there laying on a bed of pink silk was a pair of silver earrings with a tiny red rose dangling from each. Hally stared in awe, unable to speak, not only had she never before received a Valentine gift but to find her first as beautiful as this was amazing. Wes took her silence as a sign of dislike.

"Don't you like them?"

He asked worriedly. Hally immediately turned into his arms and hugged him tightly.

"I love them, they are absolutely beautiful. And the other things too. Here I have something for you too."

She leaned over the side of the armchair and brought up the presents she had put there and gave them to Wes. He studied the two packages unable to decide which to open first.

"This one."

Hally said pointing to a small soft gift. Wes gave her a questioning look then proceeded to unwrap the present. He peeled off the outer paper and found red tissue paper underneath.

"Mmmm… maybe there's nothing in here."

He teased. Hally gave a soft laugh as he gently separated the tissue and his expression on finding the gift made Hally burst into giggles.

"Hally Mackeller you are kidding me."

This brought the attention of the other two couples.

"You too mate?"

Rhys called across the room and Clia giggled.

"And me."

Said Gregg, Corrinne chuckling in the background. The boys each held up their gifts. Wes' was a red pouch in silk with 'Big Boy' printed on the front. Rhys had a red and black silk thong with 'Cheeky' along the waistband and Gregg had a red velvet pouch with 'Love machine' printed on. The boys laughed with the girls for a few minutes and joked about when they were supposed to wear them. Then Hally turned Wes' attention to her other gift which was a long thin package. Wes carefully unwrapped the gift and lifted the lid from a box. Inside he found an identity bracelet engraved with

'Hally and Wes'

"Do you like it?"

She asked shyly. Wes leaned towards her and gave her a long kiss.

"I love it Hally."

Finally Hally handed him the card she had bought and as he slit open the envelope she began to blush as she thought about the words she had written. For some reason she hadn't thought she would be this close to him when he read it. Wes studied the card then looked up and gave her a soft loving look.

"Do you mean it?"

He asked, his voice barely a whisper. Hally felt her cheeks begin to heat up as she nodded then buried her face into his shoulder. He held her tightly and for some time they didn't speak. After a while Hally mumbled to him.

"You know I think I will go and change out of this dress, it's getting a bit uncomfortable now."

"What you mean into something even more sexy?"

Wes replied. Hally looked up startled and quickly Wes murmured words of reassurance.

"Babe, I'm kidding. Honestly, just teasing you."

His smile was warm and genuine, so relieved, Hally climbed off his lap. In the dim light she couldn't quite make out what Corrinne and Clia were doing so she just called out.

"I'm getting changed, what about you two?"

Clia and Corrinne both mumbled something incoherent to Hally but then stood up and the three girls made their way upstairs.

"So did he like his present?"

Clia asked as they got to the top. Both Hally and Corrinne said yes at the same time making them all laugh.

"What about Rhys?"

Hally enquired.

"Well he hasn't stopped snogging me since."

She replied with a huge smile. Corrinne and Clia passed Hally to their own rooms agreeing to go back down all together. Changing didn't take any of them long and soon they met on the landing togged up in their warmest pyjamas and fluffy dressing gowns with matching slippers.

"Bet they get a bit of a shock when they see us now."

Clia joked as they made their way down. On re-entering the living room the girls noticed the boys had three sleeping bags rolled up on the floor and had also changed out of their smart clothes. They were all now wearing jog pants and T-shirts. Hally looked at Wes a frown asking the unspoken question.

"We told you we were on strict orders for best behaviour."

Wes told them.

"The rooms are just for you girls, we are going to bunk down here."

Corrinne jumped onto Gregg's lap taking the wind out of him and Clia folded herself next to Rhys, tucking her feet under her.

Hally kneeled on the floor in front of the fire and unrolled one of the sleeping bags and unzipped it.

"Could you pass those cushions please?"

She asked Wes. He did as asked and when she had them satisfactorily arranged settled herself on the sleeping bag and patted the space next to her. Wes joined her and together they snuggled.

"I don't want to sleep in that room by myself."

She whispered. Wes leaned on an elbow and looked down into her eyes.

"Hally, I can't…"

Wes started to say, but Hally cut across him.

"I don't mean that, even though I think it would be nice, I mean, I just want to stay here by the fire with you."

Wes beamed at her then lowered his head and gave her a long deep kiss. Hally felt her body react instantly and she pressed herself close to him. Even through her dressing gown and pyjamas she could feel her breasts tingling as they touched his chest. She could also feel his body reacting too and this excited her even more. Wes kept his hands still, just holding her, but Hally took hold of one and moved it to cover a breast. She felt his kiss deepen as he gently rubbed her breast on top of her clothes. She thought she would explode, then he stopped and pulled away from the kiss.

"No Hally, not here, not now."

He whispered, his body defying his words.

"But…"

She couldn't speak, she wanted to cry, shout but hold him tight all at once. She desperately wanted him to do more, to touch her everywhere. She was burning, so she pressed harder into him. Wes held her but didn't move, his own body sending messages to his brain and to Hally. Hally wiggled into him and then suddenly again that momentous explosion of feeling flooded through her. She bit down on her lip so as not to call out and at the same time felt Wes tense and a soft 'Huh' came from him.

As the feeling subsided Hally didn't feel shy or embarrassed or confused this time. Instead she lay snuggled in the sleeping bag holding Wes with a smile of complete satisfaction on her face. Wes didn't speak, nor move, he just kept his arms around her. Hally knew something had happened to him this time too and felt proud that she could do that to him. If he felt anywhere near what she had felt then that had to be a good thing, she thought. Wes moved slightly and Hally looked up into his eyes.

"Are you alright?"

He whispered.

"I feel absolutely wonderful. What about you?"

She whispered back, the television muting their conversation to the others.

"Hally, it felt very good even though it shouldn't..."

Hally stopped his words with a kiss.

"It's ok...I know how you feel about all of this and what just happened...well...it's enough."

Wes smiled and held her, she closed her eyes and they just lay snuggled in each other's arms. As sleep began to envelope her, Hally thought about the words she had written in Wes' card.

Wes, my Valentine because that is what love is.

He had liked what she had written, had asked if she meant it and today and especially tonight; she thought he had showed her that he felt the same. Content and feeling very grown up she let sleep take her.

The drive home seemed to be much quicker than the outward journey. The boys had made tea and toast for them all and cleaned and tidied before locking up and loading the car. Conversations were comfortable and normal and Hally guessed that meant nothing serious had happened between her friends and their boyfriends. In the end, all of them had simply stayed in the sitting room snuggled up sleeping as the fire gradually died down. Hally had awoken a couple of times during the night to movement and saw first Gregg then Rhys quietly pick up a sleeping bag.

They arrived at Hally's house a little after eleven and Wes unloaded her bag carrying it through to the kitchen. The others were going home but Corrinne and Clia had arranged to come round to Hally's later. Wes had to work at five, so he said he would spend a bit more time with her before getting off to see his family before work. The house was empty when they went in, but there was a note on the table from her parents saying they had taken

Nathan to his football match. Hally switched the kettle on and as she took mugs out of the kitchen Wes came behind her and put his arms around her.

"Last night was great."

He whispered as he nuzzled her neck. Hally smiled feeling a sense of power running through her.

"It was for me too."

She told him turning in his arms. He kissed her deeply but didn't let it linger too long. Then a sudden thought came to her and a question bubbled up and came out before she could stop it.

"Wes have you…are you a virgin?"

Wes leaned back, surprise on his face.

"Um…well…actually, no"

He told her. She didn't know what she had expected his reply to be but it still gave her a jolt and a sudden overwhelming feeling of jealousy invaded her whole being.

"Hally?"

Wes looked at her, obviously seeing something on her face.

"I…oh…who?"

Was all she could say. Wes could see she was upset but as he was about to reply the door opened and Nathan bounced in covered in mud chanting 'I scored a goal!' over and over. Mum and dad followed, dad trying to stop Nathan spreading the mud everywhere.

"Oh hi you two. Have a good time?"

Mum asked as she put Nathan's football bag into the utility room and not noticing the slight tension between them.

"Yes it was great."

Hally replied turning and taking two more mugs from the cupboard and busying herself making coffee. Wes turned to dad who was trying to prise muddy clothes from Nathan who was still chanting and wriggling.

"Need a hand?"

He asked smiling. Dad gave a sigh.

"Phew, thanks but I think I've got it now."

He lifted an over excited Nathan and tucked him under his arm.

"Right bath."

He told him as he moved out of the kitchen. Words of protest from Nathan were lost on the way. Wes turned back to Hally and found her holding a mug to him a strange look on her face. Mum was now putting Nathan's kit into the washing machine.

"There's a coffee here for you mum."

Hally called out. Mum called out thanks and then Hally nodded in the direction of the lounge and Wes followed her through. When they were again alone he said.

"Hally, are you alright?"

"Yes of course I am. It was just a bit of a surprise. I don't know why though, you are nineteen now, I mean I expect you've had loads of girlfriends and done stuff."

Wes moved over to her and put his hand on her arm.

"No, it's not like that."

"Wes it's ok. Look I don't think I want to talk about this now, not with my parents likely to come in."

Wes nodded in agreement a firm look on his face.

"But I am going to tell you."

They sat on the sofa and chatted about other things, but there was a sense of discomfort that Hally had never felt with him before. She believed it was her causing it and knew she was being unfair but couldn't get rid of the feeling that he had let her down. Eventually Wes told her he had to go and would see her tomorrow at school as he had lessons after lunch. She went with him to the door and kissed him goodbye in the usual way. When she closed the door and turned mum was standing looking at her.

"Ok, what's wrong?"

Hally was shocked. She thought she had fooled her mum.

"What do you mean?"

"You sounded falsely cheerful when I asked if you'd had a good time."

Hally sighed deeply.

"We had a great time, everything was perfect. It was just when we got back, I asked Wes if he was a virgin, I know stupid question to a guy his age. Of course he's not. It just sort of…well I felt…feel really jealous. Is that normal?"

Mum came over and hugged her tightly.

"My darling, of course it's normal. You feel a great deal for this boy and for months now he has been your boyfriend, all yours like it has always been that way. Now you find he's had a very intimate relationship with someone else in the past and it feels like he's been unfaithful."

Hally felt tears slowly trickle down her face.

"That's exactly how I feel. Is it bad?"

She sobbed into her mum's shoulder.

"No my angel, it's not bad. Just so long as you understand that Wes hasn't done anything wrong. It was his past, you are his here and now."

Mum told her wisely. Hally looked up wiping the tears away.

"Will he like compare… if I decide you know to…?"

Hally asked her mum shyly. Mum pulled her back into a hug.

"Oh baby, no I don't think he would even think about that. If or when it happens it will be between you two and that in itself will make it special."

Corrinne and Clia came round early in the evening and settled themselves in Hally's room to completely analyse the Valentine Day. Rhys and Gregg had left them with a huge box of chocolates from all three of them and the girls were nibbling as they chatted.

"So what about Rhys?"

Corrinne asked. Clia popped a whole chocolate in her mouth and deliberately made the other two wait whilst she chewed and swallowed.

"Well…a lot of snogging, a lot. He did give me a love bite though."

She pulled her hair away from her neck and showed Hally and Corrinne a mark just below and slightly behind her ear.

"What about you Hally?"

Corrinne said. Hally bit into a chocolate and looked at her friends in such a way they knew she had something to tell.

"Come on give."

Clia demanded. So Hally took a deep breath and poured out her experience.

"Wow! What was is like?"

Clia asked.

"I can't describe it, it just felt, well like a bomb going off inside."

Hally said blushing deeply.

"So not like when you… you know… touch yourself."

Corrinne asked hesitantly.

"No not really, sort of but more…oh I really can't explain."

Hally said with a sigh, then with a cheeky smile.

"You will have to find out for yourselves."

The girls fell about laughing and the chocolate box starting sliding to the edge of the bed almost as though in slow motion. Each of them attempted to catch it but failed and the whole box landed upside down on the floor. Clia kneeled down and lifted what was now the bottom of the box. It came away from the plastic tray that held the chocolates and the girls laughed even more when they saw all of the chocolates held in place by the tray but touching the floor. Corrinne quickly scooped up a magazine that was on Hally's desk and opening it out, slid it under the tray. With one hand on top of the tray she carefully lifted the whole thing up. All was going brilliantly until she tried turning it over. Then the tray wobbled and the magazine gave way and the chocolates landed in a pile on Hally's bed. The girls couldn't contain themselves, they laughed and laughed, holding their stomachs and wiping tears from their eyes.

Eventually the laughter subsided and together they began to put the chocolates back into the tray trying to find the right slots for each chocolate. Some they managed easily, others were like a jigsaw puzzle, they had to find the slot that the chocolate fitted.

"Better not tell the boys about this."

Clia stated. The other two nodded in agreement and settled themselves back on the bed to continue their conversation.

"So what else Hally?"

Clia asked. Hally looked up from perusing the chocolates, a startled expression on her face.

"What do you mean? I've told you what happened, all of it."

"But there's something else. You forget sweetie, we have known you for like ever, we know when something is not right."

Clia told her gently. Hally put the chocolate down and gave a huge sigh.

"It's stupid really…"

Corrinne and Clia waited patiently.

"I found out this morning when we got back here that Wes is not a virgin."

Before either of her friends could comment Hally carried on.

"I told you it's stupid. I mean why wouldn't he be at his age. But I've never really thought about it before and when I did I got angry like he'd cheated on me. Then mum and dad came home and we couldn't talk about it anymore and then he had to go. I haven't texted him and he hasn't texted me, so I'm sort of…well I don't know what's going on. It's like our first row but without an argument, do you get what I mean? So, I'm being stupid right?"

Corrinne and Clia both put down their chocolates and moved to Hally's side.

"I suppose it would be too much to think he hadn't been with someone before. But no it doesn't make you stupid Hals. I think because you are a virgin it just feels weird that he's not. I mean I don't really know and we haven't talked about it, but I'm sort of thinking that if Gregg isn't then I probably will feel the same, even though I haven't been going out with him as long as you and Wes."

Corrinne said trying to comfort her.

"That's pretty much what mum said."

Hally replied. Clia sat for a moment with a slight frown, then said.

"I'm not certain, but I think Rhys actually is a virgin. I mean he hasn't said he is, it's just I asked about old girlfriends and he hasn't been out with anyone that lasted more than a couple of weeks. He's really quite shy."

Hally looked at her friend and saw in her eyes that she felt deeply about Rhys and was very happy for her, even though at the moment she worried her own relationship was teetering on the edge of destruction.

"You know, in all this time the only thing Wes has told me about old girlfriends is actually just about one. She broke his heart is all I know, and even his parents were affected when she broke up with him."

Corrinne took Hally's hand and patted it like an adult comforting a toddler.

"Well I bet that's it then. This girl, I bet she was the one that he, you know did it with. But Hals, he loves you now. (Hally frowned in disbelief.) He does, the way he looks at you, protects you, worries about you. That is true love my girl, you better believe it."

Still not entirely convinced and not sure if thinking that Wes' old long time girlfriend had been the intimate one, Hally tried to put her confusion aside.

"So should I text him?"

Corrinne and Clia both spoke at the same time saying the same thing.

"Too right you should."

This brought laughter and Hally felt a lightening in her stomach. Her friends were always there for her to prop her up no matter what. So she reached for her phone and quickly tapped in a message.

im sorry i over reacted its not your fault you did nothing wrong xxx

She pressed send and it seemed that only seconds went by when her phone beeped indicating a message. Quickly she opened it and read aloud.

babe it is my fault but you must know that you really are the only girl i want to be with in every way xxxxx

Hally's smile spread across her face and she felt like she was floating on air. Suddenly everything was perfect. Corrinne and Clia smiled too happy that their best friend was again happy.

CHAPTER 15

Wes' Secret

The girls found they couldn't eat many of the chocolates because of all the chocolate treats the day before. Instead Hally went downstairs and prepared a plate of sandwiches which she put on a tray with some savoury snacks. Mum and dad were in the kitchen, Granddad too, with Nathan, supervising his tea and eating sandwiches themselves. Usually on Sunday, the family had a roast with Granddad and then tea in the evening, but today Nathan's football match had disrupted their normal routine so instead, mum had served a cold buffet lunch.

"You look a lot more cheerful"

Mum said to her with a smile. She hated seeing her daughter miserable, it always made her feel low too.

"Yes I am."

Was all Hally said back but with a broad smile that said so much more.

"Teenagers."

Granddad said with a smirk. Hally planted a kiss on top of his head as she headed back to her room.

After Corrinne and Clia left that evening Hally went into the lounge where her parents were cuddled up on the sofa. Granddad had also gone home. She tucked her feet underneath her in an armchair and hugged a cushion like it was a teddy bear.

"How is he?"

Hally asked her parents. They knew straightaway whom she was referring to.

"Oh, some days he's like his old self but others I find him just sitting staring out of the window at the garden."

Mum told her.

"They say time heals, but mum and dad were together for such a long time, I don't think he will ever truly heal."

She continued a slight catch to her voice. Dad pulled her to him more tightly and kissed her cheek.

"It will get better for him darling, especially with you there to help him. And of course we will do all we can too."

Hally watched her parents, love radiating from them and a tiny fantasy flashed through her mind. Her and Wes sitting snuggled on their own sofa, a child tucked up safely in bed. She felt herself begin to blush at the thought and tried to cover it up by rubbing her eyes and putting on a fake yawn.

"You alright Tink?"

Dad asked.

"Yes thanks dad. Just a bit tired, yesterday was a long day. Actually I think I'll go to bed now, I don't want to be nodding off in class. The teachers won't like that."

She gave a little giggle and stood, stretching as she rose from the chair. She kissed both her parents goodnight and made her way upstairs.

Nathan was being difficult and mum was trying to get him ready for school. Then it was Hally trying to feed him his breakfast and Wes sitting across the table drinking coffee and reading a newspaper. Nathan was her child and mum was nowhere. She was still fifteen but somehow Nathan was her son. It all seemed perfectly normal. She felt something move and looked down, her swollen belly was shifting, the baby was kicking. There was a bang as Nathan knocked his cereal bowl onto the floor and Hally woke up. Relief flooded through her as the dream faded and she realised the bang was her little brother pulling his bedroom door shut.

Hally climbed out of bed and pulled on her dressing gown. It was still slightly dark outside, the winter hanging on. She looked out into the garden and saw frost covering the lawn, the weekend signs of spring pushed back. For a moment she simply looked, letting the dream wash over her and wondering what if anything it meant. Could she really see herself and Wes together for that long.

"Oh I hope so."

She said out loud. Then turning from the wintery scene outside she began to ready herself for school, which seemed very strange after the dream.

Corrinne and Clia met Hally at their usual spot, the pavements white and the air crisp. A watery winter sunshine was trying to force its way out and as the girls chatted and made their way to school it finally won and shone brightly. So by the time they reached the school gates the frost was already beginning to melt. Hally had given her friends a detailed account of the dream and all three had spent the journey offering up meanings.

"Well I think it means you two are going to get married and have loads of children."

Corrinne said matter of factly. They all laughed, but inside Hally was thinking exactly the same thing, or rather she was wishing that it would be that way. She hadn't heard from Wes since his text the previous day, but he had said he would see her today so she put her worries aside.

The school morning was as normal as it could be, registration, assembly, first lesson, break then a double before lunch. The last lesson had been Maths, so Hally and Clia went to Corrinne's Maths room and met her there. They all three made their way to the dining hall as it was still too cold to sit outside to eat their lunch. They found a table that was occupied by two year seven girls who gave them a frightened look and shoved the lids on their lunch boxes preparing to get up and leave.

"It's ok. Stay there, we are just going to sit at this end."

Hally told them gently. They gave her a shy smile and re-opened their lunch boxes and continued eating and chatting.

"Were we ever that small?"

Clia quietly asked the other two.

"I suppose we must have been."

Hally replied.

"It seems so long ago doesn't it?"

Corrinne said.

"Mmmm…and this is our final official year. Weird isn't it?"

Clia said pensively.

"Do you think we will miss it? You know if we go to college rather than sixth form."

Corrinne asked.

"I won't."

Hally stated.

"I mean it's a great school and we all know some really nice people here, but well, for me too much bad stuff over the years. I think I need the change."

"So you're definitely going to college then?"

Corrinne asked her a note of fear in her voice that Hally noticed immediately.

"Um…I think so, but well I don't want to be anywhere you two aren't. So, well we don't have to decide now anyway."

Hally replied. Corrinne smiled her warm caring smile that Hally loved so much.

"Well I know I am going wherever you two go. I really don't think it matters if it's sixth form or college."

Clia nodded.

"Me too."

They smiled at each other and tucked into their lunch, swapping and sharing as usual.

"Hi babe."

A voice very recognisable came from behind Hally. She turned and saw Wes standing with a smile on his face.

"Hi."

She said back, her heart racing with joy. He leaned over her and gave her a peck. They were not supposed to do this in the dining room so he did it quickly before a lunch time supervisor could pounce on him. Then sitting by her side he took a bite from her sandwich.

"Mmmm… your mum makes lovely sandwiches."

He said.

"Actually I make them myself. She has enough to do getting Natty's lunch together."

Wes grinned.

"Oh well in that case, maybe they're not so good."

Hally took a little swing at him and they all laughed. Then Hally noticed the year seven girls were staring at Wes in open admiration and she whispered to him.

"Looks like you have a little fan club."

Wes looked up and blushed which made Hally, Corrinne and Clia laugh and the year seven girls to hurriedly look away.

After lunch Wes walked some of the way to their lessons with them then headed off to his business studies class. He promised to wait for Hally after school and walk her home as he didn't have to work. Hally's last lesson was English, they were reading Shakespeare's 'Macbeth' and Hally loved it. Mr Austin had set them written tasks alongside the reading of the play and Hally thoroughly enjoyed the work. Mr Austin had quietly asked how she was getting on with everything and she was able to tell him honestly that she was doing well.

Wes was waiting in the corridor as promised at the end of the lesson. Without asking he took her bag from her and threw it over his shoulder with his own backpack. Clia smiled cheekily and piled her own bag onto him too, Corrinne then followed suit. Wes grinned and pretended to be weighed down.

"What, so I'm a pack horse now am I?"

He said good naturedly. The girls laughed and Hally lifting her head in a haughty fashion looked down her nose at him and said.

"Why of course man servant. Do you complaineth?"

The corridor suddenly filled with loud laughter from all of them, Wes dropping the school bags as he bent over creased with laughter. The girls had tears running from their eyes as Mr Austin came out of his classroom to see what was going on. His raised eyebrows asking the unspoken question.

"It's…it's…ok Sir, Hally just got all Shakespearian on us."

Corrinne told him through her tears of laughter. Mr Austin looked at them in complete confusion, as an adult he simply could not relate to the joke, so instead he just smiled, nodded and said.

"Oh good."

Then turned back to his classroom. This of course gave cause for more laughter which slowly subsided as they all finally managed to exit the building.

As the four walked away from the school Hally felt too relaxed and comfortable to worry about anything between her and Wes.

He had his arm over her shoulder and was chatting normally to her, Corrinne and Clia.

"So, Scott thought a flow chart was something to do with plumbing…"

Wes told them, which they all found amusing.

"Well what's he doing A level business studies for then?"

Corrinne asked quite indignantly.

"Haven't you been listening Corrie?"

Wes asked her gently.

"Well, I was kind of off in a little daydream."

She replied with a grin. They all laughed and Hally went on to explain what Wes had been talking about.

"Scott Andrews, you know, the little guy with learning difficulties. He somehow found his way into Wes' class and sat at the back thinking he was in his vocational study group."

"Oh I get you now. Poor guy what happened?"

Hally gave a deep sigh and smiled at her friend patiently explaining further.

"Mrs Bates, the special needs teaching assistant?….You know her?"

Corrinne's frown became a huge smile.

"Oh Yeah!"

Hally giggled.

"The penny drops. Well she tracked him down eventually and took him to his own lesson."

Corrinne, smiling brightly replied.

"All's well that ends well."

Clia burst out laughing.

"Corrinne, what is it with you today. Sweetie what planet are you on?"

Corrinne looked at all of them with a wide innocent expression.

"Planet Gregg."

She simply stated.

Hally and Clia linked their arms through hers and with Wes with his arm still over Hally's shoulder they clumsily plodded on home.

The early morning sunshine had stayed and now the sky was

completely blue and cloudless. Corrinne and Clia went their way as normal and Wes and Hally continued on to Hally's house. The rest of the trek home was filled with chat about the rest of their school day and especially about Corrinne.

"She really has got it bad for Gregg hasn't she?"

Wes said to Hally.

"Yes, even though she has other friends at school, she never hangs out with anyone except Clia and me. And since she's an only child I think she's sometimes lonely at home. I mean her parents dote on her and her mum has only really gone back to work in like this past two years, and that's still only part time, so she's mostly at home when Corrie gets in, but I suppose it's not the same."

Wes nodded in understanding.

"I know where she's coming from. I spent most of my life as an only child and even though I had loads of mates it wasn't the same."

"Bet you were the popular one at school, with the popular group, girls scrambling to get you to go out with them."

Hally stated without any malice in her voice.

"Well…I suppose I was…"

Wes pulled her to him with a wide smile.

"But…I grew up and now I have all I want."

Hally felt like she was walking on cloud nine as they arrived at her house and walked in the back door.

Mum was at the sink rinsing potatoes and Nathan was playing at the table with an action figure, his homework book open by his side. Hally leaned over to see what her little brother should be doing and saw a list of words that he was obviously meant to be learning how to spell. Mum turned, drying her hands at the same time.

"Hi you two, how was your day?"

Hally and Wes both answered that everything had gone well and then mum said.

"Nathan, put that toy away and look at those words."

"Awww…but…"

He complained.

"No buts, this is the second week you have not learnt your spellings."

She gave him a very serious frown but as Hally looked at her she smiled as she turned away from her son. Hally knew mum wasn't really cross with him but could act that way and it worked. Nathan trying to show protest plonked his toy down and picked up his pencil.

"I don't know this one."

He mumbled. Hally took off her coat and draped it over a chair then sat next to her little brother.

"I think I'll get off home if that's alright Hally?"

Wes said. Hally smiled up at him.

"Ok, call me later please."

Wes leaned down and kissed her.

"Yuk!"

Came loudly from Nathan and Wes laughed ruffling his hair as he turned and left Hally to her task.

"So, let's see how you can remember this word."

She told Nathan.

Wes called later that evening and they spent an hour on the phone chatting about nothing in particular. Clia had phoned earlier and told Hally that Rhys, Gregg and she were meeting up at Corrinne's and would she and Wes be coming too. However, Wes explained that his parents had to go out and he had to babysit Ellie. Hally felt a little peeved by this as it would be the first time her two friends had spent the evening with their boyfriends as a foursome. So far, they had managed to either spend time as couples or the whole six had got together. But she pushed her feelings aside and told herself she was being selfish. Just because Wes couldn't be with her didn't mean her friends couldn't enjoy a night as a foursome.

However, as much as she tried, she felt left out. What would they be doing? Would they be curled up watching television? No, more likely sitting in Corrinne's bedroom talking about all sorts of things. Things her and her two friends always talked about.

Folded into an armchair with her head buried in 'Macbeth' Hally tired to concentrate on the text. But it kept escaping her and she found herself reading the same lines over and over and not taking them in. Her parents were in the study chatting online to friends so she felt very alone. She knew her feelings were somewhat irrational, but she couldn't shake the deep fear that again invaded her; that the knot that held her, Corrinne and Clia was slipping. She could not imagine her life without that connection. Memories flooded through her. They had all been through many things together, their parents were friends, they had spent birthdays together since they were tiny. They had been on days out together, and oh so many other memories that she couldn't track them in her brain. She felt overloaded as she laid the book down and put her hands over her face rubbing to relieve the tension that had crept over her.

Hally picked up the television remote control and flipped through the menu to try and find something that she would be able to concentrate on. She had completely given up on Shakespeare, it was too complicated for her tonight as thoughts of Corrinne and Clia jabbed at her mind. She found a police drama and watched for a few minutes, soon realising she had no idea what was going on. She flipped to a movie, a simple romantic story, but that made her feel miserable. She turned to a documentary about an endangered species of animal but even though the African landscape was captivating, the narration went over her head. Nothing could take away her thoughts and she felt irritable and tense, unable to settle. Just as she thought she might as well go to bed, there was a knock on the back door. She stood up and went into the kitchen. Looking through the glass from the outside in were Corrinne and Clia. For a weird moment Hally believed she was imagining them. Then she thought somehow she had conjured them there and stood staring in disbelief. The girls looked at her mouthing silently to open the door. Hally pulled herself together and yanked open the door.

"We couldn't leave you by yourself."

Clia announced as she came in.

"But what about the boys?"

Hally asked feeling very guilty.

"We spent a bit of time with them, so they can't complain. But Hals, we never see them like, just us two and them two. It's either us three together, or us six together, or well you know when we get them by ourselves. It just didn't feel right. No we should be here. You be we be, we be you be"

Corrinne told her so sincerely, Hally felt tears bubbling up. Hally pulled her friends into a hug and though she still felt guilty was genuinely happy that her friends had come to see her.

"So were they annoyed?"

Hally asked tentatively.

"No actually. They just said it was ok. I thought Rhys was going to be mad, but he was his normal self and told us they should probably do some studying anyway, 'cos they've got some building assignment to get on with for college."

Clia told her. So feeling a lot happier, Hally and her friends moved into the lounge for their usual girlie chat.

Before Hally realised, February had ended and March had begun. Spring had really taken a hold now and flowers were peeking up everywhere. Bright yellow daffodils, colourful crocuses, pure white snow drops, a variety of pansies and tiny purple grape hyacinths all swayed in the March breeze. School mornings were less irksome as the sun was bright and the temperature mild. However school work was becoming much more difficult with various course work dates close. Wes was having to spend as much time as possible studying for his exams, working and spending time with Hally.

Because of this Hally insisted that he take two or three nights a week and just stay at home. He hadn't liked the idea, but she was determined to make sure she wasn't going to be the cause of him failing his exams again. She also hadn't broached the subject of his previous exam failure or questioned him about the girl he had lost his virginity to and he hadn't offered that information. However she resolved that those questions would one day be asked and she would get answers. Some of her reluctance to ask was down to not being sure she really wanted to know. She was worried that she would find out something that would change what she had with Wes and she wasn't sure she could risk that. However, the questions still nagged at the back of her mind and she knew that sometime soon she would have to raise them.

One Friday evening late in March, Hally stood in front of her bedroom mirror checking her makeup and outfit. Wes was taking her out that evening for a meal as a special treat because he told her he had neglected her so much lately. She had protested that he had done nothing of the sort but he insisted. So, feeling very pleased and hopeful that the night out would be full of romance; Hally had consulted with Corrinne and Clia about what she should wear. She settled on one of Corrinne's dresses which was new and which Corrinne had not worn. At first Hally refused saying Corrinne should at least wear it before she did, but her friend brushed that off with.

"No you wear it. I only bought it because mum had seen it in the shop and wanted me to have it. I mean I do like it, it's lovely, but we both know it will look better on you than me. Actually that's what went through my mind when I bought it."

So without further argument, Hally accepted the loan of the dress and now looking in the mirror was very pleased that she had.

Wes was due to pick her up at seven thirty and so Hally went downstairs just after seven to wait. Mum and dad were in the kitchen watching Nathan play in the garden through the window. They stood side by side, each holding a cup of coffee smiling together as Nathan bounced around on a space hopper. They both turned as she came in.

"You look so lovely. So grown up."

Mum said to her with a tiny catch in her voice.

"Yes you do Tink. It's hard to believe that you are still so young."

Dad said quite seriously. Hally beamed at her parents pulling a chair away from the table and sitting down.

"What's Natty up to?"

Hally enquired as mum giggled.

"He's just bounced himself off and landed on the grass."

Mum replied. Dad laughed out loud.

"Now he's stamping his foot because every time he tries to get back on, the thing springs out of his way."

Hally stood and moved next to her parents, giggling at Nathan's antics. Finally her little brother tossed aside the toy and plodded to the back door. He came in sulking and mumbling.

"Don't want that nomore. It don't like me."

"Anymore and doesn't like me."

Mum corrected.

"Doesn't like me then."

He said screwing up his face.

"Oh well, bath time then."

Dad said with a grin, knowing full well what the reaction would be.

"No…no… I'm still playing out."

Nathan rapidly replied and whipped around and trotted back to the garden, grabbing the space hopper and jumping back on making them all laugh.

"What time is Wes coming?"

Mum asked through her giggles. Hally looked up at the kitchen clock.

"Should be here soon."

She said.

"Do you want a drink while you wait?"

Dad offered.

"Mmmm…. A nice glass of red I think."

Hally replied cheekily.

"Yeah in about two and a bit years."

Dad replied just as cheekily. They laughed together and Hally said.

"Actually a cup of tea would be nice."

Dad moved across the kitchen and switched the kettle on dropping a teabag into a mug. Hally glanced up at the clock and saw it was just seven thirty and felt tiny bubbles of anticipation building inside her. She always got excited when she was seeing Wes and more so when they were going out, it made her feel grown up.

Dad placed a mug of steaming tea in front of her and turned back to the window with mum. Hally wrapped her hands around the mug feeling the warmth from the beverage. She let it cool slightly before sipping as the last thing she needed was a burnt tongue to go into a restaurant with.

"He's late."

She murmured to herself not realising she had spoken out loud.

"Only a little bit."

Dad replied.

"Oh… did I say that out loud?"

She said blushing. Dad nodded.

"It's just, well he's never late actually, not even a tiny bit."

Hally replied worriedly.

"Baby, don't worry, Wes has never yet let you down."

Dad told her, coming over and squeezing her shoulder. Hally leaned against her father's hand and sighed.

"I know, just being daft."

A half hour later Hally was worried. Again she took her phone out of her bag and checked it was switched on. Again she opened messages, but there were no new ones. Again she typed in a quick message.

wes where are you

Again she pressed send and waited but there was still no reply. Something was wrong, she knew it and her parents knew it. They had finally coaxed Nathan in and dad was up supervising his bath. Mum was now sitting at the table with Hally trying to keep her calm. She placed the landline handset in front of her daughter and quietly said.

"Phone him Hally."

Hally was twiddling her fingers.

"What if he's just not coming? What if he's broken up with me and can't face telling me?"

She was close to tears and panic was evident in her voice. Mum took her hands, stilling them and gently told her.

"Baby, he wouldn't do that. Now phone."

Mum released her hands and shaking badly Hally tried to press the buttons on the handset. It took three attempts to put in the right number and seemed forever before it connected and began to ring. On and on it went with no answer. Hally hung up and pressed the number again to be sure she had got it right. Again ring, ring over and over with never an answer. Tears readily falling Hally hung up again and laid the phone down.

"No one is there."

She sobbed dejectedly. Then it hit her with a suddenness that rocked her like an earthquake. Why wasn't there someone there? Ellie would be in bed, so either Wes or one of his parents would be at home.

"Oh my God! What if he's had an accident or something? I mean there's always someone at home 'cos of Ellie. If they're all out, something's happened."

Her voice was rising to near a scream and mum quickly stood up and put her arms around her trying to comfort as much as was possible.

"Baby, baby, sh…don't jump to conclusions. Do you know any of his parents' mobile numbers?"

Hally shook her head. She had never ever thought she would need to know. Now she realised she should have asked for them. Dad came into the kitchen with Nathan trailing behind in his pyjamas and dressing gown.

"What'smatta Hally?"

Nathan asked seeing his sister's tears. Mum didn't have the heart to correct his speech this time. Dad took Nathan and sitting down lifted him onto his lap.

"Hally's just a bit upset now Nathan ok? Do you want some milk and biscuits?"

Nathan glanced up at his dad nodding quickly. So dad stood and put his son on the chair and went to fetch a large colourful glass and filled it with milk. He came back with a plate of chocolate biscuits and placed both in front of the child, lifting him back onto his lap.

It was ten past eight and Hally and her family still sat waiting at the kitchen table. Nathan had partly grasped the gravity of the situation and sat on his father's lap munching biscuits and gulping his milk but without fidgeting or asking questions. Mum had pulled her chair as close to Hally's as she could and was quietly trying to comfort her daughter. Hally was repeatedly alternating between the landline and Wes' mobile without getting an answer from either. Finally with mascara streaks down her cheeks she dejectedly laid down both phones and sat with her head down. She had worn herself out crying.

"The girls."

She whispered. Mum looked at her.

"What about them baby?"

"I should have thought, Gregg or Rhys must have Michael's number, they work for him."

Hally grabbed her mobile and rang Clia first. It took a little while for her to answer and she was about to give up when she heard her friend's voice.

"Hi Hals…"

She got no further. Quickly and with desperation in her voice Hally cut in.

"Is Rhys with you?"

"He's on his way. Hally what's wrong?"

Clia had obviously caught the note in Hally's voice.

"I'll call you later, for now I have to ring Corrinne."

Before Clia could reply Hally hung up and pressed the speed dial for Corrinne. She answered immediately.

"Hi…"

But also got no further.

"Is Gregg with you please?"

In her own mind Hally realised the word 'please' was not just an act of politeness it was a plea.

"Yes, he's here…"

Again Hally cut across.

"Could you put him on, it's really important."

Corrinne didn't hesitate or ask any more questions. She knew Hally too well to know when she was serious. Gregg came on the phone and Hally verbally sighed.

"Oh Gregg, do you have Wes' dad's mobile number please?"

"Hold on, let me get my phone."

He replied. The few seconds of waiting felt like hours to Hally but finally Gregg was back on reading out the number.

"Thanks Gregg, look tell Corrie I'm sorry I can't talk I'll call her later and explain."

She didn't wait for a reply but hurriedly hung up and rapidly punched in the number Gregg had given her for Wes' dad. At first Hally thought he wasn't going to answer either, but after several rings Michael spoke.

"Hello."

Just one word. Hally suddenly felt very afraid but managed to speak.

"Michael it's Hally where's Wes?"

It was all she could think to ask.

"Hally, we are all at the hospital."

He said very quietly and with worry evident in his voice. Fear flooded through her and she felt the blood drain from her face. Mum grabbed her hand tightly and dad leaned forward still holding Nathan.

"Why?"

Hally said in a very tiny voice, so much so she wasn't sure Michael had even heard her.

"It's Ellie Hally, she's very poorly."

Michael told her his voice trembling with emotion. Hally couldn't react; relief washed over her like a tidal wave rapidly replaced with a sick feeling which completely enveloped her.

"Oh my God. I…can I come over please?"

Her parents sat still, frowning but not interrupting, knowing their daughter would explain when she could. There was a moments silence then Hally said so simply.

"Please Michael."

Again she waited and finally the tiniest of smiles broke through the lines of fear on her face.

"Thank you."

Was all she said and hung up. She turned to her parents, pushed back her chair and stood at the same time telling them what she knew.

"I'll drive you Hally."

Dad said passing Nathan to his wife and reaching for his keys on top of the fridge. Hally hadn't even thought about how she was getting to the hospital until dad said this. She felt disjointed, in shock, fear for the toddler passing through her in waves, but with a guilty nagging at the back of her mind. Why hadn't Wes at least texted her?

With dad at her side Hally made her way through the doors to the main reception desk at the Colingford General Hospital. A smartly dressed woman smiled at her and asked if she needed help. Hally stuttered and stumbled her words and finally dad took control and explained why they were there. The woman tapped a keyboard and then gave them directions to the paediatric department. The hospital was busy as they made their way along corridors and as they neared their destination noticed the walls were brightly decorated with posters and pictures.

The paediatric department had its own reception and again they explained to a receptionist and again waited whilst she tapped her keyboard. From there they were directed to an intensive care ward but were unable to gain entry as the door was security coded. A nurse answered the buzzer and dad again explained what they were doing there. She told them to wait. After a few minutes Michael came through the door and led them to a family room. Kate was waiting inside and stood up and gave Hally a short hug.

"What's wrong with Ellie?"

Hally asked at the same time wondering where Wes was.

"They think it might be meningitis."

Kate replied holding back her tears. Hally put a hand over her mouth and dad put an arm around her shoulder. Tentatively and trying to be sensitive too Hally quietly asked.

"Where's Wes?"

Both his parents looked at each other. Then Michael said.

"He's in with Ellie…giving us a break."

There was something in the way he spoke that gave Hally a feeling that she wasn't being told everything.

"Can I see him…and Ellie?"

She asked without any confidence in her voice at all. Again Wes' parents glanced at one another making a silent decision. Kate nodded and Michael said.

"Ok I'll take you through."

Hally sighed and dad told her he would wait for her in the family room. Michael led her towards a side room and explained how she had to wash her hands and use alcohol gel before she could go in. A stupidly unintentional thought jumped into her mind. 'I can have alcohol on my hands but I can't drink it.' She pushed it out of the way as she pushed open the door to the room.

Wes had his back to the door holding Ellie's tiny hand. The little girl had tubes coming from her nose and a bag hung from a frame nearby, a tube leading to an IV drip going into her arm. There were little patches attached to her small body sending information to a monitor that bleeped constantly and all sorts of other equipment around the room. Wes looked over his shoulder and gave a start, his face paling visibly.

"Hally…what are you doing here?"

Hally thought this was a very strange question, wasn't the answer obvious?

"Well…when you didn't come round or call or anything I got worried and well…I found out about Ellie."

She told him. He looked at her, but there was something in his look that just wasn't the Wes she knew.

"I'm sorry Hally I should have let you know."

It was said without any real conviction and Hally had the awful feeling that something was going over her head.

"It's ok Wes, you had your sister to think about."

Hally said softly hoping he would notice her concern. However Wes only glanced at her then laid his head down on the toddler's tiny hand that he was still grasping. Hally didn't get it. If Nathan was this ill she would be out of her mind too, but she didn't think she would just blank out Wes. If anything she thought she would need him there to prop her up and get her through it. She moved over to his side and placed a hand on his head, gently stroking his hair. Then in a very weak voice she said.

"Have I done something wrong Wes?"

He didn't reply at first, just a slight movement of his head indicating no. Then he looked up at her pain written across his face.

"You shouldn't be here Hally."

Hally stepped back, his words burning like fire, as she stammered.

"Wh…wh..at..why?"

Wes turned and looked up at her never letting go of Ellie's hand.

"I didn't want to have to tell you like this."

He said, his eyes glistening with unshed tears.

"Tell me what?"

Hally asked close to tears herself, fear clutching her heart like a vice. Wes looked away, brushing soft dark curls away from the tiny girl's face. The toddler lay in the middle of the bed strapped to the monitors; the only sign she was alive her rapid breathing and the bleeping machine. Hally had to ask again.

"Tell me what Wes?"

He didn't look at her so she moved to the other side of the bed where she could see his face and waited. He glanced up at her then away again, and with his eyes downcast and in a very flat voice said.

"Ellie is not my sister. She's my daughter."

Hally couldn't move. Shock flooded through her body and she felt like the world was rocking backwards and forwards. A tumultuous explosion of disbelief went through her, this was a really bad joke, but Wes wasn't looking at her. She couldn't speak, could barely breathe, her stomach rolled like she was on a roller coaster, but this was no theme park, and still Wes didn't or wouldn't look at her. She wanted to scream at him, to shout and demand to know why he was doing this to her, but she couldn't do any of that. She was in an intensive care hospital room where a little baby girl lay fighting for her life, and all the while her life had just collapsed.

Hally stumbled into the family room, dad standing immediately when he saw her chalk white face, Michael and Kate heading for the door believing something had changed in Ellie's condition. Dad took her into his arms and she folded like tissue paper on a breeze.

"Baby what's happened, is it Ellie?"

All Hally could do was shake her head no. Words were lodged in the back of her throat, her tongue felt swollen and unresponsive, she couldn't tell her father what she desperately wanted to. Dad gently forced her into a chair and poured her ice cold water from a tank near the wall. Handing her the small cup, he helped her sip the contents brushing her hair away from her face. She began to shiver uncontrollably and dad realised she was most certainly in a state of shock. He took off his coat and wrapped it around her.

"Hally, baby what's happened?"

Hally shook her head as if trying to dislodge something caught in her hair and finally managed a whisper.

"Da..da…daddy…c.c.could..y.you..t.t.take.m.me..h.h.home."

She tried standing and wobbled against her father. He held her up and gently led her towards the door. As they reached it, it opened and Michael and Kate came back in. They saw the state Hally was in and Kate opened her mouth to speak but dad shook his head.

"I don't know what's going on but I'm taking her home."

He told Wes' parents firmly and without waiting for a reply, all but carried Hally out of the hospital.

During the drive home, dad kept giving Hally curious little glances but didn't ask any questions. As he had helped her into the car she told him she wanted to explain everything but wanted to wait until they were home and mum was there too. Dad was very worried about her but agreed to her wishes and drove in silence. He had the heater on high but could see his daughter still visibly shaking. He had wanted to phone his wife and warn her but Hally wouldn't let him go until she was settled in the car and then all she wanted him to do was drive straight home.

Mum sat anxiously waiting at the kitchen table when dad and Hally came through the door. As soon as she saw her husband practically carrying their daughter she leapt up and came to Hally's side. Together, Hally's parents led her into the lounge and settled her on the sofa. Mum disappeared but returned quickly with Hally's duvet. She kneeled in front of her child and removed her shoes, then wrapped her in the duvet, dad sitting by her side hugging her closely.

"What's happened?"

Mum asked. Dad shrugged and slightly shook his head.

"We had to go to intensive care and Wes was with his little sister, so his dad took Hally through and after quite a while she came out in this state of shock. She said she wanted to tell us together."

Mum sat down on the other side of Hally and pulled her close, holding her head against her shoulder.

"Baby, do you want to tell us?"

Hally nodded into her mother's shoulder tears soaking into her mum's top. Then her voice quivering she blurted out.

"Ellie is Wes'."

Mum looked at dad and he frowned, realisation dawning on both their faces. Dad opened his mouth in a silent 'Oh!'. Mum held her daughter tightly, anger bubbling inside her but holding it in for Hally's sake.

"Hally, are you saying Ellie is Wes' daughter?"

Mum asked keeping her own feelings masked. Hally nodded without speaking.

"And you had no idea before?"

Dad asked, realising he had been completely tactless when his wife glared at him.

"Sorry Tink that was a stupid thing to say."

He quickly added before Hally could reply.

"Mum could you help me get undressed?"

Hally mumbled and completely out of context to the subject. Mum leaned forward and gave her a loving smile.

"Of course baby. And dad will make you a hot drink."

Back on the sofa wrapped up in her nightwear and duvet Hally sipped hot coffee with her parents either side of her. She had finally stopped shivering and shaking and felt a little calmer. Many things were going through her mind but the one burning question she voiced to her parents was.

"Should I have guessed?"

"I really don't see how you could have."

Mum answered her truthfully.

"It's not like you spend a lot of time round there, or even with Ellie. I mean Wes is here so often."

Dad told her trying to give her comfort. Still, her mind kept nagging that she should have seen signs. She was angry with herself for not spotting them and even more angry with Wes for keeping this enormous secret for so long.

Hally sat with her parents until nearly midnight. She had talked and talked about the times she had met Ellie, few though they were. How she called Wes Pappy Es and Michael Pappy Ikle and his mother's explanation for this. Was that a sign? She talked about the way Wes had spoken when Ellie had been sick with a tummy bug. Was that a sign? She told her parents she had believed Wes wholeheartedly when he spoke about being an only child for so long. And she told her parents how she just realised she had never ever heard Wes refer to Ellie as his sister. Should she have known then? Guessed? Tuned in? None of it was fair nor straightforward.

"How could he do this to me mum?"

Hally cried.

"I would like to know that too my angel."

Mum replied.

"So would I."

Dad added.

By the time Hally finally went to bed that night it was getting on for one in the morning. She hadn't heard from Wes at all nor his parents and felt as if she was being punished for something but had no idea what. She had sent brief messages to both Corrinne and Clia telling them she really needed them to come round early the next day. They sent messages back that they would be there as soon as they got up. This was the only consolation to what had turned out to be one of the worst days in Hally's life so far.

Hally believed she would not sleep at all and expected to be tossing and turning for the rest of the night. However, whether through complete exhaustion or just her own mind switching off, she managed to fall into a deep sleep until about six. For the first few seconds of being awake, Hally's world was as it always had been. Then reality flooded in and the memories of the previous day bombarded her with pain. She turned her head into the pillow but her sorrow went so deep that tears wouldn't come. Wes, her wonderful boyfriend that wanted to be only with her was gone from her life, at least that's how she saw the situation; she couldn't even begin to imagine how things could be as they were. He hadn't even called her, texted her, ok, Ellie was very ill, but surely he could have at least sent her a quick message saying something.

Hally dragged herself out of bed and quietly made her way downstairs. She had tried to go back to sleep but Wes' face as she had last seen him kept swimming in front of her every time she closed her eyes; so she had given up. The house was quiet as she made her way to the kitchen. She knew it wouldn't be that way for long, her parents would be up soon and so would Nathan who never seemed to sleep later than seven even at the weekend. She stood at the window waiting for the kettle to boil watching the birds pecking around the lawn. The sky was overcast and heavy looking like her heart felt. The click of the kettle switching off diverted her attention from the garden and she turned to pour water onto a teabag. Her phone which was in her dressing gown pocket chirped an incoming message making her jump. Hot water spilled onto her hand and she gave a squeal of pain. She quickly turned on the cold tap and let the water run over the angry red welt that had already appeared on the fleshy part of her hand near her thumb. The water eased the soreness a little and she left it to run as she took her phone out of her pocket with her other hand. Her heart began to race as she saw a message from Wes and quickly opened it.

i need to see you i need to explain xxx

Awkwardly and unsuccessfully Hally tried to tap a reply with one hand, so she laid her phone down and pulled her scalded hand from underneath the cold water. Almost immediately the soreness returned but she ignored it as she wrote a single word back.

when

She pressed send and waited. She heard a gently rushing noise and at first couldn't determine its origin, then she realised she had left the tap running. As she turned it off she also realised that she hadn't even asked about Ellie. Guiltily she quickly wrote another message.

how is ellie

And as she pressed send her phone beeped notifying her of an incoming message.

now

Was all the message said. Hally's breath caught in her throat. She desperately wanted to see him, but was unsure of how she would react when she did. She wasn't even sure how she felt at that moment.

"Are you going to drink that?"

Hally was so startled her phone jumped out of her hand and

for a few seconds a comic act of weird juggling went on. Luckily she was able to stop the phone falling into the sink and holding it tightly turned to her mum who had just come into the kitchen.

"Umm…drink what?"

Hally managed to mumble as her heart began to settle to its normal rhythm.

"Your tea baby."

Mum replied gently.

"Oh… I forgot…I spilt hot water on my hand and then Wes texted me."

Hally replied in a flat voice. She still wasn't quite with it.

"Oh darling let me see."

Mum said as she came over and gently took Hally's hand examining the burn.

"Mmm… doesn't look like it's going to blister. Did you run it under cold water?"

Hally nodded and looked up into her mum's eyes.

"He wants to see me now."

She stated.

"But?"

Mum replied.

"Mum, I don't know what I'm going to say to him, or even how to react when I see him."

Hally said tears beginning to flow down her cheeks. Mum pulled her into a hug and said.

"Baby, first you need to be sure that you do want to see him now. The rest you will discover when you do."

Hally clung to her mum, quietly sobbing.

"Do…you… think I should see him?"

She asked hoping her mum would be able to tell her what to do as she was so unsure.

"Well, it might be best to get it all sorted out now. You know waiting could just make it harder."

Hally nodded into her mum's shoulder still holding on tightly. There was a bang from behind and both looked up to see Nathan rubbing his elbow.

"Ouch! Who put that chair there?"

He exclaimed sulkily. Hally stood back a little ready to let her mother tend to her brother, but mum didn't let go immediately. Instead she turned her head and said to her son.

"It has always been there Nathan. You need to be a bit more careful or you're going to really hurt yourself."

Holding out his arm Nathan screwed up his face and looked at mum with wide eyes. Then in his sweetest voice he said.

"Mummy could you rub it please? It really hurts."

Hally's heart melted, her own problems pushed aside for a moment. Before mum could respond to Nathan Hally moved to her brother and knelt down.

"Come here Natty, let me rub it."

Nathan wasn't particular about whose attention he was getting so long as someone eased the bump on his elbow, so he leaned into Hally and let her look at the spot where it hurt. A small red mark had appeared that would most likely become a bruise later and Hally gently moved her thumb across it. It only took a few seconds before Nathan was happy again.

"Sbetter."

He beamed hopping onto a chair to wait for his breakfast. Hally's phone went off again and she saw another one word message.

well

Mum raised her eyebrows questioningly. Hally tapped in 'ok' and pressed send.

"I've said ok. Do you think that's right?"

Mum nodded as she placed a glass of juice in front of Nathan who took no notice of his sister's and mum's conversation. Food was the only thing on his mind.

Wes arrived in record time. Hally was still in her nightwear and both her parents were now in the kitchen. Dad wasn't too keen on Wes coming round but didn't voice his opinion too strongly. In his heart he knew Hally had to get a full explanation, but he was very angry with Wes for hurting his daughter. He felt like Wes had betrayed his entire family as they were all very fond of him. It was like a slap in the face. Whilst Hally had gone to the bathroom, mum had told her husband that she felt the same, but that they had to try and stay out of it, that Hally would let them know if she wanted them to get more involved. Reluctantly dad agreed and so he sat quietly when Wes arrived.

As usual Wes came to the back door and mum let him in. He looked embarrassed and very nervous as he said hello. Mum tried a small smile but dad just nodded without speaking. Hally gave him a pained look and indicated he follow her to the lounge. As they entered the room, Wes tried to put his arms around her but she moved away from him and sat in an armchair. Never before had they sat in the room on separate seats. Wes lowered his arms and his head and dejectedly dropped onto the sofa.

"Would you sit with me?"

He asked in a voice that trembled. Hally felt her heart pound but resolved to keep her distance. She didn't want his charm and strong loving arms to cloud what was inevitably going to be a difficult time, so she shook her head. Wes sighed deeply. Hally sat looking straight at him and was finally able to speak.

"So how is Ellie?"

Was all she could say. Wes looked up and replied, his voice still wobbly.

"She's out of danger. It wasn't meningitis, luckily, but she does have a serious virus, so they're keeping her in. Her temperature has dropped a bit but it's not back to normal yet. Mum and dad are still at the hospital."

Hally felt a degree of strength begin inside and when she spoke her voice was clear and steady.

"So, shouldn't you be there too then?"

Wes placed his hands over his face and then Hally noticed his shoulders were shaking. Then she heard him sobbing and suddenly his whole body was shaking uncontrollably. Hally couldn't leave him by himself. All the times he had held her through so many painful times, been there to comfort and protect her. Now, whatever happened in their future, she still loved him and he needed her comfort. Quietly she moved to the sofa and sat next to him, pulling him to her. He came without resistance and leaned into her, wrapping his arms tightly around her. She held him as he cried stroking his hair and letting it slide through her fingers.

Some time went by as they sat in silence, Wes crying in Hally's arms. Gradually his sobs began to subside and his shaking steadied. He clung to Hally as though he were drowning at sea and she was his life preserver as his tears eased and lessened to occasional sobs. Finally Hally shifted her weight and Wes sat up a little straighter. Hally reached for the box of tissues that was on a nearby side table and handed them to him. Wes pulled a wad from the box and held them to his red and puffy face. He tried not to look at Hally, embarrassment evident in his eyes. She saw his discomfort and spoke for the first time in what seemed like hours.

"It's ok to cry Wes."

Wes could only nod, his breath coming in odd little gasps as his body recovered from the long spell of tears.

"I'll get you some water."

She told him standing. He held her hand and shook his head so she lowered herself back to the sofa.

"It's..I'm..don't…go"

He stuttered. He pressed more tissues to his face and then took a very deep breath.

"Hally you must hate me."

He managed quite clearly. Hally shook her head but he still had his face covered and couldn't see her. So she said

"I don't hate you Wes. I'm hurt and confused and very angry and I don't know what to say, but I don't hate you."

Wes screwed the tissues into a ball in his hand and looked at her with eyes still gleaming with unshed tears.

"I so wanted to tell you. A long time ago, but I just couldn't. I just kept thinking one day soon. Stupidly imagining that you would just smile your beautiful smile and tell me it was fine, so what if I had a daughter? It wouldn't affect our relationship. God how dumb could I be? I mean of course it would be a shock no matter when I told you. But I had hoped to break it to you in a way that perhaps wouldn't freak you out and then you would get used to it."

Wes was squeezing the ball of tissues in his hand. Hally placed her own hand over his and stilled the fidgeting.

"Tell me everything now please?"

She whispered gently. Wes took another deep breath, leaned

back against the cushions and closed his eyes for a moment. Then he looked at her and began.

"I was just sixteen, so was my girlfriend. She was a bit older than me."

Wes paused, already struggling to explain. Hally shifted on the sofa.

"Look, I'm going to get us some drinks and tell my parents that we are going to need some time, ok? So you stay here (she held out her hand) and give me those tissues, and work out how you are going to tell me."

Without waiting for a reply Hally stood up and left the room. Mum and dad were still in the kitchen and looked up expectantly when she came in.

"I'm ok. I'm just getting us some coffee, I'll tell you everything later. Wes is pretty upset and we have only just got started. I think it's going to take quite a while."

Hally told them busying herself with mugs and coffee. Dad frowned.

"Huh…he's upset…"

"Colin, leave them to it."

Mum told him gently and he didn't say anymore. Hally gave her father a desperate look and seeing the strain on his daughter's face he came over and kissed her cheek.

"Ok angel. I won't say another word. We will just be here if you need us."

Hally smiled gratefully at her dad and poured hot water into the mugs, then carrying them carefully she returned to the lounge.

Wes was again leaning back against the cushions with his eyes closed. He looked worn out, the puffiness around his eyes mixed with dark circles from lack of sleep made him look ill. Hally set the mugs down and he opened his eyes and gave her a little smile. Tucking her feet under her, Hally sat next to him waiting for him to begin what she knew was going to be long story. Wes reached for his coffee but changed his mind, not wanting even the simple act of drinking to delay what he had to tell her. So instead he turned to face her and began.

"We had been going out for a long time. I was only thirteen

when we first met. She had moved and just started at my school. Like you said before, I was part of the popular crowd and this girl, Sophie, was gorgeous and slotted right in with the popular girls."

Hally felt fear grip her heart. This girl was everything she despised in a girl, someone she just knew was vain, could get any boy she wanted and would dump when she'd had enough. She hated her without even knowing her for she had captured Wes' heart, taken everything she could from him and left him. How could he ever feel like that about her? However she didn't voice any of this as he continued.

"All the way through we had an on/off relationship. She kept getting all stroppy if I even spoke to another girl yet she was ok with flirting with any and all the guys. I broke up with her a few times but she would come crying back with how sorry she was and how much she loved me. I was a sucker and head over heels and couldn't see how manipulative she was."

Hally sighed, feeling a little sorry for the young Wes. She had seen the popular girls at school do exactly the same to boys. Dana and Penny and their crowd had especially been like that in years eight and nine, now things were very different. Wes continued.

"Of course at that age we couldn't really go out. I mean we went to the cinema and cafés and hung out in the parks with our crowd. Mostly we spent time at either my house or hers. Her parents were a bit strange, they didn't have a lot to do with her but they spoilt her. She had an older brother but he was out most of the time. When they had her they were over the moon at getting a girl but seemed to just ply her with stuff and not love."

Hally gave him a scathing look.

"I'm not defending her, really, I'm just telling you what it was like."

Hally relaxed a little.

"Sorry."

She said sheepishly. Wes gave her a smile that melted her heart but didn't let him see this in her expression.

"She had new clothes all of the time, not like Corrinne does, I mean she demanded them. And she had to have matching shoes and bag with every outfit. She had really expensive makeup and used to get her nails done at a fancy nail place and her hair done at the top salon in Oxford. Honestly, I don't know why I put up with it all. I didn't have loads of money yet she would always expect me to pay when we went out. One time I bought her this perfume for her birthday, and she looked at the box and didn't even open it because it wasn't the latest celebrity perfume. That was one time I broke up with her. Then she came sobbing back saying she was so sorry and the present was lovely. I stupidly took her back, but you know, she never did open that perfume."

Wes sighed then picked up his mug of coffee, sipped it but put it down as it had gone cold.

"Do you want some fresh?"

He shook his head, not wanting anything to interrupt them

"Well when she was at my house she was all sweet and lightness. I've always had a good relationship with my parents and we can talk quite openly, but well, I was a young teenager with a big ego. I didn't want to tell my parents or let them see how she treated me. Do you understand Hally?"

She thought she could see his point. It must have been hard for a boy like him, popular with the crowd, probably the dominant one of his peers, feeling used and manipulated by his girlfriend. How could he tell his parents otherwise? So she nodded that she did understand and he carried on.

"Well they thought she was wonderful. She would come in and give my mum a hug, make dad a cup of tea and chat about all sorts. She never showed her shallowness ever, when my parents were around. I don't know if it was deliberate or whether she just enjoyed the attention she got from them, (a sad frown crossed his face and he paused) I think maybe it was deliberate, but still I stayed with her."

Wes took a deep breath and took Hally's hand raising it to his lips and kissing it lightly. She didn't resist this time.

"Go on."

She encouraged. She already had a million questions but they could wait.

"Well I suppose being with her became a habit. Some of our friends had paired up, her new best friend had got together with my closest mate, so we kind of drifted through the next couple of years. She was very forward and pushy, always going on about how sexy she looked and how so many lads gave her 'come on' looks where ever she went. I wasn't comfortable with the whole sex stuff. I mean, you know we did stuff, touching and kissing, but I wasn't ready to go the whole way. She used to take the mickey out of me, she even told her friend once that I couldn't get it up "

Wes blushed with embarrassment and humiliation and Hally felt a powerful surge of pure hatred for the girl who had stolen his heart and then destroyed it. She took both his hands and squeezed them tightly.

"Oh Wes. That's just so horrible. How could anyone do that?"

Wes gave her a loving smile and shrugged.

"Well, again stupid idiot me just let it go. But it got to me so I started getting a bit more, you know close. We got near to going all the way a few times, but it was difficult. It was always at her house and her parents were always home. Then it was my birthday, she was already sixteen. We had been out, a whole group of us. We had been to a pizza place then the park for a bit, but it was too cold to stay out for long. So me and her, we went back to her house and for once her mum and dad were out. She started snogging me as soon as we got in the door and putting her hands down my jeans. I got... well I don't have to tell you what I got...but we ended up on the lounge floor. She took off her jeans and underwear and pulled me on top of her. I didn't even get my own jeans off, she tugged them down and without even thinking it happened."

Wes took his hands out of Hally's and covered his face, tears dripping between his fingers. Hally sat motionless unable to give him comfort for she didn't know what he was crying for at that point.

"Wes...what is it?"

With his face still covered he mumbled through his sobs.

"It was awful. It was over and done with in an instant. We had barely started when I... well you know...came..."

The last word was little more than a whisper, but he carried on.

"Sophie started laughing. 'What was that?' she asked me. I couldn't look at her. but I managed to ask her what she meant. She laughed again and told me it was feeble and couldn't I have just waited a bit. I didn't know what to say. I managed to get up and pull my jeans up without having to look at her. She got dressed and stood up looking in the mirror, fluffing her hair and wiping at her smudged makeup. Without even looking at me she told me it had been a waste of time. I had been so quick that she hadn't even had time to get properly worked up herself. I tried to apologise but she put her hand up in front of me. I won't ever forget what she said then and how she said it."

Wes stopped, took his hands from his face and with tears glistening on his cheeks faced Hally and said.

"She said. 'Wesley you are such a loser.' Just like that with a look of distaste on her face, then 'You better get yourself sorted. That was the worst sex I have ever had.' I just stood there. It took a few seconds for it to sink in. When had she done it before. I somehow managed to ask that and she gave me such a contemptuous look and told me it was the times we broke up. At first that didn't register, when we broke up it was like two or three days at a time, and then it did sink in. She had said times, not just once before and my mind sort of went into turbo speed, we had broken up several times so did that mean she had been with someone else every time?"

Wes' pain and humiliation was tangible to Hally. She unfolded her feet and stood up repositioning herself on his lap. He wrapped his arms around her and held her like his life depended on it. She held his head in her hands and kissed the top of his head. Anger and hatred for Sophie filling her soul.

"You don't have to tell me anymore right now."

She whispered to him. He pulled back and looked into her face.

"Yes I do. I need you to know everything."

Hally nodded and let him continue.

"I knew then that it had to be over. All the times she had been a bitch and we had broken up I had let her come back to me. But this was too much. Not only did I realise what a really nasty person she was; but finding out that she had cheated on me many times was the limit. I mean I know we technically broke up, but to me it was still cheating. So, at first I couldn't speak. Then I got angry and told her I never wanted to see her again. I told her she was an evil bitch and that it wouldn't do her any good to come running back this time because it was over. Do you know what she did?"

Wes asked Hally indignantly. Hally shook her head and Wes continued.

"She had the absolute nerve to turn away from me and say 'Whatever'. I stormed out of her house and walked and walked until I was so cold and tired. I finally went home and when I got there my parents were waiting. Mum gave me a worried look and asked where I had been. I was confused 'cos I wasn't late in but then she told me Sophie had phoned in floods of tears. She told my parents we had a row and I had stormed out. That she didn't really know what it was about, something little that she'd said and I over-reacted to. I was actually lost for words. Mum made me a hot drink and asked me to tell her about it. Finally I knew I could talk to her about all of it, to both of them. So we sat down and I poured out everything. It was really difficult, especially about the sex stuff, but they listened without comment until I finished. They were both stunned. Sophie had duped all of us and they were hurt too. They blamed themselves for being so taken in, but I managed to convince them it wasn't their fault. They both hugged me and told me they would help me as much as possible to get through it."

Wes again took a break and again Hally asked if he wanted another drink. His voice had become husky through crying and talking and so he agreed, but told her he only wanted water. Hally went to the kitchen and found a note from mum saying they had taken Nathan to football training and were then going to the shops, and that Corrinne and Clia had come round and she had told them to call back later. Hally looked at the clock and saw it was already past nine. She hadn't realised how long she and Wes had been in the lounge and then she remembered texting the girls asking them to come round early. She went back to Wes and explained about the note and that she had to text Corrinne and Clia and let them know what was going on. Wes gave her a worried look.

"Oh not everything, not yet, just that we are talking."

He gave her a relieved look as she quickly keyed in the message and sent it each of her friends.

so sorry i know i said come early but wes came round and we really need to talk promise to tell you all later love you xxxx

She then settled herself back on his lap and after a long drink of water he carried on.

"So anyway. I kept away from Sophie. At first she tried the old 'I'm sorry, I didn't mean it' stuff, but I wasn't interested. Then she turned it around and started telling her friends I had dumped her straight after having sex with her. Of course they believed her and in a way it was true, and for a while I got a lot of flak from them. I told my close friends exactly what had happened and they were with me, even the girls I was close to, so it didn't really cause me much trouble. In some ways I was relieved it was finally properly over. It was like I could breathe again and I realised that for so long I had been under this girl's control. Anyway everything seemed to settle down, it was quite nice being single and just hanging out with my mates. Then about four months later Sophie and her parents came round my house one evening. Mum and dad didn't want to let them in; but they were all indignant and stating what they had to discuss could not be done on the doorstep. So my parents took them through to our lounge. They didn't offer seats or drinks just let them stand in the middle of the room. Mum and dad stood either side of me and dad said. 'Well?' Sophie's mum crossed her arms in front of her and lifted her shoulders as though no one had ever dared speak to her like that before. Sophie's dad puffed out his chest, pointed at me and said 'He got our little girl pregnant'"

Wes' voice shook at the memory and he drained the water from the glass. Hally felt the shock of the news as if she was actually there and she shivered in reaction to it. Wes rubbed her shoulders aware of how it all sounded to her. It took a few moments before he was able to carry on. Then with another deep breath he said.

"We just all stood there. It was like a freeze frame in drama, like someone would appear and start asking students what feelings were going through so and so's mind at that point. Mum was the first to speak and honestly, it would have been funny if it hadn't been so damn serious. She pulled herself up as tall as she could get and well you know, being so short anyway, well she lifted her chin and said straight out. 'Your so called little girl got herself pregnant. She's been at it like a rabbit with half the boys in town, so she should know how to use contraception by now.' Sophie's parents reacted like they were one person, or rather like a fish. Their mouths opened and closed exactly at the same time like they were gasping for air, but they couldn't speak. I don't think anyone had ever made a derogatory remark about their daughter."

Wes smiled a real smile for the first time since she had seen him at the hospital. It lifted her spirits too and as she looked at him imagining the scene she gave a little giggle. Wes joined in and briefly they laughed together, almost as though nothing was in between them. Then it was over and Wes got back to telling Hally about his past.

"Well they stood like that for some time and then dad piped up with 'Anyway, how does she know it's even our son's?' I hadn't thought of that, but of course after what she'd told me it wasn't exactly an unreasonable question. But it was Sophie who answered. She pressed herself close to her father and in a little girl voice said. 'Daddy, that's a lie. I only did it with him 'cos he said he'd break up with me if I didn't. Of course it is his, I had my period just before we did, you know, and since he dumped me straight after, well. And I've been too upset to even think about any other boys.' Her dad patted her arm and told her it was all ok they believed everything she said. They completely overlooked what my mum had said about the other boys. Well my mum and dad were furious; I didn't know what to say and just stood there like a plank. Her mum noticed this and pointed at me again and said. 'I see he has nothing to say for himself. So what are you going to do about this mess?' Before I even got the chance to answer mum stepped up to Sophie's mum and looked right up at her. She jabbed her finger towards Sophie's mum and in a really quiet but angry voice said. 'Don't you point at my son. He's not going to do anything until she (indicating Sophie) has had this child and we get a paternity test. Then if it is his, he will take responsibility then.' Sophie's mum was shocked into silence. I mean mum might be little but she can pack a punch without raising her voice or hand."

Again Wes smiled, love for his mother showing in the way he spoke of her. Hally was very glad that he had parents he could rely on just as she had and began to get an understanding of the situation they had all found themselves in. It didn't alleviate the hurt and anger at Wes for keeping all this from her, but she was beginning to see why he had.

"So what happened after that?"

Hally prompted. Wes gave her a little squeeze.

"Well Sophie's mum looked down at mum and haughtily announced 'If she has it'. Then she took Sophie's hand like she was a little girl and headed for the door, her dad following. Mum followed them and shut the door before any of them could say any more. Then we all sort of sat down and took deep breaths. I was in as much shock as mum and dad and for a while none of us spoke. Then dad got up and went into the kitchen. He came back with three bottles of lager, he handed one to mum and held the other out for me. He said 'I know you're not old enough, but one will be alright.' Then for a little while we just sat quietly and sipped. Of course I had to say something and the only thing that came out was I'm sorry. Mum came straight over to me and hugged me. She said 'Darling you have made a very big mistake, a stupid big mistake, but whatever happens your dad and I will support you.' Well that just made me cry and then we were both crying and hugging and then dad came over and put his arms round both of us."

Hally could imagine the scene at Wes' home. It sounded like the many times her own parents had hugged and cried with her, giving her support and comfort. She stayed silent, waiting whilst Wes took a break from telling his past and just remembering it. She didn't have to wait long before he was ready to tell her more.

"We didn't see or hear from Sophie or her family for months. There was the obvious gossip at school, some of her friends going round telling anyone who would hear that I had got her pregnant and then dumped her. I got quite a lot of stick over that. I told my close friends the truth and they sided with me, but school became really difficult. Sophie had gathered quite a large group of girlfriends and they definitely had it in for me. Sophie herself wasn't even at school, someone said her parents had taken her out and brought in a home tutor. By that, me mum and dad sort of guessed that she was carrying on with the pregnancy. Anyway, exam time came round, and things eased a bit because we were not in school all of the time. So I had a chance to get on with my revision and sit my GCSEs without being hassled so much. It was actually a relief to take the exams because I didn't have to see these girls all of the time and be subjected to their bitching."

Hally made a huffing sound and Wes looked at her.

"What?"

He asked. She gave him a little frown.

"Wes you were being bullied, why didn't you say something to your teachers?"

Wes looked at her confused.

"You know I never looked at it like that. I mean I hated the constant comments and name calling, but never considered I was being bullied by them. I just sort of tried to block it out and get on with each day."

Hally took his hands and held them. She looked deep into his eyes reading the pain he had endured and completely understanding how it had felt. Though circumstances were very different, she herself knew only too well what it was like to have to live almost day by day wishing some people would just disappear. She also knew that the type of bullying they had both suffered was the most difficult for schools to deal with. Low level but constant name calling, jeering, teasing and ridicule. Never physical, but the mental torture went deeper than any punch or slap could. Now sitting on his lap she knew that it was because of their own inner strengths and the love and support from their families, that they were both able to come through fairly unscathed, but there were still some scars.

"I know exactly what you mean."

Hally told him and for a moment there was nothing between them and they smiled at each other. Then Wes became serious again and continued.

"So, the exams were finally over and those of us hoping to go into sixth form had to spend a bit more time at school than those who didn't. Luckily for me, Sophie's gang all wanted to go to college to do hairdressing, or beauty or nails, which meant none of them would be in school anymore. Wow what a relief, at last I thought things were getting back to normal. I suppose then I didn't even think about the baby, I didn't even know when it was due. Well the holidays started and we had a week in Spain 'cos dad had a big job starting and he could only take one week off. Then when we got back, actually it was the morning after, there was a knock on the door and it was Sophie's parents. She wasn't with them, but the baby was. Mum had answered the door and when she called out to dad and me, her voice, well we thought something had happened to her. We both rushed to her and saw it was Sophie's parents. They stood there with a pram and a huge bag. Her dad just looked at us and then stated without any emotion at all. 'Well it's a girl. Here she is. All you need is in the bag. She's a week old and we haven't had her registered yet, we'll leave that to you. But you should know that in two weeks time we are emigrating to Australia, the whole family and we won't be back, nor do we want anything to do with your daughter (he looked right at me). Sophie wants to forget this whole business. In the bag is also a signed letter from our solicitor relinquishing any and all rights and responsibility to the child.' Then they just left, turned round and walked away leaving the baby asleep in her pram."

Hally was speechless. She couldn't believe how anyone, especially a mother and her parents could just walk away from a new born baby without showing the slightest sign of emotion. They had treated the child like an object, something that could just be disposed of, like an old sofa that someone was giving away. Hally could not comprehend how Wes and his parents must have felt.

"We were all flabbergasted, completely shocked at the callousness of what they had done. Mum was the first to recover and told dad to pick up the bag and got me to help lift the pram into the house. I didn't know how to react, what to say, or what to do. I didn't even know if the baby was mine. At that point there was just a tiny baby with no name and it seemed no parents. It was almost like you see on the news where a baby gets left and the mother's done a runner. But obviously this time, the father was probably present. Anyway, the baby was still asleep and looked as though she had at least been looked after. Mum went through the bag and found bottles and sterilizer, baby milk, nappies and clothes and various other bits and pieces. She also found the letter. Dad turned to me and said 'Well son, first we get a paternity test then go from there.' I still couldn't speak. Mum put her arm around me and said 'Wes this is all going to be ok. If she's yours we will work this out as a family.' So at that moment all I could do was nod and look at the tiny baby in the pram not knowing what to believe."

There was a sound from the kitchen and Hally realised that her parents were home and that she was also still wearing her nightwear. The morning had virtually passed without notice, Wes talking and her listening intently. Hally stood and went into the kitchen to see her parents leaving Wes in the lounge. Mum was putting shopping away and dad was as usual struggling to remove muddy football clothes from Nathan. Mum glanced up.

"Everything ok?"

She asked, noticing Hally still in her dressing gown. Hally nodded.

"We are still talking. It is a very long and complicated story and I will tell you everything as soon as I can."

Mum smiled and said.

"Do you want me to bring some sandwiches and drinks in a bit?"

Hally realised she hadn't eaten and thought Wes probably hadn't either.

"Thanks mum that would be great."

She gave her mum a kiss on the cheek and returned to the lounge to Wes who gave her a worried and almost frightened look.

"They hate me don't they?"

He said almost in tears again. Hally sat back on his lap and brushed his hair away from his face.

"No they don't. They were angry and concerned for me, but mum's bringing us some food and drinks in a little while. She wouldn't do that if she didn't care."

Wes leaned into her and closed his eyes resting for a while.

There was a knock on the door and mum came in with a tray, on it two mugs and a plate of chocolate biscuits.

"I'll get the sandwiches in a minute."

She said with a gentle smile. Hally and Wes both thanked her and she returned to the kitchen.

"See, she's fine."

Hally told him. He gave her a tiny smile but didn't look very reassured. So, tugging lightly at his hair she said.

"Look Wes, my parents will be ok with whatever I decide. They will be there for me and offer me advice, which I usually take because it's usually what I'm sort of thinking anyway."

Wes gave her a very anxious look.

"What do you mean whatever you decide? Are you thinking of breaking up with me?"

He was on the verge of tears and Hally realised she had said the completely wrong thing.

"Oh Wes I didn't mean it like that. I mean I have a lot to think about, you know all you're telling me."

He nodded dejectedly.

"Well I'd better tell you the rest then."

"Look, I have to go to the loo and I think I'd like to get out of my night clothes. So let's take a break, mum will bring the sandwiches in bit."

Wes looked terrified.

"You're going to leave me on my own? Won't your dad come in here and make mince meat out of me?"

Hally stifled a giggle.

"No he won't. Don't be daft. Look I'll go and tell them where I am and that you need a catnap, actually you look like you do. Then I'll be back. You know how fast I can get ready."

Reluctantly Wes let her go and she disappeared into the kitchen. He leaned back into the comfort of the sofa and closed his eyes. He was very tired and almost immediately he dropped into sleep. Hally on the other hand felt wide awake as she let the hot shower flow over her. She intended to keep her word and quickly dried off and dressed, dragging a comb hastily through her hair. She trotted downstairs and back into the lounge. Mum had already been in and left a tray of very tasty looking sandwiches. Wes was where she had left him, but was sound asleep. For a few minutes she just watched him. He looked peaceful and handsome and her heart swelled to bursting point at the love she felt for him. But she felt afraid and she trembled for nothing could ever be the same. Placing her hand on his shoulder, Hally gently shook him awake. He blinked at her, at first confused about where he was, then he sat up quickly.

"Oh. I suppose I actually did drop off."

He mumbled rubbing his face. Hally could see he was still worn out, but knew they needed to get everything out in the open now.

"Mum brought sandwiches."

She said, pointing to the second tray on the coffee table. There were also two cans of cola there too. Wes leaned forward taking a plate and a handful of sandwiches. He bit into one with relish and smiling said.

"Mmmm your mum makes really nice sandwiches."

Hally smiled wistfully. Wes had said very nearly the exact same thing just a few short weeks ago, yet now it seemed a lifetime ago when everything was perfect and she didn't know about Ellie. But that was a false perfect, she thought, and with a crushing feeling she felt tears well up in her eyes. She put her sandwich down, unable to eat anymore, the bite she had taken almost getting stuck. Wes noticed the change in her and put down his own plate.

"Hally babe, what is it?"

The tears bubbled over and flowed down her cheeks. Wes tried to put his arm around her but she put out her hand to stop him. He looked at her, grave concern etched into his face. He couldn't do anything to help her, to soothe her.

"I'm sorry. It's just…"

She sobbed. Wes reached for her again and this time she let him pull her to him sobbing into his shoulder.

"Everything… is… different now. It was all so good…I… thought…I…it was perfect…now none of it was real"

Wes held her and his own voice trembling said.

"I know Hally and I am so sorry. But please don't ever think it's not real. What we have is very real. What I feel for you will not change. I know I should have told you a long time ago, to give you the chance to decide what you wanted to do about it. Now please, let me tell you the rest and maybe then you can at least forgive me a little and see that I am still the same person."

Still sobbing, Hally nodded. Wes handed her the tissues and her plate of sandwiches. She took both and after drying her eyes, sat back and nibbled at her partly eaten sandwich. Wes swallowed and took a deep breath.

"So, mum took time off work and they paid for a paternity test, which came back confirming she was mine, so at least Sophie had told the truth about that. Together we chose her name and with some legal advice got her registered. It was very difficult for me. I was sixteen going on seventeen and was a father. Mum gave up work all together to look after Ellie full time and I felt very guilty about that. But they wanted me to carry on with my studies. But right then, school was not high on my list. The more time I spent with Ellie the more I knew I loved her. She was just a normal baby, doing all the stuff babies do, but she was mine and I adored her. I had never in my wildest dreams thought about having a baby, my life had been all about hanging out with my mates; getting good exam results and probably going on to uni. Now all that had changed. But there were problems too. Even though Sophie's friends were no longer at school they were still about. I knew a lot of people right across the city and so did my parents and even though we weren't ashamed of what had happened, some people did make our lives difficult. Then the following spring I failed my first year's exams and that's when mum and dad sat me down and suggested we think about moving away and starting fresh. It was a lot to take in. I had lived in Oxford all my life, my dad ran his business from there and we all had a large circle of friends. But they were very sure that none of it mattered. They wanted a settled life for me and Ellie and mostly they wanted me to be able to have a life with new friends who wouldn't judge me because of my past. So, they looked into moving and found this town. We visited quite a few times and checked out everything from school for me, how dad's business would work, medical facilities and pre-school and other things for Ellie. It was never our intention to make anyone believe that Ellie was my sister, nor to keep her parentage hidden. Mum and dad just didn't want to broadcast it for my sake. They wanted me to have as normal a life as possible. Of course we now realise that was going to be impossible. I had no idea that I was going to meet you and fall for you.(He blushed deeply and Hally's heart skipped a beat at his words) I had no idea that I would find such a wonderful group of friends and be so readily accepted and now I just hope I haven't ruined every…every…thing."

Wes' words trailed off into tears and his whole body began to shudder. The plate he was holding slipped off his lap onto the floor, the remains of a sandwich falling apart spilling ham and lettuce onto the carpet. Hally sat motionless for a moment, then she quietly put her own plate on the table and reached for him. He came readily into her arms clinging to her and she clung back as desperate for comfort as he was. Tears now flowed down Hally's cheeks too and for some time the only sound was Wes' deep sobbing and Hally's soft crying.

CHAPTER 16

Sweet Sixteen

Mum peeked around the lounge door and saw her daughter and Wes holding each other and crying together. Her heart went out to both of them, but especially to Hally. She wanted to go in and offer her own comfort but knew at that moment it would not be appreciated. No, Hally would come to her when she was ready so instead she soundlessly closed the door and went back to her husband in the kitchen. Nathan was playing in the garden so she was able to speak openly.

"They are both crying. Oh Colin I hope they get through this."

Colin pulled his wife onto his lap and nuzzled her neck.

"Darling we can only be there whatever happens. You know Hally, she will deal with this in her own sweet way and so far (he crossed his fingers) she has made good decisions."

May kissed him and nodded in agreement, but it didn't ease the icy grip of fear that had taken hold of her heart.

"She's so young. I mean I know she's going to be sixteen very soon, and I know I was already very in love with you at that age… but"

Colin tickled her ribs and she giggled.

"You were? I didn't think you fancied me that much."

He said with a pout.

"Oh well, you know I had to keep you on your toes."

She told him with a cheeky smile. He tickled her again and then hugged her tightly.

"May Mackeller, you…"

Together they laughed and hugged until Nathan came into the kitchen asking for a drink. As mum was pouring juice for her son dad said.

"Talking of her birthday have you had any thoughts on what we are going to do?"

"Well I was thinking about hiring the community centre and having a party, but with all this I don't know."

She replied. Nathan gulped his juice and asked innocently.

"All what?"

Dad ruffled his hair and smiled.

"Nothing for you to worry about little one."

Nathan ducked away from his father.

"I'm not little, I'm nearly nine."

He stated indignantly. Mum and dad smiled at each other and mum said reassuringly.

"I know sweetheart, it's just you will always been our little one (Nathan went to protest) as is Hally."

She told him. This seemed to satisfy him and he finished his drink and dived back outside. Mum and dad laughed happy that their youngest child's life was still so simple.

In the lounge Hally and Wes still clung to each other as their sobs began to subside. This time they shared the box of tissues dabbing at their cheeks without speaking. Wes' dropped sandwich still lay on the carpet, the edges of the bread just beginning to curl. The remaining sandwiches sat undisturbed on the tray. Neither of them spoke or moved, they just sat silently sharing their hurt and distress. Hally glanced up at Wes and saw he had done the same to her, but rapidly averted his eyes when he saw her looking. She gave the tiniest of smiles and nudged him with her knee.

"Do you want any more to eat?"

She asked tentatively. Wes looked down at the discarded sandwich.

"First I think I'd better pick that up or your mum's going to kill me. Then I think I'd better eat some more after the effort she went to making them."

Hally smiled more brightly.

"Yeah, me too."

They leaned forward at the same time to pick up the sandwich and the plate and their heads came together with a bump.

"Ouch!"

Hally exclaimed putting her hand to her head.

"Ouch too!"

Wes said but instead of rubbing his own head he reached out and gently rubbed her bump. Hally leaned toward him and he kissed her full on the lips. She responded by kissing him back and everything magically vanished in that one moment. His kiss captivated her and she knew somehow they would get through this. She wanted that more than anything; knew it wouldn't be easy, knew there would be difficult times ahead. But knew that she didn't want to lose him, that right now even with all he had told her, her life would be much better with him in it.

As the kiss ended Wes leaned back and looked at her. His eyes were bright with unshed tears, but he looked a whole lot happier. Hally felt his happiness and it spread through her giving her happiness too. Wes cupped her face in his hands and smiled at her his face lighting up when she smiled back. He lifted a few tendrils of hair from her cheek that were damp from her tears and tucked them behind her ear. It was such a small act but one that sent shivers of delight down her spine. She pressed her own hands against his and kissed the inside of one palm. Afraid to disrupt this quiet peaceful time between them but knowing he still had the final part of his story to tell Wes whispered.

"Hally, are you ready to hear the last of it?"

She wasn't ready, all she wanted was this moment to go on and on, but she knew she had to let him finish. She still held his hands against her face but nodded. So gently rubbing her cheeks with his thumbs and in a soft voice concluded his secret.

"Well it took some time to organise, especially selling the house and so by the time we were ready to move I had finished my re-sits and passed. We sat with Mr Hopkins and told him why we were moving and what my academic situation was and he was great, happy to have me if I didn't mind being a year older than the others. I was just glad to have the chance to finish my A levels. So just after Easter we moved here and I found the job at the café so I could help mum and dad with the financial side of bringing up Ellie too. Mum looked into doing some accounting work from home and it all worked out well. I didn't have to start school until

September, Ellie was happy and secure and I met you."

Wes paused and looked at Hally. He stopped rubbing her cheeks and kissed them instead, ever so lightly. Hally closed her eyes, enjoying his touch. She stayed that way letting his words wash over her. She knew she loved him and at that moment she just wanted to say it out loud, but she still didn't really know how he felt. He'd said he had fallen for her, but did that mean the same thing as being in love with her. Right then, she couldn't trust her own judgement to know and if she disclosed her love for him and he didn't feel the same, well it would destroy her. She opened her eyes and Wes carried on speaking.

"At first I was very afraid to get close, especially because you were so much younger than me. But I soon found out that I couldn't control my feelings, actually it was pretty much straight after I met you. I wanted so much for you to know about Ellie, but I thought you would run a mile. I was torn between the risk of telling you the truth and you leaving me or keeping it from you. To begin with, mum said it was best not to say anything, but she quickly realised what you meant to me and we talked loads of times about telling you. I was all geared up for it that first time you met them, then I chickened out. Mum wasn't pleased about that, but she stuck by my decision."

Wes took his hands from her face and put them on her shoulders.

"You see Hally, I knew almost from the start. I love you."

Hally's eyes popped open. At first she thought she had imagined his words having thought so hard about him saying exactly that. But the look he was giving her told her she had actually heard him say it, he loved her. A huge beaming smile spread across her face, she had to hear him say it again, just to be sure it wasn't her imagination.

"What did you say?"

She asked, her voice unsteady. Wes looked into her eyes and without hesitation said again.

"Hally I love you."

Hally wrapped her arms around his neck and held him tightly. Nervously and feeling heat rising in her face she whispered in his ear.

"I love you too Wes."

He held her, instinctively knowing she was blushing and not wanting to make it worse for her by making her look at him.

"Phew, I'm so very pleased to hear you say that babe."

He told her.

After a few minutes of just holding each other Hally sat back and looked at him. Things had changed again, now she knew for sure he loved her and she loved him, she didn't believe knowing about Ellie was going to be as big a problem as she had thought. She knew him having a child would have an effect on their relationship because now she would have to get to know Ellie in a different way. A sudden little jab of panic coursed through her, what if Ellie didn't like that she was with her father? She pushed it aside, wouldn't even contemplate a problem of such magnitude. After all, Ellie had always known who Wes was and hadn't reacted badly when Hally had been there with him. No, she wouldn't create problems where there were none.

Wes' phone chirped and Hally jumped. He grabbed it and answered it, mouthing silently one word to Hally 'Mum'. He listened intently, first a little frown creasing his brow then a wide smile breaking out on his face. Hally realised it must mean that Ellie was a lot better. She felt quite guilty now that all the time Wes had been telling her about Ellie she hadn't thought about the toddler's condition. She should have, and she should have made sure Wes had contacted his parents to check in on his daughter. She sat back feeling wretched, she had no idea about bringing a young child up and the heavy responsibility that came with it. Wes finished on the phone and turned to her, his smile disappearing when he saw her face.

"Hally what's wrong?"

"Oh Wes you must think I'm just a selfish cow."

She mumbled. He looked totally confused.

"Hally why on earth would I think that?"

"Because all day you have been here pouring out your deepest and most important secret, and not once did I tell you to phone your parents about Ellie."

She turned her head down and away from him, not able to

look in his eyes. She was sure all she would see in them would be disdain. Wes took her chin and lifted her face to his. He smiled his usual loving warm smile.

"Hally, I told my parents I was going to explain everything. That it would probably take a long time. Ellie was safe, they were with her and the doctors told me she was completely stable and in no danger. Mum only phoned me to let me know they are discharging her this afternoon so to call them before I head to the hospital in case they've already gone."

"Really?"

Hally asked in a small voice.

"Yes really."

Wes replied planting a kiss on the end of her nose. Hally giggled then said in a serious tone.

"Wes I'm ok honestly, but I think perhaps you should go to the hospital now, You know, be with her when they let her go home. She's probably quite scared even with your mum and dad there, she probably just wants her… daddy."

The last word gave her pause as she said it.

"Hally are you sure? What if you come too?"

Hally shook her head.

"No, I should stay here. I mean mum and dad are going to need to know what's been going on and I have to speak to Corrinne and Clia too, they're probably worried sick about me."

Wes looked worried himself.

"We are alright aren't we Hally?"

She smiled at him and kissed him gently on the lips.

"We are more than alright Wes. I just want you to get Ellie home and I really do need to speak to my parents and the girls. I have to tell them, we never keep things from each other."

The look Wes gave her was full of pain.

"Oh God, Wes I didn't mean it like that. I just meant we have always told each other everything and I…well…that can't change. Do you get what I'm saying?"

Wes nodded.

"It's ok Hally, I know you didn't mean it to sound the way I took it. It's my fault, I'm the one who has been keeping secrets. Yes of course you must tell them and Gregg and Rhys too, they should know as well. This has been kept quiet for far too long. I suppose when I was a young teenager it was probably the best way, but now, well I should just be proud that I have a little girl."

Hally and Wes tidied the lounge and carried a tray each through to the kitchen. Dad was in the garden with Nathan and mum was tackling a pile of ironing. She looked up as they came in but didn't ask any questions. She knew her daughter would divulge all in her own time.

"Wes is off to the hospital. Ellie is being discharged a bit later."

Hally told her mum putting down the tray and taking the other from Wes.

"Oh she's alright. That's very good news."

Mum replied with a genuine smile. Wes smiled back and at the door kissed Hally.

"Can I see you tonight?"

Hally nodded.

"Call me when you want to come over."

Mum called dad in from the garden and Nathan stomped in behind him sulkily. Dad explained that Nathan was moody because they had been playing football and now he had no one to kick the ball to. Mum took her son and lifted him into her arms. She hugged him and he tried to resist at first but she persisted, gently tickling his ribs and making him wriggle. Soon he accepted the attention, putting his little grubby hands around her face and giggling with her.

"How about we load 'Crewman's Space Adventure' into the DVD player and I make you some popcorn. We need to have a chat with Hally. Will you be a good boy and watch it quietly?"

Mum asked swaying him gently. Nathan beamed.

"Yes please."

Was his answer, so dad took him into the lounge whilst mum placed a pack of popcorn into the microwave.

Hally sat at the kitchen table with her parents, tea and biscuits in front of them. Nathan was settled in front of the television watching a very exciting space adventure film and mum had added a chocolate bar and glass of lemonade to go with his bowl of popcorn. Hally looked at her parents, both giving her concerned looks back. She smiled at them and said.

"I'm alright honestly. Wes has told me everything and yes it's a lot to take in and I'm still shaken up about it all. But well, he went through a really horrible time and so did his parents. He was actually thirteen when he first met Ellie's mother."

Dad raised his eyebrows and mum took Hally's hand and leaned towards her, her other hand wrapped around a mug of tea.

"Ok baby, we're listening. Tell us everything right from the beginning."

Mum said gently. So Hally took a sip from her tea and began to retell Wes' story.

It took a lot less time telling her parents about Ellie than it had for Wes to tell her. She told it as closely to how Wes had, not wanting to edit a great chunk of his life in any way. At first she hesitated a little, but after a few more sips of tea; the words came easily and as usual she was comfortable telling her parents even though it was a very sensitive issue. When she finished dad sat back and simply said.

"Crikey. The poor lad."

Hally felt as though an extremely heavy backpack had been lifted from her shoulders. Although she hadn't said, or shown it, she had been terrified that her father would not accept any explanation Wes gave her. Now his words reassured her that her dad would not sit in judgement of Wes and so make it difficult for them to carry on with their relationship. Mum stood and refilled the kettle. As she turned from the sink to put it back on its stand she said.

"Do you really think you can cope with this Hally?"

It was said gently and only with concern, not in a way that questioned Hally's maturity or decisions about Wes. Hally smiled sweetly to her mum.

"I think so. But then who knows? I mean I can only say that I want to try and I know it's not going to be easy. But well, if I give up on Wes now because of this I'll never know if we could make a go of it. I know I'm just coming up sixteen and that's really too young to be thinking about the future, but....(she began to blush but held on to her resolve) well I do love him…and…he told me he loves me."

Mum came over and put her hands on Hally's shoulders. Dad leaned forward and with his elbows resting on the table he linked his fingers together. He glanced up at his wife and she knew that he was thinking about her words to him, sixteen wasn't such a young age to be in love. It was just that these days, it did seem very young, teenagers had so many more opportunities for their future, so many things they could do with their lives before settling down and having a family. Yet here was their daughter, not quite sixteen but willing to stay with her boyfriend and be part of his ready made family. Hally could feel the exchange of silent words between her parents and began to worry. Were they going to try and put the breaks on between her and Wes? Dad put his clasped hands to his lips and sighed, then he looked at Hally and spoke.

"Tink, yes you are still very young, we have always tried to encourage you to make your own decisions and we think we've done a pretty good job of bringing you up because you take our advice and use it to help you."

He paused and Hally thought, here it comes. Then he carried on.

"We think you know what you want to do about this and that's fine with us. Just please try and not let it take over your life. I mean your exams are coming up and you have said you want to go on to college instead of sixth form, it would be good if you still did that. I mean whatever you choose we will be behind you…"

Dad unusually found it hard to say what was on his mind and Hally felt a little sad that she was the cause of it. Mum was still standing holding her shoulders and she leaned forward a little.

"What your dad is trying to say…"

Hally put her cheek on her mum's hand and spoke before she could finish.

"Mum, I know what dad is trying to say."

She leaned forward and put her own hands out to her dad. He covered her small ones with his large.

"Daddy, I do love Wes, but I am going to stick to my plans for when school finishes. Me and the girls were chatting about this a while ago, I think we will all go to college together; and just because I know who Ellie is now is not going to make me change my mind. I would never do anything without asking you and mum first about it, I might be nearly sixteen, but I'm not yet ready to take on the world on my own."

Dad smiled and kissed her hands softly. Mum gave her a big hug and then turned to make more hot drinks.

A little later and by herself in her room, Hally looked at her reflection in the mirror. Her hair was all over the place. She hadn't dried it after her shower and with all the holding each other and crying it had dried in all directions. She took her comb and found her hair was quite tangled in some places, so holding parts of it she gently teased out the knots until it was smooth and shiny even though some bits still stuck out. She smiled to herself laying the comb down and spoke out loud.

"Well you're not going to make that look any better unless you re-wash it."

She giggled at her reflection. Then she reached for her phone and tapped in a quick message for Corrinne and Clia.

could you come round now ive got so much to tell you

Only a minute went by before she received a message back from Corrinne telling her they would be straight over and she guessed that meant they were both together. She smiled again grateful that she had such wonderful friends.

Hally was still in her room when the girls arrived and they both came in looking very worried. Corrinne immediately pulled out of her large bag a box from the bakery which had three cream cakes in it. She then took out a bag of chocolate chip cookies and a packet of chocolate covered sweets. Hally laughed.

"What's all this for?"

"Well something is obviously going on between you and Wes so we thought treats were essential."

Corrinne stated. Hally smiled again, suddenly uncertain of how to begin. She took a deep breath and said.

" Phew…going on is an understatement. You are not going to believe what I have to tell you. In fact, I think I'd better go and get us some cola 'cos this is going to take some time."

Both Corrinne and Clia frowned but didn't ask anything as Hally trotted downstairs to get the drinks. She came back quickly and all three settled on Hally's bed, where she again relayed Wes' story.

Corrinne and Clia listened intently without speaking or asking questions. She could see the shock in their eyes, sometimes anger at the callousness of Sophie's acts and the pain they felt knowing she had been so hurt by it all. Finally, the cream cakes eaten, some of the cookies but the sweets untouched Hally finished with.

"So, that's it. Wes is a dad."

Clia as ever was the first to speak.

"So Hally do you really think everything will still be ok between you and Wes? I mean it's a lot to take on."

Hally wasn't at all cross with her friend's question. She knew Clia was only thinking about her. So she patted her hand and replied.

"Actually I really have no idea, but I really do want it to be and after he said he loves me, well I think he means it. And like I said, I don't think I have to worry about Ellie, it's not like I'm going to take him away from her."

She tried to inject as much confidence into her words as she could but the look her friends were giving her told her she hadn't been entirely successful. However, Corrinne tried to bolster her up with.

"I think it will all work out just right. You and Wes have something special, we can all see that."

Hally smiled, accepting Corrinne's words as a talisman to her future happiness.

For the rest of the afternoon the girls chatted about Wes, about Ellie and about how Corrinne and Clia were getting on with their own boyfriends. Hally had told them that Wes wanted the boys to know about Ellie and they agreed to explain it all to them. This was a relief to Hally as she didn't think she wanted to have to go through the whole tale again; even though she knew it wasn't her responsibility and Wes would willingly do it himself, she felt better that the girls would speak to Rhys and Gregg for them both.

"But that Sophie sounds like one of the plastics in Dana's old gang."

Clia said.

"Yeah, she would have fitted in very well."

Corrinne replied, but Hally frowned and shook her head.

"Actually I don't think she would."

Both Corrinne and Clia looked at her with perplexed expressions. So she carried on.

"Well Dana was the leader of the whole group and from how Wes has described Sophie she would never have been satisfied being one of Dana's minions. Sounds like she had to be the centre of attention all of the time. You know the sort, look at me, look at me (her voice high pitched and squeaky making Corrinne and Clia laugh). So no I don't think she would have fit in at all. Dana and her lot were definitely plastics, well even without Dana they still are; but this Sophie just sounds like a spoilt little cow that took everyone in."

She finished with a little shrug and Corrinne and Clia both nodded in agreement.

Mum came up and asked Corrinne and Clia if they wanted to stay for dinner and Hally was very pleased when they accepted. She very much wanted to keep her friends close to her as she didn't want to be alone with her thoughts. For even though she kept telling herself that things were going to be fine, in the back of her mind she had doubts. She doubted Wes' words of love and kept wondering if he had only said it to appease her. She didn't doubt her own feelings at all and wondered how she could handle such a big feeling, not wanting it to consume her and again wondering how a person could be so happy but sad at the same time. All of this flew through her mind at a rate she couldn't measure but could at least push into a corner whilst she had people around her to distract her.

Hally, Corrinne and Clia came downstairs and into the lounge where Nathan had a pile of toys on the floor recreating the film he had watched earlier. Hally knelt down next to him and felt so much joy from her little brother's happy play. She picked up the character toy she had given him for Christmas and Nathan turned to her.

"Oh no Hally. He's hiding in a special place on planet Zipto waiting for Gripper 'cos he's gonna stop him from taking the Zipto people's stuff."

Hally quickly apologised and replaced the toy exactly where it had been and then standing up moved over to the sofa where Corrinne and Clia already sat.

"Whoops nearly destroyed Zipto then."

Clia said to Hally with a grin. Hally raised her eyebrows to her friend and stifled a giggle. For a while the three girls partly watched television and partly watched Nathan play; reminding Hally of when Wes, Rhys and Gregg all sat on the floor playing with him.

The family sat in the kitchen with Corrinne and Clia and tucked into a delicious dinner. Hally had spent many hours cooking with mum but was still in awe of how she managed to put together meals that were always varied, healthy and tasty. As they ate they chatted about various topics, Nathan's football to which he joined in enthusiastically, and a funny incident mum and dad had encountered in the supermarket. There was no talk about Wes' daughter or the secret he had kept for so long and Hally was grateful for this.

"So Tink, what do you want to do for your birthday this year?"

Hally swallowed a piece of potato and raised her eyes to the ceiling mulling over the question. After a bit of thought she said.

"Well, I think I would like a barbeque with just family and close friends."

Mum looked at her daughter.

"You don't want a party then, it is your sixteenth?"

Before Hally replied dad chipped in with.

"Your mum thought about hiring the community centre."

Hally smiled brightly at her mother.

"That's such a lovely thing to think of, thank you, but well, I just don't really want such a big event. I mean last year was terrific here at home, but we all remember what happened there, and this year what with Gran not being here (there was a slight catch in her voice) I think it would be a lot more special with just a few of us. That way granddad will come too, he won't come to a noisy teenage party."

Mum's eyes glistened and she hastily wiped a hand across her face before anyone could notice. All but Nathan did notice but didn't comment. Instead dad covered his wife's hand with one of his and Hally's hand with his other.

"You two amaze me."

He told them emotionally, not in the least bit embarrassed that Corrinne and Clia were present. Nathan continued shovelling food into his mouth, seemingly oblivious to the subject being discussed, but surprising them all by mumbling with a mouthful of food.

"Girls."

They all laughed, mum trying to admonish Nathan for talking with his mouth full.

"So a barbeque it is then."

Dad announced and Nathan interjected with.

"Good, I love barbeques and it means I won't have to put up with loads of Hally's friends trying to make me dance."

This was said clearly and without food in his mouth, but the others still found it amusing. Corrinne ruffled his hair and he tried to duck away from her. She giggled and said.

"We can still dance at a barbeque you know?"

Nathan gave her a frown that clearly stated she had no chance and brought more laughter to the table.

Hally told mum and dad she and the girls would clear the kitchen and to go through and spend the time with Nathan. Mum kissed her on the cheek and taking a cup of tea did exactly that. As the three girls loaded the dish washer, washed up saucepans, dried and put away they chatted about Hally's upcoming birthday.

"I want your families there too."

Hally told them. Corrinne and Clia accepted with smiles.

"What about Wes' parents and Ellie?"

Clia asked tentatively. Hally stood holding a tea towel twiddling with a corner.

"Well that's one of the reasons I want my birthday at home, so they can all come too. I mean I haven't even spoken to them since I found out and have no idea what they will say. And of course Wes doesn't know yet either and I will have to talk to my parents too."

Corrinne patted her arm and said.

"Your parents will say it's a very good idea then keep a really close eye on you to make sure you don't get upset."

Hally smiled knowing her friend's words were absolutely true. Her phone chirped in her pocket and she pulled it out knowing it would be a message from Wes. She opened the message menu and quickly read what he had sent.

"He's coming round at seven."

She told the girls a little nervously.

"Do you want us to make ourselves scarce?"

Clia said. Hally shook her head.

"No, in fact what were you two planning tonight with Gregg and Rhys?"

Corrinne looked at Clia questioningly. Clia answered.

"We hadn't really planned anything. I mean together that is, Rhys said he would come round tonight but what about you Corrie?"

"Same thing."

Corrinne replied.

"So do you want to call them and ask them if they want to come here?"

Hally asked. Both gave her an inquisitive look and so she explained.

"Wes wants everyone to know about Ellie and I think it would be easier if we were all together to tell them. I know you two said you would tell them, but maybe Wes should be the one. Also (with a brighter look) we can discuss my birthday."

Her friends grinned and both took out their phones and rang their boyfriends. Hally found it amusing at the way each of her friends arranged the evening with her boyfriend. Corrinne sweetly asked Gregg if he would come round to Hally's because they were all going to be there; whereas Clia simply announced to Rhys that they were all going to be at Hally's and added importantly that he should be there too. However, each boy agreed a time to come round.

"I better text Wes and let him know."

Hally said sounding a little worried. She quickly tapped in the message to Wes and waited for his reply. It didn't take long.

ok hally that's cool i should tell the lads myself anyway and i could really do with your help doing that.

Hally sighed with relief already feeling better about the evening ahead.

Wes arrived exactly at seven and gave Hally the usual hug and kiss. Mum and dad smiled and said hello and he looked at them embarrassment all over his face. Hally, Corrinne and Clia stood side by side, Hally nervously waiting to see what her parents would say. Mum put her hand on Wes' arm and gently squeezed it.

"Wes we can't say we are not shocked by what Hally's told us, but we do understand. Your parents needed to protect you and your…daughter. So please don't be embarrassed, or nervous, we are not going to bite your head off."

Wes smiled at mum and managed a meek 'Thank you'. Dad stood up from the armchair and came over to him. He held out his hand and Wes took it.

"Things happen son, things that can't be changed or undone. I only ask that you are now always open and honest with our daughter."

Wes looked at dad and nodded.

"I hurt Hally by not doing that. I won't ever let that happen again. She means too much to me."

He said the last part blushing furiously and thankfully Nathan came bursting into the room relieving his discomfort.

"Mum mum! can I stay up a bit later tonight?"

Mum turned to her son.

"Please. Remember your manners."

She said a little sternly. Nathan screwed up his face at being reprimanded.

"Pleeease."

He said giving his mum his widest most innocent look. This inevitably achieved the intended and she bent down to her son.

"Before I agree what for?"

Nathan launched into an explanation of a programme that was coming on television that would go beyond his usual bedtime. Mum listened and then agreed he could watch it sitting on the sofa in the study because Hally and her friends would be in the lounge. Nathan didn't argue, in fact he was quite pleased because he knew both his parents would be in the study too and dad especially would most likely watch the programme with him. So he smiled, wrapped his arms around his mother's neck and gave her a kiss on the cheek.

"Come on let's get you into your pyjamas then."

She told him taking his hand and leading him from the room.

"I'll give you a hand."

Dad said following.

Rhys and Gregg arrived together with a large pack of soft drinks a bag of snacks and a new DVD. Corrinne and Clia greeted their boyfriends and the six moved into the lounge ready to settle down and watch the film. However before the two boys unpacked the goodies and the DVD, Wes told them to sit down because there was something important he had to tell them. Rhys looked worried but Gregg just looked puzzled.

"Everything's ok with work isn't it?"

Rhys asked hesitantly. Wes looked a little puzzled himself then realised Rhys thought he had something to tell him from his father.

"Hey mate; this is nothing to do with your job. My dad would tell you himself if there was anything you needed to know. No this is about me."

Rhys gave a very audible sigh of relief and Clia nudged him and smiling whispered.

"Numpty."

Rhys grinned at her and sat back to let Wes get on with his explanation.

The group were well into the pack of soft drinks by the time Wes finished, the snacks and DVD untouched. He had not gone into as much detail as he had with Hally and there were no signs of tears. Hally felt that he probably felt a lot better telling his story again after keeping it a secret for so long. Almost like lifting a huge weight from his shoulders she thought. Rhys and Gregg both sat almost stunned into silence by his tale.

"So that's all of it"

Wes said turning his palms face up and sighing.

"Wow mate, that's one heck of a big thing to keep to yourself."

Gregg announced.

"Yeah, sounds like this bird was a real bitch."

Rhys told him. Hally looked at Corrinne and Clia and together they smiled. She sensed they understood as she did, that it was very important to Wes that his friends didn't rebuke or chastise him for keeping it from them or offer any opinion about him being a father. Hally believed she was as relieved by this as Wes obviously was, from the smiles and looks he and the other two boys were giving each other. She thought this could very well bring them all closer together.

Gregg was about to unwrap the DVD when Corrinne put out a hand to stop him. He looked at her a question in his eyes and she giggled. Taking the disc from him she laid it to one side but started pulling the snacks from the bag.

"Hally wants us to talk about her birthday."

She said pulling a bag of tortilla chips open.

"So we're not going to watch the film then?"

Gregg asked whipping the packet from her. She giggled again and pulled them back out of his hand.

"Maybe, but Hally's birthday is more important."

The others laughed at this little interchange between them. Hally and Clia knowing full well that Corrinne would win the packet of tortillas from Gregg. They were right and once Corrinne had complete control of the packet she then passed it around to all of them leaving Gregg until last. He took a handful with a loud 'Humph' and they all laughed again.

"So what's happening on your birthday then?"

Wes asked, so Hally explained her idea.

They all agreed that Hally's idea of a barbeque was a very good one. Hally extended invitations to include Gregg and Rhys' families too which were met with enthusiasm. Gregg had two brothers one thirteen years old and one ten. Rhys had twin younger sisters a year younger than Nathan so with Ellie there would be a few children to run around the garden and play with. Wes had no doubts that his parents would willingly take part in Hally's birthday celebrations.

"They really want to talk to you themselves about Ellie."

He told her as they were all putting together plans and ideas for the barbeque. Hally's nerves jolted but she had expected this.

"You'll be with me though won't you?"

She asked and he told her he would be right by her side. This comforted her and she leaned into him lovingly.

"So DVD right?"

Gregg said rubbing his hands together. They all laughed and agreed it was time to settle down to the movie.

Late Sunday morning Hally sat in the kitchen with her family, including Granddad. Dad had gone round and picked him up early so they could all have breakfast together. Nathan didn't have a football match on so it looked like being a normal Sunday. The main difference being that Granddad had to be told about Wes and Ellie. Gratefully mum did the telling relieving Hally of this difficult task. Now they sat at the table, tea and biscuits in front of them. Nathan was happily playing in the garden making his toys act out some daring feats in his sand box.

"Well I'm not as shocked as you thought I would be."

Granddad stated after mum finished telling him. Hally, mum and dad looked at him in surprise.

"What do you mean dad?"

Mum asked. Granddad gave her his lovely gentle smile.

"Your mum had some inkling that the boy had some secret. Don't ask me how she knew; maybe her illness gave her some sort of sixth sense, all I know is she said to me a few times. 'Will watch out for our Hally when I'm gone. Wes is a lovely lad but he's keeping something from her.' Well I didn't want to say anything, you know in case she was wrong."

He gave a little shrug and looked at each member of his family.

"She said something like that to me too."

Hally said barely above a whisper and very close to tears. Mum covered her hand and squeezed it gently.

"It's ok baby, really. You couldn't possibly know before Wes told you."

Hally looked down at the biscuit she was holding.

"I know, but I should have taken notice of her and asked him sooner. I mean there were things I was determined to ask him about, like his exams but I kept putting it off."

Mum gave her hand a little shake.

"Hally don't put so much onto yourself. It was Wes' responsibility, and just because mum had a feeling about something doesn't mean you let her down by not acting on it."

Hally still felt wretched, and then Granddad spoke out.

"My angel, if you are going to beat yourself up about this then give me a couple of punches too because I didn't do anything about it either. I just let it go, partly because I didn't want to interfere with you and your boyfriend, and partly because I just didn't know how to go about it. I suppose I should have talked to your parents, but you were happy, I didn't want to do anything to disrupt that."

Hally stood up and moved to her Granddad's side. She put her arms around him and hugged him tightly. In her heart of hearts she knew she was being too hard on herself, but more than anything she didn't want Granddad to feel he had let her down, he was the most caring loving person in the world.

"Ok Granddad, let's have a punch up together."

He laughed as they play threw punches at each other like two very untrained boxers.

The front doorbell chimed making everyone jump a little. It was very rare that anyone used the front door as everyone they knew came round the back. Only the postman and strangers used the front. Mum got up and went to answer the door and seemed to be gone for quite a while. Just as dad was about to go and see where she had got to, she came back into the kitchen followed by Wes, his parents and Ellie. Hally looked at him in surprise.

"Mum and dad thought it would be rude to come round the back."

He stated simply and quietly. Dad stood up offering his hand to Wes' parents and introductions were made. Immediately Ellie became the centre of everyone's attention and Wes hoisted her up into his arms as she began an indecipherable gabble only he and his parents seemed to understand.

"Ok, it's in the bag."

He told her giving her a peck as Kate passed a beaker filled with juice which the toddler quickly slurped on.

"How is she?"

Mum asked concernedly. Before Wes could reply Kate interjected.

"She's alright. Her temperature has gone right back to normal considering how high it was Friday. The doctor's say it was some sort of nasty virus that travelled through her quickly. We thought it would be ok to bring her out today because we're not going anywhere else."

Mum smiled nodding, as a mother herself she fully understood.

"So, would you like some tea?"

Dad asked as the lull in conversation created a tension that was almost visible. Wes' parents smiled, relief spreading across their faces.

"Hally, why don't you take everyone through to the lounge and your dad and I will get some drinks and make sure Nathan's alright."

Hally led the way and offered seats to Michael and Kate. She switched the television off which had been playing to itself, Nathan having left it on when he decided the garden was a better place to be. Wes lowered Ellie to the floor and Kate pulled several toys from the bag she had been carrying. The toddler seemed content to plonk down, grabbing toys and discarding her beaker. Wes stayed close to Ellie. Hally felt very uncomfortable, even though Granddad was with her she desperately wished her mum and dad would hurry up. As if her thoughts had summoned them they both came in dad carrying a tray. Nathan was with them, but didn't look too pleased about it. However, he behaved well and sat on the floor near Ellie and began showing her his action toys.

"We wanted to come round and apologise to Hally."

Kate said as mum passed around tea cups. Hally looked up in surprise but didn't speak and Kate went on.

"You see, at first we thought it was best she didn't know about Ellie, well she's young and we didn't know if it would…last… between her and Wes."

She took a sip of tea obviously embarrassed by her own words.

"Then when they had been together for some time we were worried that if she knew she would break up with him."

Her face flushed a deeper red. Hally felt indignant that they had placed little trust in her but remained silent with no outward signs of her feelings.

"Then when Wes wanted us to meet Hally we wanted him to explain, but he lost his nerve and though we were not happy about it we thought we should leave him to decide when. Then it just seemed to go on and on. We had a few arguments about it (Hally glanced at Wes and he looked down) we knew Hally had a right to know. But he still kept putting it off and then when Ellie became ill, well it all had to come out then."

She stopped and finished drinking her tea. Wes looked so miserable, Hally couldn't bear to see him so down, wouldn't let him feel so bad about not telling her sooner. She sat down next to him and put her arm through his.

"Thanks Kate, but it's alright. Wes knows he should have told me sooner but he was scared how I would take it. (Wes looked at her gratefully and lovingly) But now it's out in the open and we have really talked about all of it, I don't blame him. It was really hard for him, not something you can just throw into a conversation whilst watching television."

Mum and dad looked at her with soft smiles and granddad silently mouthed 'Well done' with a smile that told her he was very proud of her. Wes took her hand and leaned towards her and kissed her cheek. His parents both relaxed, visibly dropping tense shoulders. Michael then spoke.

"Hally you are a very lovely young woman. I say that because you show a maturity most girls your age haven't got a clue about. We are truly sorry for the hurt and upset this has caused you and your family and hope we can all be good friends."

Dad who was still standing replied.

"Well you're right about Hally and I think I speak for her and the rest of our family when I say we would be glad to be friends."

Everyone smiled with obvious relief. Then mum said.

"Actually, we are planning Hally's birthday. She wants a barbeque and would like you to come, so?"

Kate looked at her husband and they both nodded and she replied.

"Thank you we'll look forward to that."

More tea was made and a fresh plate of biscuits brought through. Nathan had given up showing Ellie his toys as she had taken little interest in them, finding handing out and taking back her own toys to everyone much more fun. So he settled himself down and carried on playing by himself. Wes had whispered thanks to Hally as their parents and Granddad chatted about various things. She smiled at him feeling as though she were the elder of them. Then they chatted together quietly about nothing in particular. Mum invited Wes and his parents to Sunday dinner and when they agreed she asked Hally to help her in the kitchen. Hally immediately knew this was a ploy to get her on her own as she knew her mother was very adept at putting together a meal for unexpected guests by herself.

"What?"

She asked when she was in the kitchen. Mum grinned at her.

"Don't worry. I just wanted to tell you how proud I am of you. You not only handled that very well, you gave Wes support when he badly needed it and well, his mum was kind of passing the buck a bit too much onto him and you put a stop to that. Poor Wes, he looked terrible until you stepped in."

Hally hugged her mum.

"So what do you want me to do?"

She asked.

"Nothing, just stay a bit so it won't look obvious, but honestly baby, I have everything covered."

Hally giggled but insisted on peeling carrots, so they stood side by side preparing vegetables.

Hally thought school might be awkward after the weekend until she realised that no one knew what had happened. She met up with Corrinne and Clia as usual and as they walked the route Hally told them all about the visit from Wes' parents. With a smile she told them that Sunday dinner had gone very well with Wes commenting to Hally with a wink that she had done a good job helping her mum. He had known without being told that mum had just wanted to talk to her daughter and did not need her help at all. The girls were amused especially when she told them that Wes' dad had assumed she had made the Yorkshire puddings after misunderstanding something Granddad said, and kept complimenting her.

After registration and tutor group, Hally, Corrinne and Clia made their way to their lesson which was science. The teacher had a pile of papers on his desk and after the students settled down explained they were going to look at some sample exam papers in preparation for their upcoming GCSEs. Hally found the lesson useful but unnerving. It suddenly dawned on her that her exams were now very close, really only a few weeks away; and although they had begun revision after Christmas, then they had seemed a long way off, now they seemed extremely close.

During break with Corrinne and Clia, Hally discussed her fears with her friends. It was some comfort to her to find they were as nervous as she was. So when break finished and she and Clia headed for their Maths lesson and Corrinne to hers she was already feeling more relaxed. From then on the pattern was set and all the teachers had a similar plan, to give the students as much practice as possible.

As the weeks slipped by through April revision became almost the only thing on Hally's mind. Wes too was studying hard for his final A levels and sometimes they spent evenings studying together. Most of this time was spent in silence as each was studying something different from the other and could therefore be of no help. Whereas revising with Corrinne and Clia was entirely different and reminded Hally of the previous year when they had revised for their mocks. This year was of course far more serious, but it was still very helpful to discuss questions with her two friends.

Nights not studying, when she could spend time with Wes, Corrinne, Clia, Rhys and Gregg were few, but when they did get together they relaxed and enjoyed each other's company. Hally's parents had insisted that she take some time off as they believed too much time with her nose in a book would lead to overload and exhaustion. So she took their advice and treasured those times with her boyfriend and friends. She had a brief lull in her studies over the Easter break when mum and dad organised some fun time as a family and when she actually managed to spend some more time with Wes. However, all too soon the holiday was over and it was back to school and a timetable full of exam preparation.

Hally awoke one Saturday morning suddenly realising that her birthday was exactly one week away. She went downstairs and met mum coming out of the utility room. Mum made tea and put the mug down in front of her daughter.

"You must have been worn out. It's quite late for you."

She said. Hally looked at the clock and saw it was ten thirty, she never slept this late even at the weekends. She liked to get up and have a full day believing she was missing out on part of her life. Her dad had laughed many times and told her that in a year or two she would probably change and would stay in bed until late in the afternoon like most teenagers. Hally had huffed this off exclaiming she would never be like that. But at that moment she wondered if her dad was indeed right. Then she shook off the feeling telling herself that she was just tired from all the school work. She stood up to go back upstairs to get ready and mum said.

"Your dad and I are going to the supermarket in a while. I'm going to get some of the frozen stuff for next weekend. Is there anything special you want? I mean we are getting all the fresh meat next Saturday from the butcher it's just frozen today."

Hally thought for a moment then grinned.

"Raspberry pavlova, chocolate gateaux and chocolate fudge cake."

She said. Mum laughed.

"Already on the list."

Hally giggled as she turned towards the door.

"You know me far too well mummy."

The week flew by and before Hally knew it her birthday had arrived. She woke very early and climbing out of bed she slipped on her dressing gown and slippers and quietly moved over to the window. She pulled the cord lifting the blinds and beautiful bright early May sunshine flooded her room. She thought she heard a sound behind her and glanced over her shoulder. Of course she was alone, but as the sun bounced off the picture of the baby and the angels she felt sure she had seen an angel lean over the baby and kiss her. Hally wasn't afraid, part of her believed it was a trick of the light; but another part of her believed her Gran had been there with her in that brief moment and it gave her a warm loving secure feeling.

Looking down into the garden Hally watched birds hop about the lawn pecking at things she couldn't see. There was a pair of tiny Bluetits hanging upside down on a feeder and the bird table was busy with sparrows and starlings fighting for food. She smiled to herself finding the action in the garden very entertaining. Then something must have disturbed them because all of the birds suddenly took flight and leaning forward slightly so she could see more, Hally saw her dad removing the cover from the barbeque, a bucket of water by his side. He was getting set up for her birthday celebration.

Showered and dressed, Hally made her way downstairs and found her mum in the kitchen. She glanced at the clock and saw it was too early for her brother to be up and thought her mum was trying to get some things prepared before he arose from bed. Hally said good morning and switched the kettle on to make tea. The back door was open and mild spring air came into the kitchen. Hally could hear dad whistling, smiling because there was no real tune and thought he was just competing with the birds.

"What are you smiling at?"

Mum asked.

"Dad, I think he's trying to out whistle the birds."

She replied. Mum laughed and accepted the mug of tea Hally handed her. She then carried another mug outside for her dad. He stood scrubbing the barbeque his lips pursed an incongruous sound coming from them but stopped when she approached.

"Here you go dad."

Hally said holding out the mug. Dad took it saying thank you and stopped his task of scrubbing to sip the hot drink.

"Looks like it's going to be a perfect day."

He told his daughter. Hally looked up at the clear blue sky and agreed with her father. Silently she thought it wasn't just the weather that would make this day perfect, it would be the people who came and especially one person, Wes.

Hally had decided that she wanted to wait until everyone was there before she opened any of her presents, even from her parents. The only exception was the one from Nathan. After his breakfast he had whizzed from the kitchen like an out of control firework and returned minutes later clutching a present.

"I wrapped it all by myself."

He announced handing her a small package untidily held together with tape. Hally grinned, it was an improvement on the wrapping the previous year. She carefully tugged at the tape and pulled out a red box made of card and homemade.

"Mum showed me how to make that."

He said excitedly. Hally opened the little box and found a multi-coloured beaded bracelet.

"Do you like it?"

He asked his voice getting louder the more excited he got. Hally pulled her little brother into her arms and hugged him, unusually he didn't resist.

"Natty I love it. It's gorgeous and I'm going to wear it all of the time."

She slid the bracelet over her wrist and for a moment Nathan twiddled with it. Then he whipped out of her arms and gleefully headed off to the garden to his dad.

Once again Hally stood in front of her bedroom mirror examining the way she looked. She recalled doing the same thing the year before but then had doubted the reflection that looked back at her. So much had happened since then and though she was still surprised at her shapely figure, she was so used to it now that she took it for granted. Besides, she had Wes; in fact they had been together for almost a year now and what a year it had been. She leaned toward the mirror checking her makeup. Using her thumb she removed a tiny speck of stray eye shadow and then smoothing her dress she flipped her hair over her shoulder and spoke to her reflection.

"You look pretty good."

She giggled to herself and slipping on a pair of flat ballet shoes practically skipped from her room.

The barbeque was smoking gently dad standing over it with some of the meat already beginning to cook. Granddad stood by his side each of them holding a bottle of beer chatting whilst dad turned chicken drumsticks. Mum had covered two garden tables with paper cloths, one for drinks and the other for salads, rolls and various other tasty foods. Nathan had a handful of crisps and was running around the garden chasing butterflies. The afternoon sunshine was now very warm and without a cloud in sight promised to stay for the whole day. Hally stepped onto the deck and both her parents smiled at how beautiful their daughter looked.

Wes arrived first telling Hally that his parents were bringing Ellie in a little while. He told her that his mum had just started getting the toddler ready when she pulled the lid off her beaker and spilled juice all down her. Luckily his mum had not put her in the new outfit he had bought for the party. So he decided to walk over and leave them to come when they were ready. Hally laughed imagining the scene, but secretly pleased that he was with her alone for a short time at least.

Not long after Wes arrived Clia and Corrinne turned up with their families and then Rhys with his parents and twin sisters. Nathan was not impressed, then Gregg arrived with his family and Nathan was appeased to find a new male to play with, even though he was a bit older. Finally Kate and Michael walked through the back gate, Ellie waddling along grasping Kate's hand. She spotted Wes and slipping her fingers from Kate's bounded across the garden calling 'Pappy Es, Pappy Es'. Wes caught her just as she stumbled and lifted her into his arms where she buried her face in his shoulder, suddenly becoming shy.

"Hello Ellie."

Hally said to the little girl. Ellie looked through a mass of curls at her and gave her a cheeky smile, then without warning she launched herself out of Wes' arms towards Hally. Wes reacted quickly as did Hally and between them they prevented the child from falling, Hally catching her. Ellie thought it was a hilarious game and giggling tried it again, this time towards Wes, but this time they expected it and Hally held on. Ellie squirmed in her arms, so she relinquished her hold and handed her back to her father, where this time she stayed.

A few more family friends arrived and eventually when all of the guests were there milling and chatting with drinks in their hands mum brought out a pile of presents. She called for everyone's attention and the conversations died down and the guests moved closer to the bench where she had placed the gifts.

"First, Colin and I would like to thank you all for coming to our daughter's birthday celebration."

Dad handed the barbeque tongs to Granddad and put his hand on his wife's shoulder smiling at everyone.

"We wanted Hally to open all her gifts at once and with everyone."

Mum carried on. A little voice popped up from the front.

"She opened mine already."

Nathan announced importantly and mum smiled and nodded to him.

"Yes she did Nathan."

Then she turned to Hally and handed her a beautifully wrapped present. Hally became excited and quickly unwrapped it. Inside she found a small box with a hinged lid and lifting the lid found a gold ring with a gleaming rich emerald stone at its centre. Hally was speechless, she took it out of the box and eased it onto the third finger of her right hand, it fitted perfectly. Hally hugged both her parents tightly, then Granddad stepped forward. He lifted a present from the top of the pile and gave it to her.

"This is from me and your Gran."

He told her emotionally and Hally had to bite back tears. She didn't want to cry, not today but as she took the gift she thought it was going to be impossible not to. Gently she unwrapped the package and again found a box. It was small and made from lacquered wood with a simple picture of a lily of the valley flower on its lid. Carefully and with everyone looking on in anticipation, she lifted the lid. A gold heart shaped pendant with an emerald nestled in the centre sat on a cushion of green velvet.

"It was your Gran's. I gave it to her just after she had your mum. The heart for our love and the emerald for your mum, born in May and named May."

Hally couldn't stop the flow of tears as she wrapped her arms around Granddad. Mum put her arms around her dad too and for a moment the world shrank to just those three. Finally, Hally backed away wiping her eyes and turning back to the guests.

"I'm sorry about that."

She said meekly, trying on a tiny smile and finding it fit quite well. There were lots of murmurs and mumblings of 'That's fine' and 'It's ok' when mum said with a big sigh.

"So the rest of the presents."

Hally opened gift after gift thanking each person who had given it to her. There was a new bag from Wes' parents, perfume from Corrinne and Clia and various other gifts from the guests. After opening the last on the pile and finding a huge box of speciality chocolates from Rhys and Gregg, Wes took her arm and led her to a quiet spot in the garden.

"I wanted to give this to you myself."

He whispered, taking a small box out of his pocket. Hally lifted the lid and saw a pair of gold and emerald drop earrings that perfectly matched the ring from her parents.

"I checked with your mum and dad and these are from the same collection as your ring."

He told her. Hally pulled his head towards her and kissed him lovingly.

"I take it you're pleased with them then?"

He asked with a grin when the kiss ended.

"They are beautiful Wes. I love them and I love you."

The words came easily and boldly, all her previous bashfulness gone. Wes held her.

"And I very much love you too my Hally."

All the delicious smells of hot barbequed meat filled the air and drew the guests closer to the table where dad was laying out the cooked food. He told anyone in earshot to help themselves and seemed in his element with Granddad helping. Hally sat with Wes, Corrinne, Clia, Rhys and Gregg for most of the time, occasionally wandering about and speaking to the other guests. Kate and Michael were chatting happily to Rhys and Gregg's parents and the afternoon moved lazily into evening. Dad had placed long garden candles on sticks in the borders and mum had put small tea lights on the tables. As the sun began to drop the candles were lit and a pleasant soft light was cast across the garden. Ellie had fallen asleep on Michael's lap and the other children had quietened.

"Quite a big difference from last year isn't it?"

Clia said to Hally and the others. Hally nodded.

"Yes, and you know, I think I prefer it this way. Just family and close friends."

"Why what happened last year?"

Rhys asked. Clia went on to explain and Rhys and Gregg both looked astounded.

"That Martin Cobb was in the year above us. He was always in trouble; in fact I think he got permanently excluded when he was in year eight or nine. Something about trashing a classroom. Apparently Mr Hopkins was there, the teacher had to take the rest of class out and call for help. I think that's the only time I've ever known someone to get that violent at the school."

Rhys told them.

"Oh I remember that."

Gregg exclaimed.

"The teacher was…umm…oh yeah, Miss Blake, she was new, just qualified, art teacher. I think she's left now."

The girls nodded.

"Yeah I don't recognise the name."

Hally said and Corrinne and Clia agreed.

Gradually guests came and said thank you that they'd had a wonderful time and departed. Stars appeared almost one by one in the darkening night sky and seemed to pop up as a guest left. It was as if they were leaving the garden only to appear against the velvety background of the night to continue observing the party from above. Finally it was just Wes, Corrinne, Clia, Rhys and Gregg left. Dad had left the barbeque to cool down and had gone inside with mum, Granddad and Nathan, so the six sat, each girl snuggled close to her boyfriend chatting quietly about the day. It began to get cool so eventually they moved indoors. Nathan had been put to bed and mum, dad and Granddad were in the lounge, so the six settled in the kitchen nibbling at the food that was left over. Corrinne yawned loudly which started everyone off.

"I think I need to go home."

She said to Hally. They all agreed to call it a night and Hally and Wes walked to the back gate to see them off. Wes held Hally against him and she leaned back into him waving until her friends turned onto the street.

They made their way back through the garden to the door. Just before they reached it Wes stopped and turned Hally into his arms.

"I've waited all day to do this."

He held her tightly and kissed her deeply. Instantly fire erupted inside her and her body responded as if by itself. She pressed close to him wanting to feel much more of him. She felt she couldn't get close enough, and wriggled her hips against him. She knew what doing that would do to him and was unsurprised when it did. Wes pulled back a bit and took a deep breath, but she pulled him close again. She did not want any of this to stop. A noise from the kitchen made her look up and she saw mum moving about near the sink. Hally sighed and moved away from Wes enough to break the contact. She knew there and then in the garden, with her mum close by that it was not the right time.

"I'm sorry Wes. Mum's just by the window; I can't do this here and now."

Wes nuzzled her cheek.

"It's ok Hally, don't apologise, I know. It's just not the right time. We will both know when it is."

He kissed her gently and together they strolled back into the kitchen.

It was late by the time Hally got to bed. Mum and dad had walked back with Granddad and Wes had gone home. Now with her parents in bed she stood at her window looking down into the garden where everything was quiet and still. She had stripped off her dress and stood in her underwear, aware of how her body still throbbed and burned when she remembered Wes' touch and kiss. Yet even though she knew the garden wasn't exactly the right place to take things further, she still felt uncertain that anywhere was. Yes she wanted to with every fibre in her body when Wes got so close. Also, she felt a glowing sense of power that she could make his body react too; but in the back of her mind, even when she just wanted him to take her clothes off and touch her all over and do more, she felt trepidation and uncertainty. So did that tell her that she was still not mentally ready even though her body told her she was? Hally climbed into bed feeling a mountain of confusion in her mind. She closed her eyes and tiredness took over and that night in her dreams all her reservations were thrown to the wind and she and Wes became one.

CHAPTER 17

Prom Night

The next few weeks were completely taken up with exams and Hally had little time for anything else. If she wasn't actually sitting an exam she was cramming for the next one. The school library was often jammed with year eleven students, each one trying to fill their minds with as much information as possible to help them through the next paper. Although Wes had nowhere near the number of exams to sit as Hally, his were more difficult and had more papers per subject. Corrinne and Clia spent as much time as possible with Hally, together revising, or analysing the papers they had already sat.

"I'm sure I got that equation wrong."

Clia told the other two after a Maths paper.

"Well what did you put down?"

Corrinne questioned, knowing she would be able to tell her friend if she was correct or not.

"Oh I don't know now, it's all muddled in my mind."

She wailed.

"Clia, it's done now, we can't do anything about it, so stop worrying. I bet you got it exactly right."

Hally told her gently, but silently worrying about some of her own answers.

"Yeah, I know and to think not long now and it will all be over."

Clia said with a big sigh. The other two laughed and agreed with their friend.

"Well I can't wait. It seems like Gregg and me have hardly seen each other lately."

Corrinne stated. Hally felt the same way and was sure Clia did too.

Finally with June bringing wonderfully warm weather and light evenings Hally walked with Corrinne and Clia out of their very last exam. Wes had sat his last one the previous day and was waiting at the bench with Gregg and Rhys. Wes had talked his dad into letting them off work early to celebrate the end of exams. Squealing with relief and delight, all three girls jumped into their boyfriend's arms and were kissed and spun around. Then hand in hand they trotted through the school gates to freedom. Officially they had finished school and since all three were almost certain they were going on to College they would only have to return for the award presentation evening. Outside the gates Hally stopped and looked back. The year eleven's had been given a special leaving assembly that morning and it seemed strange to be out of school before the school day finished. Other year elevens were milling about too, drifting off in pairs or groups with celebration plans of their own, but all the other year groups were still in lessons.

"So to the Hotspot then?"

Wes interrupted her thoughts. She smiled and linked her arm through his as the six set off for the town.

The café was busy when they arrived, other students having found their way there. But a surprise awaited the three girls when they went in. A table had been reserved near the window and Wes led them over and seated them all saying he would just be a minute. He disappeared behind the counter and soon came back carrying a large chocolate cake with three sparklers sizzling on top. Hally, Corrinne and Clia all looked on wide eyed but it was obvious Rhys and Gregg were in on the surprise.

"Congratulations girls on getting through your exams."

He said to them as he placed the cake on the table.

"Absolutely."

Rhys said.

"Well done."

Gregg added. Behind Wes one of the other assistants brought over a tray of drinks, plates, forks and a knife to cut the cake.

"Thanks mate."

Wes told him and offered the knife to Hally. She took it indicating that Corrinne and Clia should hold it too, so all three girls clumsily and giggling sliced through the cake. The boys clapped, taking photos on their mobile phones; and then waited whilst the girls passed out slices of cake.

The rest of the day was spent lazily wandering around the shops and just doing nothing in particular. It was really quite hot and eventually the six gravitated towards the park where the open space was a little cooler than the town centre. Mothers sat on benches and rugs on the grass chatting whilst watching their children play. Other teenagers the same age as Hally were scattered about enjoying the end of school and students of all other ages were milling about too. Hally lay back on the grass next to Wes and closed her eyes soaking up the sunshine. She felt so relaxed almost to the point of being sleepy.

"Anyone want an ice cream?"

Gregg said and Hally opened her eyes. Wes was looking down at her, the corner of his mouth twitching slightly.

"You look like you're somewhere else."

He said smiling. Hally lifted herself onto her elbows, squinting as her eyes got used to the bright sun.

"It's such a lovely day. Thanks Gregg a strawberry cone please."

Gregg and Corrinne headed off to the small shop near the lake. Rhys was teasing Clia with a stalk of grass and she was playfully batting at his hand, pretending to be cross but giggling and really thoroughly enjoying the attention. Hally smiled to herself.

"What are you thinking about?"

Wes asked her. She looked up at him, his shadow laying over her and so blocking the sun from her eyes.

"I don't think I've ever felt happier."

She sighed. Wes leaned over her and kissed her and as usual her immediate thoughts went straight to her dream that was now recurring on a regular basis. She had spoken to Corrinne and Clia about it, both offering their views. Corrinne had simply said 'Hals you know this means you want it to happen don't you?' whereas Clia had said 'Sweetie, I think you're dreaming about it because you're not sure about the real thing.' Because of this Hally was still just as confused in her own mind. But she still thoroughly enjoyed Wes' kiss and kissed him back.

Gregg and Corrinne returned carrying ice creams and laughing about something that had happened at the shop. Handing out the confections and still chuckling they managed to tell the others what they had seen. A little girl had been given the wrong ice cream, her brother getting hers instead. Their mother had been about to swap them over when the girl too impatient to wait had tried to do it. As she leaned towards her mother and the mother leaned to her, the ice cream now beginning to melt in the heat, slipped off the cone and down the front of the mother's dress. Picturing the scene Hally and the others laughed eating their own ice creams.

They left the park around six in the evening heading for home. Hally and the girls had called their parents earlier to let them know what their plans had been for the afternoon and now the three were all going to Hally's. Wes was working that evening and Gregg and Rhys were going to get some materials with Wes' dad as he'd given them the time off earlier. Mum, dad and Nathan were all enjoying the weather in the garden when they arrived. A large jug of lemonade was on the table on the deck and dad had the barbeque going.

"Thought we would eat out here this evening."

Mum said. Hally went into the kitchen and brought out glasses and filled them with lemonade for each of them.

"So how does it feel now the exams are all over?"

Dad asked. They all three spoke at once exclaiming how wonderful it was.

"Whoa! Can't understand a single thing you're saying."

Dad said backing away as though he was afraid but laughing at the same time. Hally went to her father and standing on tip toe planted a kiss on his cheek.

"Now don't go cremating the sausages."

She giggled. Dad waved her away saying.

"Cheeky little monkey."

The girls all giggled and pulled over garden chairs to sit near mum.

"So, now we can really get down to preparing for your prom."

She said to them. They all nodded enthusiastically.

"I'm so glad the school decided to change the rules this year."
Corrinne said happily sipping lemonade.
"Oh me too. I can't imagine going without Rhys."
Clia said.
"What rules?"
Dad asked coming over with a plate of perfectly cooked sausages and putting them down on the table. Nathan, ever hungry came galloping over and mum put a sausage in a roll adding ketchup and handed it to her son.
"Well, before, the year elevens had a prom and the sixth formers had their own. And you could only take a guest from your own year group who had to go to the school. Well over the last couple of years, the numbers have gone down at each prom 'cos so many people have boyfriends and girlfriends who aren't the same age or go to our school. So this year they are combining the two proms into one and we can bring any guest. Well only if they are under twenty. So of course that means I get to go with Wes and these two get to take their guys too."
Hally told her father happily, at the same time slicing open a roll and loading it with sausage, mustard, brown sauce, ketchup and onions and taking a bite.
"Well that sounds like a good idea, so long as no one brings along one of those delinquents to ruin it for everyone."
Dad said seriously loading his own roll the same way as his daughter.
"Oh, nothing like that is going to happen. We had to give the name and address of our guest when we ordered our tickets so the school could vet everyone first. They made it clear to us all that they wouldn't accept anyone who they believed would cause trouble."
Clia told dad. He nodded approval as he took a huge bite from his hot dog, the sauces spurting from both ends and splattering his clothes. They all laughed, including mum, although she frowned saying.
"Colin Mackeller you are worse than Nathan."
Dad dabbed at his shirt with a paper napkin grinning at his wife.

"I know but you love me anyway."

As though there had been no interruption in the flow of the conversation Hally said.

"Well we did hear that Penny and a couple of her friends are not going because the school said no to the boys they wanted to bring."

"Well that's a blessing then."

Mum said. Dad had now added burgers to the plate of sausages and was putting one in a bun for Nathan who was actually waiting quite patiently, he too with sauce down his T-shirt.

"You're having some salad and rice with that darling."

Mum told him spooning some onto a plate. Nathan pressed his lips together tightly but didn't argue with his mother. Lately he had been trying the fussy with his food trick but mum was far too tough to let him wear her down. He had tried throwing the odd tantrum, folding is arms, refusing to pick up his cutlery, and clamping his mouth tightly shut when he didn't want to eat a particular food. However mum held firm and using various tactics was winning the battle. Now he took the plate and giving a sulky look slowly put tiny amounts of salad and rice in his mouth. After a while when he thought no one was looking, Hally noticed him forking larger amounts in and smiled to herself.

Later that evening when Nathan was tucked up in bed and the barbeque was cooling down, Hally sat with her parents and friends on the deck enjoying the summer evening. It was still very warm and small moths and night insects fluttered about especially close to the tea lights on the table. Mum and dad had a glass of wine each and the girls were sipping mum's lemonade, which they all preferred to the sweeter shop bought soft drinks.

"Have you two got everything for the prom?"

Mum asked Corrinne and Clia. Hally wondered why her mum was asking this because they had discussed their outfits many times with mum present.

"Yes I think so."

Said Clia.

"Mmm…me too."

Corrinne agreed. Mum nodded and then stood up.

"Won't be a minute."

She said disappearing into the house. Hally looked at her friends and shrugged. Dad smiled.

"Just wait."

He said. A couple of minutes went by then mum returned with a bag in her hand. She sat back down and took a sip of her wine prolonging the curiosity now aroused in all three girls.

"What have you got there?"

Hally asked.

"Just a little something for all of you."

Mum said lifting three identical boxes out of the bag. The girls gave her very surprised looks and dad gave them a very knowing look. Mum handed each girl a box and they looked at each other, none of them wanting to be the first to open their box. Silently they came to an agreement and almost at the same time lifted the lids. All three gasped with delight. Nestled on silk cushions each girl found a beautiful delicate tiara, each one identical, tiny bright crystals gleaming in the candlelight.

"Mum these are gorgeous."

Hally said emotionally.

"Oh thank you!"

Corrinne exclaimed. Clia sat speechless and as they looked at her they saw tears flowing down her cheeks. Mum was instantly on her feet putting her arm around her daughter's friend.

"Clia, what is it?"

Clia wiped away her tears and with a little sob said.

"Oh I just got all choked up. Stupid I know. It is beautiful, thank you so much."

Mum gave her a little hug and returned to her chair.

"You three have had a tough year. Not just school. Corrinne and Clia, you have given Hally so much support through so much and you have helped us as a family through a very difficult time. You are both like daughters to Colin and me. So well we wanted to give all three of you a little gift just to add to how special your prom night is going to be."

The girls stood up and hugged both of Hally's parents then settled back down taking the tiaras out and trying them on, exclaiming to each other how gorgeous they looked and how the boys would be stunned.

So it was with visions of sparkling jewellery, ball gowns and handsome boys that Hally went to bed. She slept deeply and dreamed of princes and princesses, dancing and glamour.

Hally woke to a tapping sound and bleary eyed tried to locate the noise. Light was coming through the blinds but glancing at her clock she saw it was only just after five. The tapping came again and a little more alert she raised herself up in bed and looked around the room. There was no obvious source of the noise and she turned her head gauging where exactly it was coming from. It seemed to be emanating from near the window. Climbing out of bed she quietly crossed the room, an idea of the source forming in her head, and not wanting to disturb it if she was right. She reached the window and without touching the blinds carefully peeked through a tiny slit. A chaffinch was perched on her window ledge pecking quite furiously at the glass for no apparent reason. Hally stood silent and motionless watching the little bird. Eventually it gave up its seemingly pointless task and flew away, so Hally raised her blind and looked out. The sun was already bright and promised to be another hot day. Now she was fully awake she had no intention of going back to bed, so very quietly she gathered her things and went to the bathroom to get showered and changed.

With her hair still wet from the shower, Hally quietly made her way downstairs. No one else was up yet and she felt as though she were completely alone. It wasn't an unpleasant feeling, she didn't feel lonely. In fact she felt great. School was over, the summer was shaping up to be a scorcher; she had weeks of not having to worry about homework, or getting up for school and well yes, the exam results were a bit of a worry, but they were ages away, and she had Wes.

In the kitchen she unlocked the back door and opened it wide letting in the early morning sun and fresh sweet air. She poured juice into a glass, found a pack of croissants and took one out, and wandered into the garden settling on a lounger on the deck nibbling at the pastry. Dad would be up in about an hour to get ready for work so she had some time to just sit and do nothing. Birds were flitting about the lawn and feeders, the starlings as usual squabbling over scraps of food. Hally watched enjoying the activity. She loved that her garden offered such a haven to all sorts of birds. Her mum had always tried to encourage as many species as possible by hanging out a variety of foods and planting various flowers and shrubs. Consequently, many types visited the garden all through the year. Hally had often asked her mum about them and now had a fair idea of which bird was which.

"Morning Tink"

A voice said behind her making her jump and the birds to fly off. She turned and saw her dad standing near the door a mug in his hand.

"Oh you made me jump."

She said to him and he smiled.

"You're up very early."

He stated. Hally nodded and relayed the tale of the tapping chaffinch.

"Yes lots of birds do that. They see their reflection in the window and think it's another bird, a rival. They think they are attacking it."

Dad imparted to her.

"I was wondering what it was doing. Now I know, thanks dad."

He came over and gave her a kiss on the top of her head.

"Your welcome. Now I suppose I'd better get some breakfast and get sorted for work. Your mum will be down in a minute."

He turned leaving her to continue watching the birds. Before long they began to appear back on the lawn and feeders.

About mid morning Wes texted her saying he had been asked to work because someone had called in sick. She was a little disappointed but knew he tried to get extra hours when he could so he could treat her and especially his daughter. So she texted him back saying it was fine. Corrinne and Clia were coming round later anyway, and then they were going into town, so she would probably see him as they were most likely to go to the Hotspot. Mum had gone round to Granddad's after dropping Nathan at school so Hally had the house to herself. She thought she would help her mum out, so she ran the vacuum cleaner around the house and dusted too. Her mum never asked her to help with the household chores, but over the years had let her do little things when she wanted to, so now Hally often offered help.

Corrinne and Clia turned up at about eleven. None wanted to linger so Hally locked up and they all headed straight for town. It was something else that was new and exciting, to be going to the shops on a school day. It was different to going at the weekend or during the holidays and they all felt very grown up and independent. They saw adults they recognised without children in tow and expressed to each other how different and relaxed they looked shopping alone. The coffee shops were different too, the clientele made up of business people taking a break, small intimate groups of grown ups chatting and relaxing and single shoppers resting, with bags leaning nearby. The girls thought it was like a different world, and one which they could share for a short time, at least until the school holidays started.

The three headed for Chandlers deciding that they all needed new makeup especially for the prom. Inside the shop they went down an aisle to the stand that held their favourite brand. For some time they examined testers, checking out eyeshadow, nail polish, eyeliner and foundation. There was a box of tissues on the stand to wipe away the makeup they tried and discarded. Finally Hally held out a trio of cream eyeshadow to Corrinne and Clia. It was a selection of glittering shades of blue.

"What do you think?"

She asked her friends. They both examined her choice, and then Corrinne said.

"That's perfect Hals. Those colours will go great with your blue eyes. I think I'm going for this one."

She held up a similar trio but in shades of green. Clia sighed.

"Can't decide between these two."

She held up a purple set and a silver one.

"The purple."

Corrinne and Hally said together and they all laughed. They examined lipstick shades and settled on one each, then Hally said.

"I don't think I'm going to bother with foundation. This weather has given me such a great tan already I think that will be enough."

"Yeah, probably a waste of money, all it will do is make your face look a different colour than the rest of you."

Clia said. They all giggled.

"What like Pamela Sedgeley? Her makeup makes her look orange."

Corrinne said. They giggled some more and Hally added.

"Yeah but what makes it worse is the line around her jaw line. She only puts it on her face and never blends in it."

"Like an explosion in a juice factory."

Clia said making them all laugh even more.

"Poor thing."

Said Hally whilst still laughing.

"I bet no one has ever shown her how to put it on properly."

Their laughter began to subside as they headed for the counter to pay for their purchases.

After visiting a few more shops and finding accessories they couldn't do without for the prom, they headed for the Hotspot. It wasn't as busy as usual and the girls guessed this was because it was a school day and was mostly populated by students. They found a table easily and Hally went to the counter to get some drinks. Wes was not behind the counter and Hally was disappointed.

"Where's Wes?"

She casually asked the assistant who served her.

"Oh he's just gone to the bank to get some change. He'll be back in a bit."

Hally was relieved, not sure what she had felt not seeing him there. She took the drinks back to the table and the girls asked the same question. Sitting down she told them where Wes had gone, then with her eyes downcast went on to tell them how her tummy had tumbled when she saw he wasn't there.

"It wasn't like just a disappointed feeling. It was…oh this is going to sound awful…it was suspicion. He told me he was working and when he wasn't here I wondered if he told me the truth."

She felt very sad at that moment. Clia covered her hand briefly.

"Hals, you know he dotes on you. But there are bound to be times when you feel a bit mistrusting. I mean, he didn't exactly lie about Ellie but he didn't come clean either, not 'til he had to.

Don't get me wrong, I adore Wes, he's lovely and I don't think he would do anything underhand, but well it's only natural to get suspicious sometimes."

Hally sipped her cola and looked at her friends.

"Do either of you two ever feel like that?"

Corrinne mulled over her answer, but Clia gave hers very quickly.

"Anytime Rhys doesn't text when he says he will, or come round on time I think that's it, he's finished with me. Then of course, he turns up with an explanation and I know I've been daft. I don't say anything to him about how scared I get 'cos I don't want him to think I'm possessive and frighten him off."

She finished with her lips pressed together and a little shrug.

"Blimey Clia, I had no idea you were so insecure. Did you know this Corry?"

Corrinne shook her head.

"No, I didn't have a clue. You shouldn't have kept that to yourself Clia."

Clia gave a little smile and said.

"I know, but it sounds so stupid when I say it out loud."

Hally gave her arm a little shake.

"You are always telling me not to bottle stuff up you dipstick. Anyway Corry, you didn't answer."

Clia turned towards Corrinne her head slightly to one side waiting for the question to be answered.

"Well Gregg never makes me feel insecure, if anything it's the other way round. You know, he often says he can't believe his luck going out with me."

Hally and Clia smiled brightly at their friend. They were both very happy that Corrinne had someone who loved her for herself. A previous boyfriend and a very short relationship; had made it clear that he only wanted her to go out with him so that she would do his homework for him and get him good grades. Another thought she was very wealthy because she always had the latest fashions and gadgets. He didn't even get to take her out, so for Gregg to feel like he did was very good news for Corrinne.

The door to the café opened and Hally looked around a smile

breaking out as she saw Wes coming through. He saw her and waved with one hand, the other holding a cloth bag that looked quite heavy. He moved behind the counter and went out the back and on returning came over to their table. He leaned down and gave Hally a peck on the cheek saying hello to Corrinne and Clia. Hally pressed her face against his cheek for a moment feeling very guilty about her suspicious mind.

"You ok?"

Wes asked. He always seemed to have the knack of knowing when she had something on her mind.

"I'm fine. Just missed seeing you when we came in."

She said it a little over brightly and Wes gave her a tiny frown before replying with.

"Ok. I have to get back to work but I'll see you tonight."

She smiled a normal smile and kissed him, and then he made his way back to the counter.

After the Hotspot the girls strolled around a few more shops mostly window shopping. Hally spotted a cute apron with 'You don't cook You create' printed on it and couldn't resist buying it for her mum. She didn't often buy presents for her family except the usual celebrations but thought this would please mum. The afternoon was very hot so the three casually made their way home arriving before the school day finished. Although it hadn't been spoken it was important that they did this, giving them more of a sense of no longer being school girls, but young adults.

Mum was in the garden having a cold drink and a few moments to herself before heading off to pick Nathan up. Her face lit up with delight when Hally gave her the apron and went to stand up to get the girls drinks. Hally stopped her insisting she stay on her sun lounger and 'Catch some rays' whilst she could. Instead Hally fetched cold drinks from the fridge and found Corrinne and Clia already stretched out in loungers one opened and ready for her. Mum asked how their shopping had gone and lazily the girls showed her what they had bought. A short time later, mum reluctantly pulled herself up and donning flip flops headed off to collect Nathan from school.

Wes came round just after six and found Hally still relaxing in the garden. Mum had laid out a buffet dinner of cold meats and salads and as usual there was plenty so Hally handed him a plate and he loaded it with food.

"Haven't you been home?"

She asked watching him tuck in. Wes swallowed a mouthful of chicken and lowered his fork.

"Only for about an hour. I went to say hi and then came straight over."

He told her.

"What about Ellie?"

She said it as casually as she could, still finding it difficult.

"Happily playing in her paddling pool. Luckily I was still in my work gear 'cos she had great fun soaking me to the skin. Most of the hour I spent playing with her, then I got changed and came over. She'll be going to bed soon."

Hally watched his face and as always noticed the change in expression whenever he spoke about his daughter.

"So what was up with you in the café?"

He took her completely by surprise and she felt herself begin to blush as she tried to come up with an answer.

"What?…oh…umm…nothing."

She stammered. Wes put his plate down and leaned towards her raising his eyebrows.

"Now come on Hally. I can tell you know."

She sighed deeply and looked away. When she glanced back he was still looking at her expectantly. So she took a deep breath.

"I don't know, honestly. When you weren't there I…"

She couldn't finish. She felt embarrassed and guilty. Wes seemed to click on to what she was trying to say.

"You weren't sure if I had told you the truth."

He said it as a statement not a question and his tone was filled with disappointment and not anger. Hally felt terrible, she would have preferred him to yell at her. She couldn't look at him, he took her chin and lifted it.

"Believe me Hally, I know I didn't tell you about Ellie but I have never lied to you about anything. We have been together for almost a year now and in all that time I have never wanted to tell you a lie."

This made Hally feel even worse and she felt tears threaten. Wes saw her distress and pulled her to him. Mumbling into his shoulder she said.

"I didn't think you were lying, not really, it was just a little feeling that I can't really explain."

She managed to look up at him.

"It's like I still can't believe you are with me. Clia said she gets like that about Rhys."

Wes laughed and Hally thought he was laughing at her. She frowned and tried to pull out of his arms but he held on.

"Hey, I'm not laughing at you. It's Rhys, he's always worrying that Clia is going to break up with him, and Gregg, he's even worse."

Hally looked at him wide eyed.

"What about you?"

Wes looked at her lovingly.

"I try not to think about you breaking up with me. I feel lucky every day that you are my girlfriend but sometimes I get scared, I think as you get older you will start to go off me. Or when you go to college you will meet so many other guys that one might take your fancy."

It was Hally's turn to take his chin and turn it to her. She gave him a little kiss on the lips and said.

"What are we like? All of us seem to get insecure at times don't we. Maybe that's part of having a relationship."

Wes smiled then picked up his plate and once again tucked into his food.

Later that evening after Wes had gone home, Hally sat with mum and dad on the deck enjoying the summer evening. It was still very hot and none of them wanted to go inside let alone go to bed. Hally had thought a lot about her conversations with Corrinne and Clia that afternoon and then with Wes that evening. She looked at her parents and decided to ask how they felt about insecurities. Mum glanced at her as though expecting her daughter to ask something.

"Mum."

"What's on your mind angel?"

Mum asked. Hally was taken by surprise a little, how did her mother always know something was bothering her.

"Nothing really. Well, when you and dad were going out, did you ever get scared that one of you would break up with the other?"

Her parents looked at each other and grinned. It was dad who answered.

"Me, I used to get all nervous when I saw her, for ages after we started going out, and thought your mum would think I was a right wimp and would want a bloke who was all tough."

Mum giggled and took her husband's hand.

"I didn't know this for ages though. When he finally told me, about nine months after we starting seeing each other I was quite surprised. I'd only had one other boyfriend and that only lasted three months. Like you I was only fifteen when I started going out with your dad. So when I got your dad I was just over the moon, I wasn't going to let him go."

Hally felt relieved that it was not just her generation that found relationships difficult.

"Tink, it's normal and part of getting to know someone to feel a bit insecure at times. I think it would be arrogant to think you could take for granted another person's feelings. So long as you don't let any insecurities get too intense and spoil what you have."

Dad told her gently. She looked at her parents and then asked.

"So when do you stop feeling like that?"

Mum answered this time.

"Angel, there's no set time so I can't answer that. I suppose time is the only real answer and how a relationship develops. Honesty and communication are probably the key though."

Hally nodded understanding what her mum was saying and knowing in her heart of hearts that she and Wes could be together for ever like her parents. It was a thought that brought warmth and comfort to her whole being.

The run up to the prom came with heavy rain. The temperature was still high which made the days muggy and storms impending. On the morning the day before the prom, the storm finally arrived, fierce, furious and full of power that threatened to shake the world apart. Hally sat looking through the window watching the rain pour onto the garden waiting for Corrinne and Clia. Today they were going to try on their makeup and experiment with hair styles. The boys had been barred from the house for the whole day and evening so their girlfriends could surprise them the next day.

Whilst she was waiting Hally went into a little daydream. Instead of trying on makeup and hairdos for the prom she and the girls were preparing for her wedding. It was not in a prom dress she would surprise Wes with, but as a bride in a beautiful floating gown of ivory silk and layers of net and lace. He would be nervously getting his own suit ready with his best men, Gregg and Rhys and Corrinne and Clia would be checking last minute details on their own bridesmaid dresses. A loud rumble of thunder and a quick succession of lightening flashes brought her out of the daydream at the same time the gate opened and Corrinne and Clia came trotting to the door.

"Phew, that is some storm out there."

Clia exclaimed shaking rain drops from her jacket and stepping out of her sandals.

"I didn't notice."

Hally replied. Corrinne looked at her strangely but only said.

"Where shall I put my umbrolley?"

At first Hally didn't react then she realised what her friend had said.

"Umbrolley?"

She asked with a grin, Clia looking amused too. Corrinne replied in a very serious tone.

"Mmm, my umbrolley."

Both girls looked at her as though she had gone a little crazy. She looked at them as though they should know exactly what she meant and turning her eyes upward said.

"Well, it's such a mini one you can't really call it an umbrella so it's my little umbrolley."

Hally and Clia burst into giggles.

"What?"

Corrinne asked innocently but with a smile twitching at the corner of her mouth.

"Well just put your…umbrolley in the sink."

Hally told her.

With the storm still raging outside the girls sat in the lounge with all of their makeup and accessories laid out on the coffee table. Mum had taken Nathan to the swimming pool as he had a day off school for a teacher training day; so he couldn't get in their way and promised to keep him occupied when they got back. They all sat on the floor cross legged holding their hair this way and that to see which style suited best.

"So how come you didn't notice the storm that was right over your head Hally?"

Corrinne asked. Hally grinned at her friends and went on to tell them about her daydream. For a while after, they all three indulged her fantasy, each adding to it until the imaginary wedding was as big as a celebrity's nuptials and the honeymoon was on a Caribbean island. This led to planning Corrinne and Clia's weddings to Gregg and Rhys and by the time they finished all three girls were having fairytale weddings with definite happy ever afters. Finally they got back to the task in hand. That of finalising the plans for the prom the next day.

Saturday morning arrived dry and with blazing sunshine, the storm pounding through the night and eventually dying down at about two in the morning. Hally climbed out of bed feeling fresh and excited. She had managed to sleep through most of the storm and so wasn't at all tired. She showered and made her way downstairs to find mum already making tea and toast in the kitchen,

"Granddad is coming round this morning. Your dad and him are going to take Nathan out for a while so I can get a few things sorted around the house."

Mum had already arranged with Wes, Corrinne, Clia, Rhys and Gregg's parents to all come round and have photographs and champagne and so see them all off in the car for the prom. Hally was really looking forward to this, it made the event even more special and she was grateful to her mum for organising it.

Corrinne and Clia were dropped off by Clia's brother Don at eleven. The girls came in carrying bags and boxes and Don followed holding long zippered dress protectors. Mum took them from him and hung them next to Hally's. They all thanked Don, Clia standing on tip toes to peck her brother on the cheek.

"See you later sis."

He told her.

"Are you coming round here too?"

She asked excitedly.

"Yep and I'm bringing Tillie with me."

Clia's eyebrows went through the roof.

"When did that happen?"

She asked. Don grinned widely.

"Last week."

"About time too."

She told her brother as though she was the elder sibling. Still smiling Don gave a little wave and headed out of the door. Before Hally or Corrinne could ask Clia announced.

"You remember the girl I called when we were trying to find out who Wes was? Well that was Tillie. At long last my big brother has finally seen sense and got together with her."

Mum prepared sandwiches and salad for the girls at lunchtime and laid it out on the deck. Dad and Granddad were back with Nathan and dad had given him strict instructions to stay out of the lounge. Nathan sulkily agreed even though everyone, him included, knew he would be far happier out in the garden anyway. Nibbling on a sandwich Hally examined the polish on her nails.

"Do you think this colour is right?"

She asked. Corrinne and Clia examined the colour and both agreed it was perfect and would contrast beautifully with her dress. Mum, dad and Granddad joined them, mum bringing another tray of sandwiches and calling Nathan over for food too.

Corrinne and Clia's parents arrived late afternoon and the three mothers discussed the most practical way for the three girls to get ready. It was decided that Hally's mum would help the girls dress because of lack of room, then the other two could come up and see their daughter's and help with finishing touches. So later in the day mum took Hally, Corrinne and Clia up to her bedroom to finish getting ready. She told the girls Hally's room was too small and because she had an en-suite bathroom too, it would be much easier to check makeup and hair. None of the girls complained.

With mum's help they put on hold up stockings, shoes and finally the dresses were removed from their covers. Hally and mum held Corrinne's dress high and gently lowered it over her head and raised arms. It was emerald in colour, strapless and made from crushed taffeta. The bodice was gathered and beaded and the full long skirt looped and overlaid. Mum carefully zipped the dress up and Corrinne examined her reflection in mum's full length mirror.

"You look stunning."

Mum said. Next it was Clia's turn and again Hally and her mum held the dress Clia had chosen. Her dress was lilac organza with a gathered crossover bodice, drop waist and full length pickup skirt. When she was zipped in and the dress smoothed down, Clia gave a little twirl in front of the mirror. Smiling mum said to her.

"You look stunning as well. Now Hally your turn."

Corrinne helped mum with Hally's dress. Hally stood still her arms raised anticipation bubbling inside. She had never worn a ball gown before and she was very excited. The dress was lowered over her head, smoothed and zipped. Hally stood looking down at herself. The dress was light blue and made from satin and tulle. The bodice was beaded and low cut and it had a satin cincher waist with a full length ball skirt. She swung the skirt from side to side feeling like a princess about to meet her prince in a fairytale. Mum brushed at a few tears that had escaped her eyes and took her daughter's hand.

"You look beautiful my angel."

Hally bit back her own tears, not wanting to spoil her flawless makeup and gave her mum a little smile.

"Thank you."

She whispered.

Mum went out of the room and downstairs to fetch Corrinne and Clia's mums. The girls stood checking their reflections, making sure no stray hairs had escaped and were out of place and that their makeup hadn't run in the heat. Mum had opened the windows as wide as they could go but there wasn't much breeze and Hally was very glad they were in mum's room because they would have been sweating profusely in hers. Mum came back with the other two mothers and Hally and her own mum stepped back so they could fuss over their daughters. Finally each mother placed a tiara on her daughter's head and announced they were definitely ready. As they made their way out of the room Hally turned to her mum holding a finger up.

"Just one moment."

She said. Mum looked at her curiously.

"I just want to go into my room for a moment."

Mum nodded and said.

"Ok, we'll wait here, don't be long."

Hally swirled around and into her own room closing the door. She walked over to the picture on the wall and gave a little turn swishing the skirt of her dress. Looking up at the angels she whispered.

"What do you think Gran? Will I do?"

She smiled to herself as though acknowledging an answer and then left the room.

The mums led the way downstairs, the girls following careful not to tread on the hem of the girl in front. The rest of the families were still in the garden dad handing out drinks as the perfect host. As Hally stepped onto the deck, both dad and Granddad stopped talking and looked at her. They both came over and showered her with compliments. Corrinne's father took her hand and told her she was very beautiful. Clia's dad, her brother Don and Tillie crowded round her lavishing her with compliments. Hally's dad then went and brought cold drinks for the mums and the girls.

Not long after, the group heard noises coming from behind the gate and it was obvious the boys and their parents had arrived. The girls ducked back into the kitchen wanting to make an entrance to their boyfriends. Looking through the window they all watched as Wes, Rhys and Gregg came into the garden. All three looked tall, handsome and very grown up. All three were wearing black tuxedos, with dazzling white dinner shirts, cummerbunds in silk and bow ties. The dads shook their hands and the mums kissed their cheeks and then they looked around for their girlfriends. The girls moved gracefully out onto the deck towards their man.

"Wow, what can I say Clia? You look absolutely gorgeous."

Rhys exclaimed kissing her on the lips. She smiled and returned the compliment.

"Stunning, beautiful, gorgeous, lovely…can't think of any more."

Gregg told Corrinne also kissing her. She wrapped her arms around his neck and kissed him back. Wes came forward to greet Hally and stood looking at her. He took her hand and gently kissed the back of it.

"You are more beautiful than any words can say."

He told her. She flicked her eyelashes at him and gave him the biggest smile ever.

"And you are the most handsome man in the universe."

The parents arranged their offspring in various combinations and poses to take numerous photographs. The girls stood together, then the boys, then couples and all six. Hally's dad brought out a tray with champagne and goblets and more photos were taken as the cork was popped and flew high into the sky. Each holding a small glass of champagne the girls were photographed individually with the climbing rose as background. Then again, couples, parents, other family members and finally the six.

"Phew, now I know what a model must feel like."

Hally said to her friends. They all giggled watching the boys who had huddled together and were whispering.

"What are they up to?"

Clia said. The boys broke apart and came towards them, each one with a hand behind his back. They stood in front of the girls and all together gave each girl a small transparent box. Inside each box was a delicate orchid corsage. The girls smiled and hugged the boys and after placing the flowers on their wrist more photographs were taken.

"The car's here Hally."

Dad announced and the whole group moved through the house to the front where a gleaming, sleek, black stretch limousine had just pulled up.

The six stood next to the car having yet more photos taken

whilst their families and neighbours stood and watched. Eventually one by one, the boys handed the girls elegantly into the car and climbed in after them. Slowly the driver edged away from the kerb as they waved from the windows and moved off down the street. Their destination was The Old Crown Hotel in the centre of town which the school had used many times before and knew provided excellent food and entertainment for the students.

Cars of all descriptions were parked and lined up waiting to park outside the hotel. Girls dressed in gowns of various styles and colours emerged from the cars and as they mingled, looked like a beautiful rainbow, floating and shifting as they glided towards the entrance. Some with male escorts, some just in all girl groups. Most of the boys were in black tuxedos, but a few had added colour of their own and come in white, blue and maroon. All looked happy and excited for the evening ahead. Hally and Wes walked arm in arm followed by Corrinne and Gregg and Rhys and Clia. On the way in they met up with other students and the girls all squealed and complimented each other's dress. The boys nodding or shaking hands with other lads they knew. The entire party was gently herded through the entrance lobby and into a large hall by teachers and hotel workers. The room had a dance floor at its centre and round tables surrounding the floor, all seating six. There was a table plan on a large board and each group or couple found their names and headed for their designated table. Hally and her group found their table right on the edge of the dance floor and sat down. Each table had a flower arrangement and menus in the middle.

The meal comprised of three courses with three choices of starter, main and dessert. Hally really didn't take much notice of the taste of her food but found it pleasant enough. She was far more interested in watching the other students, chatting with Wes and her friends and waiting for the meal to end and the band to begin. Finally when the tables were cleared a local band of three men and two women began to tune up their instruments and check their microphones. The lead singer introduced the group and then they began to play. At first no one moved from their tables, they all just sat and listened, some singing along a little, others tapping their feet. After a few songs, a small group of girls moved onto the dance floor, staying close to the edge and tentatively jigged to the music. When the song ended they sat down again, but as the next song started they got up again and were joined by a few other groups. Gradually more and more people got up and headed for the dance floor, less and less sitting down between songs. Eventually the whole party was in full swing, the tables left empty until students and guests needed to sit and rest or get drinks.

Hally, Corrinne and Clia danced close to their table. Sometimes the boys joined them but mostly sat out of the more vigorous tunes preferring the slower melodies where they could dance up close to their girlfriends. Occasionally other girls they knew would come over and chat or dance, but most of the evening was spent with just them and the boys. When the band took a break, Hally and Wes wandered out of the tall French windows at the back of the hall into the garden of the hotel. The air was sweet and fresh after the stuffiness and heat of the hall as they strolled hand in hand along the pathways, shrubs on either side of them. They saw other couples and groups of girls and boys all getting away from the heat too as they found a solitary bench and sat down. Wes draped his arm over her shoulder and she leaned against him.

"It's a great night isn't it?"

She whispered.

"Wonderful."

He replied and took her in his arms and kissed her deeply. As usual his kiss ignited the fire within her and she wrapped her arms around his neck and kissed him back. He rubbed his hands up and down her back sending shivers throughout her body. She did not want him to stop and felt bereft when he backed away.

"Too many people around."

He whispered huskily and even though she wanted to grab him and put her hands all over him, she knew he was right. After all they didn't want to get thrown out for not behaving. Taking her hand Wes led her back inside and the evening continued happily.

The limousine was waiting at midnight when they all emerged from the hotel. They piled in, all tired and no longer so concerned with elegance. The girls' feet were sore from dancing in high heels all night much to the amusement of the boys. Hally slouched on one of the seats her legs stretched out across Wes. He pulled her shoes off and rubbed her toes. It tickled but soothed at the same time. Corrinne and Clia followed suit both sighing as their shoes were removed and their feet freed from constriction. Gregg took one of Corrinne's feet in between both his hands and held it away from him.

"Phew Corry, do I have to rub these, they're a bit whiffy."

Corrinne took a swipe at him but he ducked laughing loudly. Rhys looked at Clia and opened his mouth to speak. She pointed at him.

"Not a word."

She warned. He laughed and said.

"Would I?"

Clia nodded. Instead he covered his mouth with a fist and pretended to cough but with a very audible.

"Smelly feet."

Laughing, Clia took a swing at him but missed as the car bumped over a hole in the road. This brought more laughter from all of them which continued as they arrived at Corrinne's house. Gregg and Corrinne climbed out saying goodnight and the driver pulled away from the kerb heading for Clia's house. As she lived close to Corrinne this didn't take long and soon she and Rhys were also saying goodnight.

Alone in the car, Hally snuggled up to Wes and closed her eyes. She didn't think she could ever feel as content as she did just then. She had almost dozed off when the driver pulled over outside her house. Wes climbed out and took Hally's hand to help her out. She still had her shoes in her other hand so once out of the car, Wes lifted her and carried her to the house. In his arms she fumbled in her bag for her key and finally plucked it out and opened the door. Wes lowered her onto the carpet and she plodded tiredly towards the lounge, her hair having come loose and her makeup smudged. Mum and dad were still up watching television and smiled when they saw her.

"The princess has turned into a frog."

Dad mocked her. Hally giggled and plonked down next to him

on the sofa lifting her feet and draping them over the arm. Wes sat down in the armchair.

"Did you have a good time?"

Mum asked.

"Absolutely wonderful."

Hally told her parents closing her eyes and resting her head on her father's shoulder. Wes looked at her and said.

"She's worn out, been dancing most of the night. I should get off home."

Hally opened her eyes quickly but didn't get up.

"Oh do you have to?"

She said in a little girl voice. Wes laughed and nodded.

"Yes I do and you need to get some sleep."

Hally pouted. Dad nudged her and said to Wes.

"I'll run you home, you look done in too."

Wes thanked him and stood up. He leaned over Hally and gave her a kiss and when she tried to get up to go with them he stopped her telling her she should go to bed and he would see her tomorrow. Reluctantly she let him go and he headed off out the back door with dad.

Dragging herself to a sitting position on the sofa Hally turned to her mum and asked if she would help her get out of the dress. Mum told her she would and took her daughter's hand pulling her up. Hally put an arm through her mum's and let her lead her up the stairs to her bedroom. Once inside mum unzipped her dress and gently eased it over her head. She turned to hang it up and when she looked back Hally was already under her duvet with her eyes closed.

"Did you take your stockings off baby?"

Mum asked gently lifting a tendril of hair away from her face. With her eyes still closed Hally nodded, so mum leaned over, kissed her goodnight and left the room turning the light off.

CHAPTER 18

What Next?

A few days after the prom Wes rang her telling her he had some news for her. He told her his parents had arranged to take Ellie to a holiday park for a long weekend break so would have the house to himself for a few days. Hally at once became excited and apprehensive at the same time. She texted Corrinne and Clia and asked them to come round and knowing their friend they responded almost immediately.

"So what do you think I should do?"

She asked her friends as they sat on the deck enjoying the sunshine.

"Hals what do you want to do?"

Clia asked her.

"Well I know what I'd like to do, but don't know if I should."

She replied.

"You know, maybe you shouldn't try and plan anything. Just see what happens and how you feel at the time."

Corrinne told her.

"Has Wes asked you to stay over?"

Corrinne asked and Hally realised that he had actually only told her he would have the house to himself. He hadn't mentioned anything about her staying with him.

"Actually no. Oh I don't know what to think anymore."

Hally said dejectedly.

"Hey sweetie, don't let it get you down. It's not a big deal."

Hally knew her friend was right but lately how she felt every time Wes came near her was becoming a very big deal. Just then Wes came through the gate and seeing him their conversation stopped in its tracks.

"Are my ears burning?"

He asked with a smile and a kiss for Hally. She blushed lightly but it was Clia who replied.

"Just girl talk."

Wes grinned and then said.

"Did Hally tell you about my parents going away?"

Corrinne and Clia both nodded.

"So Hally, are you going to ask your mum and dad if you can come and stay over?"

He said it casually. She was surprised and didn't quite know what to say.

"Umm..."

She stammered. Wes looked at her with concern.

"It's alright babe, if you don't want to I won't be upset. I just thought we could spend a bit of time alone. I bought that new DVD you wanted to see and well it would be nice to just curl up and watch it quietly."

Hally now looked concerned.

"It's fine Wes really, I just didn't know if you wanted me to stay over. Of course I'll ask them. I'm sure they will say yes anyway."

Corrinne and Clia gave her a little knowing smirk, both aware that Hally had skirted the truth completely but withholding their friend's secret.

After dinner that evening Hally waited until Nathan asked if he could get down and her mum had cleared the table of the plates. She sat holding her glass of orange juice reluctant to broach the subject but anxious to hear what her parents had to say about it. Swallowing the last of her juice Hally took a deep breath and said.

"Mum, dad, Wes' parents are going away next weekend and he wants to know if I can stay over. What do you think?"

Mum finished loading the dishwasher and came back to the table sitting next to her daughter.

"Well it's really up to you my angel. Do you want to stay over or do you want us to say no?"

Hally picked at a crumb on the table.

"I want to stay over."

She mumbled hesitating and not sure of what to say next. Dad stood up saying.

"I'll leave you two to have a chat."

Then he headed for the lounge giving mum a knowing smile on the way out of the kitchen.

"But you're a bit scared."

Mum finished for her. Hally looked up at her mum relief washing over her that her mum so understood and nodded.

"Baby, you are the only one who knows what you want. I can't tell you if it's the right time or not. All I can say is be sure, be very sure and be very very careful. You know what I mean?"

Hally nodded again.

"Oh definitely and I'm not saying it will. But will I know mum? I mean what if I think I do then I don't, is that wrong?"

Mum took her hand and held it tightly.

"Hally, whatever you feel at any time is never wrong. Wes is a lovely lad and he will respect whatever decision you make at any time."

Hally felt a little better, she always did after her mother's advice, but was still just as confused inside.

As the weekend approached Hally spent much of her time discussing it with Corrine and Clia. Wes had spoken to Rhys and Gregg and between them arranged for all six of them to spend the Friday night at his house having a barbeque leaving the Saturday night free for him and Hally. All three girls were pleased about this as they only had another week before the school holidays. To them this meant their grown up time was near an end as all the other students would be out and about too. So it was with fun in mind that they all made their way over to Wes' on Friday night armed with bags of snacks and soft drinks, leaving Wes to arrange the hot food. The evening was again hot and with the barbeque burning steadily and music playing not too loudly; the six had yet another night enjoying each other's company.

They all left together, Corrinne, Clia, Rhys and Gregg saying goodnight to Hally and Wes where the roads divided. Arm in arm the two continued on to Hally's house and just before they reached it, Hally stopped and turned to Wes. She linked her arms around his neck and rose up on tip toes to kiss him lightly on the lips. Then shyly she whispered.

"I would have stayed tonight too, but was a bit embarrassed 'cos the others were there."

She felt herself blushing. Wes pulled her close to him and whispered back.

"Hally, babe, I know what you mean. I thought about it too but felt sort of awkward broaching it. You know, seeing them off at the door."

They laughed lightly together, both a little embarrassed at what they knew was likely to happen when Hally did stay over.

Saturday dawned bright and warm and Hally climbed out of bed making her way to the window to look down into the garden. She watched the birds pecking the feeders and spotted a tiny wren flitting about in the shrubs. She turned to her back pack and wondered what to include for the night at Wes'. At home she slept in her undies during the hot summer nights and even sometimes in winter, but had no idea what she would do at Wes' house. She didn't even know if she would be staying in his room. They had been together for nearly a year now and yet still she felt a certain amount of trepidation when it came to asking some things. Finally she decided to take the bull by the horns and texted Wes. Quickly before she could change her mind she tapped the keys on her phone.

am i staying in your room tonight and what do i bring to wear xxx

She pressed send and waited. It didn't take long before her phone beeped an incoming message.

babe the room is up to you and if you want to wear full body armour i wont mind lol xxxx

Hally burst out laughing feeling immensely relieved and finally looked forward to the coming day and night.

The day at Wes' was quiet and enjoyable. They sat in the garden soaking up the sun, drinking soft drinks and watching rabbits bouncing about the field that the garden backed on to. Wes made them sandwiches at lunch time and cooked them steak with salad for their dinner. They finished off with chocolate ice cream in the garden before settling in the lounge to watch the DVD Wes had bought. He put popcorn in the microwave and a box of chocolates on the table and snuggled Hally to him as the film began. It was a very enjoyable movie, a romantic thriller and when it ended they sat for a while chatting about the parts they enjoyed the most. Wes held her and kissed her and stroked her hair.

"Are you tired?"

He asked softly. Hally shook her head.

"Do you want to go to bed anyway?"

He asked. Shyly she nodded and standing up he took her hand and led her from the room.

In his bedroom, Hally suddenly felt very nervous. Wes sensed this and put his arms around her. He held her to him just giving comfort and easing her tension.

"We won't do anything you don't want."

She leaned into him and ran her fingers through his hair.

"I'm alright, just a bit nervous."

She whispered.

"How about I go to the bathroom and leave you to get yourself, well, where you want to be."

She smiled and breathed out, not realising she had almost been holding her breath. Wes turned and went out of the room. As soon as he left, Hally stripped off her skirt and top and climbed into his bed pulling the duvet over her. She kept her underwear on not wanting to feel completely naked. This way she wasn't dressed much differently to when they went swimming and she had a bikini on. A little time passed and Wes came back. With no hint of self consciousness, he pulled his T-shirt over his head and stepped out of his jeans. Leaving his boxers on he slipped under the duvet next to her. Hally lay back on the pillows feeling very self conscious and nervous. Wes leaned over her and began to kiss her gently moving his hands up and over her body. All at once she was on fire and turning pressed herself up against him as close as she could. She immediately felt his own body respond and knew now was the right time, the very right time. She relaxed completely letting his love envelope her and soaked up every tiny touch he gave her. When she thought she would burst Wes whispered in her ear.

"Are you sure about this?"

"More sure than I have ever been about anything."

She whispered back. Gently Wes unclipped her bra and slid her panties down. Hally closed her eyes. She felt him move away slightly and began to panic a little; sure he had changed his mind. Then eyes still closed, she heard a small tearing sound and realised Wes was unwrapping a condom, something she hadn't thought about. With eyes still closed she felt him move on top of her settling himself between her thighs. There was a moment of sharp pain, she winced, and Wes stopped but she urged him on. Then she was completely taken by emotion so strong she thought she would explode. Then it was over.

Sleep wouldn't come although Hally was sure Wes was completely and soundly asleep beside her. He still held her in his arms and she was reluctant to move in case she disturbed him. However, she needed to go to the bathroom, so very slowly she slipped out of bed and tip toed out of the room. There was a tiny amount of blood on the inside of her thighs which she was totally unconcerned about. She looked at herself in the bathroom mirror and was surprised she didn't look any different. She didn't really know what to expect but felt a sense of disappointment and had no idea why.

She quietly returned to Wes' bedroom and found his dressing gown hanging on the back of his door. She wrapped herself in it and wandered over to the window. There was a wide cushioned window seat and the windows were open. She sat down pulling her knees up to her chin and wrapping her arms around them. The curtains were open as the room looked over open fields so there were no worries of anyone being able to see in. The moon was bright and she could see right across the fields, sitting quietly and drinking in the peaceful summer air. It smelled different to when she sat at her own bedroom window; being on the edge of town the scents were more country than those of garden flowers. For some time she stayed that way until she felt herself growing sleepy. Then quietly she slipped back into bed beside the still sleeping Wes and managed to drift off into a peaceful sleep.

Wes woke her with toast and orange juice. He kissed her

sweetly and looked in her eyes questioningly. She thanked him for the breakfast but didn't feel ready to talk about the night before. Even though she felt comfortable about it, talking about it was an entirely different thing. Wes didn't press her sensing the turmoil inside. So instead he left her to eat and get dressed and went downstairs to wait for her. She joined him soon after and they decided to go for a walk up the lane that ran along the side of the house. Wes put a couple of bottles of water into his back pack and hand in hand they set off.

Hally was again astounded at the beautiful country sights that were so close to her home but which she had never realised were there. They walked for some time Wes pointing out different landmarks and came upon a small wood with a stream flowing through. They rested against a fallen tree and sipped at the bottles of water chatting about nothing in particular. Then they made their way back to Wes' and spent the rest of the day in the garden before Wes walked her home in the evening. She had already decided she wanted to talk to her mum as soon as she got home and explained this to Wes. He said he was ok with that and kissed her at the back gate and waved until he reached the road and turned the corner.

Hally walked into the kitchen but mum wasn't there. She headed for the lounge and when she found that empty decided her parents were probably in the study on the computer. She made her way there and heard them talking as she neared. She popped her head around the open doorway and called out hello. Both looked up from the computer, and mum who had been leaning over dad's shoulder patted her husband on the arm and said.

"Tell them I'm with Hally."

Colin said ok and began tapping the keyboard. To Hally this meant they had been chatting online to friends and dad was explaining where mum had gone.

Mum and Hally went into the kitchen, mum flicking the switch on the kettle and lifting mugs down. Hally felt comfortable with her mum and had no hesitation in discussing what had happened between her and Wes. But she also didn't feel the need to rush, so she sat at the table and waited until mum made two mugs of coffee and sat down with her.

"Are you alright?"

Mum asked. Hally wrapped her hands around the hot cup and pressed her lips together gathering her thoughts.

"Yes and no."

She said. Mum waited without speaking. Then Hally said.

"I mean yes because of what happened, but no…well…because I didn't really feel anything. Well I mean it was sort of disappointing. All that build up then, well nothing really. Am I normal mum?"

May took her daughter's hand and smiled at her lovingly.

"My angel, you are completely normal. The thing is, for women, it can take time. The first time can be strange and not very exciting. In fact the other stuff, touching and so on can often give you a much better feeling."

Hally nodded knowingly, so mum carried on.

"After a while you will find it gets better and much more enjoyable. It just needs a little patience and I suppose practice."

Hally sipped her coffee and squeezed her mum's hand.

"Do you mind that I did?"

She asked a little note of worry in her voice. Mum sat back and looked at her.

"Hally no I don't mind. I've known it's been coming for a while and the fact that we can talk about it shows me how mature you are and how you really thought about it first. The only thing I'm a bit sad about is that you are growing up."

Mother and daughter smiled each showing the other how much love they had between them.

Corrinne and Clia were at Hally's the next morning barely after she had got up. They came in grinning with raised eyebrows waiting expectantly for a detailed account of her night with Wes. Nathan was still getting ready for school and they had to wait until mum took him. The second they were out of the house they both practically shrieked at Hally.

"Well?"

Hally deliberately acted blasé and replied.

"Well what?"

Corrinne and Clia both clasped their hands tightly together and screeched.

"Hally, come on give. What was it like?"

Hally giggled and handed the girls a bottle of cola each then sat down and told them all about it.

"So, it wasn't all that then?"

Corrinne asked with obvious disappointment.

"Mum said that's normal and it always gets better."

This brightened her friends up.

"Well that's a relief then. So it's worth it really then?"

Clia asked. Hally nodded realising that although her experience hadn't been the fiery, romantic passionate night she saw in films; it had been a whole lot more. It had been filled with love and she told her friends this.

Hally and Wes celebrated their first year together with their friends and later on their own Hally found that her mum was right. Wes was if anything more loving and caring than ever before and Hally wondered again where they were heading. It wasn't something she worried about, just a question that came to her late at night when she was alone. She didn't want to voice it to anyone because she knew no one would have an answer. It was one of those questions that could only be answered by time. For now the present was important, was good and happy and she was content.

The summer seemed to fly by, the weather showing occasional signs of change. The nights were slowly drawing in and were becoming a little chillier only so much as needing a light jacket or jumper when they all stayed out after dark. Hally loved the warm summer days and the summer nights spending them sometimes with just Wes; other times with Corrinne and Clia and often all together with Rhys and Gregg too. They had all become very close and didn't feel the need to join other groups. One evening they sat on rugs in the park just as the sun was going down. Wes had his arm draped around Hally, Clia was leaning against Rhys' chest and Corrinne was lying with her head on Gregg's lap.

"Well tomorrow decides part of my future."

Wes said. They all knew what he was talking about. The A level results were out the next day and although he wasn't going on to university; he still needed certain grades for the course he had chosen at college. Hally pressed his hand against her lips.

"You've worked hard this year. I think you will pass with flying colours."

"What about our results? They're out next week."

Corrinne said sounding very anxious.

"Corry you always get top grades."

Hally replied.

"Doesn't mean I will this time."

She said pessimistically.

"You will."

Clia announced. Hally sat forward.

"You know what? I reckon we are all going to do really well. I mean we have put a whole lot into this last year and these three (she indicated to the boys) have supported us all the way. We will be fine."

"You are forever the optimist."

Wes told her giving her a squeeze.

"I never used to be, you ask those two."

She replied. Corrinne and Clia both nodded in agreement.

"So you are definitely going to college here then?"

Gregg asked Wes.

"Yes, I can't imagine being away from the two people I love the most, Hally and Ellie."

Hally felt herself light up inside. It was the first time ever she had heard Wes say he loved her to other people and it made her glow. They all chatted some more then as it got late the boys walked the girls home.

Hally was up and ready to meet Wes to go to the school to collect his exam results. Already the local radio was reporting from the school telling the listeners how the students were gathering, anxious and nervous. Hally felt nervous for Wes at the same time sure he had done well. As they neared the school gates they saw Corrinne, Clia, Rhys and Gregg waiting with beaming smiles.

"Thought we would come and give you some support."

Rhys said.

"Your dad said we could go into work later and that we had to remind you to phone him and your mum the moment you get your results."

Wes grinned even though Hally could see he was nervous.

Inside the school hall, the students gathered in groups, some with their parents waiting impatiently. Finally the envelopes were handed out and the local media descended on random students to await their opening. Wes' hand shook slightly as he slit his envelope and pulled out the sheet inside. He quickly glanced over it and a smile broke out on his face.

"All 'A's."

He said. Hally leapt into his arms and he swung her around. A man thrust a microphone in his face and said.

"Looks like good news. Would you like to tell us how you did?"

Hally looked at the reporter and felt her stomach churn. It was the same one who had tried to interview her after Dana's death. Wes noticed her distress and turned away from the man but he persisted, talking to his cameraman at the same time trying to push Wes into a conversation.

"This young man has obviously got good news; tell us what do you plan to do next."

Wes shielded Hally and replied with.

"I don't want to talk to you. Please go away."

"Is that your girlfriend? Aren't you the girl involved in that suicide last year?"

He didn't get any further. Mr Austin quickly intervened and steered the reporter away from them; sending him to a group of girls who were more than willing to appear on television. Hally overheard him saying. "Hi my name is Daly Fesandelo, what grades did you get?"

Hally was determined not to let the reporter spoil or overshadow Wes' achievements. She took his arm and kissed him, then smiling stood with the others whilst he phoned his parents and gave them the good news. They all heard his mum squeal with delight and his dad loudly offer congratulations. Then Gregg and Rhys said they had better get off to work, so together they walked from the school and headed for Hally's house, Gregg and Rhys going in the opposite direction. Mum was at home and gave Wes a hug and kiss on the cheek and made them all drinks before she set off for Granddad's. Wes' phone chirped, it was his mum. She called to tell him that she and his dad had booked a table at Gesslers that evening for all of them as a celebration treat.

Hally walked into Gesslers that evening with Wes holding her hand on one side and Ellie's tiny hand on the other side. His parents were there, her family was there and Corrinne and Clia with Gregg and Rhys. Wes lifted Ellie into a high chair between himself and his mum and the whole party settled down to order. It was a very enjoyable meal, sometimes quite noisy as Ellie made herself heard.

"Well next week it will be the girls' turn."

Hally's dad stated during the meal.

"Perhaps we should all do this again then, obviously with Corrinne and Clia's families too."

He added.

"I'll call them tomorrow and see what they say."

Hally's mum said.

"Maybe we should wait and see what we get first."

Hally said, Corrinne and Clia nodding in agreement.

"Well I'll just ring them anyway. I'm sure you will all get very good grades."

Mum told them. The girls left it at that not wanting to argue.

The week went by very quickly and before they knew it the day of their results was upon them. Hally had woken very early and had received text messages from both Corrinne and Clia telling her they had been up for hours too. Wes was coming round to walk to school with her and she was meeting the girls at their usual point where their roads met. All three had declined offers from their parents to accompany them and again Wes' dad had given Gregg and Rhys time off to go with them. They met up and nervously set off for the school.

There was a lot of activity both outside and inside the school gates. Hally glanced around and was thankful to not see the local television van anywhere near. She thought that maybe the GCSE results were not as compelling news as the A levels. They made their way into the school hall and stood with their arms linked waiting for the results to be handed out. The boys stood nearby unable to ease their apprehension. After what seemed an age the envelopes were handed out. Hally stood holding hers unable to open it. Corrinne had ripped hers apart and was struggling to pull out the paper. Finally it came loose and she studied it. At first she stared at the sheet not speaking.

"What?"

Hally said. Corrinne offered the paper to Hally and she read it out.

"A star for Maths and A for everything else."

Clia jumped in the air and grabbed Corrinne, Hally doing the same, bouncing around laughing.

"Now you two."

Corrinne told her friends. Clia held her envelope towards Hally.

"Together."

She said. So they both slit them open and pulled out their results.

"A star for English lit and language, B for Maths, A for the rest."

Hally said waiting to hear Clia's results.

"A for English lit and language, B for Maths, A for the rest."

Clia said. More squealing and hugging and bouncing ensued with the boys joining in. Finally Wes took Hally in his arms and kissed her.

"Well done. You really deserve that after the year you have had."

She held him tightly then took out her phone and called her parents.

That night they all met up again at Gesslers to celebrate the achievements of the girls. The parents sat proudly next to their daughters, Hally's Granddad next to her mum, and the boyfriends and their families smiled and offered congratulations. Hally ate her meal enjoying every bite. Between mouthfuls she looked up and down the table. She had every person near her who was important to her. Wes' dad had asked her the simple question 'What next?' and she had answered simply with 'College' but that wasn't really the answer. The answer was out there somewhere but it was unknown. Who could say what was next, her future wasn't mapped out; she hoped Wes would be a part of it, she hoped for a lot of things; especially that Corrinne and Clia would always be nearby and still like sisters. She hoped her family would always be happy and be proud of her. As she watched the party enjoying the celebrations, chatting and laughing, as she saw Wes glance at her lovingly and her parents smile at her proudly, she thought that right then it didn't matter. The here and now was all that was important, what next would come and she would face whatever challenges it brought with it. Granddad tapped her on the shoulder leaning behind mum so he could speak to her.

"Your Gran would be very proud of you."

He told her.

"I know. What do you think she would say to me right now?"

He smiled.

"If you listen you will hear her, I do."

He said simply. Hally smiled back and briefly closed her eyes. Granddad was right, she heard her Gran's voice, sweet but strong, telling her she could cope with whatever life threw at her. Opening her eyes and smiling, Hally knew her Gran was right.